DRAGON

*A powerful story of love and adventure set
against the cauldron of World War II*

DALE S. EDWARD

Dragon
© Dale S. Edward

Print ISBN 978-1-66783-351-4
eBook ISBN 978-1-66783-352-1

Apollo aka "Wolfie" vom Hirschel

Dedicated to Wolfie

In loving memory of my faithful friend
and companion.

Apollo aka "Big Boy" vom Hirschel

CONTENTS

ACKNOWLEDGEMENT

THE AUTHOR WISHES TO THANK THE WASP ORGANIZATION for their patience and helpful assistance during the writing of this novel. The National WASP WWII Museum is dedicated to honoring the life and legacy of the Women Airforce Service Pilots and preserving the legacy of Avenger Field on which most of them trained. Their mission is to educate and inspire all current and future generations with the history of the WASP – the first women to fly America's military aircraft – women who brought honor to our nation and forever changed the role of women in military and civilian aviation.

National WASP WWII Museum

210 Avenger Field Road

Sweetwater, Texas 79556

325-235-0099 www.WaspMuseum.org

Photo by WaspMuseum.org - WASP pilots, L to R, are Francis Green,
Margaret (Peg) Kirchner, Ann Waldner, and Blanche Osborn

PROLOGUE

THIS BOOK IS BASED, IN PART, ON THE TRUE STORY OF THE
Women Airforce Service Pilots (WASP) organization. At the beginning of
World War II, America was caught unprepared, and there was a critical shortage
of skilled male pilots needed for combat duty.

At the recommendation of Jacqueline Cochran, a well-known woman
pilot, First Lady Eleanor Roosevelt contacted General "Hap" Arnold, commanding general of the United States Army Air Force, and suggested that he
use women pilots in noncombative roles as ferry pilots. General Arnold liked
her idea, and the recruitment of women began immediately.

The women became highly trained and transported newly built aircraft
from factories and military bases to the east and west coast to support the war
effort. They flew over sixty million miles, transported over twelve thousand
planes, and ferried every type of aircraft in the military inventory.

It was a dangerous job, and thirty-eight women were killed in the line of
duty. Sadly, they faced prejudice and discrimination because of their presence in
a traditionally all-male military, and there were several incidences where WASP
planes were sabotaged, resulting in the pilot's death.

At the end of the war, General Arnold promised that a grateful nation
would never forget its debt to these women. At airbases all over America, they
hung up their parachutes and packed their bags. Despite his pledge that the Air
Force would never forget them, they did . . . and so did America.

In 1977, with the support of Senator Barry Goldwater, the women were granted full military status for their service, and in 2009, President Obama and the United States Congress awarded them the Congressional Gold Medal. The following year, two hundred surviving WASP members accepted their award from House Speaker Nancy Pelosi and other Congressional leaders.

IN MEMORIAM

Photo by National WASP WWII Museum L to R Cornelia Fort, Katherine
Dussaq, Gertrude Tompkins-Silver, Mary Howson

HONORING THE THIRTY-EIGHT BRAVE WASP PILOTS THAT
made the supreme sacrifice in defense of their country. May they never
be forgotten.

Jane Delores Champlin
St. Louis University, Missouri
Killed June 7, 1944, while on a training flight near
Avenger Field, Texas

Susan Parker Clarke
Secretarial School, NYC
Killed July 4, 1944, on a ferrying flight near
Columbia, South Carolina

Marjorie Laverne Davis
Hollywood, California
Killed October 16, 1944, on a cross-country
training flight near Walnut, Mississippi

Katherine Kay Applegate Dussaq
Whitman College, Washington
Killed November 26, 1944, on an administrative
cross-county flight near New Carlisle, Ohio

Marjorie Doris Edwards
Santa Barbara State College, California
Killed June 13, 1944, while on a cross-country
training flight near Childress, Texas

Elizabeth Jayne Erickson
University of Washington
Killed April 16, 1944, in a mid-air collision at
Avenger Field, Texas

Cornelia Clark Fort
Sarah Lawrence College, New York
Killed March 21, 1943, in a mid-air collision near
Abilene, Texas

Frances Fortune Grimes
University of Pittsburgh, Pennsylvania
Killed March 27, 1944, on take-off in an attack
bomber from Otis Field, Massachusetts

Mary P Hartson
Portland, Oregon
Killed August 14, 1944, while flight testing a trainer
at Perrin Army Air Base, Texas

Mary Holmes Howson
Smith College, Massachusetts
Killed April 16, 1944, in a mid-air collision at
Avenger Field, Texas

Edith Clayton Keene
Pomona Junior College, California
Killed April 25, 1944, on a training flight near
Mission, Texas

Kathryn Barbara Lawrence
University of North Dakota
Killed on August 4, 1943 - bailed out but her
parachute failed to open at Avenger Field, Texas

Paula Ruth Loop
Oklahoma A & M
Killed July 7, 1944, in a crash near
Medford, Oregon while on a ferrying mission

Alice E. Lovejoy
Scarsdale, New York
Killed September 13, 1944, in a mid-air collision
near Brownsville, Texas

Peggy Wilson Martin
Seattle, Washington
Killed October 3, 1944, on an engineering test
flight near Marianna, Florida

Leah Ola McDonald
Wayland Baptist College, Texas
Killed June 21, 1944, while flying an attack bomber
near El Paso, Texas

Virginia Caraline Moffatt
Los Angeles, California
Killed October 5, 1943, while on a routine
flight near Cal Aero Academy Airfield at
Chino, California.

Beverly Jean Moses
AJB Business School
Killed July 18, 1944, in a mountainous area near Las
Vegas, Nevada

Dorothy Mae Nichols
UCLA, California
Killed June 11, 1944, on a cross-country flight near
Bismarck, North Dakota

Jeanne Marcile Lewellen Norbeck
Washington State College
Killed October 16, 1944, while flight testing near
Shaw Army Air Base, South Carolina

Margaret Burrows Sanford Oldenburg
University of California
Killed March 7, 1943, on a routine training flight
near Houston, Texas

Mabel Virginia Rawlinson
Western Michigan College of Education
Killed August 23, 1943, in the crash of an
attack bomber

Gleanna Roberts
University of Iowa
Killed June 20, 1944, on a routine training flight
near Lorraine, Texas

Marie Michell Robinson
National Park Junior College, Washington, D.C.
Killed October 2, 1944, in a crash in the mountains
near Victorville, California

Dorothy Faeth Scott
University of Washington
Killed December 3, 1943, in a mid-air collision near
Palm Springs, California

Elizabeth Mae Scott
Pasadena Junior College, California
Killed on July 8, 1944, on an engineering test flight
near Waco Army Airfield, Texas

Margaret June Seip
Lawrence College, Wisconsin
Killed August 30, 1943, while on a routine training
flight near Big Spring, Texas

Helen Jo Anderson Severson
South Dakota State University
Killed August 30, 1943, while on a routine training
flight near Big Spring, Texas

Marie Ethel Cihler Sharon
Jefferson High School, Oregon
Killed April 10,1944, on a training mission near
Tecumseh, Nebraska

Evelyn Genevieve Sharp
Millstone, Montana
Killed April 3, 1944, when her engine failed on
take-off near Cumberland, Pennsylvania

Gertrude Vreeland Tompkins Silver
Pennsylvania School of Horticulture
Lost at sea on October 26, 1944, on a cross-country
flight near Los Angeles, California. She is the only
WASP pilot never to be accounted for.

Betty Pauline Stine
University of Arizona
Killed February 25, 1944, on a cross-country
training flight near Tucson, Arizona

Mary Ann Toevs
Eastern Washington State College
Killed February 18, 1944, on a ferrying flight near
San Jose, California

Mary Elizabeth Trebing
Oklahoma A&M College
Killed November 7, 1943, in a crash near
Blanchard, Oklahoma

Mary Louise Webster
Central Washington State College
Killed December 9, 1944, on a routine
training flight

Bonnie Jean Alloway Welz
University of California, Los Angeles
Killed June 29, 1944, on an administrative flight
near Randado, Texas

Betty Louise Taylor Wood
Sierra Junior College, California
Killed September 23, 1943, in the crash of an
attack bomber at Camp Davis Army Airfield,
North Carolina

Hazel Ying Lee Yim-Qun
Portland, Oregon
Killed November 23, 1944, in a mid-air collision at
Great Falls Army Airfield, Montanav

DRAGON

CHAPTER 1
THE MOSEL RIVER VALLEY

THE YEAR IS 1965 AND FALL WEATHER HAS COME EARLY TO southern Germany. Below the snow packed peaks of the Swiss Alps, runoff from the summer snowmelt and thawing glaciers forms rivulets that slowly wind their way across steep, rock-strewn slopes before cascading through towering forests of Beech trees.

The scenic Mosel River begins its serpentine path in the Vosges Mountains in northern France, and travels north into Germany before emptying into the Rhine River near the picturesque town of Koblenz. It flows at the bottom of a deep gorge surrounded by low-rolling hills and dense green forests, forming a beautiful river valley. Here and there, small villages overlook its rocky shoreline, and ruins of ancient castles, partially hidden by thick vegetation, dot the landscape.

Lush, terraced vineyards descend the steep southern-facing slopes, creating a Riesling wine of exceptional quality. This region was first cultivated by the Romans in A.D. 300, and over the following centuries, countless battles were fought here by invading armies seeking to control this fertile land. Today, the valley is one of Germany's most famous wine districts.

A paved driveway flanked by wooden rail fences winds its way through forested glens and green meadows, ending in a cul-de-sac in front of a private estate. Well-kept lawns and flowering gardens surround an impressive two-story stone mansion that sits close to the edge of a deep gorge. Built in the late 1880s, it reflects the grand style of fifteenth century architecture with its narrow arrow slits and battlements reminiscent of a time long past. Nearby, an imposing look-out tower with a pointed copper roof rises above the tall trees.

The back of the mansion has a large terrace that overhangs the gorge's steep slope and commands a stunning view of the winding Mosel River and the fertile valley below. The centerpiece is a sunken fire pit surrounded by comfortable wooden chairs. Nearby planters overflow with a rainbow of flowers that cascade onto a natural stone deck.

An attractive, well-dressed woman in her mid-forties sits at a wrought-iron table. She has shoulder length auburn hair and wears amber-colored designer sunglasses. As she sips her morning coffee, her twin teenage daughters approach on horseback, trotting slowly down a long meadow that parallels a paved airstrip. The girls are riding two magnificent Hanoverian show jumpers and are cooling them down after having completed a challenging cross-country course.

As they near the mansion, they pass an airplane hangar. Parked in front is a blue and white Beechcraft King Air, a six passenger ultra-modern turboprop plane. They enter a paddock near the mansion, and after removing their saddles and bridles, they open a heavy wooden gate. Carved deeply into the weathered wood is a heraldic shield with a winged dragon in the center. The girls are wearing tall black boots, tan breeches, and white blouses, and climb a flight of stairs that leads to the terrace.

Lynnetta, a willowy eighteen-year-old with blonde hair and emerald-green eyes, speaks in French. "Good morning, Mother."

"Good morning, girls. How was your ride?"

"Wonderful! Natalie and I just finished the new cross-country course."

Natalie, her attractive twin sister, chimes in. "But I was faster than Lynnetta!"

Lynnetta frowns. "You were just lucky this time."

Her mother asks, "What did you think of the new course?"

"I liked it a lot, especially the uphill section, but Natalie had trouble at the creek crossing."

She looks at her daughter's muddy riding breeches. "So, I see!"

"Where is everybody?" asks Natalie.

"Christian is with your father at the winery, and your uncle should be here soon. Are you hungry?"

"Yes! We're starving!" responds Lynnetta.

"Good. Have Gertrude fix you something."

They bolt for the kitchen, and their mother calls after them in German. "Change your muddy clothes first!"

Natalie answers in German. "Yes, Mother."

The woman sits down in a comfortable chair and her wide-brimmed hat flutters in the light breeze. The scent of flowering roses drifts across the terrace, and she closes her eyes, enjoying the warm sun. Soon the droning of a distant plane shatters the peaceful morning. It flies above the wooded river shoreline, and the noise from its powerful engine reverberates across the valley, echoing louder and louder as it approaches.

She awakens and focuses on it as it emerges from the mist, revealing the outline of a Swiss made Pilatus PC-6 Porter, a ten-passenger turboprop float plane that services the remote villages upriver. She watches intently as it passes by and continues up the gorge. It soon disappears into the distance, and she closes her eyes and dozes off once again.

CHAPTER 2

THE SUMMER OF 1943

A GENTLE BREEZE BRUSHES AGAINST A VAST SEA OF GOLDEN wheat. Baked by the relentless heat of the sun, it sways back and forth across the low rolling hills of North Dakota. A group of school children chatter amongst themselves as they walk down a dirt road toward a distant farmhouse.

High amid the puffy white clouds, the droning sound of a military fighter breaks the morning silence. Suddenly, the engine backfires and flames shoot out from under the cowling. Inside the cramped cockpit, the pilot desperately tries to work the radio, but the fire has burned the wiring and it's dead. The pilot slides the heavy bulletproof canopy back to let in fresh air, and a trail of thick black smoke tracks far behind the plane.

What started as a rough running engine has now turned into a full-blown emergency. The pilot reaches to the instrument panel, turns off the engine, and the flames die down. As the stricken fighter glides silently toward an unknown fate, the pilot scans the rugged terrain, looking for a place to make a forced landing. The altimeter slowly unwinds from 7,000 feet, and the plane is trimmed for a long, shallow glide. Minutes later, several immense buildings appear in the distance.

From his commanding view, a frantic air traffic controller watches the plane through his binoculars. As the fighter approaches, a thin trail of black smoke etches into the clear blue sky. He quickly reaches for a red telephone and alerts his emergency rescue crews. Sirens wail as they race to their vehicles.

An officer enters from a side door and asks, "What's happening?"

"We've got a fighter coming in, and it doesn't look good. I don't think he's going to make it!"

The officer picks up a pair of binoculars and focuses on the stricken plane. "Can you contact him?"

He speaks into his microphone. "Approaching fighter. Do you read me?" and pauses. "Approaching fighter. Do you read me?" but there is no answer, and his radio only crackles with static.

The pilot stares with difficulty through the oil-streaked windshield. A dense forest lies directly ahead, followed by an immense cleared area with several large aircraft hangars partially built. The airbase is under construction, and bright yellow earthmoving equipment grades the dirt runway.

As the plane approaches, the controller watches in horror as it sinks behind a cluster of tall trees. "Oh, no! He crashed!"

Moments later, it bursts through a narrow gap and clears the perimeter security fence with only a few feet to spare. It makes a perfect landing, decelerates down the dirt airstrip in an immense cloud of dust, and turns out onto a grassy area. Smoke pours from the engine compartment, and flames dance on its red-hot exhaust manifold. Crash crews race across the base with their emergency lights flashing, and a group of student pilots run after them.

A young pilot calls to his friend. "I've never seen a plane like that. What is it?"

His friend responds. "It must be one of our new fighters!"

"But what's it doing out here?"

The student pilots arrive, and stare in amazement at the deadly looking fighter, a plane that they've only heard about but have never seen. The massive plane is painted olive green and towers above them. With a forty-one-foot wingspan and carrying eight fifty-caliber machine guns in its wings, it's an impressive sight by any standard.

Firemen dressed in shiny silver suits arrive, and immediately spray fire retardant onto the engine, causing a cloud of white steam to spiral skyward before dissipating into the clear summer air. Droplets of burning oil drip from the cowling, forming a black pool that smolders in the grass. Rivulets of oil streak across the bulletproof windshield, and smoke damage clouds the interior windows.

Inside the plane, the pilot struggles to slide the canopy back, then exits the cockpit dressed in a brown leather flight jacket, parachute, and tall boots. The pilot jumps to the ground, unclips an oxygen mask, and the astonished group stares in silence at a pretty woman.

A firefighter approaches her. "Are you alright, mam?

"Yes, I'm okay."

He unbuttons the front of his heavy firefighting jacket. "We were fortunate to get the fire out quickly. I'm amazed that you kept it flying for as long as you did."

"Thanks." Lt. Betty Bauer walks to the front of the plane and stares worriedly at the scorched engine cowling. "That doesn't look good."

He stands next to her and looks at the damage. "It might not be as bad as it seems. It looks like you may have broken an oil line, and it was spraying on the exhaust manifold."

His positive attitude is reassuring. "I hope you're right."

"This might take a while," and he motions toward his fire truck. "You can wait at flight ops if you like."

She unbuckles her parachute and lays it on top of the wing. "Thanks for the offer."

"I'm glad to help, mam," and they walk toward his vehicle.

The fire truck lurches from side to side as they pass an enormous hangar that is under construction, and she asks, "By the way, where am I?"

"Well, mam. You're smack dab in the middle of nowhere. They're building a new airbase here," and he points off to the left. "Over that way is Fargo, North Dakota."

He pulls up to the flight operations office, and she steps out of the vehicle. "Thanks for the lift," and he waves goodbye as he drives off.

Betty crosses the unpaved street. As she enters the building, an officer looks up from his desk. "Are you the officer on duty?"

He pushes his chair back and stands. "Yes, mam. I'm Captain McKenna. Glad to see that you made it in okay."

She shakes his hand. "Thanks, I'm Lt. Bauer."

"What brings you this way?"

"I'm ferrying a plane to Walker Army Airfield in Virginia, and my engine caught on fire. Could you have a mechanic look at it?"

"Sure, you bet. Let me find someone." The captain starts to leave the room but stops in the middle of the doorway. "It's about lunch time. Are you hungry?"

"Yes. I've been flying since early this morning."

"Great. I'll be back in a few minutes to pick you up. You can leave your flight gear here if you like."

The cafeteria is noisy and crowded with Army personnel and civilian workmen. Any woman would be an unusual sight, much less a female fighter pilot. Amid many looks of surprise, she follows him to the officer's mess line, and they push bright metal trays along as the cooks fill them. The captain gestures toward a nearby table and is quick to notice the attention that she is getting. "Sorry for all the stares, but you seem to be the star attraction today."

Betty is very attractive and wears a white blouse and khaki-colored pants. "That's okay, I'm used to it," and she pulls out a chair.

The captain sits down across from her. "That sure is a beautiful plane you're flying. What is it?"

"It's a Republic P-47 Thunderbolt. It was specifically designed to take on the German fighters. With 2,000 horsepower, and a top speed of 410 mph, she's a potent high-performance plane."

"That's impressive!"

He notices the insignia on the front of her leather flight jacket. It's a large red circle with a winged female character wearing goggles in the center. "I'm not familiar with your squadron."

"I'm a WASP ferry pilot," and she sees a confused look on his face. "The Women Airforce Service Pilots. Have you heard of us?"

"Sorry, we're kind of off the beaten path out here."

"That's okay. The Army has done very little to acknowledge us."

"How long have you been ferrying planes?"

"They formed our squadron a couple of months ago, and I've been racking up a lot of hours since then. And you?"

"I was accepted into medical school a week before the attack on Pearl Harbor."

"And now you're out here counting gophers, huh?"

"Yep. Our talents seem to be lost when it comes to the Army."

A half hour later, a mechanic approaches them. "Sorry to interrupt, Captain, but you wanted to know as soon as we found something."

"You're not interrupting, Sergeant."

"I've got good news, sir. It was only a loose oil line, but it's kinda odd. A wire locking system always secures them, but it looks like someone removed it. It vibrated off and sprayed onto the hot exhaust manifold. We replaced some burned wiring, but the radio is dead, and we don't have any way of fixing it."

Betty looks up at him and smiles. "Thanks, Sarge. I can get by without it. How long will it take to fix?"

"She's ready right now, mam."

It's after lunch, and Captain McKenna drives Betty out to her plane. She steps out of his jeep. "Thanks for everything."

"Sure thing, Lieutenant. Glad that we could help."

She walks over to her P-47 and looks up at the blackened cowling. A mechanic approaches her. "Sorry about the fire damage, mam, but we're not set up to paint anything."

"That's okay, Sergeant. As long as she can fly."

"Oh, she'll do that just fine!"

"Thanks. I appreciate the work that you did." She slips into her parachute, reaches around her leg for a strap, then stands upright and pulls on it, securing it in place.

He wipes oil from his hands. "Glad to help, mam."

Betty steps into a toe hold in the side of the fuselage, walks up the wing, and climbs into the cockpit. She gets comfortable, then checks her flight controls by moving the stick back and forth while pressing the pedals with her feet. She signals the mechanic that she's about to start and the propeller cycles a few times, building up oil pressure.

The massive radial engine whines loudly as it coughs while sucking fuel-laden air into the intake manifold and bursts into life. The huge thirteen-foot four-bladed propeller blasts an enormous cloud of dust and debris behind it, and the deafening roar quickly transitions into the steady drone of a well-tuned high-performance engine.

Betty maneuvers the huge fighter onto the gravel taxiway and idles past rows of trainers and other parked aircraft. Had her radio been working, she would have been talking to the control tower, but today they will communicate using a signal light. The tower shines a bright green light in her direction, showing that she can safely take off, and she pushes forward on her throttle and rotates the heavy fighter out onto the dirt runway.

Even though it's only mid-day, the afternoon is hot, and mirages dance above the long gravel runway. Betty locks her parking brake, checks her flight controls one last time, then revs her engine to full power. It shatters the quiet morning for a few seconds, then drops back to idle. She releases her brakes, pushes the throttle forward, and the heavy fighter rolls down the airstrip, creating an enormous cloud of dust that stretches out far behind it. Nearing the end of the runway, she pulls back on the stick, and the speeding plane rockets into the sky.

Hours later, and with nightfall fast approaching, she descends to Walker Army Airfield near Newport, Virginia. As the sprawling complex grows larger through the whitish blur caused by her plane's spinning prop, she reaches forward, pulls the throttle lever toward her to lower her airspeed, and the fighter begins a slow descent. To her left, she sees the control tower, and dips her wings to show that her radio is not working. Immediately, a green light flashes in her direction, giving her permission to land. She smiles to herself, knowing that Captain McKenna must have called ahead to report she was coming in without a radio.

She dips her wings in acknowledgment, and banks onto the base leg of her landing pattern. Written across the end of the runway are huge words that read, "*WHEELS DOWN*", a reminder for pilots not to forget to lower their landing gear. She pulls back on a shiny metal bar next to her seat, and the plane's massive flaps slowly extend downward. The ground rushes up, and her tires screech as they spin up to one hundred miles an hour.

A jeep waits for her at a turnout and its yellow emergency lights flash brightly, warning others to stay alert. Attached to the back bumper is a large orange and white checkered flag that flutters in the light breeze. She follows him and weaves her way through the busy network of taxiways. He motions toward an empty parking space, and a waiting mechanic guides her fighter to a stop.

Betty slides her canopy back, unbuckles her safety belt, and climbs out onto the wing. She has been to this base several times and recognizes the mechanic as he approaches. He's wearing grease-stained coveralls and chews at the wet end of an unlit cigar. "Is this my baby?"

"You bet, Sarge. She's all yours."

"How did it go?"

"I had an engine fire from an oil line that fell off, but I stopped and got it fixed. Umm, oh yeah, and the radio is dead."

He stares at the fire-scorched cowling. "That looks pretty bad. Are you sure you're okay?"

"Yup," and she walks down the wing and jumps to the ground. "It's all in a day's work. Would you mind dropping me off at flight ops?"

"Can do."

She sits down in his jeep, and as they pull away, he gives her a quick glance. "You look a little tired."

"I'm okay. I just haven't had a day off in a month, but tomorrow, I'm going to sleep all the way back to Texas."

It's the following morning, and the bus station is busy with Army personnel waiting to board buses that will take them to destinations all across the country. Betty is wearing a khaki-colored jumpsuit with her name tag and pilot's wings sown on the front and stands in a long line. Soon her bus arrives, and the driver steps out. A soldier at the front hands the driver his ticket, and the line slowly shuffles forward.

Betty enters the nearly full bus, and the stench of stale beer, body odor, and cigarette smoke overwhelms her. She makes her way down the narrow aisle to the back of the bus and sits next to a sleeping airman. His eyes are already closed, and his head rests against the window. With every seat filled, the driver climbs aboard, and the door hisses shut. He slowly weaves through the crowded station, and a few minutes later, pulls out into heavy traffic. Betty was looking forward to catching up on some much-needed sleep, but the ruckus caused by the noisy soldiers continues until sometime well after midnight.

During the night, they stopped several times, and the bus is now half full and unusually quiet. The first rays of sunlight flood across an endless desert and a low-lying mist envelops the sagebrush-covered countryside. A lone coyote trots through the dark shadows toward its hidden den.

Hours later, the rumble of a rough section of road awakens her. She twists out of the cramped position that she had been sleeping in and stands in the aisle, arching her back to relieve the cramps in her neck. Still sleepy, she finds an unoccupied row of seats and sits next to a window. The bus sways rhythmically from side to side as it rumbles across the featureless landscape, and she soon falls into a deep sleep.

CHAPTER 3
LIFE IN NAZI GERMANY

BETTY WAS BORN IN BERLIN TO JEWISH PARENTS THAT WERE both medical doctors, and her early years were a wonderful time. She loved school and had many friends; however, in 1935, the dark clouds of war appeared on the horizon. Hitler's creation of the Nazi juggernaut followed his meteoric rise to power, and they sought to purify the Aryan bloodline. The Nazi's reign of terror quickly swept across the country like wildfire, and a wave of anti-Semitism turned German against German. Many cultures and religions would soon experience extreme persecution and, for many, death.

During this time, Betty was bullied at school because of her Jewish name, Elisheva Goldberg. Unhappy and fearful of her schoolmates, her only escape from the incessant personal attacks was the school's library. She loved to read, and it was there that she could immerse herself in a stress-free environment. Betty excelled at mathematics, and when she accidentally discovered the fascinating world of electricity, she was amazed to discover that mathematics was used to describe its invisible power, and her lifelong interest in electricity was born.

When she was fourteen, the Nazis began arresting Jews and others that they considered "undesirable", and the violence against them spread quickly. Jewish businesses were closed, their personal property confiscated, and death squads roamed the streets, randomly killing anyone that they suspected of being

Jewish. The constant bullying of Jewish children by Hitler Youth gangs soon turned into deadly violence.

Too afraid to leave after school, Betty would study until late in the afternoon before leaving for home. On a bleak winter day, she left the library at dusk and, as usual, she took a different route home, cutting through side streets and alleys, before walking down a dark and deserted avenue. The shops were closed, and ahead of her was a small neighborhood park with a massive tree at its center. Its dark, leafless limbs were silhouetted against the silver-gray evening sky.

As she neared it, she saw three schoolboys and a young girl hanging from the branches. A hangman's noose strained at their necks as their lifeless bodies twisted in the light breeze. Their hands were tied behind their backs, and the boy's pants were pulled down to their ankles, revealing that they were circumcised, a Jewish custom that the Hitler Youth used to identify male Jews. A crude sign pinned to the girl read, "*No One Is Safe!*".

Just then, a gang of tough-looking teenagers in uniform emerged from an alley next to the park carrying flaming torches. They were dressed in dark winter coats and waved a large red Nazi flag. An older boy held a hangman's noose in one hand, with a coil of rope wrapped over his shoulder. They had captured two young boys and were dragging them to the hanging tree.

Several of them spotted Betty and yelled for her to stop. Frozen in fear and terrified, she dropped her schoolbooks and dashed into a nearby alley, but quickly discovered it was a dead end. Realizing there was no way out, she ran from door to door trying to open one, but without success; however, the very last door opened, and she burst into the building and locked it behind her.

She peeked through a crack to see if they had seen her and watched in horror as they entered the alley banging on the doors, looking for her. Suddenly, one of the older boys walked directly toward her. The flames from his torch cast an eerie glow across his angry face, and his eyes seemed to penetrate the old wooden door.

He slowly turned the doorknob, but it remained firmly locked. Then he cursed and shook it violently, as if he knew she was hiding there. Terrified,

Betty held her breath while staring through the crack directly into his face, only inches away. Across the alley, his friends gave up their search and called to him as they left. He angrily banged on the door with his fist, then disappeared into the darkness.

The night was freezing cold and snowing and she remained hidden for another hour before mustering enough courage to leave. With no sign of the boys, she ran as fast as she could and arrived at her home exhausted and hysterical.

That night, Betty's parents realized it was time to leave Germany and emigrate to America, but the journey would be difficult, and it would take time for them to prepare. It was now too dangerous for Betty to continue going to school, so they decided to send her to live with her mother's sister in Paris, and she would wait for them there.

On a rainy afternoon, they took her to the train station and promised they would all be together in a few days. They hugged and kissed her one last time, then helped her board the train. She quickly found a seat by a window and, as the locomotive slowly pulled away from the platform, she waved a tearful goodbye to them. The train's whistle blew as it rapidly gained speed, and soon it disappeared into the mist.

It was March 18, 1935. Betty had never traveled alone before, but she made friends with a German family that had two girls about her age, and the time passed quickly. By mid-morning the following day, she arrived in Paris, and her aunt was there to meet her.

She anxiously waited several weeks for her parents to arrive, but they failed to appear. Then one day, her aunt received a letter from a relative, and she was horrified to learn that the Gestapo had arrested them, and their fate was unknown. Unsure of what to do next, her aunt wrote to a family friend, who lived near San Francisco, California, and he agreed to help her.

It was a time of great uncertainty in France, and her aunt was concerned about their future. She, like many others, felt it was only a matter of time before Hitler invaded their country. She thought about leaving but needed to care for her invalid husband who couldn't be moved.

Fortunately, an American professor and his wife were staying with her and were about to return to Chicago. They were fond of Betty and volunteered to help smuggle her to America using a false passport that showed her to be their daughter. The professor, his wife, and Betty left Paris by train to the port of Le Havre, France, where they boarded a steamship bound for New York City.

CHAPTER 4
GROWING UP IN CALIFORNIA

AFTER CROSSING THE ATLANTIC OCEAN, THEY ARRIVED IN New York and cleared customs without incident. Then they take a taxi to the impressive Grand Central Terminal in Manhattan. The Main Concourse, with its grandiose French Beaux-Arts architecture, high vaulted ceilings, and massive size, astonishes Betty. Long lines of people stood on highly polished pink marble floors on their way to every corner of America.

The professor purchased tickets for them on an express train called the *20th Century Limited*, a luxury service to Chicago and from there, Betty traveled alone on the streamlined passenger train, *The City of San Francisco*, on the Overland Route to Oakland, California.

She was only fourteen years old, and small for her age. The bullying at school had left her introverted and fearful, and now she was alone in the world and far from home. Her only possessions consisted of a bag with an extra set of clothing, a tattered doll, and a well-read copy of *The Frog Prince*.

Her journey to California would cover twenty-four hundred miles in sixty-three hours and for Betty, who only spoke a little English, traveling alone in a foreign country was a terrifying experience. As the train speeds across the vast expanse of America's Heartland, it lurches from side to side, only slowing down when it neared one of its few stops. Betty's favorite seat is in the lounge car next to an oversized window, and she spends hours there staring at some of the most desolate regions of the United States.

Unsure of what waited for her in California, she struggles with anxiety and fear of the unknown. Her only friend in the world is a small doll that her mother had given her, and she clutches it tightly as she watches the barren landscape pass by.

Two days later, the train pulled into the rail station in Oakland, California, and the conductor rushes through the cars, shouting that they have arrived. Betty gathered her things, pinned a card to her coat that had her name on it, and left the train. Karl Bauer, a family friend, quickly spotted her in the enormous crowd and called to her. She ran to him in tears, and he held her in his arms for a long time. When she felt better, they boarded the ferry. As it motored out into the immense bay, they walked to a windy railing to look at the distant city of San Francisco; however, Betty never let go of Karl's hand.

From the ferry terminal, they drove south a few miles to Karl's home in nearby San Mateo. He was a single, fifty-year-old man that lived in a modest two-bedroom house near his warehouse on the outskirts of the city. He had emigrated to America many years ago from Germany, and after arriving in San Francisco, he worked as a baker at a large hotel until he saved up enough money to buy a small electrical construction company. After a few years, his company expanded into a mid-sized business.

Betty and Karl had an instant connection with each other, and she soon referred to him as Uncle Karl. He was extremely sympathetic to her situation and was quick to provide her with a safe home where she could start a new life and, after a few months, she settled into a daily routine. As time passed, she realized that something dreadful must have happened to her parents, and she was now alone in the world. She had escaped the Nazis, but in the process, she had lost everything; her family, her country, her language, and her religion were gone, and it was a terrifying experience.

With the summer ending, it was time to start school, and her first day was challenging. She didn't know a single student, and to make things even more difficult, she spoke broken English with a heavy German accent. During this time, the newspapers published countless stories of Nazi atrocities, which appalled the American public. As sentiment against Germans became widespread, she was again shunned by her schoolmates.

Betty's adolescent years were a very painful time for her, and the years of bullying had left her friendless and unhappy. To make matters even worse, Karl's dentist recommended she wear braces, which made her an easy target, and once again, the terrifying bullying started.

One day, she came home crying, and Karl discovered what was going on. He knew something had to be done and told her she was the daughter that he would never have, and that he would like to adopt her. Betty was overwhelmed with emotion as she would no longer be an orphan, but part of a family once again, and she tearfully accepted his offer with a long hug. He also suggested that she change her name from Elisheva to Elizabeth.

She agreed but wanted to think about it. During this time, Betty Grable was the number one box office draw in the world. Grable, whose first name was also Elizabeth, was a very successful woman, and she had made a lasting impression on Betty. With her adoption completed she became an American citizen, and her new name became Betty Bauer; still German, but much more Americanized.

With her identity taken care of, Karl purchased a spacious three-bedroom house with a swimming pool in an upscale neighborhood in nearby Palo Alto. Then he hired a professional speech coach to reduce her heavy German accent. After moving into their new home, he sent her to a private school known for its high academic standing and that ended the bullying and discrimination

Betty loved the year-round warm California weather and used their swimming pool daily. Although she was late to develop physically, her long workouts soon sculpted her body from a pudgy adolescent to that of a tall, attractive young woman, and that summer her braces were removed. Throughout her years of pain and suffering, she learned to be a survivor and to cherish her independence, and it was a quality that would serve her well later in life.

However, her isolation came at a significant cost, because the social skills that she should have learned from interacting with other children her age were completely missing. Compounding the situation was the fact that Karl did not have a wife or girlfriend, so she didn't have a matriarchal influence in her life. This concerned him greatly, and he was unsure what he should do about it.

One sunny Sunday afternoon, he invited his long-time friends Camille and François over for a barbecue as he had done many times before. While Betty was swimming laps, they sat at a poolside table shaded by a large, colorful umbrella, and Karl worriedly confided his concerns about her; however, Camille was quick to come up with a workable solution. She and her husband owned a popular dance studio, and she suggested Betty take lessons as she had seen many of her students gain poise and self-confidence while studying dance. Best of all, it would also expose her to other teenagers her own age. Karl immediately liked her idea, but he didn't want to push dancing onto her. Somehow, she would have to try it on her own, but it was a radical concept for an introverted young girl.

However, the ever-resourceful Camille quickly came up with an idea. The following week, she took Betty shopping for school clothes, and on the way home, she mentioned she needed to pick up something at her studio. While she pretended to look in her office, Betty watched her class with great interest as the students appeared to be having fun dancing together. They were about to leave when Camille asked if she would like to try a new dance, and before she could say no, she started dancing with her. To her utter amazement, Betty thoroughly enjoyed herself, and before the music stopped, François cut in and expanded her confidence with a little more complicated routine.

A handsome older boy watched her from the sidelines and when she looked at him, he smiled at her, but she was embarrassed and quickly glanced away. After the music ended, he walked over to her and introduced himself. While they were talking, the music started playing, and without even asking, he took her hand and danced with her. No boy that handsome had ever even talked to her, much less danced with her, and the experience was thrilling.

On their way home, Camille built up her confidence by telling her she had done exceptionally well and invited her to attend a class for beginners. To her great surprise, Betty suddenly bubbled over with excitement and told her she would love to try it. After just a few lessons, she overcame her bashfulness and eagerly looked forward to her next lesson.

Betty became passionate about dancing and was a gifted student. She continued taking classes throughout high school, and in her senior year, her dance group took first place in a regional championship, much to Karl's amazement. Dancing had given her confidence and increased self-esteem, and as a result, she was one of the most popular girls in her class.

To earn extra money, she began working part time in Karl's office. From studying electricity in the library, she had gained a lot of theoretical knowledge, and now she could put it to good use. Karl was amazed to see that she could read the complex electrical schematics, and he paid her well for her work. She would review an upcoming project's plans and specifications, order the components, and then have them ready to be loaded out by the construction crews when the job started. She became so proficient that his project managers would ask her for technical advice when they ran into trouble.

At the end of her senior year, Betty had the highest academic standing in her class, and it was a great honor for her to be chosen valedictorian. However, the highlight was when she won a full scholarship to Stanford University. Its electrical engineering department was one of the best in the nation, and the school was located only a few miles from her home.

That summer, Karl invited her to work in the field with his installation crews. She accepted with great excitement and soon learned the practical applications of electricity. Although young, and a woman, the all-male crews welcomed her. Karl continued to mentor her with an invisible hand and never tried to force anything on her. Instead, he had a subtle way of doing things. He wanted to teach her the value of saving some of her earnings, and to make it interesting, he told her that at the end of each year, he would match whatever savings she had put away. His plan worked, and her savings quickly built up.

Betty's freshman year at Stanford was an exciting time. She was popular, loved the university lifestyle, and maintained a high grade point average. One weekend, she discovered the thrill of flying when a boyfriend took her for a ride in his plane. The experience was exhilarating and flying became her passion. She joined a flying club at the local airport and studied hard to get her private pilot's license and by the end of the following year she had earned her multi-engine rating and her commercial pilot's license.

As her passion for flying grew, she bought a used open cockpit Stearman Model 75 biplane. It was painted bright blue with yellow wings and was powered by a reliable Pratt & Whitney R-985 engine that produced three hundred horsepower. One day on a routine training flight, her instructor showed her a few aerobatic maneuvers, and she was hooked. Her biplane was perfect for aerobatics, and she became addicted to the experience.

Betty loved flying in an open cockpit plane with the wind in her face and the rush of adrenalin from the invisible g-forces that pressed against her body. She experienced a freedom of flight that she never knew existed, and she loved the psychological stresses that gripped her. It was intoxicating, especially when the ground wasn't where it should have been. From the pilot's perspective, it could be above the aircraft, or in front, or maybe to the rear. Aerobatics required an advanced set of piloting skills, and she was up for the challenge. As soon as she finished with her schoolwork, she was flying, or in the field, working for Karl's company.

Although he was initially reluctant, Betty soon had Karl out on his first flight, and it was a thrilling experience for him. The Pacific Ocean was not far away, and the sunny shoreline was one of Betty's favorite places to explore. It was only a short flight across a low-lying coastal mountain range and flying at four thousand feet in an open biplane was quite an adventure for him.

Below them were green wooded glens and yellow sun-burned meadows. Steep canyons carved into the rugged mountains sheltered magnificent redwood trees, and babbling brooks meandered through the dense forest before emptying into the ocean. Betty liked to land at an unimproved dirt airstrip near the sleepy town of Half Moon Bay, and from there it was a short walk to a seafood restaurant that overlooked the rocky shoreline. Afterward, they would fly low along the spectacular coastline before returning to Palo Alto.

Her happiness lasted until her second year at Stanford, when she focused her studies on engineering. However, discrimination would once again raise its ugly head, only this time it was gender-based. Society's perception was that women should stay at home and raise a family, which was what many did. While quite a few women were studying at the university, there was always a significant gender imbalance in their fields of study. Women dominated the humanities, and men held a majority in science, technology, engineering, and mathematics. This time, the discrimination was much more subtle, but it was there, hidden in plain sight.

When she applied for entry into the electrical engineering program, she was told it wasn't a suitable profession for a woman, and they suggested she consider one of the many humanities. Stunned by their decision, she was unsure what to do until she thought of her Jewish mathematics professor. Over time, they had become friends, and he knew her very well. Betty met with him to explain her situation, and he offered to help if he could. She showed him her grades and her honor roll status and explained that she had been earning extra money tutoring some of the electrical engineering students in the classes ahead of her. He understood her predicament and asked her to check back with him in a few days.

Betty's years of hard work hung in the balance, and she worried she may have arrived at an impasse. Soon it was time to meet with her professor, and she was extremely nervous; however, he smiled and told her he had good news. He had presented her case to a review committee, and the school reversed its position, and accepted her into the electrical engineering program, but she would be the only woman in her class.

The following years were outstanding for Betty. She graduated with honors and immediately applied for admission into Stanford's doctoral program in electrical engineering. A short time later, she received a letter from the university stating that they had accepted her, and she was excited beyond belief. Her passion for electrical engineering continued to grow, and they were her best and most rewarding years.

For the first time, she was in a serious relationship with a fellow student. His name was Robert Swanson, but she called him by his nickname Robby. He was about to graduate as a medical doctor, and they had talked about getting married after graduation and buying a home. Betty continued doing well at school and was taking on more responsibilities at Karl's company when a news flash came across the radio.

Japan had attacked Pearl Harbor!

Their lives, and the lives of millions of others, changed in an instant. Robby was only two months away from graduating and immediately enlisted in the Navy. The day after graduation, he left to fight in the war, and Betty was heartbroken as her plans for marriage and a family were put on hold indefinitely.

In the beginning, he would write to her almost every week, but he was soon assigned to a task force somewhere in the Pacific and was in the middle of some of the worst action of the island-hopping campaign.

Although the Marines did the actual fighting, the doctors served in forward medical aid stations dangerously close to the action. As time passed, his letters became more infrequent, and sometimes they would be months apart because of the remoteness of his unit's location. Then one day, Robby's mother called her. She was crying and told her she just received a telegram from the War Department stating that Robby had been killed.

Betty was devastated, as her life had once again changed forever and she learned to become more cautious about protecting her heart, especially during a time of war. A year later, she graduated from Stanford, and Karl was there to congratulate her when she received her doctorate in electrical engineering. Her schooling had been a long and arduous journey, but it also was a time of great personal growth. It had been the best of times, and sometimes the worst of times, but through it all, her bond with Karl had grown even stronger. That night, he treated her to dinner and a show in San Francisco, and as always, they had a fabulous evening together.

With school out of the way, Betty needed to decompress and think about what she would do next. The popular resort town of Palm Springs was only four hundred miles away, so she decided to take a brief vacation and relax in the warm sun. When she arrived, she took a taxi to a nearby resort, and by that afternoon was relaxing by a sunny pool, wondering what to do with her life. Karl wanted her to help expand his company as there was plenty of wartime construction going on in the Bay Area; however, she appreciated the many opportunities that America had given her and wished that there was something she could do to contribute to the war effort.

One evening, she went to see a movie and, as usual, the theater showed a newsreel covering the latest news, which included an announcement that the Women Airforce Service Pilots group was looking for experienced women pilots. They were needed to ferry military planes from aircraft factories for shipment to the war zones. And with that, she knew what she wanted to do. Betty sent in her application, and someone soon contacted her. She met with a recruiter, signed some paperwork, and was told to report to Avenger Field, an Army Air Force airbase, near Sweetwater, Texas, for three months of training. When she arrived, her commanding officer noticed her years of flying experience and she was immediately assigned to regular duty as a ferry pilot.

CHAPTER 5
AVENGER FIELD, TEXAS

IT'S THE SUMMER OF 1943. THE MORNING SUN PEAKS OVER A distant mountain range as a dusty military bus pulls off to the side of the road. Its air brakes hiss as it comes to a stop in front of Avenger Field near Sweetwater, Texas. The desolate, wind-blown, semi-arid base is well known for its jackrabbits and rattlesnakes, and its ram-shackled buildings reflect years of exposure to the unrelenting sun and desert winds. A large sign reads, *"Home of the Women Airforce Service Pilots"*. The bus's door swings open, and the driver exits, followed by Betty. He unlocks the luggage compartment and hands her duffel bag to her. "Here you go, miss. Have a nice day."

She gives him a tired "Thanks," and steps back as it pulls away in a cloud of dust and disappears into the distance.

Avenger Field is an Army airbase about two hundred miles west of Fort Worth, near the center of Texas, and is used exclusively for training WASP pilots. Over 25,000 women applied, 1,830 qualified, 1,074 completed training. . . and Betty was one of them. The trainees received 560 hours of ground school and 210 hours of flight training, including classes in Morse code, meteorology, military law, physics, aircraft mechanics, communications, and navigation.

Most of the cadets were white, except for two Chinese Americans, two women of Hispanic descent, and one Native American woman. Although qualified, all African American applicants were rejected. Sadly, the WASP pilots did not qualify for military benefits and only received two-thirds of the pay that the men did. Each member paid for their own transportation, the cost of their uniforms, and for room and board.

The pungent smell of sagebrush fills the warm morning air, and Betty takes a deep breath. She opens a pocket on her flight suit, removes a case holding her sunglasses, and adjusts them before walking over to the checkpoint. She hands an armed military police officer her identification papers, which he briefly glances at, and enters the airbase.

It's Sunday morning, and the main street is deserted. A loose panel of rusty metal roofing material rattles in the light breeze, and a startled jackrabbit bounds away in fright. She walks over to a building with an American flag flying in front of it and hauls her duffel bag up a couple of steps. Attached to the front is a large painting of Fifi, the WASP logo. She opens a well-worn door with a sign over it that reads, "*Base Operations*" and enters the building.

The inside is distinctly military in décor, with light institutional green walls and a polished dark brown linoleum floor. At the far end, a woman stands on a low stepladder, filling chalkboards with information. A window fan blows fresh air into the room, and several women sit at desks quietly typing, while others sort out paperwork.

As she approaches, the woman behind the counter looks up and smiles. "Hello, Betty. I haven't seen you for a while."

"Hi, Cheryl," and she slides an envelope toward her. "They've been keeping me pretty busy," and signs in. "How are things here?"

"It's been crazy. We're moving planes from all over the states now. They're making them faster than we can deliver them."

A side door bursts open, and a WASP pilot wearing a pressed Army issue khaki skirt and blouse enters the room. She's a pretty brunette with blue eyes, a slim build, and speaks with a Canadian accent. "Betty! It's good to see you! Someone said they saw you get off the bus."

Sharron is Betty's best friend, and she's happy to see her. "Hi! How are you?"

"Busy, as usual. How 'bout you?"

"I'm tired. I never thought I would be so glad to get back to this place."

Sharron takes her by the arm. "It's a beautiful morning. Come on, and I'll fill you in on the latest."

They walk down a sidewalk lined with white rocks. On each side are wooden barracks painted desert tan with green asphalt shingle roofs. Ahead of them is a large lawn with women sunbathing on army blankets, while others gather under a willow tree talking in small groups. They sit down on a shaded bench and Betty stretches out her legs. "Oh, that feels good. That bus seat was impossible to sleep in."

Sharron laughs. "I know what that's like!" and smiles. "We're going to the club tonight. Why don't you join us?"

"Thanks, but I'd rather catch up on my sleep. I haven't had a day off in a month!"

"Aw, come on. It'll be fun. Life can't be all work. You need to get out and about more often!"

Betty is too tired to argue. "Well, okay. I would like to see the girls."

"Great! I'll see you at dinner," and she starts to leave. "Did they give you another assignment?"

"No, and hopefully not right away."

It's later that evening, darkness has fallen, and a cool breeze has replaced the unrelenting heat of the day. A white 1939 Ford convertible drives down the deserted main street of the small town of Sweetwater, located just a few miles from the airbase. It stops in front of the Avengerette Club, a brick building with a neon sign that glows red and shows the outline of two people dancing.

Two men sit at the bar talking to a local woman, and music from an old jukebox plays softly as a lone couple quietly slow dance, lost in their own world. The girls chat among themselves as they walk to a table, and the waitress soon arrives. "Hi, ladies. What would you like to drink?"

Sharron seems to be in charge of the evening's entertainment and orders. "The usual, Virginia."

Pamela, a cute brunette from North Carolina, laughs. "Like they had something else to choose from."

The waitress gives her a stern look and walks back to the bar. Sharron is happy to be away from the base. "Aren't you glad you changed your mind?"

Betty looks around at the nearly empty room and shakes her head. "I'd forgotten how deserted this town can be."

An officer that was sitting at the bar approaches their table. He has a friendly smile and walks up to Betty. "Excuse me, miss, but would you like to dance?"

He surprises her, and she stumbles for words. "Oh! Ah, no thanks. Maybe later."

Undaunted, he looks over at an attractive girl from California. "Hi, Linda. How about a dance?"

"Sure, Hank. I'd love to," and the two of them hold hands and walk out onto the floor, enjoying a lost moment away from their lives in the Army.

Sharron pushes Betty's arm. "Are you crazy? That guy was a dreamboat!"

Betty shakes her head. "I know. I know. I just need to relax for a minute."

The waitress returns with a tray of chilled glasses filled with Coca-Cola and sets them on the table. Sharron reaches into her purse, covertly removes a bottle of clear liquor, and pours a small amount into each glass. Betty laughs at her antics. "I'd forgotten this is a dry county. Where did you buy that bottle?"

Sharron winks at her. "There's a little old lady in town that sells it for two dollars a bottle."

Betty laughs, then makes a toast. "To the best of friends!" and they raise their glasses.

Sharron takes a sip. "Did you hear they arrested Kathy when she landed at Fort Collins?"

Betty is surprised. "What are you talking about?"

"When they saw that a woman was flying a fighter, they assumed she had stolen it, and they threw her in the stockade!"

"You're kidding, aren't you?"

Sharron laughs. "No, I'm not. It really happened. Now when she flies in there, she puts on a fake mustache so she'll look like a guy! It's hilarious."

Dotty, a tall redhead from Florida, chimes in. "Why do men think it's so strange to see a woman flying a plane? We're just trying to help the war effort."

Betty looks around and asks, "Where's Evelyn?" The group falls into an uneasy silence, and she frowns. "What's wrong?"

Sharron speaks in a low voice. "Evelyn was killed a week ago in a new plane with less than twenty hours on it. She was flying over rugged terrain and radioed that her engine had locked up, and that was the last they heard from her."

Betty can't believe it. "What did the crash report say?"

Sharron leans toward her and whispers. "They discovered her engine froze because someone put sugar in her fuel tank. It crystalized in the fuel injectors and stopped the flow of gas."

"How did that get into her fuel tank?"

"Because one of the mechanics put it there!"

Betty has a worried look and lowers her voice. "I think someone sabotaged me on my last flight."

Sharron is astonished. "Sabotage! What do you mean?"

"I was ferrying a new P-47 and an oil line came loose. It sprayed onto the exhaust manifold and started an engine fire. I was lucky and barely made it to an airfield. The mechanic said someone had removed the locking wire!"

"Oh, my Gosh!"

"There's been other strange malfunctions, too. I just never put it together until now. Why would our own people want to murder us?"

Sharron looks over her shoulder to make sure no one was listening to them and speaks in a low voice. "This isn't the first time something like this has happened. A lot of men in the military resent women doing what they consider men's jobs. We're supposed to be at home raising a family. It's gender discrimination on a grand scale." She continues with sadness in her voice. "I'm taking up a collection for Evelyn's burial expenses. The Army won't pay for anything because they classify us as civilians."

Betty is disgusted. "Count me in," then stands. "I need some time by myself. I'll catch a taxi back to the base."

Sharron gives her a hug. "Sure, sweetie, get some sleep. You'll feel better in the morning."

Visibly shaken, Betty walks toward the front door. Unfortunately, Evelyn wasn't the first WASP pilot killed in the line of duty. It was a dangerous job, and everyone was aware of the risk that they were taking. More than a thousand pilots flew many types of aircraft, and in all kinds of weather. Eventually, mid-air collisions, mechanical failures, pilot error, and fires would claim the lives of over thirty women. Most of them were just like her; they were young, they loved to fly, and they wanted to help their country.

It's a sunny fall morning several days later, and Betty and Sharron sit at a table in the mess hall having breakfast with two other WASP pilots. A light breeze billows the curtains, and the scent of flowering desert plants drifts through the open windows. The room is filled with the sounds of women talking, and the noisy banging of pots and pans echoes from the kitchen.

Cheryl approaches them with a tray of food, and Betty motions to her. "Hi. Please join us," and she pulls out a chair for her.

"Thanks." She hesitates for a moment, knowing Betty's not going to like her news. "I'm sorry, but they rescheduled you."

"Oh, no. So soon? I was hoping I'd have another day or so to rest up," and sets down her cup of coffee. "Did you see the orders?"

"Yeah. You're picking up a B-25 in Houston and delivering it to New Castle Airbase in Delaware."

Sharron whistles. "Wow! A twin-engine attack bomber!"

"It's about time. We trained on them months ago. When do I have to be there?"

"You leave on the afternoon bus."

CHAPTER 6

FLIGHT TO NEW CASTLE ARMY AIR BASE

AN OLIVE-GREEN MILITARY BUS PULLS OFF A BUSY HIGHWAY and approaches a checkpoint at the main gate to Scott Army Airfield on the outskirts of Houston. It comes to a full stop, and the driver hands his papers to a smartly dressed military police officer. He glances at them, returns the paperwork, and motions them forward. It continues down the street, passing a column of troops dressed in white tee-shirts, crew cuts, olive drab trousers, and shiny black boots. They march at the side of the road in perfect unison, and a drill sergeant calls to them loudly. "To your left, to your left, to your left, right, left."

Betty stares blankly out the window as the bus passes them and a short time later, it stops at the operations center. She enters the building and takes a seat in a large briefing room along with other WASP pilots. They are dressed in khaki uniforms, brown leather flight jackets, and many wear dark green aviation sunglasses. In front of them is a low stage, and on the walls are maps and weather charts. A young lieutenant stands by a side door. Suddenly, he snaps to attention and yells. "On your feet!" and they stand as the briefing officer enters.

"At ease, ladies. Please take your seats. As you already know, we've got a flight of six B-25s going up to New Castle." He turns to a large map of the east coast of the United States hanging on the wall behind him and uses his pointer.

"This is your route. It's about thirteen hundred miles, and you'll be close to your maximum range, so be sure and monitor your fuel supplies."

As he traces out their proposed route, he adds anecdotes that pertain to their upcoming flight, and finishes his brief comments. "I don't expect any complications. Just stay together and follow the lead aircraft. The weather boys say it will be clear all the way. Any questions?"

A pilot raises her hand.

"Yes?"

"When do we leave?"

"Zero nine-hundred tomorrow morning. Well, that's about it, ladies. Have a pleasant flight." The women stand in unison, return his salute, and follow him out of the briefing room, talking amongst themselves.

The next morning comes soon enough, and the slight delay has given Betty the opportunity to rest and recuperate. She is up early, has a light breakfast, and takes a walk to look around the base. This is her favorite time of the day, and it's a habit that she's had for quite a while. It gives her a chance to pull her thoughts together and get organized for the day.

An hour later, Betty is dressed in a black sheepskin flight jacket and is wearing a parachute. Although warm on the ground, the weather at altitude will be freezing cold. The airbase is very busy, and there's a lot of activity with planes coming and going from every direction. Ahead of her, and parked in a row, are six twin-engine B-25 bombers surrounded by ground crews.

The Mitchell B-25 is a medium class bomber, manufactured by North American Aviation at its plant in Inglewood, California. It's an impressive sight with its twin seventeen hundred horsepower radial engines and bristles with heavy machine guns. It has a wingspan of sixty-seven feet and is supported by a tricycle-style landing gear. The nose has a large greenhouse-type canopy and forward mounted machine guns. A comfortable cockpit provides the pilots with an unrestricted view, and the plane's twin vertical rudders give it a very distinctive look.

Betty walks down the row of planes, scanning the tail numbers. Spotting her plane, she approaches it just as a member of the ground crew pulls out the plane's wheel chocks. He comes to attention and salutes her. "Morning, mam."

She returns his salute. "Good morning," and pre-flights the plane by walking around it to inspect its flight surfaces for wear.

A smiling WASP pilot approaches her. "Hi, I'm Susie McAllister," and the two women shake hands.

"I'm Betty Bauer. Nice to meet you."

Susie is cute with short blonde hair, blue eyes, and a bubbly, extraverted personality. She's a recent graduate from the WASP flight school and is a little nervous. "I'll be your copilot today."

Still focused on her walk-around, Betty talks to her as she ducks under the plane's fuselage. "How much flight time do you have?"

"Not too much. I just graduated."

Betty carefully inspects the landing gear and tires for wear. "That's okay. We've all had our first day at work. Climb aboard. I'll be up there in a minute."

The plane sits low to the ground, and its massive bomb bay doors are open. Susie ducks under the fuselage and tosses her gear bag inside. She climbs up a short ladder, hunches over, and maneuvers along the narrow passageway before stepping into the cockpit. Betty soon follows and buckles herself into her seat. She reaches up to the overhead instrument panel and flips on several toggle switches. She's logged quite a few hours in the B-25 and is relaxed and confident at the controls.

Susie reviews her navigation charts, goes through her weather advisories, then checks their fuel supplies. "We've got full tanks, and we're ready to go."

Betty is the most experienced pilot and will be the flight leader today. She glances down at her watch. "It's time to get under way." Her crew chief is standing on the ground in front of the plane, and she waves to him, indicating she is about to start her engines. She reaches forward to adjust her altimeter, then opens the cockpit's side window and calls out. "Clear One!" alerting her ground crew that engine number one is about to start. She presses the starter button and there's a loud cranking noise as the massive radial engine cycles several times before bursting into life. A few moments later, the second engine starts, and a huge cloud of whitish-gray exhaust swirls around the plane.

A heavy vibration flows through the plane as the two powerful engines warm up, producing a deafening roar that resonates against the nearby hangars. The B-25 is notoriously loud because the factory upgraded it to larger engines at the last minute, and there was only enough room for very short exhaust stacks.

Betty presses the microphone button on her control yoke and contacts the tower. "Army eight six ready to taxi."

The tower responds. "Army eight six, cleared to taxi to runway zero niner."

She confirms. "Roger," and pushes her throttles forward. Her crew chief salutes her as she passes him, and she returns his salute. Behind her, the other planes move out and form into a long and impressive line. A few minutes later, she stops at a holding point short of the runway and waits. To her right, a huge four-engine B-17 Flying Fortress is on final approach, and she watches intently as the giant bomber flies past her. Its wheels touch the pavement with a screech, and dark puffs of smoke from its tires swirl around the landing gear as the plane decelerates.

Betty is next in line and revs her engines, checking them for any problems. The B-25 shudders violently for a moment, then she lowers the rpm. The glass-lined room at the top of the control tower is busy with four air traffic controllers all talking at once. A calm sergeant holding a microphone and wearing headphones stands at the window with a commanding view of the entire complex. He looks down at the long string of B-25 attack bombers. "Army eight six, you are cleared for take-off."

Betty confirms her instructions by repeating them back to the air traffic controller. "Army eight six, cleared for take-off," then looks over at Susie. "Ready?" and she nods in the affirmative.

She pushes the throttles forward and the bomber slowly moves out onto the runway, pivots to the left, and lines up with the centerline. She breaks to a stop and increases her engines to full power. It's a technique she learned from an instructor that was a Navy carrier pilot. It proves that they aren't likely to fail, and it also shortens her normal takeoff distance considerably.

A moment later, she releases her brakes and, without the weight of a typical bomb load of twenty-four hundred pounds, the B-25 races down the runway. She pulls back on the control yoke, and it gently lifts into the air. One by one, the other planes in her group take off and catch up to her. They fly in a double 'V' formation high above the blue Atlantic Ocean, with Betty's plane in the lead. It's sunny and cold at ten thousand feet, and they settle in for the long flight ahead of them.

She looks over at Susie. "Feel like taking it for a while?"

"Thanks. I can't wait."

"Okay, she's all yours, but let me show you a trick I learned. The B-25s have a tendency to fly nose up. Just give her a little flap, and it'll level her out."

Susie checks the flap setting and sees that she has already set it for level flight. "Thanks," and she glances at Betty. "What led you to join?"

"I started flying in college. I joined because I wanted to contribute to the war effort. How about you?"

"I always wanted to know how to fly. After college, my father sent me to a private flight school and when I heard about this program, I volunteered. He pulled some strings, and they accepted me right away."

"He must be an important man to do that."

"Yeah, I guess so. He's a Senator from Vermont, but please don't tell anyone. I want to do this on my own."

"Don't worry. Your secret is safe with me."

Susie scans her gauges. "It's about time to switch out our auxiliary tanks," and she rotates the fuel selector handle. "We're looking good, and we've got a nice tailwind. I heard our next plane won't be there until Monday, which gives us the weekend off."

"What are you thinking?" asks Betty.

"Well, it's close to New York City. Have you ever been there?"

"No. Have you?"

"Sure, it's a real hoot. We could catch a couple of shows on Broadway."

"That sounds like fun!"

"Super! Daddy said the Ziegfeld Follies and Oklahoma are playing, and Bob Hope might be there, too. We can stay at my parent's penthouse. We'd only be minutes away." She reaches over to the radio and spins the dial. "Let's see. There's gotta be a good station here somewhere," and the music of Glenn Miller playing "In the Mood," fills the cockpit.

Several hours later, Susie is flying, and she reaches over and shakes Betty's shoulder. "Wake up. We're coming up on New Castle."

She opens her eyes and stretches. "Thanks. How's our schedule?"

"We're right on time, and we've got fuel to spare."

The late afternoon sun paints the skyline orange as they approach New Castle Army Airbase in Wilmington, Delaware. The huge complex is a major material staging area for the war, and it's a beehive of activity, with aircraft arriving from all over the country. One by one, their flight of B-25s land, and turn off the runway.

Betty is on the radio with the other planes. "Follow me down to Staging Area 27. We're supposed to park there."

Her speaker crackles with the voice of another WASP pilot. "Roger that. We're right behind you," and they follow each other in a long line.

An airman in a jeep leads them to a busy area where ground crews wait. Betty rolls into her parking spot and shuts down her engines. As she finishes updating her logbook, she looks over at Susie. "You did a great job today. You're a natural pilot."

"Thanks. That was really exciting!"

They exit their plane through the bomb bay doors and approach the operations center. As darkness engulfs them, powerful lights turn on, giving the busy airbase an eerie, unnatural look. Work continues at the same never-changing, hectic pace, day, and night.

As they walk, Susie unzips her heavy jacket. "It'll be nice to get out of this flight gear and freshen up."

"Yeah. I know what you mean."

They enter the operations center and head for the women's shower room. It's very busy, and women in white bathrobes hurry past them. They remove their heavy flight jackets, and Susie closes the door to her wall locker. "This is my first time at New Castle. Where do we go from here?"

"The Operation Center, and then we'll find something to eat."

The cafeteria is a huge room filled with men and women eating together, and they slide their trays along the serving line as cooks place food on them. Susie looks around for a table. "I don't think I've ever seen so many good-looking guys." Several airmen walk past them, and she nudges Betty. "Let's check out the Officer's Club after dinner."

It's later that evening, and they enter the busy club. The enormous room has a bandstand at the front, and a huge dance floor surrounded on three sides by tables. The band plays loudly as they work their way through the crowd, searching for a table.

Susie looks around excitedly. "Boy, this place is hopping!" She turns to follow Betty, but bumps into an airman walking toward her.

He apologizes. "Oops. Excuse me, miss."

She looks up to see a nice-looking officer staring at her. "Sorry. It was my fault. I wasn't watching where I was going."

"First time to the club?"

She flirts back. "Yes. We just flew in."

"Not in one of our transports, I hope."

"No. A B-25."

"Was that your flight late this afternoon?"

"Yep. That was us."

"I'm impressed! By the way, I'm Jerry."

"Nice to meet you. I'm Susie."

He calls to his buddies sitting at a nearby table. "Hey, guys. These ladies brought those B-25s in this afternoon," and he turns back to her. "Come and sit with us. I'd like to buy you and your friend a drink."

Susie waves excitedly at Betty. "Over here!"

A tall pilot with a southern drawl stands up. "Hi. I'm Marty. This is Hank, and that's Bret."

"I'm Susie and this is Betty," and they join them.

Jerry is excited and looks at Betty. "We're headed to Illinois to train on B-25s. What are they like to fly?"

"You tell them, Susie. You're the expert."

"Expert! Wow, fill us in!"

Susie quickly falls into the role of an expert. "Gosh. I love flying the B-25." She talks with her hands, and the pilots hang on to her every word. "The secret to flying a B-25 is that they have a tendency to fly nose up, so you need to give her a little flap, and it'll level her out."

Marty smiles at Betty. "They're going to be talking about flying all night. How about a dance?"

She is more relaxed now and accepts. "Thanks, I'd love to."

They slow dance with the other couples, and for a moment, the war is far away.

CHAPTER 7

THE ATLANTIC CROSSING

THE FOLLOWING DAY, THEY ENTER THE BUSY OPERATIONS center and scan large bulletin boards covered with schedules and weather advisories. Susie locates their orders and calls to Betty. "Here we are!"

She joins her and reads the notice. "Hmm, it looks like they canceled our flight. So much for our trip to Broadway!"

"Oh, no!" cries Susie, disappointed by the news.

Betty continues reading. "This is strange. We're scheduled to fly, but it doesn't say what we're flying, or where we're going. I've never seen orders like this!"

Later that afternoon, twenty-four WASP pilots sit in rows of chairs in a large, nearly empty briefing room and wait patiently. Susie nudges Betty. "Where is everybody? And why are the military police guarding the entrance?"

"I don't know. Something's not right."

A side door opens, and a colonel enters the room as the WASP pilots stand and come to attention. Col. Westly is an older man in his late fifties and looks more like a college professor. "At ease, ladies," and they sit down. "I'll come right to the point. Our B-17s are arriving here faster than we can deliver them to England, and we are extremely short of male pilots. WASP pilots have never attempted the Atlantic crossing because it leads directly into the war zone, or I should say . . . almost. I'm sure you know it's the Army's policy not to allow women to enter combat zones, but our fly boys desperately need these planes."

He walks over to a large map of Europe and taps his pointer on it. "What I'm suggesting is that we use WASP pilots to ferry these bombers to England. Ireland is closer, but they are a neutral country, so we're not allowed to land there. Our plan is for you to fly from here to Labrador, which is about 1,000-miles and refuel.

"After that, you'll make the 2,500-mile Atlantic crossing. Your planes will be fitted with portable gas tanks in the bomb bay, so you'll have plenty of fuel. Because of the great distance, each plane will be crewed with a pilot, a co-pilot, and a navigator."

The colonel pauses, then walks to the front of the stage. "You're already checked out on the twin-engine B-25. The question is. Can you fly the bigger, and much harder to handle, four-engine B-17?"

A WASP raises her hand. "We can do it, Colonel. Just give us a chance."

He smiles. "Let's see how your training goes before I make a final decision. That's all I have for the moment. Report to Hangar 34 after this meeting for further instructions."

Hangar 34 is an immense building and is filled with aircraft in various states of repair. The WASP pilots walk to a huge four-engine B-17 parked in front and its sheer size dwarfs the group. A flight instructor addresses them. "Because you are experienced pilots, we're going to compress your training into a week. You'll have orientation classes covering instrument flying, long-range navigation, and you'll get to spend plenty of time in the B-17.

"Our boys are dying over there, and they need these planes badly. If ever there was something you could do for your country, this is it. Are there questions?" and he scans the audience for a moment. "Alright then, dismissed!"

The WASP pilots walk out to their bombers parked in a long row on the flight line and Susie confides to Betty. "I'm really nervous."

"Don't be. You're a natural. You handled the B-25 like a pro. This one is just a little bigger."

"Yeah, but that's the part that worries me."

As they approach their plane, they see another WASP pilot talking to an officer and she turns to them. "Hi. I'm Shirley, your navigator, and this is Stan, our instructor."

They shake hands, and he goes over the flight plan with them. "This morning, I'll cover every detail inside and out until you've got it memorized. After lunch, we'll fly up the coast to let you get a feel for the plane. Shirley is your navigator, so she'll take her training on long distance and celestial navigation in a nearby classroom." He turns to her. "Do you know where it is?"

"Yes," and she holds up several papers. "I have the directions."

"Good. Why don't you meet us here at the end of the week?"

As she leaves, she smiles at Betty. "It was nice meeting you," and walks back to the hangar.

Stan explains. "We'll start with the pre-flight walk around." They duck under the fuselage, and he hands them a checklist. He points up at the plane's massive control surfaces, and shows them what type of damage, or wear, to look for. When they finish, he opens a door at the rear of the plane, and they carefully step over the ball turret that partially sticks up from the floor. It hangs below the belly and protects the bomber from fighters attacking from below. Then it's a long uphill walk on a narrow catwalk.

They squeeze past machine guns that stick out of large open windows on each side, and Stan apologizes for the cramped space. "Sorry, there's not much room inside," and he pushes a heavy fifty-caliber machine gun out of the way. "There are ten of these babies protecting her. That's where her nickname comes from—the Flying Fortress."

The women settle in at the controls, and he sits in a jump seat behind them. "Okay, ladies, she's all yours. Let's see what you've learned."

Betty grins. "I can't wait."

He flashes a smile at her. "Whenever you're ready."

She slides her side window back and calls out. "Clear One!" The engine slowly turns over a few times, then coughs to life, producing a cloud of gray exhaust smoke. The other engines start one at a time, and the huge plane shutters from the brute force of four thousand horsepower. Betty idles them for a minute, allowing the oil temperature and hydraulic pressure to stabilize, then contacts air traffic control, and they route her through a complex maze of taxiways that lead to the main runway. Ahead of her are several cargo planes waiting for clearance to depart. One by one, they takeoff and blast past her on their way to parts unknown.

Moments later, the tower gives her permission to leave, and she pushes forward on a row of four throttle levers, one for each engine. The huge bomber rotates ninety degrees to the left and points down the long empty stretch of asphalt. Betty doesn't waste any time and quickly increases her throttles to full power. The huge bomber slowly picks up speed, and at a hundred and fifteen miles an hour, she pulls back lightly on the control yoke and the massive plane lifts off the ground. The landing gear retracts, and they climb into the clear blue sky, followed by the rest of the planes in her group.

Betty and Susie handle the plane with ease, which impresses Stan, and he presses his throat microphone. "That was very nice, ladies. I think you could teach me a thing or two. Take her up to twenty-five thousand feet on a northeast heading."

The radio crackles as Betty acknowledges him. "Two five thousand, heading 045."

"Follow the coast for a half hour and then return to base."

"Roger."

After a while, she glances over at Susie. "Want to take over?"

"Thanks, Betty. I'd love to."

Back at the women's dormitory, they excitedly relive their first experience with the B-17. Dorothy is excited. "Gosh, that was incredible! I never dreamed it would be that fantastic."

Dawn blurts out. "When those engines started, I knew this was going to be a day to remember. Do you realize we will be the first women to fly a B-17 across the Atlantic?"

It's five days later, and Col. Westly addresses the seated class inside the hangar. "I want you ladies to know that you've done very well, and you should be proud of your accomplishments as pilots. This is the last day of training and your final check ride. Lt. Bauer has the most flight time and will be your Group Leader."

Susie is sitting next to Betty and gives her a gentle nudge. "Good job!"

The WASP pilots exit the building and walk along the flight line toward their planes. Shirley, their navigator, catches up to them. "Well, ladies. One more check ride and then we face the long crossing."

Susie doesn't have a lot of flying experience and whispers to Betty. "Jeez, I'm so nervous. What happens if I mess up?"

"Come on now, don't psych yourself out. You're a natural, remember?" She reaches into her flight jacket, pulls out a small teddy bear, and hands it to her. "Here, I want you to have my good luck charm."

"Oh, no. You should keep it."

But Betty is adamant. "No. I insist. I'm depending on you. You can give it back to me later if you want to." She puts her arm around Susie, and they walk toward their bomber. "Don't worry. You're going to be an expert by the time we get to England."

"Thanks, Betty. I really appreciate it."

Everyone has a successful final check ride, and the girls wait anxiously outside the headquarters building for Betty to return from her meeting with Col. Westly. Mildred paces back and forth. "She's been in there a long time. Maybe something went wrong."

Suddenly, the door swings open, and Betty and their flight instructor, Stan, approach them. He has a big grin on his face. "Congratulations, ladies! Everyone passed with flying colors!" and the aircrews explode with excitement and congratulate each other. He continues. "Betty has a flight certification for each one of you, and I would like to give you something special myself." He hands out a small, gift-wrapped box to each of them. "It's been a pleasure flying with you!"

Susie opens her gift. It's a shiny new silver dollar with a WASP insignia soldered to the back side and she gives him a huge hug. "Thank you so much."

The women excitedly talk amongst themselves, and Betty calls out to them. "Last chance to get some rest. We leave tomorrow morning at 0800!"

The next day soon arrives, and a chill fills the morning air as winter is fast approaching. Their massive four-engine bombers lumber down New Castle's long runway and slowly lift into the cloudless sky one at a time. Betty climbs to seven thousand feet, and throttles back her engines, waiting for the other planes to catch up. Below them lies the vast Atlantic Ocean, and the reality of what they are about to attempt sinks into Susie.

"This is going to be the longest flight I've ever made."

"Yes, but this is only the prelude to the Atlantic crossing, which is more than twice as long." Then she calls Shirley on the intercom. "How are you doing back there?"

Shirley gazes out her frost-covered window. "Actually, I'm pretty comfortable."

Betty presses the microphone button on her control yoke. "Can't say that about up here. What's our estimated time of arrival?"

"It's 1,000-miles to the Royal Canadian Air Force station in Labrador. It should take us about five or six hours depending on the winds. I'll give you course corrections and a revised estimated time of arrival in route."

"Thanks."

She stares out the window and looks over at Susie. "It looks like beautiful weather for this leg of our flight."

Susie is mesmerized by the vastness in front of them. "What a view! You can see forever!"

"Yeah. It'll be mid-afternoon when we land in Labrador. We'll top off our fuel tanks and get an early start tomorrow morning. Then it's 2,500-miles to England, with nothing under us but ice-cold water."

Susie laughs. "Well, I hope the bathroom works. We can't just land in some farmer's field like I used to do."

"Didn't you worry about getting caught?"

"I didn't think anyone would ever know, but when I landed several hours later, I had dry pig poop splattered all over the plane and the ground crew quickly figured out that I had made an unscheduled stop. Turns out that it's not easy to remove, and I took a lot of ribbing because of it."

"That's funny! Actually, I thought about doing the same thing several times."

As they climb past ten thousand feet, they put on their oxygen masks and conversation is now more difficult. White contrails from their formation contrast against a gunmetal-blue sky and the cold Atlantic Ocean is far below them, covered by scattered low-lying clouds. At twenty thousand feet, they catch a strong tailwind, and the skin of the bomber is well below freezing; however, they are wearing high-altitude flight gear and remain warm.

Several hours of monotony pass, and Betty radios the other bombers on a shared frequency. "We're about a half hour out of Labrador. Descend to six thousand feet and follow me."

Forty-five minutes later, the faint outline of land appears on the horizon. The airbase is located on a desolate spit that protrudes out from the low-lying coastline and extends into a calm bay. As it comes into view, they see several enormous hangars and an assortment of weathered wooden buildings. A long, enclosed hallway connects the three-story control tower to a large Quonset hut, a lightweight prefabricated structure made of corrugated steel. It has a semicircular cross-section, which is sealed at each end by insulated plywood walls.

Betty approaches the runway that the Canadians built specifically to support Americans transporting heavy bombers and radios for permission to land. She stares at a dozen Martin B-26 twin-engine medium bombers parked off the taxiway. "It looks like we've got company down there."

Susie glances up at the threatening sky. "Yeah, but the weather is getting worse by the minute."

Betty is surprised to see the rocky snow-covered hills behind the airbase. "We're pretty far north. It looks like the Canadian winter has already started."

She lands, taxis to a vacant parking area off the taxiway, and the rest of the bombers follow her. Betty shuts down her engines, and there is total silence as they remove their headsets and stow their charts. Susie stares at the desolate wind-blown base as large snowflakes hover outside the cockpit windows. "This is one lonely airbase! All those planes and there isn't a single person in sight!"

Betty laughs. "As long as they've got hot showers, I don't care about the rest."

Stiff and tired from the long flight, they clamber out of the cockpit and work their way down the narrow catwalk. A blast of frigid Arctic air greets them as they leave their plane, and they crunch through a light layer of snow as they hurry toward the buildings. The other aircrews follow them with their heads bowed to avoid the icy gusts of arctic air.

The women enter the building that connects the control tower to the Quonset hut through a side door, and the howling wind slams it shut behind them. Betty looks back at her group. "Is everybody inside?" Several women shiver and nod in the affirmative. "Okay, let's get checked in."

They walk down the cold, deserted hallway and enter a large room filled with noisy aircrews laughing and talking; however, at the sight of twenty-four attractive women, they fall silent. Betty notices a sergeant carrying a clipboard and walks over to him. "Hello, I'm Lt. Bauer."

"Hi, I'm Nick. Give me a minute and I'll check you in." He looks over at the silent airmen and smiles. "Sorry about them. You're the first female pilots ever to stop here. When they get over the shock of seeing women, you won't be able to get rid of them!" He points toward the noisy kitchen in the back of the room. "Take a seat. We'll be serving chow in a few minutes."

Several of the male pilot's approach, and an officer with a southern accent, introduces himself. "Hi, I'm Josh."

Susie gives him a big smile and makes the introductions. "I'm Susie. This is Shirley, and our group leader, Betty." Introductions are made and Betty follows the sergeant to his office. "We're just spending the night. We'll be leaving in the morning."

"Yes, mam. I'll have your tanks topped off after dinner."

The following day, they find themselves fogged in and grounded, but later that afternoon, the fog dissipates, and the forecast is for clear weather by evening. This is the news Betty's been waiting to hear, and she's excited at the thought of getting back into the air again. She looks over at Susie. "We might be leaving soon. Let's check on our plane."

It's still snowing, but the winds have died down and they crunch through the light snow to inspect their bomber. Ahead of them, a maintenance crew sweeps snow off the bomber's wings and Betty scans the horizon. "The weather is getting better. We might be cleared to leave in a few hours."

Susie rubs her hands and shivers in the icy wind. "I can't wait!"

By late afternoon, the visibility is improving, so Betty calls her aircrews together. "They expect the fog to clear soon, so we should be able to leave after dinner, which means an overnight flight. That should put us in England around sunrise tomorrow morning. If you want to take a quick nap, now would be a good time."

After dinner, the women say goodbye to their new friends and exit the building. They approach their planes, and Betty does her usual walk-around and pre-flights it. Susie enters the cockpit to check on their fuel supplies, and Shirley sits down at her navigation station and organizes her nav charts.

Minutes later, Betty arrives, and they go through their checklists. She signals her crew chief that she's about to start her engines, and he waves back at her. A mechanic standing under her wing starts his portable generator, then connects a power cable to an outlet in the belly of their plane. He steps back into view and signals for her to start her engines.

Betty flips several toggle switches, and the whirling sound of electric pumps fills the cockpit. Satisfied that all is well, she starts her engines and, one by one, they turn over and burst into life with a thunderous roar. She is on the radio talking with the other planes as they warm up in preparation for the long flight ahead.

There is no traffic in the area, so they roll onto the runway one at a time and soar into the clear evening sky. After adjusting her seat, Betty settles in for the long flight ahead of them and looks over at Susie. "Better make yourself comfortable. We're going to be at this for a while."

Susie is writing something on her clipboard. "Yeah. It should take us about twelve hours."

Shirley heard them talking on the intercom. "We should have a headwind most of the way, but you might want to check the winds at different altitudes. The weather guys only know what other pilots have reported."

Betty adjusts her compass heading and settles back in her seat. "Good idea. I'm sure it can change quickly this time of the year."

It's several hours later, and the sun has set. At twenty-five thousand feet, the outside temperature has fallen well below zero and glittering stars fill the evening sky. Susie returns from the bathroom, and slides into her seat. "Boy, it's really cramped back there. I can't imagine what it would be like if you were under attack."

"Yeah. It would be terrifying. Can you take over for a minute? I want to talk with Shirley."

"Sure."

Betty walks back to Shirley's navigation station. "Well, don't you look comfortable? Do you know where we are?"

"Yes, exactly," and she holds up her sextant. "When the night is clear like this, it's easy to get a fix on Venus. We've got a forty-mph headwind, but that will probably keep changing. An ETA at sunrise is still a good possibility."

It's now well past midnight, and the night is cold and clear. Looming on the horizon is a huge storm center with massive white thunderheads that tower high above them, and lightning flashes through the clouds, creating an eerie light show. It's a breath-taking sight; incredibly beautiful, and just as deadly. . . and it lies directly in their flight path. Betty is flying and Susie is asleep. She stretches and rubs her eyes. "I was really tired. What's happening?"

Bolts of lightning flash ominously through the massive storm center and momentarily illuminate the dark cockpit and the B-17 buffets heavily in the rough air.

Susie stares at the storm in fear. "What's that!"

Betty fills her in. "There's a tremendous thunderstorm ahead of us. We can't fly over it, and it's too large to go around."

Susie quickly pulls out a map of their route. "Iceland could be an alternative. What do you think?"

The turbulence shakes their bomber violently, and Betty struggles with the controls. "I thought of that, but the weather looks just as bad in that direction. It's a toss-up, I guess. Our orders are to go to England, so I'm going to stick with that."

Susie stares out the window at the massive cloud formation. "Wow! That's a frightening sight. What do we do now?"

Betty worries. "Pick up any loose items and pray we get through this!" She presses her microphone button and talks to the other planes. "Okay, girls. We're in for a rough ride. Punch through this storm and regroup on the other side. Spread out so you don't bump into anyone."

One by one, the other pilots confirm and vanish into the dark clouds. A light rain soon turns into a heavy downpour, and thick sheets of water flood across their windshield, reducing their visibility to zero. They strain their eyes, trying to see into the darkness when suddenly, from out of nowhere, the enormous belly of a B-17 appears directly above them. Susie looks up and screams a warning. "Watch out!"

Betty dives steeply to avoid the other plane, and it vanishes back into the darkness. The near collision was unnerving, and she takes a deep breath. "Thanks, Susie. That was a close call!"

The thunderstorm rages on for another hour, when a heavy sheet of hail suddenly slams into them in a deafening roar, nearly breaking their windshield. As they penetrate deeper into the clouds, the turbulence worsens and the B-17 lurches about. Several times, they drop hundreds of feet in an instant, only to catch an updraft and surge upward just as quickly.

Loose gear and personal effects fly about the cockpit as Betty struggles to maintain their course. The full force of the storm now engulfs them, and it takes all of their combined strength to keep it in level flight.

A powerful downdraft drops their plane several hundred feet, and Susie screams. "Ahhhhhhhhh."

Suddenly, a bright lightning bolt arcs through the dark night in a blinding flash and hits their bomber just ahead of the windshield. Electrical sparks shower the interior, and smoke from burning wires fills the air. Their cockpit lights blink off and on, and then it's pitch-black. Betty reaches over and flips switches on the power panel, trying to reactivate them, but to no avail. Susie gets up out of her seat, grabs a fire extinguisher, and works frantically to put out several fires, but in the darkness, it's difficult to see.

Betty calls out to her. "What's happening?"

She sprays fire retardant on the flames, then inspects the cockpit with her flashlight. "I think they're out. Guess I've heard too many terrifying stories about aircraft fires."

The bomber pitches about violently and Shirley works her way forward to the cockpit. "What happened! Are you okay?"

Betty struggles with the control yoke. "Yeah. A lightning strike hit us just in front of the windshield."

Susie shines her flashlight on the instrument panel. "Does this help?"

"Yes, thanks. That was a bad one. The controls are okay, but I think we lost our radio."

Betty glances at Shirley, who is standing next to her. "How is your nav system?"

She disappears and returns moments later. "Everything is dead."

Susie flips several overhead switches. "Yeah, our radio is out, too."

Shirley tries to bolster their spirits. "It'll be morning pretty soon, and we should be out of these clouds. I'll be able to get a fix on our location."

Hours later, the violent thunderstorm has subsided, and they fly into the bright morning sky. Over the loud drone of the engines, Betty radios Shirley. "Well, it looks like we are coming into clear weather. Can you get a fix on our position?"

She rubs her frost-covered window and peers through her sextant. "I'm working on it now. Give me a minute."

The morning sun peaks over the cloudy horizon to the east, filling the cockpit with bright sunlight. However, far below them, darkness still covers the land and low clouds obscure the landmarks. Their situation makes Betty nervous, and she radios Shirley. "Do you have a fix yet?"

"Almost, but I'm worried. That storm might have thrown us off course."

Betty doesn't like her news, and it gives her an uncomfortable feeling. Minutes later, the sun rises above the horizon, and shines down on the snow-covered countryside far below.

Flying at twenty-five thousand feet, the exhaust from their four engines forms large billowy-white vapor trails that stretch out behind them for miles.

Susie scours her maps, trying to find a landmark. "Damn it. We're not supposed to be over land. I can't figure out where we are!"

Suddenly, Shirley calls out excitedly. "Betty! Reverse course immediately! We are over Germany!"

Instantly Betty begins a wide 180-degree turn toward England and minutes later, they hear a loud rhythmic banging on their fuselage. Susie looks over at Betty. "What's wrong now?" Just then, a gray German fighter flashes past the nose of their bomber, and she screams. "Look out!"

Smoke permeates their cockpit, and Betty struggles to trim the plane. "He must have hit something. The controls are mushy and we're losing altitude."

Again, the rhythmic banging sound of machine-gun fire tears into their bomber as a second fighter makes a high-speed pass from behind them. Betty cries out. "Oh, no! There's two of them!"

She tries to dive to avoid the attacking fighter, but her bomber is slow to respond, and the fighter's machine guns rake the length of their fuselage. Their windshield explodes, and glass and pieces of metal shower the cockpit. The huge plane shutters violently, an engine catches on fire, and a propeller flies off another. Dense smoke fills the air and is slowly sucked out of the shattered cockpit windows.

Betty fights to control the plane, but it noses down, and the altimeter spins wildly. An icy wind blasts through the blown-out windshield, and large pieces of torn aluminum bang violently against the fuselage. The noise is deafening, and she yells. "I've lost control! We're going down!"

Susie is slumped to the side, and Betty shakes her shoulder. "Susie! Listen to me! We have to bail out!" She struggles to pull her back into her seat, but her eyes are closed, and blood drips from the corners of her mouth. The little teddy bear she gave her lies on the floor in a pool of blood.

Betty is terrified. "Oh, no!" She frantically pushes her microphone button and calls to Shirley. "Are you alright?" but there is no answer.

Another one of her engines is now fully engulfed in flames and the bomber is in a flat spin. It descends through a broken layer of clouds and flies out into the clear winter sky. Betty is losing altitude quickly and realizes that it's time to abandon the plane. She struggles with the safety harness release lever, but it's jammed, and she can't get out of her seat.

Again, the rhythmic banging of a strafing run reverberates throughout the plane, and she shuts her eyes, knowing she is about to die. The German fighter closes in on her lumbering bomber, but he's going too fast, and overshoots his target. He passes above her at high speed, then rolls over into a steep inverted dive to the side.

Betty watches in disbelief as a thick trail of smoke streams from behind it. Red tracers are clearly visible as they arc through the sky from behind her, and they flash brightly as they track across the fighter's wings. Suddenly, its engine bursts into flames, and the pilot rolls the plane over and bails out.

A moment later, a black British fighter flashes past her. Its machine guns and 20 mm cannons unleash a vicious hail of bullets at the second German fighter that's coming at her head on. Bright red tracer rounds arc out into the sky from both planes as the two fighters duel it out head-to-head. Suddenly, large pieces of the German fighter's wing fly off and it spins out of control and disintegrates in a violent explosion.

Betty struggles to shut down her burning engines and slowly flies out of her flat spin; however, she's losing altitude quickly. The British fighter returns and drifts in close to her. The pilot points toward a plowed field in the distance, and motions for her to crash land there. She struggles to line up her crippled B-17, but her controls finally fail, and the snow-covered ground races toward her.

Her bomber clips the treetops, takes the thatched roof off a farmer's barn, and digs a long, deep furrow into a plowed field. It skids along the shoreline of a large lake, creating a gigantic wave of mud and water that engulfs the plane and extinguishes the engine fires. The smoldering wreckage comes to rest in the shallows near the edge of the lake, and an enormous cloud of steam and black smoke rise into the early morning sky.

Betty is unconscious and a smoky vapor fills the cockpit. She's slumped over her control yoke, but slowly recovers, only to see electrical cables hanging down in front of her. They arc against the bomber's metal frame and ignite fluid leaking from a broken hydraulic line. Flames shoot upward, and she recoils from the intense heat. It's one of her great fears; being trapped in a plane that is on fire, and it terrifies her.

She struggles with her safety harness, but the jarring crash has pinched her seat so tightly against the fuselage that she can't extract herself. The flames grow much larger, and the heat is unbearable. She places her boots on the instrument panel and pushes hard against it.

Suddenly, her seat breaks away from the floor, and she scrambles to check on Shirley. She stops in front of her navigation station and is horrified. "Oh, no!" A long section of the plane's fuselage had been ripped open by the machine gun fire and Shirley's body lies crumpled on the floor in a pool of blood.

Betty immediately runs down the narrow walkway toward the back of the plane. The acrid smell of burning electrical wires, and the pungent odor of high-octane aviation gas fills the air, making it a very dangerous situation. When she reaches the rear door, she throws it open, and stares at the ice-covered water ten feet below her. Without pausing, she unbuckles her parachute, strips off her heavy flight jacket, and jumps.

Her bomber had ripped through the thin layer of surface ice, and the freezing water surrounding her has a purple sheen caused by avgas dripping from her wing tanks. She struggles through the chest-deep water, knowing that the plane could explode at any minute, and with great effort, slogs toward the shoreline. She forces her way through snow-covered cattails and stumbles out into the frozen field, but soon trips and falls to the icy ground.

Gasping for air, and too exhausted to continue, she rolls onto her side as blood from a nasty head wound streams across her face. Glancing back at the smoldering wreckage of her plane, Betty is stunned to see the extensive damage that the fighters had inflicted. Their cannon fire had literally chewed the fuselage to pieces. How it continued to fly was a miracle.

Suddenly, a German half-track emerges from the forest carrying heavily armed troops and approaches her at speed from across the lake. It's followed by a six-wheeled armored car, and they race toward her. Terrified, she jumps to her feet and runs just as the bomber detonates violently in an enormous fireball of orange and red flames. The force of the explosion heaves the huge plane out of the water and throws it high into the air, creating a massive cloud of black smoke that boils upward into the clear winter sky.

The shock wave from the blast knocks her to the ground, and large pieces of flaming debris rain down all around her. The immense column of thick black smoke towers above her, blocking out the sun. Fueled by adrenalin, and a powerful instinct to survive, she staggers to her feet and stumbles blindly across the frozen field. As her senses slowly return, she sees that the twin-engine British fighter has landed on a nearby dirt road and is taxing in her direction. Betty runs toward it just as the half-track crests a distant hill, firing at her from its roof-mounted heavy machine gun.

Bullets hit all around her, sending chunks of frozen ground flying into the air, and the British fighter returns fire with its cannons blazing. The half-track bursts into flames, as heavily armed soldiers flee the armored car and fan out along the ridge, firing their rifles at her.

The twin-engine fighter rotates back toward the dirt road and rolls to a stop, creating an enormous cloud of loose snow and debris that slams into her, nearly knocking her down. The pilot frantically motions for her to get in, and she stumbles toward the plane. Betty dodges a huge spinning propeller and runs to an open hatch below the cockpit. As she struggles to pull herself into the plane, a mortar explodes in a nearby ditch and a tall column of mud and water rains down on her. She struggles to hang on as the plane lurches about but loses her grip and tumbles to the ground. The pilot realizes the next mortar could hit his plane, and its engines roar as he tries to return to the dirt road.

Betty struggles to her feet and runs toward the open hatch. At the last second, she lunges at a handhold and pulls herself inside the moving plane. It screams down the dirt road and departs in a deafening roar. Fully airborne it climbs steeply, then disappears into the low clouds. She works her way up to the cockpit and slips into the copilot's seat.

The pilot concentrates on his flying and doesn't look over at her. "Are you okay?"

"Yes, I think so."

Startled by the sound of a female voice, he does a double take at his new passenger. "You're a woman?"

Betty removes her leather helmet and brushes the mud and snow off her flight suit. "That's what I've been told."

"Bloody hell! It's too dangerous out here for a woman."

She is soaking wet and blood streams from the nasty gash on the side of her head. "Actually, it was an accident."

He takes off his scarf and hands it to her. "Here, take this. You're bleeding."

"Thanks," and she wipes the blood from her face.

"How about your crew?"

"They didn't make it. We were working feverishly to get back to England, and a split second later they were dead."

"I'm sorry. I know what that feels like. How did you end up in Germany?"

"Lightning knocked out our radio and nav system, and we became lost in a nighttime thunderstorm."

"I didn't know you Yanks used women in combat."

"We just ferry planes. By the way my name is Betty Bauer."

The pilot focuses on flying and gives her a quick glance. "Nice to meet you, Betty Bauer. I'm Andy McQueen."

She finishes cleaning up with help from his scarf which is now covered with blood. "Sorry, but I think I've ruined your scarf."

"That's okay. I've got a couple more. Why don't you keep it as a souvenir of today's adventure?"

Betty's mood perks up, and she admires her surroundings. She's familiar with a lot of different planes, but not this one and she's intrigued. "I like this plane. What's it called?"

"It's a de Havilland Mosquito, and one of the fastest fighters in the war."

"What's she like to fly?"

Andy doesn't break his concentration and stares out the windshield. "Well, she's a lot more difficult to handle than that flying dump truck of yours. Do you want to give it a go?"

"Yes! I'd love to."

They are traveling at speed just above the icy waters of the English Channel, and the white cliffs of Dover race toward them. Andy waits to the last second before giving her the controls. "Okay, let's see what you can do," and he drops his hands from the control yoke.

Betty is quick to realize that he's trying to scare her and delays a couple more seconds. "Let's see," and she fiddles with the flight controls. "How does this work?"

Andy is panic stricken. "Pull back on the bloody stick! NOW!"

At the very last second, she pulls hard on the control yoke, and they barely miss crashing into the towering white cliffs. The fighter screams up and over the top of the cliff, banks steeply on its side, then rolls over inverted before slicing back to the ground.

Andy was totally unprepared for the maneuver and hangs on for dear life; however, he quickly regains his composure. "Bloody hell, woman! You could have killed us! Where did you learn to fly like that?"

"When I'm not flying dump trucks, I ferry fighters."

"Blimey! You could have told me!"

She teases him. "Well, you didn't ask."

Andy thinks about it for a moment, then laughs. "You're right. I deserve it, and your flying skills are impressive!"

"Thanks."

A deep blanket of snow covers the rolling hills below them, and Betty looks down at the ground. "I wasn't expecting England to be so beautiful."

"Wait until summer when the fields are green. The countryside is quite stunning."

CHAPTER 8
RAF STATION KENLEY

AHEAD OF THEM IS KENLEY STATION, A FIGHTER BASE located twenty miles outside of London on the coast. As they approach, Andy is on the radio with the control tower, and lands the Mosquito on a Marston Mat runway, a perforated steel matting material developed by the United States. He parks near a row of fighters, cuts his engines, and they exit the aircraft. He glances at the deep cut on the side of Betty's head. "I think you should have the doc take a look at that."

"Thanks, but I'm okay. Just a little shaken up."

They walk along the edge of the flight line toward a stately three-story stone mansion now being used as their headquarters. As they approach the building, Andy salutes an elderly gentleman walking toward them.

General Buckley is the Base Commander. "Ah, good to see you, Andy, my boy. I heard you made a couple of kills today."

Andy responds casually. "Two 109s, and I also picked up a hitchhiker. General, I'd like you to meet Lt. Bauer."

He extends his hand. "Pleased to meet you, Lieutenant."

"Thank you. It's my pleasure."

"So, you're the Yank that crash-landed that B-17?"

"Yes, and thankfully, Andy was there to rescue me."

The general raises his eyebrows and smiles. "I'm sure he's quite good at saving damsels in distress."

Betty asks, "General, if you don't mind, I'd like to let my squadron know I'm alright."

"Of course, my dear."

Andy looks at him. "We're headed there now, sir."

"Nice meeting you, Lieutenant, and I hope to see you again."

As they walk amongst the fighters parked on the flight line, Betty gives Andy a puzzled look. "Your kills didn't seem to impress him. How many do you have?"

He nods toward a Supermarine Spitfire parked nearby. On the pilot's side are eighteen iron crosses painted on the fuselage. "That's my plane."

"You're a triple ace? I'm impressed. Why didn't you tell me?"

Andy quips at her with a smile. "You didn't ask."

They walk toward a large stone building with a sign on the roof that says, "*Communications Center*". As they approach a busy clerk, he looks up and salutes Andy smartly. "Ah, Wing Commander! It's good to see you!"

Betty is surprised. "Wing Commander?" then laughs. "I know, I didn't ask."

He enjoys joking with her and extends his hand. "Let's call it even and start over."

"Okay, it's a deal."

The handsome wing commander is tall and older than Betty. He has black hair, dark eyes, a mustache, and walks with a noticeable limp because of a war injury. He has been flying with the Royal Air Force for ten years, and at thirty-six, he's considered the old man of the squadron. He addresses the clerk and speaks with a Welsh accent. "Graham, this nice lady needs to contact her unit in Texas."

"No problem," and he pushes a pad of paper across the table. "Just fill out this form, and I'll get right on it."

Betty starts to write, but she is freezing cold, and her hand shakes uncontrollably. Andy reaches over and takes her pencil. "Here. Let me help you with that." He completes her message and hands it to the clerk. "Thanks, Graham. We'll check back with you later."

They exit the building and walk down the front steps. Betty is soaking wet and shivering, which concerns him. "You're going to need some warm clothes and a place to stay. Let's see if the nurses can put you up." He stares at the bleeding wound on the side of her head. "And I think you could use a couple of stitches."

"Thanks. I'd sure like to get out of this soggy flight suit, too."

Andy motions toward a building. "The base hospital is just up ahead. You can clean up there."

A military ambulance is parked in front, and they enter the building. Mattie, the head nurse, greets them. "Hi, Andy. Do you need to be patched up?"

He is embarrassed and stutters. "No, no. This is Lt. Bauer. She needs a place to stay. Can she bunk with your nurses?"

Mattie is in her mid-thirties, speaks with a heavy Scottish accent, and has fiery red hair and green eyes. "Hi, I'm Mattie."

The two women shake hands, and Betty feels an immediate connection with her. "I'm Betty. Nice to meet you."

"Of course, you can stay here with us," then notices her head wound. "Oh, my! I need to look at that!" and gives Betty the once over. "Lass, you are a mess! Come along. We've got a lot of work to do," and the two of them walk down a long hall.

Andy calls after them. "I'll be in my office."

An hour later, they leave the hospital and cut across an icy lawn toward a three-story vine-covered stone building. Mattie is wearing the uniform of a British nurse; a teal blue skirt and blouse with a white bib that clips onto each shoulder and, in the center, is a large red cross. Betty is wearing a tan skirt and a white blouse that she borrowed. "I really appreciate all that you've done for me, and your nurses are a lot of fun to be around. They invited me for a drink after work today."

"Nursing can be very stressful, but that doesn't keep them from having fun when they can. I think you're going to fit in with us just fine."

They walk up the entry steps and pass a sign that reads, "*Headquarters*". Betty is no longer wearing a soggy flight suit covered with dirt and grime, and her looks have changed radically. She's radiant in her pressed skirt and blouse and wears her silver WASP wings. Several officers walk toward them and give her a double take as they pass by.

Andy steps into the hallway and sees them approaching. "Well, well. I'm impressed!" His loud voice alerts others in the building, and doors open to see what's going on.

All the attention embarrasses Betty, and she replies shyly. "Thanks."

He motions toward a side door. "Come this way. We can talk over here."

They follow him into an alcove with a large window that overlooks the flight line. He reaches into his pocket and produces an unopened brown envelope. "This was just delivered to me," and hands it to her.

Betty eagerly opens the envelope. "It's a response from my unit." As she reads, there is sadness in her voice. "No one made it to England. The Germans shot one down, two are missing, and four landed in Iceland. Because of severe weather this time of the year, they have temporarily postponed our transport flights." She continues reading with a frown. "Because of my injuries, I'm to stay put until the others arrive." She looks up at Andy. "But I'm not injured. What did you say in that message?"

"Ah, well . . . all I said was that your copilot and navigator were killed, and that you were wounded," and he points to the bandage on her head. "Right there."

"But it's only superficial! I'll be fine in a week or two."

Mattie comes to his defense. "The doctor suspects you might have a concussion. It can happen when you hit your head that hard, so we need to be careful."

Andy has taken a liking to Betty and would like to see her stay a little longer. "Mattie's right. There could be complications. I'll show you around while you convalesce. I promise you won't be bored."

"Well . . . maybe," and she slowly warms up to the idea.

Mattie is concerned. "He's right Betty, and you're in a state of exhaustion too. Come on. Doctor's orders. A little rest and recuperation are all that's needed."

As they walk down the hall, Mattie confides to her. "Actually, I'm short staffed. You could be a big help if you don't mind."

Betty's mood immediately picks up. "Really? I'm happy to help if I can."

"Good!" and she looks at her watch. "It's about lunch time. Are you hungry?"

"Yes, I am."

Andy has a suggestion. "The special today is bangers and mash, and I'm buying."

Betty glances at Mattie. "What's that?"

"You've got a lot to learn about the British, lass. That would be sausage and mashed potatoes to you Yanks. It's a classic dish here in Britain."

"Are there any other dishes I need to know about?"

"Well, there's toad-in-the-hole, blood pudding, bubble and squeak, and roly-poly, but a word of warning . . . I'd stay away from haggis for now."

Their food sounds strange to Betty. "What's haggis?"

Mattie smiles, knowing what her response is going to be. "It's fermented sheep organs cooked while encased in the animal's stomach lining."

"Oh, my gosh! I won't be able to sleep tonight!"

Several days later, Andy walks up the steps to the Headquarters building and bumps into Mattie, who is just leaving. "Hi Mattie, I haven't seen you for a while."

"I've been busy. We're getting a lot of wounded from the London bombing raids."

"How is Betty doing?"

"That girl is phenomenal, and my nurses love her. She wanted to help, so I trained her in wound care."

Andy is surprised. "Really! How did she do?"

"Very well. As you know, after surgery, our patients need to have their bandages changed regularly, and when they're discharged, they need to return as outpatients until they're completely healed. She changes their bandages, cleans their wounds, and checks up on their general health. If she sees a problem developing, she alerts a nurse. It takes a huge load off me, and the nurses as well . . . and she's a natural at it.

"She's already the most popular of all my nurses. Some of the injured actually come in here asking for her. And why not? She's beautiful, smart, has a great bedside manner, and a figure that's to die for."

Several days later, Andy enters the base hospital, which is busy as usual, and the receptionist at the front desk greets him. "Good afternoon, Wing Commander. Can I help you?"

"Hi Connie, I'm looking for Lt. Bauer."

She turns in her chair and points behind her. "She might be in post-op down that hallway. You'll see the sign."

"Thanks."

He walks down the long corridor past open doors that lead to several patient bays. The rooms are painted white and are filled with wounded servicemen in various states of recovery. Many of them are British Army soldiers that were injured during Nazi bombing raids on London. Just ahead of him, an overhead sign reads, "*Postoperative*". As he approaches, the door swings open, and two medical attendants exit, pushing a gurney carrying a patient. Betty, dressed in her nurse's uniform, follows them. She notices Andy approaching and smiles at him. "Well, what a surprise! How have you been?"

"They keep me busy, and it looks like you found something to do."

"Yes, and I like it a lot."

Andy walks with her. "How's your head wound?"

"Oh that. I'm fully recovered, thanks."

The hallway is busy with doctors and nurses coming and going. A nurse passes by and pats her on the shoulder. "They're looking for you, hun. We've got wounded in the emergency room."

She turns to Andy. "Sorry. I better go."

He calls after her. "How about a drink tonight?"

"Sure, I'd love to."

"Officer's Club at eight?"

"I'll see you there."

It's the end of Betty's shift, and she and the other nurses are relaxing in their barracks. Her friend Heather is changing out of her nurse's uniform. "We're going to the Officer's Club tonight. Want to join us?"

"I'd like to go with you, but I'm meeting someone there."

"Is it that handsome Dr. Hunter in ER? I've seen him chatting you up."

"He's fun, but we're just friends."

Heather wants to know more about her mystery man. "Come on, Betty. Who is it? You can tell me."

Betty tries to keep her personal life private, but it's impossible under the circumstances, and confesses. "I'm meeting Wing Commander McQueen."

"Wow! He's a dreamboat!"

"It's not like that. He's married and a lot older. We can have fun together without it being a date. You should try it sometime."

"I've never had a "just-a-friend" fella before, so I don't know what that's like. What are you going to wear on this non-date?"

Betty opens the metal door to her wall locker. "My uniform."

Heather stops what she's doing and turns to her. "Oh, no! That's not a good idea. I've seen some of his friends. They're the socially elite around here, and you wouldn't want to embarrass him."

"Hmm. I didn't think about that."

"You need something better than your uniform."

"Yeah, like there's a dress shop nearby."

Heather tries to be helpful and thinks for a moment. "The last time I was in London, I bought something that just might fit you."

She walks over to her locker, looks through her clothes hangers, and spins around, holding a stunning black cocktail dress up to her neck. "Voilà. You're going to look great in this," and pauses, "but we need to do something about your hair."

It is almost 8 pm, and Andy waits patiently at a table in the Officer's Club. A loud band is playing, and the dance floor is filled with couples dancing to the fast music. Minutes later, Betty and the other nurses enter, and she sees Andy. "There he is. I'll see you back at the barracks."

As she approaches, he stands and pulls out a chair for her. Betty removes her tan Mackintosh raincoat and gives him a hug. "Sorry I'm late."

"That's alright. I just got here."

Betty is radiant in her black low-cut cocktail dress and piercing emerald-green eyes. She usually wears her hair up for practical reasons, but tonight it flows down to her shoulders. Her new look shocks Andy. "Whoa, you are stunning! Where did you find that dress?"

Betty brushes her auburn-colored hair back from her face and sits down. "Oh, I borrowed it from a nurse."

"Well, she certainly has fantastic taste in evening wear!"

Andy catches the eye of the waitress, and she walks over to him. "What will you be having?"

He asks Betty, "What would you like?"

"Do you have white wine?"

"Yes, and you, sir?"

"Guinness Draught, please."

The waitress takes their order and disappears into the busy crowd. Andy is curious. "Well, how are you settling in?"

"The girls are super to be around, and I like them a lot."

"Mattie told me you've become quite skilled at your job. I'm sure she appreciates your help."

"Maybe I should have studied something in the medical field. My parents were doctors, so I guess healing is in my blood. Occasionally, you see some terrible things, but it's an incredibly rewarding feeling to have helped someone."

Andy is happy to be alone with her, but a handsome medical officer sitting with a group of doctors at a nearby table calls to her. "Hey Sparky!"

She sees him and waves. "Hi! I want you to meet someone."

The doctor excuses himself from his group and approaches their table. Betty makes the introductions. "Dr. Hunter, this is Wing Commander McQueen," and the two men shake hands.

Andy pulls out a chair. "Please join us," and Dr. Hunter sits down.

"This fantastic woman completely revolutionized our operating room." and he turns to Betty. "I want you to know that we appreciate your hard work. I still can't believe what you did."

Andy looks confused, and Betty brings him up to speed. "I delivered a patient to the operating room the other day, and I noticed how poor the surgical lighting was. So, when I had some time off, I had a friend drive me to the salvage yard. I explained I was from the base hospital and asked if it would be alright if

I looked around for something to upgrade our lighting. I found the parts that I needed and was able to cobble together a couple of impressive surgical lights."

Dr. Hunter interjects. "She's being modest. We were working with an antiquated lighting system. At times, it would die out in the middle of surgery and the nurses would have to assist with flashlights. Sparky also rewired the entire operating room. She's an incredible woman!"

Betty is bashful. "You save lives every day. You're the one that's amazing."

He pushes his chair back and stands. "I'm sorry to interrupt. I just wanted to extend a big thanks from all of us," and he offers his hand to Andy. "It was nice meeting you."

"My pleasure."

As he walks away, he smiles at Betty. "Have a nice evening," and he returns to his group.

Andy winks at her. "Well, you seem to have a new admirer."

But she is quick to dismiss his comment. "Oh, no. We just joke around to relieve the tension sometimes."

"Ok, if you say so. Why did he call you Sparky?"

"That's a nickname for an electrician."

"I thought you were an electrical engineer."

"When I was in college, my uncle owned an electrical construction company. One day, he asked me if I wanted to earn a little extra money helping him out and I worked in the field for three and a half years while I was going to school. It was an incredibly valuable real-world experience."

Andy takes a sip from his drink. "What other secret skills do you have?"

"It might look like that, but I'm just an average person caught up in extraordinary times."

"Well, how about a dance, and let's forget about saving the world."

"I thought you'd never ask."

He stands. "After you, Sparky."

As they pass Blake's table, she smiles at him, and they walk out onto the crowded floor. The lights are low, and they sway to the gentle rhythm of the music.

CHAPTER 9
A WOUNDED ENEMY

IT'S FOUR O'CLOCK IN THE MORNING, AND A PATIENT IS wheeled out of surgery on a gurney and taken to a private room. The attendants are followed by an armed military police officer. Betty is on the night shift and watches curiously as they pass by her. Mattie is working at a nearby desk, and she approaches her to find out what's going on. "Why are the police here?"

"The patient is a German fighter pilot that they just shot down. Would you check on him?"

"Yes, of course."

Betty walks down the hallway, stops at the door to his room, and nods at the police officer guarding the entrance. She enters and uses her flashlight so as not to disturb the patient who is badly wounded. His eyes are bandaged, his arm is in a cast, and his leg is in traction suspended above his bed by a complicated apparatus of weights and pulleys. She makes a minor adjustment to one of the positioning cables, then quietly slips away.

The pilot slowly regains consciousness and speaks in German. "Where am I?"

She freezes, not sure if she should respond. It's not a secret, but no one knows she speaks German. She ignores him and tries to sneak out of the room, but the wounded pilot calls out again. "Is someone there?"

Betty switches off her flashlight, returns to his darkened bedside, and answers him in German. "You are in an RAF hospital near London. An explosion blinded you. Your arm is fractured, and your femur is broken, which is why you are in traction. Over time, you will make a full recovery."

He lays in bed motionless. "Am I blind?"

"No. Your vision should return in a day or two."

"Who are you? You speak perfect German."

"I was born in Germany."

"You seem far away. Can you come closer?"

"Of course," and Betty walks to the side of his bed.

"What is your name?"

"Nurse Bauer. And yours?"

"My name is Adrian von Schönburg."

Unsure if she should be talking to the enemy, she slips back into the shadows. "You need to rest. I'll check on you later."

It's the end of her shift and Betty sticks her head into Adrian's room, but he is fast asleep, and she quietly closes the door. The dark December morning is windy and freezing cold, and she increases her pace as she walks toward her barracks. She's tired and looking forward to a hot meal and a warm bed.

The following evening, she reports for work and checks in with Mattie to see what she has planned for her. "Hi. How are things going?"

"Good. Our German pilot has been asking for you, but we don't know what he wants. Do you speak German?"

"Yes, some."

"If you could check in on him, I would appreciate it."

"Of course."

Betty picks up her clipboard with a list of patients for her to see and pushes her cart ahead of her. She nods at the military police officer standing at the door and enters the room. Adrian is sitting upright, resting against several pillows. She smiles and greets him in German. "Good evening. Are you feeling better?"

"Yes, and I appreciate your kindness last night."

"I'm just doing my job," and she pushes her first aid cart to the side of his bed. "I need to check the bandages covering your eyes. Do you mind?"

"Please do. The flashing lights have stopped."

"That's a good sign." She lowers the room's light and carefully removes his bandage. "How is your vision?"

He blinks his eyes several times. "Everything is slowly coming into focus."

"Good. I'm going to keep the room light down low for a while. How does your leg feel?"

"Very numb."

Betty reviews the information on his patient clipboard. "You've had a serious injury. There will be a lot of pain for the next week, but I can give you something for that."

"I hate to be a burden, but could I ask you a favor?"

She hangs the clipboard on the end of his bed and looks up at him. "That's what I'm here for."

He motions toward a newspaper laying on a chair across the room. "Could you tell me what they are saying about the war?"

"Yes, but I have to do my rounds first. I'll be back in a couple of hours and we can talk then."

It's later that evening. Betty knocks on Adrian's door and peeks into the darkened room. "Are you awake?"

"Yes, please come in."

She enters and walks to his bed. "I need to change your bandages every day for the next few weeks."

"Thank you. I heard you talking to the other nurses in the hallway. You have an unfamiliar accent."

Betty unwraps the bandage on his leg as they talk. "I'm an American."

"Why is an American nurse working here?"

"It's complicated."

"I'm sorry. I didn't mean to pry."

She carefully removes the bandages on his leg and replaces them with new ones. As she works, he scans through his newspaper, then holds a page up to her. "What are they talking about here?"

"It talks about the Allied invasion of Sicily, and the collapse of the Italian Army. Many German troops have been diverted from the eastern front to help defend Italy."

"That's not good."

"Nothing about war is good," and she pushes her medical cart to the side. "I'm finished. We can talk again tomorrow."

As time passes, Betty changes his bandages daily, and their strange friendship slowly develops. One evening, she stops at his room and knocks on the door. "Are you awake?"

He glances over the top of his newspaper as she approaches. "Yes, please come in."

"If you don't mind, an officer would like to talk to you."

"I have been expecting someone in authority," and he sets his paper down.

Betty opens the door and calls to Andy, who is standing in the hallway. "Please come in," and she returns to his bedside.

He enters the room, and she speaks to Adrian in German. "I will translate for you. This is Wing Commander McQueen."

"It's a pleasure to meet you," and he extends his hand.

Andy walks to his bed and the two men shake hands. "Thank you. Are you feeling better?"

"Yes, Nurse Bauer is taking good care of me."

"Can I have your name and rank for our records?"

"Of course. Captain Adrian von Schönburg, Staffelkapitän."

Andy asks Betty, "What is that?"

"He's the squadron commander of a fighter group."

"Can you ask him what happened the night he was shot down?"

Adrian describes the events of that evening. "It was well after midnight, and there was very little moonlight. I was leading a flight of night fighters when an unknown number of Spitfires intercepted us over the English Channel. The combat spread out across the sky, and we must have drifted over land.

"I shot down two before someone attacked me. My fuel tank exploded, and I immediately rolled over and dropped out. I parachuted into some trees, fell to the ground, and was knocked unconscious. When I came to, I was partially blind, and had a broken arm and leg. A farmer was standing over me holding a wooden pitchfork, and now I'm here."

Andy finishes writing in his notepad and tucks it into his jacket. "Tell him thank you, and I hope his leg gets better." He starts to leave, then asks, "If you have a minute, I'd like to talk to you outside."

"Certainly, I'll be right there," and she turns to Adrian. "The wing commander wishes you well."

"I could tell it surprised him to hear you speaking German. It seemed to make him uncomfortable."

"Maybe, but for now, you need to rest."

Betty leaves the room and walks over to Andy, who is waiting for her in the hall. "Why didn't you tell me you spoke German?"

"I don't know. It just never came up. I studied it when I was in college."

Andy is pensive. "There's something different about him. Let me know if he says anything."

"Of course."

The following night Betty stops at Adrian's room to change his bandages, and they speak in German as usual. "How are you feeling tonight?"

"Much better. Thank you."

She removes a meal tray from his bed and places it on a nearby table. "Let's see how things look," and carefully examines his leg wound. "I'll get word to the doctor, but I think it's about time to take you out of traction."

"I hate being in this thing, but at least it keeps me here, and not in a POW camp."

"That's still a couple of weeks away."

Adrian watches her as she changes his bandages. "Do you have a husband?"

She shakes her head. "No."

"I have a wife and two young daughters," and he pauses for a moment. "I don't want to get you into trouble, but I would like to send them a brief note to let them know I'm alive and well. Is it possible? It would mean a great deal to me."

"I don't think there is a postal service between Britain and Germany."

"She lives in Paris, and the French are your allies."

Betty finishes wrapping his leg. "Really? I can't promise anything, but I can give your message to the Wing Commander."

"Thank you. I'm sure they are extremely worried about me."

He writes a simple note stating he is in a prisoner of war camp near London recovering from minor injuries, and hands it to her.

The following day, Betty checks in on him. "How are you feeling today?"

"Ah, Nurse Bauer. Good afternoon. As you can see, they removed the traction device. I assume that was your doing?"

"Yes. I reported that you were making exceptional progress."

"Thank you. I appreciate your help."

"I gave your note to Wing Commander McQueen. He said he would forward it to your wife. Apparently, there's some sort of code of honor between fighter pilots."

"That meant a lot to me. I won't forget your kindness."

A few weeks later, Betty is at work when she sees Andy walking down the hallway toward her and greets him. "Hi. I want you to know that the captain was extremely appreciative that you mailed his note."

"If that happened to me, I hope someone would do the same for me. Speaking of the captain, how is he doing?"

"The doctors fitted him with crutches, so we couldn't hold him any longer and the military police removed him yesterday. I wasn't here, so I don't know the details."

Days later, Betty is at work, and the hospital is very busy. She pushes her cart filled with a variety of bandages and antiseptic solutions that she needs to clean her patient's wounds. The medical staff fills the corridor, and they hurriedly walk past her. In the crowded hallway, and coming her way, is Dr. Blake Hunter. He's about her age, with light brown hair, blue eyes, and wears glasses.

He is highly skilled and has a great reputation as a surgeon. In the operating room, he's extremely focused, but the rest of the time he can be lots of fun and doesn't take life too seriously. Betty has become quite fond of him, although he has never even come close to asking her out.

He steps in front of her cart, and she comes to a stop. "Are you coming or going?"

"Sometimes it's hard to tell," she says flirtingly.

"You work too much. I'm here all the time and I see you here every day."

"It's because of that thing. I forget what they call it . . . oh yes . . . the war."

"Well, I think we both could use a day off. How would you like to drive down to the Thames and feed the seagulls?"

"I don't know. They need me here."

Dr. Hunter has a broad grin on his face. "Somehow, I knew that would be your answer, so I checked the duty roster. We're both off tomorrow, so don't be a stick-in-the-mud, and throw caution to the wind for once."

As they talk, attendants roll a gurney past them with a screaming patient. Betty cringes and shakes her head as they pass by. "You know, a day off sounds pretty good right now."

"There you go, Sparky. It's not a dreaded date or anything that serious. We'll just have some fun."

She smiles. "Knowing you, you're probably up to something!"

"Ah, you know me all too well. How about we meet after breakfast tomorrow?"

The following morning Betty leaves the mess hall just as Dr. Hunter pulls up in a slightly battered, and almost comical 1937 Austin Ruby. She looks in the window and can't hold back her laughter. "Is this your car?"

"Yes, I won it in a poker game. It runs, and that's all I care about. Hop in."

She sits down and glances at the interior. "This looks like something out of a cartoon. All you need is a clown in the back seat!"

He presses the starter button and grins. "Very funny!" He grinds the Austin into gear, and they drive off belching a cloud of smoke from a broken exhaust pipe. As he picks up speed, he hands her a chrome-plated window crank. "If you want some air, you'll need this. It keeps falling off."

Betty laughs and takes the handle from him. "I thought you doctors could afford to buy anything you wanted?"

He struggles to shift gears and looks over at her. "Ahh, yes, but times are tough, you know. I had a chauffeur once, but he was called to duty. It took me a week to figure out how to drive this thing."

"Well, I was just joking. It's got character. How far is the Thames?"

"About thirty miles, but we're going to take a detour to the Isle of Sheppey. Do you know of it?"

"No. I've never heard of it."

Dr. Hunter fights the steering wheel to avoid the many potholes, then looks over at her just as they hit a deep hole, and the Austin lurches from the impact. "Last time I drove this car, I broke down and had to get towed back to the base by a farmer's plow horse. The guards were laughing so hard they didn't even try to stop me."

"Oh, my gosh. That's hilarious! And it's something only you would do!"

The sun is out, and they drive through the frozen countryside. High walls of loosely stacked stones surround the snowy fields. Scattered along the edges are dark leafless trees, creating a surreal black and white landscape. A half hour later, they arrive at Queensborough, a small village at the convergence of the Thames Estuary and the North Sea. He drives into an empty parking lot, parks in front of a sleepy marina, and looks over at Betty. "Well, what do you think?"

The colorful fishing boats and the smell of the sea take her by surprise. "This is beautiful, but I don't see a single person."

"Yes, it's quiet in the winter, but I like it. The salty air helps me unwind, and I can get a new perspective on life."

She taunts him. "I'll bet you bring all your girlfriends here."

"No, I don't. And I'd appreciated it if you would keep it to yourself."

"Sure, no problem, Doc. I was just giving you a hard time."

A strong ocean breeze ripples the calm harbor water and he pulls out a heavy windbreaker from the back seat and hands it to her. "The weather here can change quickly. You might need this."

"Thanks," and she puts on the coat.

Dr. Hunter opens the trunk of the Austin, produces a wicker basket, and holds it up. "I brought lunch."

"Yum. I hope there's hot coffee in there."

"On a cold, wintery day like this? Of course!"

He puts his arm around her waist and motions toward the marina. "Come on, we've got a bit of a walk."

A stiff breeze swirls at Betty's hair. "Where are we going?"

"It's a surprise," and he zips up his heavy coat.

They stroll along the rock-lined shore, and Betty admires the colorfully painted commercial fishing boats. Sea gulls sitting on a low stone wall squawk and take to the air as they pass, and a strong smell of fish comes from an enormous pile of fishing nets next to their path. They walk to the edge of the marina and stop at a security gate topped with concertina wire. A sign reads, "*Boat Owners Only*". He digs around in his pocket, produces a key, and unlocks it. "Watch your step. This ramp can get slippery."

Betty stares at the fishing boats tied to the dock. "I've never been this close to a boat before, Doc."

"We're not at work anymore, Sparky. You can call me Blake."

"Okay, Blake. I'm Betty."

They continue down the floating dock to a slip containing a sleek thirty-six-foot racing sloop, and he steps aboard. "This is my baby."

She looks at the sailboat in disbelief. "Wow, you're full of surprises! It's beautiful!"

"Thanks. I've been sailing all my life. She's a racing sloop built about ten years ago. I came across her on a trip to London."

The sailboat is painted white, with a varnished wooden mast and teak deck trim, and stands out amongst the brightly colored commercial fishing boats. It has a long overhanging bow that reflects its racing heritage, and the pilothouse is low, adding to her sleek lines. Across the stern, and written in gold letters, are the words, "*Wind Dancer*", and below that it says, "*London, England*".

Blake holds out his hand. "Come on aboard," and points toward the cockpit. "You can sit over there. It will just take me a minute, and we'll get underway."

She looks around admiringly. "This is fun! I've never been in a sail-boat before."

"Well, you're in for a surprise. The sun is out, and the winds are perfect."

He unlocks a small door to the pilothouse and disappears below deck. A few minutes later, he returns wearing a heavy yellow windbreaker, and hands her a steaming cup of coffee. "As I remember, you like it black."

"I do. Thanks."

He sits down across from her and starts the engine. A low, monotonous drone reverberates throughout the boat, and the smell of diesel exhaust fills the air. "We'll motor out into the estuary, and then I'll get the sails up. Would you mind untying that line from the mooring cleat over there?"

Betty unties it and the sleek sailboat slips out into the marina. They quietly motor past rows of fishing boats, and idle toward the harbor entrance. As they pass the rocky breakwater, a group of seals nervously stir from their dry haul-outs and slip into the water. The bay is unusually calm and deep green swells gently rock the boat.

Blake turns the engine off, pulls hard at the rigging, and the mainsail slides to the top of the forty-five-foot mast. A gust of wind quickly fills the sail, and the sloop heels over slightly, cutting through the water with ease. Then he walks to the bow and unfurls the big genoa, which snaps taut as the breeze catches it. Next, he releases the colorful spinnaker, a mix of green and royal blue panels, and it balloons out in front of the boat. The sleek sailboat quickly surges forward, revealing its racing heritage. "Well, that's it. It looks like we're going to have a great day!"

Salt spray carried by the gusting wind fills the air and drifts back onto them. A blustery breeze whips at their faces, and the boat heels over hard as it knifes through the waves at full speed. Blake makes himself comfortable. "What do you think about sailing?"

"This is exhilarating! I love it!" and the chilly breeze blows Betty's long hair in all directions.

"You better put some lotion on your face. Even though it's winter, the sun and the wind can really cook you on a day like today," and he hands her a tube of lotion.

"Thanks," and she rubs it onto her cheeks. "What an incredible experience! It's wonderful out here."

"I take it you're a city girl?"

"Yes, I am."

They pass a white lighthouse sitting on a high cliff overlooking the harbor entrance and sail out into open water. A stiff breeze fills the air with salt spray, and it drifts across the deck to Betty. Blake notices some streaks of lotion on her face. "If you don't mind, you've got some of the lotion kind of piled up," and he carefully brushes her hair out of the way and gently strokes it into her skin. "There, that's got it."

Their eyes meet for a long moment, and their heads draw close. Suddenly, a powerful gust of wind heels the sailboat over and a sheet of icy green sea water surges across the deck. Blake pulls hard on the wooden tiller handle to correct their course, and the spell is broken. Filled by the strong breeze, the colorful spinnaker balloons out in front of them, almost touching the waves, as the sleek boat races through the swells at speed.

When they reach the English Channel, they tack upwind along the rugged shoreline. To the right of them, and several miles out to sea, is a long line of American freighters on their way to the London docks. The steady stream of men and materials needed to support the war is unrelenting. A large seaplane carrying depth charges shadows the convoy, and US Navy destroyers flank them for added protection. Betty watches them pass by, and they soon disappear into the morning's haze. "They must be incredibly brave to face the German wolfpacks."

"Yes, but they are taking heavy losses now. The Yanks are hunting them down with long-range bombers that can depth charge them."

She leans back against the cockpit, enjoying the sun on her face and the wind in her hair, and is lost in thought as she enjoys the moment. An hour later, Blake points toward the rugged wave-swept coastline. "How about some lunch? There's a quiet cove just ahead."

"Great! I'm famished."

Blake sails into a sheltered bay, lowers the mainsail, and drops anchor. "Let's go below and get out of this cold weather," and he opens the cabin door. The interior is warm and with narrow windows that let in just enough sunlight to make it comfortable. Amber lights and highly polished walnut paneling give it a luxurious feel. On one side is a galley kitchen, with a small dining area directly across from it, and the stateroom is forward through an open door.

Betty rubs her hands together and looks around. "Boy, it's nice and toasty down here!"

He sets his picnic basket on the table. "Go ahead, and make yourself comfortable," and spreads the contents out.

She takes off her heavy windbreaker and looks around. "I'm impressed! This is very cozy!"

"Thanks." He holds up a bottle of wine. "Do you like merlot?"

"Yes. Very much so," and she admires the interior. "I see you have all the comforts of home."

Blake jokes with her in his Australian accent. "No lawn to cut, but I do miss the barbie."

He digs a little deeper into his basket, takes out a loaf of French bread and a large stick of salami, and hands them to her.

"Thanks. Where did you get all these goodies?"

He opens the refrigerator door and looks for something. "I did an emergency appendectomy on the harbor master's son, and he insisted I take them."

"That was certainly thoughtful."

Blake finds what he's looking for. "Ah, here it is," and closes the door. "I think you'll like this locally made brie," and slices off a large wedge of it.

"Hmm, it smells fantastic! I can't wait to try it." She reaches into her pocket and produces a gift-wrapped present. "And I have a little something for you as well."

Blake takes the box with a quizzical look on his face. "This is for me?"

"Yes."

He carefully removes the wrapping and is surprised. "Swiss chocolate! Where on earth did you find this?"

"I heard you tell one of the nurses how much you miss chocolate."

"Yes, I do, but it's impossible to find." He opens the box and extends his arm to her. "Please take one."

"Thank you."

Blake unwraps a candy and slowly enjoys a bite. "Ohh. This is like a piece of heaven. I'm going to make this last for months."

Betty lifts her glass of wine. "I think we should toast to our good fortune."

"What will it be? To King and Country? A quick end to the war?"

"How about to us, and this wonderful day!" and they touch glasses. "Thanks for inviting me. I can see why you enjoy being out on the sea."

He smiles at her. "Well then, we'll do it again sometime."

"I'd like that."

After a quick lunch he pours the last of the merlot into their glasses, then reaches over to a radio built into a cabinet and spins the dial. The voice of Frank Sinatra singing *I'll Never Smile Again* with Tommy Dorsey's band fills the cabin, and Betty exclaims. "Ohh, I love him."

"So, you're a romantic, after all?"

"Can you keep a secret?"

He quips back. "Cross my heart."

"I've seen all of his movies."

"Well, we can't have Sinatra have all the fun. Do you want to dance?"

Betty loves to dance and is quick to accept. "Yes, I'd like that," and the two of them sway to the romantic music for a few minutes. As the song ends, they slowly separate, and their eyes make contact. A large ground swell rocks the boat, and she is pressed into his arms. He gently brushes her hair away from her face and kisses her softly. She runs her hand along the back of his neck, and they press their bodies together tightly. Blake stretches out on the bed, and she snuggles up against him, as they kiss passionately.

IT'S A COLD AND BLUSTERY AFTERNOON ON JUNE 6, 1944, and dark storm clouds swirl overhead. Betty leaves the nurse's barracks and walks down a sidewalk toward the hospital. She shivers and pulls up the collar on her raincoat. She's on the 8 am to 4 pm day shift and enters the building. Her friend Connie greets her. "Hi Betty."

"Good morning. It looks busy today."

"Crazy as usual. Mattie was looking for you. She should be in the emergency room."

"Thanks. I'll see if I can find her."

Betty walks down the busy corridor, and as she passes one of the operating rooms, the door bursts open, and Mattie and two nurses push a patient laying on a gurney. She calls to her. "We've got a full house. Can you help?"

"Yes, of course."

She follows them to a recovery room and helps the nurses transfer the patient to a bed. Then they push the empty gurney into the crowded hallway and disappear. Mattie rolls a blood plasma stand toward her. "The doctor will be here in a minute. Can you stay and give him a hand?"

"Sure."

It's an hour later, and Betty has been busy working with the wounded patients. She rolls her first aid cart down the hallway as several nurses pass by. Her friend Debby calls to her. "We're taking a break. Do you want to join us?"

"Yes, I could use one . . . and a cup of coffee!"

She parks her cart in an alcove and catches up to her as they enter the staff lounge. A radio is playing music when suddenly the voice of the newscaster interrupts the broadcast. "This is the BBC Home Service, and here is a special bulletin. D-Day has started. Under the command of General Eisenhower, Allied naval forces, supported by strong air forces, began landing Allied armies this morning on the northern coast of France. General Montgomery is in command of the Army group that is carrying out the assault. The Army group includes British, Canadian, and United States forces."

Betty can't believe what she's hearing. "Oh my gosh! It's started!"

The nurses rush over to the radio to listen to the rest of the report. Betty dashes out of the room and runs down the hallway. She sees Mattie coming toward her and calls to her. "Did you hear the news?"

"Yes! They said it's the largest seaborne invasion in history! We should expect to receive a massive number of casualties very soon. Can you help me pull together our staff?"

"Of course."

"My office in fifteen minutes!" and she disappears into the crowded hallway.

Several weeks have passed and Andy has returned from his trip to inspect the northern defense system. He walks down the busy corridor to post-op looking for Betty and finds her working with a badly wounded soldier. She glances up and notices him enter. "Hi. Welcome back."

"Thanks."

He stands on the opposite side of the soldier's bed. "Sorry to drop in like this. You look busy."

She works at changing the patient's bandages. "Could you hand me that roll of gauze?"

He walks over to her cart, and hands it to her. "Are you available for lunch today?"

Betty carefully rolls her patient over on his side. "Sorry. I need to look at your stitches," and the soldier grimaces. She's focused on her work, and glances up. "I take lunch at 1300. I'll see you then."

They sit at a table in the busy mess hall. Andy is like a big brother to her, and one that she wishes she had. He's twelve years older and married to an Irish woman by the name of Olivia, whom she has met several times. She and Andy share a deep bond that was created when he rescued her from her crashed bomber. Betty is more mature than other women of her age and enjoys hanging out with him and his older friends. However, when she does go out on a date, it's always with someone closer to her own age.

Andy produces a piece of paper and waves it playfully. "I've got a pass. Would you like to see London?"

"Yes, of course. I'd love to."

"We'll only be gone a couple of hours, but there's something special I want to show you. I'm on administrative duty tonight so I've got to be back by midnight."

"That sounds like fun. Count me in."

It's after work, and she and Andy walk toward his staff car. The sun sets behind a dark gray wall of fog that darkens the airbase, and Betty is curious. "Where are we off to?"

He pulls away from the curb and enters traffic. "To a night club. I think you'll like it."

A half hour later, they approach the outskirts of London, and he points to a large building. "This is one of our favorite hang-outs."

They exit the car and enter the busy club. The enormous hall is filled with cigarette smoke, and couples dance wildly to a loud band. Andy looks for someone, and sees his squadron leader, Major Charlie Barclay, sitting at a table with his girlfriend. He is tall and thin with reddish-brown curly hair and speaks with a strong Irish accent. Charlie is well-known for his practical jokes and playful attitude.

As they approach, he greets them. "Hi, I'm Charlie, and this is Shelagh."

"Hi, I'm Betty," and they lay their coats on their chairs just as the band plays music for a dance called the Jitterbug. It's a highly energetic style of dancing that became popular when Cab Calloway, an African American bandleader, developed it while working at the famous Cotton Club in Harlem; and it's currently the craze in England. The band plays loudly, and the wild dancing begins.

Charlie stands. "I love this one. We'll be right back," and they disappear onto the crowded dance floor.

Andy whispers in Betty's ear. "This is the surprise that I was talking about."

She watches the dancers, then turns to him and grins. "I know this dance, it's a lot of fun! Would you like to try it?"

"I'd love to, but I've got a bad leg."

"That's okay, Andy. We can wait for something slower."

After the dance ends, Charlie and Shelagh return holding hands and laughing. They met two weeks ago and have been inseparable ever since. She is a pretty Irish girl, slightly younger than Charlie, and is studying at the University of London.

Betty notices Mattie across the room talking with several nurses, and asks Shelagh, "My roommates just arrived. Do you want to meet them?"

She has taken a liking to Betty and smiles. "Sure."

"Excuse us, fellas. We're going to say hello to Mattie and the girls."

Andy looks up at her. "Have fun."

As they leave, a waitress arrives with a pitcher of beer and sets it down on their table. "Complements from your friend over there."

Andy searches the crowded room and sees Dr. Hunter sitting with his date. He waves to him. "Thanks!"

Charlie fills their glasses from the pitcher, and glances back toward Betty. "Wow! Where the bloody hell did you run into her?"

Andy finishes a long drink and sets his glass down. "In a cornfield in Germany."

"Come on, Andy! Don't joke around. Where did you meet her?"

"Hey, I'm a happily married man. She's fun to be with, but we're just friends. Would you do me a favor? You're a fantastic jitterbug dancer, and Betty loves to dance. Would Shelagh mind if you danced with her?"

Charlie shakes his head. "No, she won't mind."

Betty and Shelagh return, and moments later the band plays *Boogie Woogie Bugle Boy*. Three attractive women dressed in army uniforms stand at the front of the stage and sing loudly.

Charlie asks Betty, "Do you want to give it a go?"

"I'd love to!"

"Have you danced it before?"

"Yes. It was popular in America before the servicemen brought it here."

He leads her out onto the crowded floor, and they join the other dancers. The energetic tempo increases dramatically, and they dance facing each other kicking their legs out in all directions. Charlie lifts her high into the air, then swings her between his legs, and she slides away from him. He reaches out, grabs her outstretched hand, and she returns to him swaying her hips back and forth, while holding her other arm above her head. He pulls her into him, then spins her several times.

Four trumpet players at the back of the band stand and deafen the room as they dance side-by-side, stomping their feet quickly to the fast eight count beat. Betty is enjoying herself and has a huge smile on her face. Charlie twirls her in front of him, and she stops abruptly, facing him. Then she moonwalks backward before returning in a sexy move. As the dance approaches its climactic ending, he does a back flip, then spins her head-over-heels to the side, and she slides to the floor in a full split.

As they walk back to their table, he complements her. "You're an unbelievable dancer! People actually stopped to watch us."

Betty is out of breath from the strenuous dance and answers him shyly. "Thanks. You're a pretty talented dancer yourself."

Suddenly, the building shakes from the detonation of a powerful explosion, which is followed by the sound of air raid sirens. Glaring overhead lights turn on and flood the crowded dance hall with bright light. The music comes to an immediate stop, and the musicians quickly pack up their instruments as the crowd exits in an orderly but rushed manner. Andy leads their group and calls back to Charlie. "We better look for cover!"

They exit the building and the large crowd fans out into the nearly deserted street. Charlie yells to them. "There's an air raid shelter this way!"

Search lights pan the darkened sky searching for German bombers, and the sound and smell of battle fills the cool evening. Nearby anti-aircraft batteries spray the night with brightly colored tracers, and the dull thud of exploding flak shells echoes high above the city. Andy holds Betty's hand as they run toward the air raid shelter.

A nearby building is on fire and collapses, spewing large sections of burning rubble out into the crowded street. The flaming debris spreads out like a river of lava creating total chaos. He stops running, looks at the inferno ahead of them, then calls to Charlie. "Forget the shelter!" and points in the opposite direction. "My car is this way!"

Charlie yells back. "I'm parked that way too. I'll see you back at the base!"

The wind picks up, and scattered drops of rain fall from the dark clouds. Betty and Andy run cross the street and get into his car just as a powerful downpour slams into them. It beats steadily against the car's windshield, and the sedan buffets violently as the full force of the storm hits them. The enormous explosion was very close to the dance hall, and it rattled Betty. "What was that? I thought the Germans had given up on bombing London?"

"I'm not sure what happened. There was only one tremendous explosion, and I couldn't see any attacking bombers."

Betty wipes the rain drops from her face. "At least the dancing was a lot of fun!"

Andy smiles at her. "I thought you might like it."

Driven by a blustery wind, sheets of chilly rain whip across their windshield as they stare at the smoldering silhouettes of burning buildings. Flames shoot high into the sky and cast an eerie orange reflection against the low-hanging clouds. Andy stares at the skyline lost in thought. "It's surreal, isn't it?"

"Yes. And frightening too."

He gazes at the dark and stormy sky. "I'm glad I'm not flying tonight."

CHAPTER 10
A DANGEROUS MISSION

A FEW DAYS LATER, BETTY NOTICES ANDY AND CHARLIE SIT-ting at a corner table in the cafeteria and approaches them. "Hi, guys. Fancy meeting you here."

Andy motions to her. "Come and join us. How are things going at the hospital?"

"We're not busy at the moment. Am I interrupting anything?"

"No," and he pulls out a chair for her.

Charlie looks around to make sure no one is listening to them. "I just came from a staff meeting. They're really worried about this new navigation disruptor the Jerries are using."

Andy speaks in a low voice. "Yeah, they're pretty smart cookies, but we've defeated their systems before, and we'll do it again."

But Charlie shakes his head in doubt. "Maybe not this time."

Their story intrigues Betty. "How does it work?"

"Nobody knows. Somehow, they can bend our navigation beams and throw us off target. You're an electrical engineer. How is that possible?"

"I don't know. It could be a lot of things."

Charlie continues in a low voice. "The German resistance knows where the Nazis are developing the technology, and they have a spy on the inside, but they're having a hard time finding someone with the right qualifications to get to him."

Betty is fascinated by his story. "What are they looking for?"

"Well, he would have to speak perfect technical German and be able to understand complex scientific issues. And another thing . . . it's a high security installation, so he'll have to get past the guards somehow."

Several officers walk by them, talking loudly, and Charlie pauses. "It's a top-secret operation. No one ever leaves that base."

Andy is skeptical. "It sounds like an impossible mission to me."

"Maybe, but if our bombers can't find their targets, this war could drag on for a long time. A lot is hanging on this one, Andy, my boy!"

Betty leans forward and whispers. "I could do it."

Andy is shocked. "Oh, no! It's too dangerous for a woman."

"Nonsense. I'm an electrical engineer and I speak perfect German. I'd be comfortable traveling anywhere in Germany."

Andy in adamant. "Absolutely not! I won't hear of it."

IT'S THE FOLLOWING DAY, AND A SECRETARY OPENS THE door to General Buckley's office. "Excuse me, General, but there's a Lt. Bauer here to see you."

"Thank you, Liz. Tell her to come in."

She ushers Betty into his office, and he stands. "So nice of you to stop by."

"Thank you for taking the time to see me."

"Of course. Take a seat. What can I do for you?"

"I heard about the navigation disruptor that the Nazis are using."

"Yes. It's becoming quite a problem."

"That's why I'm here, sir. I believe I can help."

"I'm not sure what you mean."

"You need someone that can go to Germany and find out what they're doing. Someone who speaks technical German and is also an engineer. And that's me."

But the general is dismissive. "You are talking about a mission that could be incredibly dangerous."

"I'm aware of the dangers. I lost my aircrew in Germany, and it almost cost me my own life."

He doesn't think a woman can do the job, but he tries to be diplomatic. "It's not that easy, my dear. Missions like this require an enormous amount of planning."

She ignores his pessimism. "Their navigation disruptor works well enough that our bombing raids are completely ineffective. You have little choice, General. Thousands of lives are at stake against one if I fail."

He taps his fingers on the table for a moment. "Logically, your idea makes sense. I'll talk to our intelligence section and see what they have to say."

That afternoon Betty is in post-op talking to Mattie when a messenger enters. "I have a message for a Lt. Bauer."

Mattie nods toward Betty. "She's Lt. Bauer."

"This is for you, mam," and hands her a brown envelope.

She scans the contents, then puts it in her pocket. "Excuse me, Mattie. I'll get back to you later," and she leaves the room.

Mattie calls to her. "Goodbye, love."

Betty walks to the headquarters building and enters a door marked, "*Commanding General*". She smiles at the secretary, asks to see the general, and is ushered into his office. He has been expecting her and stands. "Come in, Lieutenant."

He motions toward another officer standing across from his desk. "Lt. Bauer, this is Captain Morgan with Special Operations Executive."

"It's nice to meet you."

"My pleasure, miss. Please, have a seat," and she sits down.

"Thank you. I take it you have been discussing my offer?"

"Yes, we have. Are you sure that you want to do this?"

"Something needs to be done, and I have the qualifications."

Captain Morgan explains. "Our plan is simple. We'll fly you into Germany at night, and the local resistance group will smuggle you into the airbase. Once inside, our agent will contact you and give you a roll of film detailing how the device works. Then you are to leave immediately. If all goes well, you should be back here the next day."

The plan is straight forward, and she agrees with him. "That sounds doable."

Captain Morgan looks at the General. "Well, what do you want to do?"

He takes a cigar out of a box on his desk. "I think this young lady can do it, but there is one thing that I'm afraid we have to insist on."

Betty is unsure of what he's thinking. "What's that?"

He lights his cigar and fills the room with smoke. "We need to put you through our basic combat training course. They will instruct you in self-defense, how to use automatic weapons, and the use of a parachute, because that's the only way we can get you there."

"Do I need all that just to pick up a roll of film and return the next day?"

"Yes. In war, you should expect the unexpected. We consider you a valuable asset, and you need to protect yourself. I'll contact Mattie and tell her you are needed at a hospital in London for a couple of weeks." He takes a long puff on his cigar, then sets it on the edge of his ashtray. "Report here at 0800 tomorrow morning, and we will begin your training."

That night, the Officer's Club is noisy as usual, and Betty and Andy stand away from the crowd. She talks in a low voice. "I volunteered to go to Germany and get the plans for the navigation disruptor."

"Bloody hell! You did what!"

Andy is extremely upset, and she tries to calm him down. "It may be hard for you to understand, but this is something that I have to do."

"Damn it! War is unpredictable, Betty! Anything can happen on a mission like that!"

She tugs at his arm. "Please, Andy. I need your support."

He knows he can't stop her and starts to calm down. "If that's what you're going to do, then at least let me fly you in."

"Thanks. And don't worry, it's not that risky. I just have to pick up a roll of film, and I'll be out the following night."

"Did they tell you when you're leaving?"

"Soon, but an officer with the Special Operations Executive insisted I take a short training course and learn how to parachute."

"The SOE? That sounds like trouble. Do you know who they are?"

"No, I've never heard of them."

"They're a secret group that trains commandos in espionage by attacking and disrupting the enemy from behind their lines."

"Well, I agreed to go on the mission, and that's what I'm going to do. My training starts tomorrow."

The following morning, Betty reports at the General's office and Capt. Morgan meets her. He drives her to a secret installation in the north of England, where she is introduced to four other women who will train with her. Their training is rigorous to the point of exhaustion, and very demanding, both mentally and physically.

They are up at dawn, and run three miles before breakfast, which is followed by long hours of instruction that sometimes end late in the evening.

During the day, they go through grueling hours of hand-to-hand combat training, and spend days on the firing range until they are proficient marksmen with pistols and submachine guns.

As time passes, they prepare for their first parachute jump. After three days, Betty knows how to do a parachute landing roll, and how to cut the shrouds in case she lands in a tree. Then they learn how to use a shortwave radio, and practice throwing hand grenades. By the end of the week, they make the first of many static line parachute jumps. Static line refers to a jump where the parachute is opened by a twenty-five-foot line attached to the plane. A few days later, they begin night jumps, and practice how to guide the descending parachute.

Toward the end of their training, they make nightly free fall jumps using a black canopied parachute, which will help conceal them when they make their night jump behind enemy lines. Betty returns to her barracks, changes into her nurse's uniform, and reports for work at the hospital.

That evening, she visits the Officer's Club and finds Andy and Charlie having a beer as usual. Andy looks up and sees her approaching. "Well, well. Look who's here."

"Hi, guys," and she greets them with a hug. "It's good to be back."

Andy is surprised. "What happened to your beautiful, long hair?"

"The German Army doesn't allow it, so they cut it."

Charlie is curious. "Well, how did it go?"

"The general completely understated the training. It was a grueling sixteen days. We started each day at sunrise with a three-mile jog over difficult terrain, then we trained in hand-to-hand combat, weapons and explosives use, and never got to bed until late at night. Now I know ten ways to kill someone. After a few days, we started our parachute training, and we ended with high-altitude free-fall night jumps."

Andy is not surprised. "I tried to tell you. Those SOE boys take their work seriously."

"Well, it seems quite unnecessary for a brief reconnaissance trip."

Andy smiles at her. "I told you war is unpredictable. Anything can happen, and it usually does," and he takes a drink from his glass of beer.

"That's what I keep hearing, but don't worry about me. I'll do just fine."

Later that day, Andy and Betty walk down the flight line, passing a row of parked Spitfires. He stops and turns to her. "I talked to the General and asked him if I could fly you in."

"What did he say?"

"He agreed, and he also told me that the SOE highly recommended you. You're a natural born spy; smart, and resourceful."

"Oh, gosh. All I want is to help end this war and go back to my quiet life."

"Are you planning to return to America when this is over?"

"I guess so. What are you going to do?"

"I'll continue working at my family's business."

Betty is curious, as he had never spoken about it. "What sort of business is that?"

"My family owns a factory that makes war materials. What would you think about staying here in England?"

"Why do you ask?"

"When the war ends, there's going to be a lot of business opportunities here, and I know influential people that can help us."

She shakes her head. "I haven't thought about it much. The end seems so far away."

"Well, think about it. This will all be over some day. We can talk about it when you return from your mission."

It's late in the evening days later. Scattered low clouds obscure the clear starlit heavens, as a black twin-engine de Havilland Mosquito night fighter taxis quietly between long rows of Spitfire fighters. Nearing the end of the taxiway, it rotates into a light breeze and comes to a stop. Its two seventeen hundred horsepower Rolls-Royce engines rev to full power, and it launches forward.

Halfway down the runway, it lifts gently into the air and silently disappears into the misty darkness.

Minutes later, they fly through the top of a thick layer of fog, and turn onto a southerly course away from Germany as a diversionary tactic. Their flight path parallels England's southern coastline for a bit, and then they climb high above the clouds.

The Mosquito is made of plywood and it's nearly impossible to see on German radar screens. Originally designed as a fighter-bomber, the model NF Mark II is specially configured for night combat missions. The plane is painted midnight black, making it difficult to be seen at altitude, and its muffled exhaust system conceals its engine noise.

Andy is at the controls, and Betty sits beside him dressed in a black jump suit. It's going to be a dangerous night flight and the red cockpit lights bathe the interior in an eerie glow. Little is said, as it will take Andy's full concentration.

In order to avoid German coastal radar stations, he flies far to the south of their target in case they are picked up and tracked by an alert radar operator. Several minutes later, they descend steeply through the clouds, and level off fifty feet above the wind-swept seas of the English Channel. It's a dangerous night maneuver designed to fly under the ever-present radar; however, Andy is highly experienced, and they soon approach their destination deep into southern Germany.

The minutes pass, and he glances down at his map looking for landmarks to confirm he's in the right area. "I'm pretty sure this is it. Look for a bridge."

Betty strains to see into the dark night. "I think the drop zone is up ahead!" and glances down at her watch. "And we're exactly on time."

Andy reduces his air speed, and in the darkness, they can barely make out the edge of the forest and the contours of the fields below them. He crosses over a mountain stream, then banks to the right and follows it until they reach a small bridge.

As he flies over it, Betty sees a bright flash. "There's the signal light!" and they roar past it, flying only fifty feet above the ground.

"I'm going to double back and pick up some altitude. You might as well open the belly hatch and get ready. I'll count to three, then jump."

"Thanks Andy. See you in a couple of days."

"Be careful. We'll stay in contact with the resistance. If anything goes wrong, scrub the mission, and get the hell out of there."

"Got it. And don't worry, I'll be okay."

Betty works her way down to the belly hatch and opens it as a frigid blast of cold air greets her. She carefully sits down with her legs dangling out the hatch, and the wind tears at her clothes. She tugs at her parachute straps to check them, then reaches down with her hand and feels the razor-sharp commando knife strapped to the calf of her leg.

Andy circles back, regains altitude, and flies high over the drop zone. If he is too low, Betty could drift into the dense forest, so he climbs to fifteen hundred feet, which will allow her time to pinpoint her landing. She adjusts her goggles, then gazes at the ground far below.

He calls to her. "Get ready! One! . . . Two! . . . Three!"

Betty slips through the hatch and tumbles through the dark sky. The night is misty, and a light rain obscures her visibility. She quickly opens her arms and legs into a spread-eagle position to stabilize her tumbling and orients herself with the ground as the strong wind thrashes at her body.

She searches for the signal light, but it's difficult to see in the rain. Suddenly, a bright light flashes in her direction, and she instantly swings her arms down to her side, pulls her feet together, and descends rapidly at a steep angle.

At six hundred feet, she pulls hard on her rip cord, which releases a small drogue parachute from her backpack. It quickly blows behind her, pops open in the stiff wind, and instantly deploys her main canopy, jerking her back violently as it snaps open.

Betty dangles below the huge black canopy and silently drifts across the dark sky. In the distance, the Mosquito drops low to the ground, and vanishes into the shadowy night. She pulls at her shroud lines, making wide descending spirals, and runs to a standing stop in a plowed field as her canopy collapses to the ground behind her.

A man dressed in dark clothing and carrying a light gun runs toward her. It's a three-foot tube mounted on a gun stock, with a light at the bottom that's activated by the trigger. The only person who can see it is the one that it's pointed at. As Betty gathers her canopy, the man approaches and whispers in German. "Come quickly."

She follows him to a small two-door sedan parked in the dark shadows of the forest, and he introduces himself. "I am Fritz," and he tosses the light gun into the trunk.

Betty whispers back. "I'm Elizabeth," and hands him her parachute. Then she strips off her black jump suit, and stuffs it into a corner of the trunk. Fritz taps lightly on the roof, and it pulls away and vanishes into the darkness.

They turn and run to a dark sedan parked in the shadows, and he opens the rear door for her. As they drive off, he nods toward his passenger. "This is Bruno."

She shakes his hand from the back seat. "Hi. I'm Elizabeth," and stares down the lonely road ahead of them. "How far do we have to go?"

"It's about an hour away."

Bruno hands her several documents. "If they stop us, you will need these."

"Thanks," and she carefully scans them with a small flashlight. There is only silence as their car speeds into the night. A half hour later, the sedan turns onto a narrow gravel road that winds through the dense forest. Soon their headlights reveal the shadowy outline of a large barn, several outbuildings, and a small farmhouse. Fritz pulls up to the house and stops. "We are here."

As they approach, the front door opens and a man in his late sixties extends his hand to her. "I am Hérr Ritter."

"I'm Elizabeth Bauer. Good to meet you."

She enters the house, and he motions toward a young woman standing at the stove. "This is my daughter, Gerta."

Betty reaches out to shake her hand, but she ignores it and gives her an enormous hug instead. "Welcome!"

Hérr Ritter motions toward the kitchen table. "Please sit down. We have a lot to talk about before morning."

Betty pulls up a chair, and the others join her. He unfolds a map and points to it. "We are here," and moves his finger along a winding road. "Not far away is a seldom used emergency airfield with grass runways that the locals call Starlight Forest. Security is tight, and it's the perfect location to develop a secret weapon. We are sure they are developing the navigation disruptor there, but we know little more."

She looks up from the map and questions him. "I was told your man would have a roll of film for me."

"Yes, but unfortunately, he was recently killed in an accident, and they've requested a replacement. But that's good news for us."

The unexpected change in plans makes Betty uncomfortable. "Why is that?"

"Because you can present yourself as a temporary replacement. It will be difficult for them to find someone, so you should have time to discover what they are doing and get back here in a day or two."

Betty doesn't like what she is hearing. "That wasn't the plan."

"What can I say? In war, things can change quickly." He reaches into his jacket pocket. "You may need this," and he slides a subminiature camera toward her. "We have a small window of opportunity to get in and get out. Find out whatever you can and get back here as soon as possible. It will be extremely dangerous to stay."

The unforeseen change in plans agitates her as Andy, Charlie, and now the German underground are counting on her to succeed. She pushes back in her chair. "Damn it!"

Hérr Ritter has a serious look on his face. "If you don't think you can do this, we should abort the mission, and I wouldn't blame you. It could be very dangerous for you . . . and for us."

"What do you mean, us?"

"Torture. If they capture you, they will discover every detail."

She taps her finger on the table as she considers the risk, then looks up. "I'll go. I should be able to find out something."

Hérr Ritter has one last warning. "The Allies plan on bombing the base as soon as the weather clears, so be sure to leave before it starts."

The lack of British intelligence frustrates her. "I just left them. No one told me they were going to bomb it!"

"What can I say? Allied bomber command alerted us that the bombing would start as soon as the rain stops." He opens a small box. "There is just one more thing," and he hands her a gold wedding band. "You should wear this."

"What's this for?"

"It will help keep unwanted attention away from you."

"You seem to have thought of everything," and she slips on the ring.

"In the morning, go with Gerta when she delivers milk. They know her, so there shouldn't be a problem getting past the sentries. Tonight, we'll fit you into a German officer's uniform and hide it in the cart. After you enter the base, she will show you where to change, and then you'll be on your own. When it's time to leave, rendezvous with her at the drop-off point. She will look for you at sunset in a day or two. Do you have any questions?"

"No. That sounds like a doable plan."

Just then, a man enters the house, and Hérr Ritter greets him. "Ah, come in, my friend," and they shake hands. "This is Dr. Krause. He will take care of your implant."

Betty is surprised. "What implant?"

"Didn't your people tell you anything?"

She feels poorly prepared and angered that British intelligence didn't inform her of the details of her mission. "What are you talking about?"

Dr. Krause takes the top off a glass vial and shakes several small gray capsules into his hand. "This is a cyanide capsule. If they catch you, the torture will be unbearable."

"Of course. The implant."

"Follow me, Fräulein. We should take care of this right away."

She excuses herself from the table, and they walk down the hallway and enter a small room. In the center is a makeshift dental chair and an overhead light. "Please, sit down. I need to drill your molar and install the cyanide capsule. If you bite down on it hard, it will crush, and death will be immediate."

Betty is not happy about these unforeseen changes to her plans, and he continues. "Please, make yourself comfortable, and don't worry, the effects of the anesthesia will be gone by morning. Do you know what your blood type is?"

"Yes, AB. Why do you ask?"

"All officers have their blood type tattooed under their arm. I will tattoo it on you before the anesthetic wears off. You won't feel a thing."

It's early the following morning. Betty and Gerta, dressed in the colorful costumes of local milkmaids, stand next to a donkey harnessed to a brightly decorated cart. It has two large wooden-spoked wheels, and its small rear deck is filled with a dozen metal milk containers.

Hérr Ritter explains. "The airfield is not far away. When you and Gerta stop at the security check point, the guards will check your papers. They know her, so there shouldn't be any problems." He removes an envelope from his jacket pocket and hands it to her. "These are your military identification papers.

No one will dare question your authority when they see that uniform." He stares at her for a moment. "You do speak technical German?"

"Of course. I'm an engineer."

"Good, because your life will depend on it."

He taps on the map. "Use this side entrance. There's not much traffic there," and points to a building. "This is Hangar 9. We think they are working on the project there. You should be able to get close enough to the plane to find out what they are up to. Remember, you need to leave before the bombing starts."

Betty shakes her head. "That doesn't give me much time. I can't promise anything."

"Whatever you discover will be valuable."

CHAPTER 11

STARLIGHT FOREST AND THE HIDDEN SECRET

IT'S A SUNNY MORNING, AND GERTA LEADS HER DONKEY AS she and Betty walk down a quiet rural road. Rolling hills, covered by a dense forest of tall European Beech trees, surround them and they soon approach the base's guard station. They stop at a vehicle barrier's white wooden arm that extends across the road. Parked next to the building is an armored half-track with a forward mounted MG-42 heavy machine gun.

A guard carrying a submachine gun approaches them. "Halt! Where are you going?"

Gerta smiles. "We are delivering milk."

"Where are your papers?"

"Here," and she hands them to the guard.

He stares suspiciously at Betty. "Who is this? I haven't seen her before."

"She's my cousin from Hamburg."

Just then, a car with a plaque on the bumper showing that it belongs to Field Marshal von Meyer, the regional commanding general, stops behind them and honks impatiently. The guard hands Gerta's papers back to her. "Here. You can pass," and he walks to the general's car.

The women continue deeper into the forest, passing buildings hidden amongst the tall trees. A patrol of heavily armed men with two Rottweiler guard dogs walk out of the shadows and wave to them as they pass. A short while later, they arrive at a large mess hall, and Gerta stops her donkey. "This is our first stop," and she points to a metal milk container. "Take that one and follow me."

They carry the containers up the steps and enter the kitchen. The smell of freshly baked bread fills the air, and a happy, heavy-set man approaches them wearing a soiled white apron. "Good morning, ladies. Please put them next to the cooler."

Gerta gives him a friendly smile. "Good morning, Klaus."

"Are you staying for coffee?"

"No. We're late, but tomorrow for sure."

He smiles at Betty. "Hello. I'm Klaus."

"Hi, I'm Elizabeth, and I've already heard about your delicious apple cake."

"Thank you! I'll look forward to seeing you both."

The women leave the building, and Gerta leads her donkey as they continue walking down the road deeper into the base. She smiles at Betty. "Klaus is a fantastic baker."

"Yes, but I think he has eyes for you."

"Oh no, we're just friends."

A while later, Gerta motions toward several buildings. "I've got more stops to make, but this is a good place for you to change." She leads her donkey cart into an alley between two buildings and removes the hidden bag containing the German Army uniform. "Just down the road is Hangar 9, where the disruptor is."

"Thank you," and Betty takes it from her.

Gerta is nervous. "Remember, security is tight, and the guards suspect anyone they don't know. I make a delivery of butter and cheese in the late afternoon, and I'll look for you here."

"Thanks, Gerta."

She gives Betty a hug and a warning. "Be careful," and continues down the road.

Betty opens the side door, crosses a large room, and enters the bathroom. An hour later, she exits dressed in the black uniform of an elite Gestapo officer. The Nazis specifically tailored it to project authority and foster fear, and it's a chilling transformation. She wears an officer's visor cap with silver piping, and a black velvet band. Above that is a large German eagle and below it is a silver death's head badge. Its skull and crossbones represent the much-feared Gestapo. Her braided shoulder boards denote her rank as a lieutenant, and on her arm is a red armband with a large black swastika set in the center of a white circle. Her trousers taper tightly into shiny, calf-high jackboots. Betty removes a Luger pistol from its holster, ejects the clip, and checks to see that it's loaded. Then she gives the base a thump with her palm, and it locks firmly into place. She expertly pulls the pistol's slide back, releases it, and it slams forward, chambering a round. Then drops it into her holster, exits the building, and walks toward Hangar 9.

The guard at the entrance snaps to attention and salutes her smartly. "Your papers please." He glances at them and hands them back. "You can pass, Lieutenant."

They Nazi salute each other, and she enters the dimly lit hangar. The only light comes from large aircraft doors, which are fully open. Parked in the shadows is an impressive looking Junkers Ju-88, a twin-engine bomber painted green with a disruptive pattern of off-gray camouflage markings. It's an agile high-speed plane that's very popular with the Luftwaffe because of its multirole capabilities. On top of the fuselage is a strange looking saucer, about three feet thick and ten feet in diameter. It's constructed of aluminum and rests on two streamlined vertical support members. Now she needs to discover how it works and leave before the Allies bomb the airbase.

A group of technicians are reviewing documents on a table, and don't notice her approaching. As she nears them, Major Krüger, a short, balding, rotund man in his mid-sixties, turns in her direction, and she snaps to attention with a Nazi salute. "Heil Hitler!"

The Major, surprised by the sight of a Gestapo officer, returns her salute. "Heil Hitler!"

She hands him her orders and responds stiffly. "Lieutenant Hausser. Temporary replacement for your engineer that was killed."

He stares nervously at her uniform. "I see. And what is your specialty, Lieutenant?"

"I'm an electrical engineer."

Betty looks closely at the plane. "Is this it? I was expecting more activity."

"This is only a decoy. The disruptor is hidden," and he returns her paperwork. "Are you familiar with our technology?"

"No. I was only told that you needed an electrical engineer."

He's disappointed. "I'm sorry, but I requested someone with very specialized talents."

Betty immediately comes to attention and clicks her boots together. "Understood, Major. I will let the Führer know you are unhappy with his decision."

As she starts to leave, he nervously grabs her arm to stop her. She looks down at his hand and glares threateningly into his eyes. "Release my arm, or I'll have you shot!"

He stammers. "I . . . I . . . did not mean to offend the Führer, but our work here is vital to winning the war," and he motions toward his car. "Please. Let me show you the plane."

They get into his black BMW sedan and drive through the base. The road winds among the tall trees before coming to a paved section that is straight as an arrow for at least a mile and the vegetation on both sides has been cleared back, creating a wide swath through the forest.

They drive to the far end, pull off to the side, and stop. Two heavily armed soldiers appear from the shadows and approach them. "Your papers, sir," and the major hands him his identification. "And yours, Lieutenant."

A second soldier looks in the back seat, then opens the trunk to inspect it. He returns their papers and waves at someone hidden in the shadows. "You can pass, sir."

There is a whine of electrical motors, and a huge camouflage screen opens, revealing a wide concrete ramp that slants downward into a massive underground hangar. They drive down it and park inside. The interior of the heavily fortified concrete structure is painted white and is brightly lit. Mechanics work on a Focke-Wulf 189 tactical reconnaissance plane, widely known as the Flying Eye, because of its glazed cockpit. It has a camouflage color scheme of light gray and whitish pink, and its distinctive twin-engine design makes it unusual looking. A large multi-pronged antenna protrudes from the nose.

Betty opens her door and steps out of the car. As she does, a huge long-haired German Shepherd attack dog emerges from the shadows. He is a fearsome sight and approaches her, barking loudly while flashing his large fangs. She freezes, unsure of what she should do next.

A man wearing a white lab coat with a red Nazi armband looks over at them. He excuses himself from a group of technicians and approaches. Noticing that Betty is unsure of how the dog will react, he calls to him in a Slavic dialect that she can't quite put her finger on. Immediately, the huge animal stops advancing, and returns to his side. The handsome officer is about the same age as Betty, and has Nordic features, an athletic build, blonde hair, and blue eyes.

He walks toward her and apologizes. "I'm sorry. My dog is just curious."

She is suddenly confronted with a reality that she never considered. As she looks at the two Nazi officers, a terrifying sense of déjà vu overwhelms her. Long forgotten, and frightening, memories of marauding Hitler Youth gangs and public executions flood into her mind, and her hand trembles out of fear and hatred for what the Nazis did to her family. She had spent a lifetime trying to suppress those terrible memories, and now it feels as though they happened only yesterday. She struggles to stay calm, takes a deep breath, and reminds herself that her mission is to get as much information as she can, and leave as soon as possible.

The officer approaches the major and shakes hands with him. "It's always good to see you, Major."

"Thank you," and he introduces Betty. "This is Professor von Hirschel, the project director."

"My pleasure, I am Lieutenant Hausser," and she shakes his hand.

"Nice to meet you. I don't get many visitors. What brings you here?"

"I am to assist you until your replacement engineer arrives."

This is not good news, as the professor doesn't need a fanatical Nazi poking around his project, especially now. They are months behind schedule, and to make matters worse, he recently discovered technical issues with the plane that will delay them dramatically. "You're an electrical engineer?"

"Yes."

"I wasn't expecting a woman. You should know that this technology is quite advanced, and I don't have the time to train anyone."

Betty snaps back at him. "I understand. Are you the inventor?"

"Yes. I have a doctorate in applied physics, and my field of interest is wave motion generators. Are you familiar with the technology?"

"No, I am not."

This is the excuse he needs to rid himself of another Nazi fanatic looking over his shoulder. "I'm sorry, Lieutenant, but I don't think you will be of much help then."

Betty responds with a defiant attitude. "As you wish. Apparently, the Führer has made a mistake," and she starts to walk away. The professor hoped she would give up and leave on her own accord, and he quickly realizes the extreme danger that he could be in if she leaves under these conditions. His pace quickens as he catches up to her. "You are the third engineer that they've sent me. The others only made things worse."

She stops and turns to face him. "This wasn't my idea. If you think I'm unable to help you, then I am happy to leave."

The professor quickly reconsiders his position. "I didn't mean to offend you," and he holds out his hand. "Please accept my apologies."

Betty stares at him for a moment, then stiffly shakes his hand. "Maybe you should review my work before you complain about me!"

"I'm sorry about that." His attitude changes dramatically, and he motions her forward. "Let me show you the disruptor. Please, come this way."

Her dangerous bluff worked, and this is exactly what she needs to know. As they walk toward the plane, she questions him. "Why is it painted that color?"

"A few months ago, we shot down a British photo reconnaissance fighter that was painted like this. We discovered it to be a very good camouflage scheme for hiding in the clouds."

They pass several mechanics that are working on the plane, and Betty asks, "Is it operational?"

"Almost, but as you can see, we are upgrading the engines to something more powerful. It has no armament; its only defense is its speed."

They walk under the fuselage. "We are extending the front section three feet to give us a bit more cabin space for the electronics, and we are also adding a nose wheel so that it will sit level, which helps to calibrate the antenna array. We've had some success against the enemy bombers, but we can only fly at night. Unfortunately, we are at a standstill because of technical issues."

Betty is unimpressed with the plane. "What type of problems are you having?"

The professor questions her. "Are you a pilot?"

She lies to him. "No, but I am familiar with aerial weapons."

"We are experiencing a lot of vibration, and the antenna array tore itself apart the last time we were out."

"What other problems are you having?"

"Our electrical schematics are a disaster. Several engineers have worked on them, but they only made things worse. Most failed to comprehend even the basics of what I'm doing and were of no help at all."

She gives him a stern look. "In their defense, it is very difficult to understand a radically new technology. Bridging the gap from your mind to paper can be very difficult."

"Maybe, but it still needs to be built. Do you think you can help?"

Betty, who is always confident, is quick to respond. "That remains to be seen. I need to review your plans and familiarize myself with your project. What is your background in this technology?"

"I completed my earlier research and theoretical modeling at the university. One day, a Luftwaffe general approached me. He had read one of my papers on advanced aerial navigation systems, and he asked if it would be possible to weaponize my concept. So here I am, a year and a half later."

"So, how does the disruptor work?"

"The Allied bombers find their short-range targets pretty much by line of sight. They use a map, a compass, and a watch to time themselves to the target. However, it is extremely inaccurate if used at night, or in poor weather, where they can't reference features on the ground.

"For longer range cities like Berlin, they use radio direction finders to home in on broadcast stations, then triangulate a course to their objective. By using my disruptor technology, I can warp the beam that they are riding by bending it and point them off the target."

"That sounds unbelievable!"

"You've probably seen it happen without realizing it."

"I don't think so."

"Let's say you and I have two rocks about the same weight. You stand on one side of a pond, and I stand on the other side, facing you. We both drop our rocks into the water at the same time, and they create waves that radiate across the pond."

"So, what am I looking for?"

"When the waves meet in the middle, they cancel each other out and disappear. It's the same with radio waves, except the disruptor is much more complicated because I have to determine the exact wavelength they are riding and then match it."

Betty is skeptical. "It can't be that easy."

He ducks under the tail boom. "Of course not. There are a lot of variables to address, and there are many issues to sort out before it's combat ready."

This is exactly what Betty needs to know. "What kind of problems are you talking about?"

"Our signal breaks up intermittently, causing the beam to return to normal. Part of the problem is that we don't generate enough signal strength, but there are other issues too."

He walks over to a drafting table strewn with drawings, and points at a thick pile of complicated wiring diagrams drawn on large sheets of paper. "These are the electrical schematics," and he slowly turns a few pages. As he does, Betty notices he is wearing a gold wedding band. He motions toward the stack of plans. "What do you think?"

She flips through the sheets, stopping occasionally to scan them. "This will take some time. Do you have an office that I can use?"

"Yes. You can work here. I have a meeting to attend, but we can go over this in more detail later in the day."

The attack dog stares intently at her, and the professor sees that she's uncomfortable. "Please don't worry about Apollo. He's just slow to make friends." As he leaves, he calls to him, and the dog obediently follows.

The professor walks out into the hangar and joins Major Krüger, who is angry. "I can't believe they sent us a woman! She has no idea of what we are trying to do. This is way over her head!"

"You might be right, but it won't be easy to find a replacement. Others have tried and failed, and now we have someone handpicked by the Führer himself."

Betty takes off her jacket, hangs it on the wall, and removes her heavy jackboots. She sits down on a tall drafting stool and flips through the electrical schematics. From the size of the large stack of plans, she realizes it's going to take a lot of time, and she looks down at her watch. Gerta is expecting to meet her, but it's too late in the day, so their meeting will have to wait until tomorrow.

Unfortunately, she doesn't have many options. Her windows reveal her every move, making it impossible to use the sub-micro camera, and she can't carry the plans because they are too large and heavy. There is a remote possibility that she could steal the plane, but it won't be flyable for several weeks. Her biggest worry is that the real replacement engineer could appear, and her charade would be over in an instant. To make matters worse, the weather is clearing, and the Allies are planning to bomb the base; and it's her greatest fear. With no current plan, she can only wait for an unknown opportunity to present itself.

The electrical schematics are large, about two feet by three feet, and complex. Betty picks up a red marking pen and starts reviewing one of the sheets. Several revisions overwrite the originals, but she is extremely thorough and takes her time crossing out electrical components that make no sense and drawing question marks here and there with arrows pointing to complex mathematical calculations written in the margins.

Several hours later, she looks up to see the professor's attack dog laying outside her doorway staring at her with his big brown eyes. He is twice the size of a normal German Shepherd and has a black saddle, an apricot-colored coat, and long hair. When Betty first met him, she was apprehensive, but now he appears to be friendly, and she decides to try to make friends with him. "Apollo, do you want to stay with me?"

At the sound of his name, he snaps to his feet and immediately comes to her, wagging his tail. He instinctively pushes past her, lays down under her desk, and she rubs her bare feet on his warm furry back.

By now it's the end of the day, and the professor sticks his head into her office. "How's it going?"

"Very good, but these schematics are poorly written."

"I was afraid of that. Others have stumbled around trying to work on them. What have you found out?"

"Look at this."

She slowly turns half a dozen pages over. Red lines, lengthy comments, and mathematical calculations cover the margins. "These are all enormous problems, and I've only just begun. I'm amazed that your invention even works!"

He is shocked at the detail of her work. "This is impressive! Maybe you can help me!"

"Yes, but it will take time." She traces a line on the plans using her finger and follows it as it winds its way across the page. "These wires go nowhere, and these components are completely unnecessary." She taps on a complex cluster of electrical symbols. "And I have no idea what this does. This is incredibly poor engineering. No wonder you are behind schedule!"

The professor turns a couple of pages and reviews her comments. As he does so, he notices her wedding ring.

Betty is very serious. "It would be impossible to go into production with these plans. They make no sense at all."

His technology intrigues her, and she realizes it has possibilities. Thinking quickly, she makes a gutsy move to stall his program, and return to England as soon as possible with the information that she has. "I'm sorry, but I must recommend we end this project. Our resources would be better used elsewhere."

The professor is shocked. "Oh, no! You can't do that!"

Just then, the office door opens, and Major Krüger enters the room. "Well, what did you find out?"

Betty gives him a stern look and motions toward a chair. "Please have a seat, Major. These plans are complete nonsense. It would take a lot of time to rewrite the schematics, rebuild the equipment, and then test it. Then there are the technical problems with the plane itself. Upgrading to more powerful engines won't work. It will only unbalance the plane and worsen its already poor flight characteristics. Even if we were able to resolve these difficulties, there still is no guarantee that the disruptor will work. Who recommended using that plane?"

The professor looks over at the major, and Betty questions him. "And what is your expertise in aviation, Major?"

He mumbles sheepishly. "A friend of mine recommended that plane."

"So, you thought a small underpowered observation plane could catch up with the Allied bombers? They cruise at two hundred miles an hour, and at an altitude of twenty-five thousand feet!"

"But we've been working on this for a year and a half! We can't stop now!"

Betty speaks firmly. "I'll decide that. I need to return to Peenemünde as soon as possible."

"Peenemünde? What are you working on that is more important than this?"

"Vengeance weapons for the Führer."

She stands and gets ready to leave, but the professor continues to defend his position. "I'm not an electrical engineer, and yes, incompetent people have worked on these plans, but I'm an expert at the science, and I know it will work. I just need the help of someone like yourself to complete the project. At least let me explain. I think you might change your mind if you understand what I'm trying to do."

This is exactly the reaction that Betty had hoped for. The sun is setting, and it's too late to meet Gerta, but she realizes that one more day shouldn't hurt, especially if she can discover the disruptor's secrets.

She pauses for a moment. "Alright. I owe you that much."

"Good. We should start with the plane."

She swivels her chair to the side, pulls on her boots, and stands. As she does so, Apollo gets up from under the table, walks through the group, and into the hangar. The professor is shocked by his friendliness. "Well, he's never done that before! He is usually extremely wary of strangers."

"He visited me a couple of hours ago and just walked in."

"I thought you were afraid of him?"

As she leaves the room, she smiles at him. "You only assumed I was. Predictability is the enemy of innovation."

Betty's brilliance intrigues him, and he is at a loss for words. Major Krüger is uncomfortable and eager to leave. "Professor, I need to return to my office. Can you see to Lt. Hausser's accommodations?"

"Yes. Of course. I'll call later and let you know what we've decided."

He nods to Betty. "Until then."

She answers dryly. "Good evening, Major," and he leaves.

The professor is apologetic. "I'm afraid he doesn't understand the science of what we are doing," and motions toward the plane. "Please. Let me show you the disruptor."

"Thank you. I'd like to see what you have done."

They cross the hangar and climb a metal ladder that leads to a hatch in the plane's belly. Betty follows him, and they enter the cramped cabin. Electronic equipment racks line both sides, floor to ceiling, and there are several cathode-ray tubes used to display the signal output created by the wave generator. Betty wasn't expecting to see the extensive number of electrical components. "This is quite impressive, Professor."

"Thank you, but once it's operational, I plan to downsize it," and he points to a large cluster of batteries under the racks. "This is our direct current power supply. It feeds to an alternating inverter that powers these instruments."

The professor moves to a complex bank of electronic instrumentation installed in the rear of the cabin. "This is the operator's station. By using this cathode-ray tube, he can adjust the signal output to match the bomber's homing frequency, and then bend it to throw them off course."

Betty plays dumb and asks, "Have the Allies figured out a countermeasure?"

"Well, all this is new. I don't think they have any idea that it's happening. But truthfully, as with most technologies, there is always a way to defeat them; however, it would take time, and time is what everyone is short of."

"This is an interesting idea, Professor."

"I'd prefer that you call me Max. Professor is a little formal if we are going to be working together."

"Alright. Please call me Elizabeth."

Betty now has a major dilemma to consider. His invention has real possibilities, but it's not operational, and that's an enormous problem. The British assumed all they would need was a few photographs so that they could engineer a way to defeat it. But it's never that simple, and now she must make a hard choice. Leave before the scheduled bombing and avoid being killed, or wounded, or stay and learn how the technology works, but that could take time, and every day exposes her to the risk of discovery and being shot as a spy. She wonders if the professor is realistic about his invention. "Do you think this will win the war for us?"

"War winning? No, but for sure, it will delay the Allies until one of the Führer's vengeance weapons is combat-ready. I understand they are developing a jet engine. Do you know anything about that?"

"Yes, but I can't discuss it."

"I understand."

Betty is uncomfortable in the small cabin. "It's claustrophobic in here. Can we talk somewhere else?"

"Of course. Let's go back to my office."

He ushers her out of the plane, and they walk across the hangar. Betty questions him. "How successful do you feel the Allied bombing raids have been?"

"I would say they have been highly successful. They have leveled dozens of our cities and industrial centers, but at an enormous cost. We've shot down hundreds of their bombers, and their losses can't be sustainable."

"Is it safe to fly near them?"

"If the escort fighters are with them, we have to distance ourselves, or risk being shot down. Normally, we shadow them until the fighters run low on fuel and turn back. Then we keep our distance and fly several thousand feet below the formation.

"They usually fly very high to make it difficult for our fighters to reach them. But when they bomb from an altitude of twenty-five thousand feet, they can miss their target by as much as five miles. If they approach at a lower level, our anti-aircraft batteries and fighters can easily shoot them down."

Betty thinks about what he said. "It would seem that you need to produce a more powerful disruptor signal and stay farther away so that you're not noticed."

"Theoretically, our range is three to five miles, depending on atmospheric conditions. We usually operate at ten thousand feet. Higher than that and we have to go on oxygen, and the outside temperature drops dramatically, which affects the equipment. If we fly well below them, we present no threat."

"Are you achieving results with your prototype?"

"Only limited success. On our first flight, we had to get dangerously close to them, but we were lucky, and they didn't spot us. A major concern has been overheating. I've had to shut it down twice, and one time it caught on fire."

Betty realizes the potential threat that it proposes to the Allies, and, in an instant, she changes her mission and decides to stay a few more weeks and help develop a fully operational system. It's an extremely risky move, but without full knowledge of the technology, she could never come up with a solution to defeat it. She motions toward the small observation plane. "If you are to succeed, then this is the wrong aircraft. You've already exceeded its design capacity."

"Really! What would you suggest?"

"Keep it simple. Get rid of it and use a fast twin-engine bomber like a Heinkel 111. With minor modifications, it could easily reach the Allied bombers. Stop trying to re-invent the wheel and concentrate on developing your technology. You can worry about finding the perfect plane another day."

"Hmm. I like your idea, and I believe I can talk the major into changing planes. Then you'll stay and help me?"

"Yes, but if it doesn't look promising, I will return to Peenemünde."

"I understand."

He opens the door to his office, and they sit down. "Now that you know what our challenges are, what do you suggest?"

"I can see the amazing amount of work that you've done with little or no technical support. Possibly by working together, we could finish what you have started."

"Thank you. I appreciate your help. How about the electrical schematics? How long would it take you to redraw them?"

Betty pauses. "It would be a lot of work, so I can't be exactly sure, possibly a month or so, but we could start manufacturing the new components as I redesign each module. When the bomber arrives, we should be close to installing the last of them."

He thinks about her plan. "I like your idea. It will eliminate a lot of re-engineering and speed up our schedule by months."

A loud snoring sound interrupts their conversation. Betty laughs and looks at Apollo sleeping under her desk. She reaches down, rubs his stomach, and he slowly wakes up. The professor is shocked. "He's never this comfortable around someone he doesn't know. Are you a dog person?"

"I like dogs, but I've never seen a German Shepherd as large as he is."

"He's an Alsatian Wolf Dog from the Black Forest. They are twice as large as a German Shepherd and are closely related to the long extinct Dire Wolf."

"Well, he's certainly a beautiful dog, but fearsome when he approaches you."

"Oh, it wasn't you. He is trained in weapon detection, and he could smell your firearm, which is forbidden down here. I'm sorry, but I need to ask you to surrender it. You can have it back when you leave."

"I understand." She releases her belt buckle and hands the weapon to him. "Sorry, I didn't know."

He opens a large safe, places it on a shelf, and turns toward her. "It's getting late. I'll show you to your quarters. We have a cafeteria here and the food's not bad."

Max takes off his white lab coat and puts on a Luftwaffe officer's jacket that shows his rank as a captain. "Your quarters are on the other side of the hangar."

Betty is curious and questions him. "Do you stay here?"

"No. I live at home.

"Where is that?"

"It's south of here in a small village where I grew up. When I agreed to work here, I requested that I be able to live off base." He closes his office door and locks it. "You will be quite safe here. It's bombproof, and well-guarded."

They walk across the hangar to the transient housing quarters, and he unlocks a door. "This will be your home while you work here," and hands her a key. "I'm looking forward to working with you, Lieutenant."

"Thank you. Your project is intriguing."

"I appreciate your interest," and he points to the rear of the hangar. "The cafeteria is open for another hour. Good evening. Tomorrow will be a new day for us."

"Yes, I agree. Good night."

Betty enters her quarters, removes her jacket, and stretches out on the bed to think things out. Her twenty-four-hour mission to recover a roll of film has changed dramatically and there are many unexpected problems; her contact is dead, and their replacement engineer could arrive any day and expose her.

When the professor gets the navigation disrupter operational, it could cause havoc with the Allies, and possibly change the outcome of the war so, she decides to stay a little longer to find out how it works so she can design a system to defeat it, but she worries about the electrical schematics. They are a disaster, and it will take weeks to rewrite them, which will put her in an extremely dangerous position. However, her immediate worry is the impending Allied bombing raid. She narrowly escaped a bombing attack in London, and it terrifies her thinking about it.

Later that evening, she walks up the concrete entrance ramp to the camouflage screen. At the top are several heavily armed guards who nod hello, and she stands with them looking out at the sky. A light rain falls from dark, low-hanging clouds and rain drips through the nearby tree branches. There will be no bombing tonight. Betty realizes that it will be much safer in the underground complex, but it won't be easy to escape when the time comes. Gerta could help her, but she's confined to the hangar, and it's impossible for her to escape undetected.

The following day she is up early, and after a light breakfast she walks to the camouflage entrance screen and looks up at the overcast sky. The weather is clearing, and she knows the bombing will happen soon, but all she can do is wait it out and hope for the best.

From her office window, she watches Max park his car nearby. He drives a military version of a Volkswagen Kübelwagen; a small four-passenger convertible. Its unique feature is its spare tire which is attached to the outside of its sloping front hood. Time passes quickly, and she continues to work on the schematics.

An hour later Apollo enters, followed by the professor. "How are you doing today?"

"Fine thank you."

She hands him several pieces of paper. "I made a list of the parts that we're going to need. Do you have a supply depot here?"

He takes her paperwork and scans the long list. "No. Not for all this. We'll have to go to the main army depot in Cologne."

"Can you send someone to pick them up?"

"I think it's better if you go. You know exactly what you're looking for," and he hands the list back to her. "I'm happy to drive. We can leave tomorrow morning if you like."

The thought of leaving the confinement of the hangar is appealing. "I'd like to see the sun again . . . and get some fresh air."

"Good. We can stop for breakfast on the way."

The Allied plan to bomb the base worries her, and later that afternoon she returns to the camouflage screen to check on the weather. It had been a beautiful day so it will probably happen tonight, and she's unsure of how safe the underground hangar is. It's a night that she's been dreading, but there is nothing she can do but wait, and hope for the best. As she walks back down the ramp, she sees Max walking toward his car and worries about his safety. The bombing will probably start after midnight, so it shouldn't endanger him.

She goes to bed early knowing it's going to be a long night and hours later, she awakens to the sound of thunderous explosions. Even though she's more than a mile away from the base, they are loud and rattle everything in her room. Distant air raid sirens wail, warning of the attack; however, the bombing only lasts for a minute, and then silence returns. She worries about the professor, but he is probably safely at home with his family. Dawn is only a few hours away, and she doesn't have long to find out what happened.

It's 8 am, and Betty is sipping a steaming cup of coffee when Max's car drives down the concrete ramp. He enters her office and is visibly concerned about her safety.

"Are you alright?"

"Yes, just a little shaken. I was worried about you and Apollo."

"We were safe at home. Unfortunately, the base suffered heavy damage and the decoy plane, and many buildings were destroyed."

Betty fakes her concern. "Oh, no!"

"If you are ready, we should leave for the supply depot."

CHAPTER 12

AIR ATTACK

MAX'S KÜBELWAGEN CONVERTIBLE IS PARKED IN FRONT OF Betty's office with the top down. She puts on her black leather trench coat and picks up her briefcase. As she approaches the car, she notices the professor's attack dog is not with him.

"Where's Apollo?"

"I left him with a technician that he likes."

"Oh. I'm going to miss him." She drops her briefcase into the back and gets in. "I think I've got everything."

Max puts his car into gear, and they drive up the hangar's entrance ramp. "I know you're skeptical, but I promise you that our final product will be impressive."

Betty tries not to become too friendly. "Time will tell, but I have to admit, I can see possibilities."

Her newly found optimism impresses him, and he realizes she's going to play a key role in completing his project. "Thank you. I'm excited to be working with you. If you had been here at the beginning, we would have been done by now."

His openness surprises her, and it puts her one step closer to discovering how the technology works. Max is happy to be alone with her. "It's such a nice day. Let's put the war aside. Alright?"

"Yes, I agree."

Betty can't help herself and is slowly warming up to the charismatic professor. She can see he trusts her, and his promise of technical explanations will be much more valuable to the Allies than a few stolen photographs. As they drive through the bombed-out base, fallen trees litter the ground and many buildings have been reduced to smoldering piles of rubble. Men with firefighting equipment work feverously to extinguish the fires, and she is shocked to see the amount of damage that the bombing created. "I've never seen such destruction. It was so peaceful here."

"Yes, it was. Fortunately, they missed the barracks area, so our casualties were minimal, and no bombs were dropped on our underground hangar, which means they don't know it's there. The major said they won't rebuild anything, so the Allies will think we abandoned the base; however, our work will continue as usual."

He slows down at the main checkpoint, waves to the guards, and turns out onto a secondary road that leads to the supply depot in Cologne, several hours away. The sun-drenched land slowly warms after a week of rainy weather and the skies are clear. The road winds its way through a gorgeous alpine forest before descending into a wide valley covered with green pastures and farmland.

Max turns off the road, and ahead of them is a small village on the edge of a river. "This is a beautiful part of the country. Have you ever been this way?"

"No. It looks like something out of a fairy tale."

"So, you're a city girl?"

"Yes, I am."

They cross a small bridge and enter the sleepy hamlet. Max follows a horse-drawn wagon piled high with hay, then turns onto a cobblestone street and parks next to an ivy-covered building. "This is one of my favorite cafés, and their pastries are the best I've ever had."

They enter, and an elderly woman approaches them. "Hello, Max. I'm glad to see you," and she gives him a hug.

"I couldn't pass without stopping for one of your pastries."

"I wish all of my customers were as nice as you," and she looks at Betty. "My, you are a pretty one! My name is Hanna."

Her compliment embarrasses her. "I . . . I . . . thank you. I'm Elizabeth. Max has been raving about your pastries all morning!"

"Well, you are just in time. My strudel is about to come out of the oven. Coffee?"

He nods to her. "Yes, please."

She disappears into the kitchen, and Max ushers Betty toward a side door. "Let's sit outside," and they walk out onto a small terrace surrounded by flowering vines. A nearby mountain stream surges over a rocky riverbed and cascades into a deep pool of crystal-clear water.

Max admires their surroundings. "This is an incredible view."

Betty looks across the river at a meadow covered in wildflowers and is lost in thought. "Yes, it's beautiful here."

He motions toward a sunny table. "Let's sit over there."

Betty takes off her hat and removes her jacket, revealing a white blouse. She runs her fingers through her auburn hair and looks up at the sky. "I miss the sun. It feels wonderful!"

"I'm sorry about the hangar, but it's for our own protection," and he smiles at her. "We can take a break any time you'd like."

"Thank you. That would be wonderful."

Max is surprised by her natural beauty and feminine demeanor, as he has only seen the serious Gestapo side of her personality. Just then, Hanna returns with a pot of steaming coffee and pastries fresh from the oven. "I have apricot strudel today. Please enjoy."

Betty looks down at her pastry. "Oh . . . I love this smell."

Suddenly, a wave of déjà vu fills her with long lost memories of her mother baking, and her father sitting at the kitchen table drinking coffee and reading his newspaper. Germany was a beautiful country, and she missed her homeland and its people.

Max stares at her quizzically. "Elizabeth. Are you alright?"

"Oh . . . sorry. I was lost in thought for a moment. What did you say?"

"It wasn't important. Please, try your strudel."

She cuts into it, takes a bite, and closes her eyes as distant memories of better days flood into her mind. "This is delicious! I'm so glad we stopped here."

Max is starting to see her in a new light and wonders about her. "Tell me about yourself."

Betty knew someone might ask about her background and she's well prepared. "I was born in Berlin, and my parents were medical doctors. After graduation, I went to Vienna to study at the College of Technology, and I graduated with a doctorate in electrical engineering. That's where I met my husband. He's a Luftwaffe fighter pilot. We were married, and shortly afterward he left to fight in the war."

Max stares at her Gestapo uniform. "Why is an electrical engineer working with the secret police?"

"My husband worried about my safety while he was gone and his father, a high-ranking Gestapo officer, suggested I work with him. When his superiors discovered I had a doctorate in electrical engineering, they sent me to the Peenemünde Army Research Center to assist them in their weapon development programs. One day, they asked if I wouldn't mind temporarily assisting on a special project. And here I am."

"I'm impressed! I didn't realize that you held a doctorate!"

Betty is bashful when it comes to talking about herself and quickly changes the topic. "What about your background?"

Max is relaxed and sees her as an intellectual equal. "I grew up in the country. My parents raised horses, and we had a vineyard. In school, I loved physics, and I wanted to be a scientist ever since I was a little boy. I completed my doctorate in applied physics at the university in Berlin and took a staff position there. When the war started, the Luftwaffe enlisted me to develop the disruptor technology, and the rest you know about."

Betty wondered about his wedding ring but decided not to ask about it. "Are you an only child?"

"No, I have a younger brother. He's a fighter pilot, and the last I heard, he was fighting the Russians on the Eastern Front."

"Are you close to him?"

"Yes, but he's not conservative like I am, and is always joking around."

"I wish I had a brother or sister. I was lonely when I was a child."

Max is curious. "What do you plan to do after the war?"

"I'm not sure, and that could be a long way off. Who knows what will happen by then?"

Max is serious. "It doesn't matter who wins or loses."

He seems to have a cavalier attitude, and it shocks her. "I'm surprised to hear you talk like that. You're an officer, and I noticed your Nazi party armband."

"Joining the party was part of their hiring package. I'm not political," and he looks at her Nazi armband. "Look at you. Are you a Nazi fanatic?"

"I didn't have a choice; you join the party or stay home and feed the chickens."

He laughs at her comment. "When I first met you, I thought you were just another crazed Nazi."

She smiles bashfully. "I thought the same thing about you!"

He looks down at his watch. "It's getting late. We better get going."

An hour later, they exit a mountain tunnel and catch up to a long convoy of military vehicles carrying troops and towing heavy weapons. Several half-tracks equipped with forty mm anti-aircraft guns protect them. The narrow, tree-lined road winds through the rolling hills and open countryside. Up ahead, a wooden bridge spans a quiet river that meanders through a scenic valley on its way to neighboring Belgium. They rumble across the bridge and follow them, waiting for a chance to pass. After a while, the driver of the truck in front of them waves his arm, signaling that they can safely pass, and Max carefully drives by the slow-moving armored column.

Halfway down the long line of vehicles, he looks up to see a lone American P-47 Thunderbolt fighter diving straight in on them at high speed. The pilot levels his wings and releases several rockets which rip into the convoy. Tracers from its eight fifty-caliber machine guns arc through the air and rake the column with deadly accuracy.

On the ground, there is total pandemonium. The German gunners spin their weapons toward the approaching fighter and begin firing. Trucks explode and turn over, throwing men and equipment into the air. Vehicles transporting troops stop, and they dive into a roadside ditch for cover. As the fighter screams overhead, it releases a bomb with deadly accuracy, and it sails toward its intended target; a transporter carrying a large Panzer tank. A huge fireball erupts, spraying shrapnel in all directions.

Unable to stop fast enough, Max hits the edge of a large bomb crater and careens off the road, narrowly missing a large oak tree. The Kübelwagen sails over the edge of the road and slams nose first into the rocky hillside, then rolls over violently. It continues cartwheeling down the steep slope before coming to rest in a creek bed.

The fighter pulls out of its dive but stays low to avoid the flak guns from targeting him and screams over them at tree-top level. Then, just as quickly as it started, the sound of its engine fades into the distance and the attack is over. Back on the road, it is total chaos. Soldiers fight fires while others tend to the wounded. Medics carrying stretchers run toward Betty and Max. Their contorted bodies lay motionless in the grass amid large rocks scattered out across the steep hillside.

IT'S EARLY IN THE AFTERNOON SEVERAL DAYS LATER. BETTY is unconscious and tosses and turns in her sleep, tormented by her recurring nightmare of a man dressed in black carrying a hangman's noose. He walks out of a huge orangish-red fireball and reaches out to grab her.

Max is sitting in a wheelchair next to her bed and shakes her shoulder. "Elizabeth! Wake up!" and she slowly regains consciousness. Perspiration covers her face, and she struggles to sit up, but falls back onto her pillow. Her vision is blurry, and her body aches in pain. She raises a hand to her forehead. "Ohh, my head!"

Max notices her blood type lettered in Fraktur; a calligraphy font tattooed on the underside of her arm, a practice that all Gestapo officers used. "Elizabeth don't move. You've been injured, but at least you're alive."

Betty is dazed and confused. "Where are we?"

"We're in a military field hospital."

His head and arm are bandaged, and she worriedly asks, "What happened to you?"

"I have some lacerations and a nasty hip wound from the shrapnel."

She struggles to make herself comfortable. "I remember the air attack and the explosion, then nothing."

"We hit a crater and careened over the embankment. Our car rolled over, and we were thrown out. It's a miracle that we're both alive. You've got several broken ribs, severe bruises like me, and a possible concussion."

Betty feels something taped to her side. "What is this?"

"The doctor fitted you with a brace to protect your broken ribs, but it's only temporary."

"How long have we been here?"

"You've been unconscious for two days. The doctor said it will take ten weeks for us to recover, and it's going to be a painful recovery."

This is bad news for Betty's timetable. "But our project . . ."

"We can work on the design revisions at my home. We won't lose that much time."

"Your home? Where's that?"

"It's about an hour away from the airbase."

CHAPTER 13
A LONG RECOVERY

A GRAY MILITARY AMBULANCE DRIVES THROUGH A BEAUTI-ful alpine forest that covers Germany's mountainous southern border. The winding road cuts into a rocky hillside, then descends to a wide meadow filled with summer wildflowers. It passes a farmer walking with a herd of dairy cows, rumbles across a wooden bridge that spans a babbling brook, then turns off the road, and stops in front of a heavy wrought-iron gate flanked by two large stone columns. Attached to the gate is a colorful heraldic shield with a golden dragon in the center. The attendant gets out, pushes it open, and they continue up the driveway. A wooden rail fence parallels the road, and beyond it are green pastures and grazing horses. At the sound of the approaching vehicle, they bolt and race across the field.

The ambulance comes to a stop in a cul-de-sac in front of a two-story country mansion, and the driver opens the back doors. Max steps to the ground holding his cane, while they remove a stretcher carrying Betty, dressed in a hospital gown. She carefully swings her legs to the side, and they help her into a wheelchair.

Max unlocks the mansion's heavy front door, and the medics roll Betty into the entrance hall. Massive wooden rafters support the ceilings, and natural stone trims the white plaster walls. The room's highly polished floor tiles glisten in the afternoon sun. The furnishings are exquisite, and paintings of pastoral scenes hang on the walls.

Betty rolls her wheelchair over to a large painting and looks up at it. "Max, your home is gorgeous!"

"It's been in our family for more than a century. After my parents passed away, I continued to maintain our tradition of raising horses and making wine."

"I'll bet it takes a lot of work."

"It does, but I have a vintner who takes care of the grapes."

"Where are they? I didn't see any driving in."

"You can't tell from here, but my grandfather built this house on the edge of a steep gorge and our side is terraced all the way to a large river. The slope is well drained and faces directly to the south . . . conditions that are perfect for growing grapes."

"Do you make the wine here?"

"Yes. When you're feeling better, I'll show you the winery."

He rolls her down a wide hallway and stops at an open door. "This will be your room," and pushes her wheelchair inside. It's a large bedroom with high ceilings, white walls, and an enormous stone fireplace. He wheels her close to a comfortable-looking canopy bed and offers his hand. "Here. Let me help you."

Betty grasps his hand and carefully stands. "Thank you." She sits on the edge of the bed and glances around. There are paintings of horses on the walls, and it has a definite feminine flavor to it. "I love this room, and the décor is exquisite."

"I hope you'll be comfortable here," and he adjusts the pillows for her.

"Thank you, Max."

"You're welcome. Relax and get some rest. My housekeeper should be here tomorrow to help us out. Are you hungry?"

"No, thanks. I'm still in a lot of pain."

"It will be bad for a while. The doctor gave you a powerful pain killer so that you could travel."

She sinks back into her pillow with a sigh. "Ohh, so that's why I feel so groggy!"

The accident and subsequent ordeal in the field hospital had been stressful for her, and the painkillers numb her body. Max is worried about her and tries to comfort her. "I'll have your uniform cleaned for you, and there are some women's clothes in the closet. Please help yourself."

"I don't know how to thank you."

"Just get better. We have exciting things yet to do." As he leaves, he stops in the doorway. "My bedroom is upstairs. Call me if you need anything."

The following morning, Max knocks on her door. "Are you decent?"

She tidies her blankets and makes herself presentable. "Yes, please come in."

He enters, pushing a cart holding a bed tray with her breakfast. "I thought you might be hungry."

"Thanks, I am," and he places it in front of her. On it is a sweet roll and a cup of steaming hot coffee, and next to her plate is a single iridescent blue wildflower. Betty picks it up. "I love these! My grandmother used to grow them in her yard."

"They're a favorite of mine, too. Did you sleep well?"

"Yes, a little. The doctor was right. It's even painful to breathe. How are you feeling?"

"I have to get off my feet from time to time, but I'm feeling better." He hands her a small pill bottle. "The doctor said to take these for pain."

"Thank you. I hope they'll help."

A knock at the front door interrupts them, and Max calls out. "I'll be right there," and turns to Betty. "That must be my housekeeper," and he leaves the room.

Several minutes later, he returns with a matronly looking woman wearing a dark blue folkloric dress. She is cheerful, a few years older than Max, and holds out her hand to Betty. "Hello, I'm Helga."

"Hi, I'm Elizabeth. Nice to meet you."

"Max told me about your accident. I'm amazed that you two survived."

"We can thank the medics for that. They were quick to get us to the hospital."

Helga smiles at her. "It was nice meeting you. I've got work to do, but we'll talk later."

"Thank you. I'd like that."

She exits the room, and Max sits down in a chair next to her bed. "You look like a new person today. How do you feel?"

"I feel better. How are your injuries?"

"My wound is painful, and it's still bleeding. I tried to change the bandage, but I can't reach it."

Betty is alarmed and sits up in bed. "Max, I need to look at it."

He is embarrassed. "It's not a pleasant sight. I can get it changed in the village."

She is an expert at wound care and knows he needs immediate attention. "You are not in any shape to drive. I worked at the hospital in Peenemünde as a volunteer, so I've seen it all."

"When did you have the time to do that?"

"They were understaffed, and I wanted to help. They trained me in wound care, and that relieved the nurses to do more important things."

"Well, you continue to be quite the enigma."

Betty is worried. "It can become infected quickly if it's not attended to."

Reluctantly, he turns sideways and slides down his pants, revealing a large blood-soaked bandage on his hip. Betty carefully peals it back. "Hmm. I should have looked at this yesterday. I'm going to need gauze pads, tape, and hydrogen peroxide. Do you have any medical supplies here?"

"Yes. I keep a first aid kit in the barn for the horses. I'll be right back," and pulls up his trousers."

As he leaves, she calls after him. "Have Helga boil some water."

A short time later, he hobbles in with the medical kit and sets it on a table next to Betty's bed. "Will this do?"

She carefully sorts through the contents. "Yes. This is fine," then expertly organizes the items that she needs. Helga enters the room with a pot of hot water and several towels. "Thank you," and turns to Max. "I need to clean your wound and change your bandages every day, or it will become infected. If we are not careful, things could get complicated."

A short while later, Betty finishes cleaning his wound. "There. That should do it," and tapes a large gauze pad over it. "I'll pull the stitches in a few weeks, and you will be good as new."

"Thank you. I appreciate your help," and he starts to leave the room. "I need to pick up Apollo."

"Be careful out there! Those roving fighters shoot at anything that moves."

"Thanks, but I'll be alright."

Late that afternoon, Betty is napping when something nudges her arm, and she wakes up to find Apollo standing next to her bed. "Apollo!" and she strokes his head. "How are you?"

Moments later, Max appears in the doorway. "Ah, there he is. Somehow, he knew you were here. When I opened the car door, he bolted for the house. I'm sorry if I woke you."

She runs her hands through his thick fur. "I missed him. Can he stay with me for a while?"

"Yes, of course."

She scratches his head lovingly. "I've grown quite fond of him."

He smiles at them. "I think he's found a new friend as well."

As time passes, Max makes brief trips to the airbase to oversee modifications to the disruptor equipment. Betty can now walk with a cane but wears a bathrobe because it's still too painful to wear normal clothes. She continues to take long naps but is no longer bedridden. Her health slowly improves, and she spends most of the day reading in a chair on the sunny terrace with Apollo at her side. Several days later, Max returns from the airbase and joins her. "Well, you two look comfortable!"

"I am, and I'm feeling better."

"Would you like a glass of our wine?"

"Yes, thank you," and puts down her book.

"Good. I'll be right back," and a few minutes later, he returns with two glasses, and hands one to her.

"It's nice being waited on," and she takes the glass.

They sit quietly, enjoying the warm afternoon sun, and Betty admires the spectacular view. "Your estate is beautiful, Max. It must have an interesting history."

"It does. A hundred years ago, my grandfather settled here with his family. They were poor, and no one wanted the land, so he was able to purchase it for very little money. He terraced the side slope to the river and planted the grape vines. Then he cleared the forest and created some of the meadows that you see today.

"At that time, farmers in the area started planting crops, and there was a need for draft horses to plow the fields, so he began to raise them. When my father took over, he continued working the land, and eventually purchased more property on the top. As the years went by, the farmers became mechanized and draft horses weren't needed, so he looked for something else to do.

"He loved to ride, so he sold the draft horses, and started raising Hanoverian Warmbloods. He became quite successful and saved enough money to build the winery you see today. That allowed him to process his own grapes and sell directly to the public without a middleman. It turned out to be an excellent financial move, and for the first-time, our family began to prosper.

"After my father passed away, I took over and when Lotar went off to school, I hired Jannik to operate the wine side of things, and now he's my partner in our wine sales. I continued to oversee our breeding program while I finished school. During that time, I hired Elke to manage the horses. She's incredibly talented, and I couldn't have done this without her help. It took three generations to get to what you see today, and I hope someday that my children will continue our traditions."

Betty takes a sip of wine. "That's an amazing story!"

She notices distant vapor trails high in the sky and watches them intently. They come from hundreds of Allied bombers headed for Berlin. "What an incredibly beautiful day. It's hard to believe that there's a terrible war going on."

They watch them in silence for a moment, then Max explains. "Fortunately, we are far south of the Allied assault forces. They are on a direct path from the Normandy beaches to Berlin, and the closest large city is hours away."

As they sit in silence, the sun sets in the west, and darkness slowly sweeps across the land. Betty is shy and has been putting off changing her bandages, but it can't be postponed any longer. "I think it's time that I took off this temporary brace. Would you help me?"

"Yes, of course," and they walk to her bedroom.

"The doctor said I could remove it when I felt better."

She motions toward a pair of scissors laying on the table. "You'll need to cut the bandages on both sides and take out the metal supports." She lifts her blouse to her bra, and Max carefully cuts through the tape. "Ohh, that feels great. I feel like I've been living in a steel cocoon."

He gently removes the metal brace, revealing her smooth stomach. "Is that better?"

"Yes, thank you. See that bottle of hydrogen peroxide on the table? Pour some on a gauze pad and wipe down the bandaged area, so it's cleansed."

He carefully sponges down her torso with great care, passing over large red areas of skin abrasions that cover huge black and yellow bruises. "These are nasty looking. I can see why you've had so much discomfort."

"I've never felt pain like that before, but at least I can take deep breaths now." Her body is sleek and smooth and it's an erotic experience for him. He finishes and sets down the scissors. "How does that feel?"

"I feel like a new person," and points to the medical supplies. "Can you wrap me with that wide tape?"

"Of course," and he carefully wraps it around her ribs.

She stands and buttons her blouse. "Thank you, Max. It's wonderful to be out of that contraption!"

SEVERAL WEEKS PASS, AND BETTY CONTINUES TO REGAIN her health. A favorite walk of hers is down the driveway to watch the horses play in the long meadow. She and Apollo stop at a wooden rail fence and watch as six young geldings chase each other through the trees and across the meadow. They gallop at full speed with their heads held high as they weave in and out of the trees and their tails flow straight back as they thunder past her.

As her strength improves, her daily walks with Apollo lengthen, and their bond grows stronger. It's late in the day when Max returns and she is in her bathrobe, sitting in a chair brushing Apollo's long coat. She looks up at him. "How are things at the hangar?"

Max sits down next to her. "We are finally making progress." He looks at them and smiles. "You two seem to enjoy yourselves."

She pets Apollo. "He is such a good-looking dog."

"Yes, and I can see he enjoys being with you."

"He's so unusual. Where did you find him?"

"Because I travel back and forth from my home, I felt I needed some sort of protection. A friend of mine suggested an attack dog, and I mentioned it to the Luftwaffe colonel in charge of this project, and he thought it was a good idea. I looked at many dogs that they were training and when I first saw him, we had an instant connection with each other."

Betty looks at Apollo affectionately. "He's so gentle. I can't imagine that he has a ferocious side."

Max reaches down and scratches Apollo's stomach. "Well, he does. They won't train dogs that are too aggressive because they can become uncontrollable. He's highly intelligent and family raised, but when he senses a threat to me, he will go into attack mode."

"Has he ever attacked anyone?"

"Yes, many times in training, and it's a scary sight. Even now, if a stranger approaches, and Apollo is uneasy, he emits a rumbling warning growl that comes from deep inside his chest, and it's frightening to hear. When he goes on alert, he can be extremely intimidating, and people keep their distance."

Apollo stands up and puts his massive head in Betty's lap. She scratches a favorite spot behind his ears and talks to him. "Well, we're friends, aren't we?"

Max looks at them affectionately. "Apollo might not look like it, but he is ever watchful of me, and now you. He's always on alert for danger and at night he sleeps in different locations where he can watch as many entrances as possible."

"Are you saying he's protecting me?"

"Yes, he has bonded with you. When you feel better, I'll show you how to work with him. He understands more than a dozen voice commands, and you will need them because he's too powerful to control physically."

She runs her fingers through his long coat. "When can I train with him?"

"As soon as you feel better. The two of you will have a lot of fun, and it will take your relationship to a whole new level." He checks his watch and stands. "I need to talk to Helga. Would you like to have dinner on the terrace? It should be a warm evening."

She looks at the beginning of a beautiful sunset. "Yes. That would be wonderful."

Betty sits at a mirrored vanity table combing her hair and decides it's time to get out of her bathrobe. She goes to a large antique armoire and looks through an assortment of women's clothing. An expensive looking skirt and an elegant dark green silk blouse catch her eye.

Max has a roaring fire going, and she approaches him wearing a white shawl covering her shoulders. Her natural beauty and expensive clothes combine to give her a radiant and very feminine appearance.

He looks up and is stunned. "Look at you!"

She blushes and responds shyly. "Thanks. I thought it was time for a change."

"Well, it's a stunning transformation!"

From their vantage point, they look down on the spectacular Mosel River and a patchwork of vineyards that cover the valley floor. She walks to the stone railing and stares at the view. "What a breathtaking evening!"

Max motions toward a comfortable chair facing the fire pit. "Please sit down. I hope you enjoy the sunsets as much as I do."

Betty admires the panorama in front of her. "Thank you. You're lucky to have such phenomenal scenery."

"It's even nicer to share it with someone that appreciates it."

As the sun disappears behind the horizon, a myriad of yellow and deep orange clouds fill the sky, and darkness slowly envelops the land. Helga appears with a bottle of Riesling wine and a tray of cheese and crackers. "I thought you two might be hungry."

Max takes it from her and places it on a small table. "Thank you, Helga."

"You're welcome. I'm on my way home. I'll see you tomorrow."

"Good night," and he picks up the bottle and pours wine into their glasses. "This is something special from our vineyard."

Betty swirls her glass several times, sniffs the aroma, and holds the glass up. "Á votre santé," and they touch glasses in a toast. She takes a sip and swirls the wine in her mouth. "Hmm, don't tell me. It's a dry Riesling . . . and the bold fruit flavors and heightened acidity suggest it has been aged."

"Yes, about ten years. So, you know your wines?"

"A little, and this is excellent."

"My family has grown grapes here for a long time. When you're up for it, I'll show you around the property."

"I'd like that. I feel a little better every day, but I still have a lot of pain."

Max is sympathetic. "I know what you mean. My hip is very painful as well."

"You have a terrible bone bruise, so it will be tender for quite a while," and she sets down her wine glass. "You said something before about your horses?"

"Yes. They are my passion and raising them goes back a long time into my family's history. I raise a breed called Hanoverians. They are powerful and elegant."

"I can't wait to see them."

"Do you ride?"

"Yes, but it's been quite some time."

"I have a bay stallion I call Gunnar. He's reddish brown with a black mane and tail, and I have a young mare called Arabella. When you feel better, she would be perfect for you."

"Thank you. It would be fun to ride with you sometime."

Betty takes a sip of wine and asks, "You seem to be quite mysterious about your wife. When am I going to meet her?"

"My wife?"

She motions toward his hand. "I noticed your wedding ring."

He pauses, then responds sheepishly. "I'm not married."

She sees that her question has caught him off guard. "Oh, I'm sorry. I didn't mean to pry."

"It's alright. My wife and daughter drowned in a boating accident three years ago, and I never took it off."

"I'm so sorry, Max."

"Tell me about your husband. How did you two meet?"

Now it's Betty's turn to be embarrassed. "I . . . I . . ."

"Please, you don't have to explain. I was just trying to be polite."

Knowing that someone might ask about her husband, she explains. "We met at a friend's party. He's a fighter pilot and returned to duty shortly after we were married. A month later, I received a call saying he was shot down over the English Channel. I don't know if he is dead or alive."

"I'm so sorry, Elizabeth."

The sun has set, and the evening is becoming chilly. Max puts another log on the fire. "Have you ever seen so many stars?"

"No, and the heavens are incredibly beautiful."

"Do you miss your city life?"

"No. Well, maybe the cultural events, but I feel completely relaxed here in your home."

"I know exactly what you mean. It would be perfect to enjoy both worlds; to live here and spend time in the city."

The two of them sit around the fire talking for quite a while, but Betty is still in pain. "Would you mind if I retired early? My side is painful tonight."

"No, not at all. I should get some rest as well. Come, I'll walk you to your room."

They stop at her bedroom, and she apologizes. "I'm sorry, but I think I tried to do too much today."

"Don't worry. There will be other days," and he opens her door.

"Thank you for the pleasant evening," and steps into her room.

"You're welcome. Sleep well."

Later that night, Max awakens to cries and murmurings coming from Betty's bedroom. He gets out of bed and walks down to her door. As he listens, he realizes she's having another one of her nightmares and enters her room. Perspiration covers her face as she struggles with some unknown demon. Not sure of what to do, he shakes her shoulder, and she immediately wakes up and clutches him tightly.

"It's alright, Elizabeth. You were just having another one of your nightmares."

She is terrified and tears stream down her cheeks. "I'm so embarrassed! It all seemed so real!"

Max holds her for a long time, then leans her back onto her pillow. "I used to have terrible nightmares as a child, so I know how real they can be."

He walks over to her fireplace and adds several logs to the fire. She looks up and sees Apollo standing in the doorway, staring at her, and calls to him softly. "Apollo. Come here," and he immediately rushes to her side.

Max looks over at them. "I think he was worried about you as well."

"Do you mind if he stays with me for a while?"

He pulls a chair next to her bed and gives her a comforting smile. "I think we both should stay with you. Just relax and know that you are safe with us."

"Thank you, Max," and she closes her eyes and falls into a deep sleep.

The next morning, the sun fills her room, and the sound of Helga making breakfast awakens her. Apollo is stretched out in front of the fireplace fast asleep, and she's surprised to see that Max is still there, wrapped in a blanket and sleeping in a chair next to her bed. She shakes his shoulder, and he slowly wakes up and stretches. "Good morning. Did you sleep the rest of the night?"

Betty is apologetic. "Yes, and I'm so sorry. I've had the same nightmare for years. It just won't leave me."

"What do you see in your nightmare?"

"The room is on fire and flames are about to consume me."

"That sounds frightening. What do you think it means?"

She lies to him. "I have a fear of being burned alive."

Max is worried about her. "Do you feel better now?"

"Yes, I'm fine, and thank you for caring."

"I'll be right back with coffee and a hot roll. I can't let the demons steal away my engineer!"

The following day, he pulls up to the front of the house in his Mercedes and walks up the stairs to the terrace. Betty is napping, and Apollo is sleeping next to her chair. She hears him approach and wakes up. "Hello, Max."

He smiles at them affectionately. "Good afternoon. You two look comfortable."

"I am. And it's another beautiful day."

He walks over to her and hands her a colorful gift-wrapped present. "I brought you something."

"Oh, Max. Thank you," and removes the colorful wrapping paper, revealing a book. "Magic Mountain! I've always wanted to read it! What ever happened to him?"

"In '29 Mann received the Nobel Prize in literature, but because of his anti-Nazi views, the Party banned his works. I heard he's living in exile in Zürich."

He sits down next to her. "I have good news. I met with Major Krüger and several high-ranking Nazis this morning and showed them your new electrical schematics. They were quite impressed with your work and would like to meet you after you recover.

"I told them that for the first time, we were making excellent progress in finalizing the technology. Sadly, the major doesn't understand the science of what we are doing. Actually, I think he was a pig farmer prior to the war."

Betty is nervous, knowing she could be easily discovered if they have anything to do with the Peenemünde Army Research Center. Stoically, she smiles and hides her concern. "How soon does he want us back?"

"I told him what the doctor said. That it would take ten weeks to recover, but we can work on the engineering here."

The thought of getting back to work energizes her. "Good. I like to stay busy."

"The major liked your idea of switching planes, but it will take several weeks before one becomes available."

Another week passes, and Betty can now walk without her cane. She and Max are on the terrace sitting at a table going over technical drawings when suddenly a Focke-Wulf 190 fighter screams low over the house, shaking the windows. It pulls up steeply, banks hard to the left in a wide, sweeping arc, and disappears into the clouds.

Betty didn't see the approaching plane, and it surprised her. "Oh, my gosh! What was that?"

"I think that was my brother, Lotar. I told you he was a little crazy!"

The fighter circles back toward them, reduces its air speed, and extends its landing gear. With full flaps and reduced power, it lands in the meadow adjacent to the house and taxis toward them. The engine shuts down, and Lotar steps out of the cockpit and onto the wing. He jumps to the ground, and Apollo runs to greet him, almost knocking him down. They play rough for a while, then he gives him a loving pat on the back and continues walking toward the house.

He embraces Max with an enormous bear hug. "It's good to see you, big brother!" then he looks over at Betty. "Well. Well. Who is this?"

Max introduces them. "Elizabeth Hausser, this is my younger brother, Lotar."

She extends her hand, but he ignores it and gives her a gentle hug. "Nice to meet you, Elizabeth Hausser."

His warmth catches her off guard. "It's my pleasure."

Lotar is just as handsome as Max, with blonde hair and blue eyes, and has the same Nordic features. Max puts his arm around his shoulder. "You're just in time for an early supper."

"Thanks. I've been flying since sunup."

"So, what brings you this way? I thought you were on the Russian front?"

As they walk toward the house, Lotar takes off his leather flight jacket and drapes it over his shoulder. "I was, but my squadron is moving back to Berlin to help protect the city from the Allied bombers, and I've got to be there tomorrow."

"It'll be fun catching up with you. What ever happened to that girl that you were so crazy about?"

"She works in Berlin, and we write to each other often. She'll be happy to see me."

Lotar sees they are walking with a noticeable limp. "Why are you two limping?"

Max explains. "It's a long story. We were on a trip to the supply depot in Cologne when an American fighter strafed our convoy. Our car caught the edge of a bomb crater, and we rolled down the mountainside. A piece of shrapnel hit me in the hip, and Elizabeth broke several ribs, but we'll be alright in a few weeks."

Lotar is concerned. "I thought you would be safe out here brother, but war is unpredictable."

"Let's put the war aside for a while and enjoy our time together."

They walk up the terrace stairs and minutes later, Helga comes out and gives him an enormous hug. "It's good to see you, Lotar. I think you're becoming even more handsome. You must drive the girls crazy."

He laughs. "There aren't many girls at twenty-five thousand feet!"

She gives him a loving push. "I see you haven't changed. Let me get you something to eat," and disappears into the kitchen.

He asks Max, "How is your disruptor going? We could use some help up there."

"As you know, there have been many technical issues that have delayed the project. The electronic packages have been the biggest challenge, but Elizabeth has changed all that."

Lotar has a surprised look on his face and turns to her. "You're an electrical engineer?"

"Yes, I am."

"Well, you're much too pretty to be an engineer."

Betty doesn't like to talk about herself and changes the subject. "How long have you been flying?"

"I spent a year in training, and I've been in combat for fourteen months."

Max is proud of his accomplishments and interjects. "Lotar has fifty-four kills."

She's surprised. "Oh! That's quite a lot!"

"Yes, but mostly Russian antiques from the first war. However, I shot down an American P-51 and three British Spitfires."

Betty asks about his exploits. "What's the secret to your success?"

"In aerial combat, there are two main situations you can find yourself in. One is a dog fight which is always dangerous. Some pilots are experts, and some are novices, and there's no way to tell them apart. Anything can happen, and usually does. It becomes a violent confrontation, and things happen quickly. Then suddenly it's over, and the sky is empty."

"That sounds frightening. And the other situation?"

"Ahh, my favorite tactic. The ambush. I learned about it from an instructor when I was training. You find someone flying alone and you swoop down behind them at full speed and blast them out of the sky at a very close range. The advantage is you save on ammunition, and they are not likely to break away and engage you."

Betty shakes her head in amazement. "And the disadvantage?"

"Well, I've had to crash land four times due to damage from exploding planes."

"Have you ever been shot down?"

"Yes, twice. Like I said, it's dangerous up there. Eventually, someone is going to jump you when you least expect it. The first time I was hit by friendly fire while I was chasing a Russian flying at a low level. And the second time I was shot down by an American P-38 Lightning near the Italian border.

"We chased each other around for quite a while. I tried everything I knew to throw him off, but he was very good. After five or six minutes, he hit my engine, and I immediately rolled over and dropped out of my cockpit. My parachute opened, and I was drifting slowly to earth when I saw he had doubled back and was heading straight for me. I thought, well this is the end for me, but at the last minute, he broke off and saluted me when he passed. It was an unbelievable experience!"

Lotar is a battle seasoned pilot, and his confidence impresses her. "To survive, you need to be supremely confident, and very aggressive. As the Red Baron famously said. 'Never pick a fight that you can't win.'"

Helga returns with Lotar's dinner. "Here's something special for you."

He reaches out and puts his arm around her waist. "I miss your cooking. The army food is, how should I say . . . boring."

She pats his back affectionately. "Are you staying long?"

"No. Unfortunately, I have to leave in the morning. Duty calls."

After dinner, Betty stands and excuses herself. "I'm sorry, but these pain pills tire me. It was a pleasure meeting you, Lotar. Good night," and they stand as she leaves.

The brothers sit around the firepit watching a crackling fire and sipping brandy. It's a dark moonless evening, and high above them, a million flickering stars dance in the sky. Max is concerned. "I didn't want to worry Elizabeth, but how do you think the war is going?"

"In the beginning it seemed like an even match, but Hitler can't win a war of attrition on multiple fronts against two large countries and their allies. It's a numerical impossibility, and we don't have the numbers."

"I didn't realize it was that bad. The news reports are quite optimistic."

Lotar has frontline combat experience and knows what he's talking about. "The Allies invaded Normandy with over a million and a half men, and they continue to move inland. They are pushing us back and are getting stronger every day. Our military is experienced, well trained, and well equipped, but we are a relatively small nation fighting on two huge fronts. We're also fighting in the low countries, as well as North Africa and Italy.

"The Americans and Soviets entered the war poorly prepared and inexperienced, but they are catching up quickly. When that happens, I'm afraid it will become a fighting retreat all the way back to Berlin, and it's going to end with Hitler's defeat."

"Do you think he would surrender?"

"No. Hitler is a war criminal and would hang if that happened, and he knows it. My guess is that he will try to escape at the last minute. He's too much of an egomaniac to kill himself as long as there is a way out."

"What about the Siegfried Line? Won't that protect us?"

"No wall in history has ever worked. There's always a weak link that can be exploited."

"Brother, you are a hardcore realist."

"I have to be, or I'd be dead by now. What about your disruptor?"

"It's only a clever manipulation of an existing technology. It will buy us some time, but in the long run, it won't win the war. In time, the Allies will figure out how to defeat it."

"So, it's only a delaying tactic?"

"Yes, I'm afraid so," and he lowers his voice. "But in developing the technology I accidentally discovered a way to cancel out radar waves. It shows tremendous potential, but it will take time to develop. I think you're right. The outcome of the war is uncertain, so I'm going to keep it under wraps for the moment."

"That's what I would recommend, big brother. Well, so much for the war," and he takes another sip of brandy. "Your friend Elizabeth is quite stunning. Where did you meet her?"

"She replaced an engineer that was killed."

Lotar is waiting to hear more. "And?"

"And what?"

"The chemistry between you two is obvious, but it seems you are both married."

"I don't know why I keep wearing this ring. Memories, I guess."

"And Elizabeth?"

"We just talked about it. She's married to a fighter pilot, but he was shot down over the English Channel, and she doesn't know if he's dead or alive."

"Well, I think she's interested in you. You need to ask her out on a date. You know, dinner and dancing."

"I wouldn't feel comfortable asking out a married woman."

"War changes all the rules. Who knows what tomorrow will bring?"

"Maybe you're right, but when I first met her, I couldn't stand her, and she couldn't stand me either."

"Why? She's beautiful!"

"She doesn't look like it now, but she's a Gestapo officer. When she enters a room dressed in that uniform, she terrifies everyone. And she has a violent temper. I saw her threaten to shoot the base commandant once, and he was visibly trembling with fear. On the other hand, she's brilliant and holds a doctorate in electrical engineering . . . and she's absolutely crucial to the success of my project."

"Well, big brother, you seem to have gotten yourself into quite a predicament!"

The following morning Betty enters the kitchen and finds Max cooking breakfast. "Hmm, do I smell freshly brewed coffee?"

He looks up from the stove. "Ah, the walking wounded arrives."

"What can I do to help?"

"Nothing. Breakfast is ready."

Betty is curious. "Is Lotar still here?"

"No. He left at first light, but he said that he enjoyed meeting you."

"I liked him very much. You're lucky to have such a loving brother."

He picks up their plates and motions toward the terrace. "Yes, I suppose I am."

She follows him, and they sit down at the wrought-iron table.

Max questions her. "How are you feeling?"

"My ribs are still painful, but the medication helps a lot, especially at night."

"That's the worst time for me too, but I'm getting better every day. I think it's time to get out of the house. Are you up for a short walk?"

Betty brightens up at the thought of it. "Yes, I'd like that."

After breakfast they walk along a cobble stone road toward the horse barn which is near the main house. Attached to the front of the barn is a colorful heraldic coat of arms. The red battle shield has gold edging, and in the center is a golden-colored winged dragon. Betty admires it. "Is this your family crest?"

"Yes, and it's quite old. The red field represents blood from the many battles that have taken place here over the centuries."

"And the dragon?"

"There is a legend that a dragon lived in this valley, and it guarded a golden treasure."

His story fascinates her. "Do you think it lived here?"

"Maybe. When my grandfather excavated the building pad for the winery, he discovered an entrance to a cave that had been hidden for centuries."

"That's exciting. Did he find a treasure?"

"No, but many stories refer to dragons that guarded golden treasures. I like to think it refers to the golden color of the Riesling grape."

"How romantic!"

They enter the massive barn, walk down a wide aisle flanked by rows of stalls, and the air is filled with the aromatic smell of fresh hay. "These are my Hanoverian Warmbloods. They're a popular horse used in show jumping and dressage." He stops at a stall and offers a large powerful looking horse a carrot. "This is Gunnar, my bay stallion."

"He's beautiful! No wonder you're so proud of him!"

Max runs his fingers through Gunnar's long mane and pats his shoulder. "He is a German national champion and has received many other awards. He's also the sire of most of our foals."

They continue walking toward the next stall and it holds a stunning black mare. "And this is Arabella. She's a powerful jumper, but very calm and confident. I think she'll be perfect for you."

For Betty it's love at first sight. "Arabella, you are a beauty!" and she turns to Max. "I've never ridden a horse as tall as she is."

"All of our horses are part Thoroughbred. They have a deep chest, a lean body, and long legs, all of which are needed for cross-country racing."

Max pulls out an apple from his pocket and hands it to her. "This is her favorite treat. She loves apples."

Betty takes it from him. "How do I do this?"

"She's very gentle. Just put it in the palm of your open hand and hold your arm out."

She follows his advice, and Arabella is quick to consume the apple. She strokes her forehead admiringly. "I've never seen such a beautiful horse."

"Arabella is young and spirited and loves the challenges of jumping."

Betty is spellbound. "She's absolutely magnificent."

They exit the barn and walk toward a wooden fence. He opens a gate, and they enter a pasture with tree-lined rolling hills, and brush-covered ravines. Several mares and their yearlings graze in the green meadow. Apollo races ahead of them and scatters a flight of Mallard ducks off a small stock pond.

Max points to a knoll shaded by a large tree. "Up ahead is a bench with a panoramic view of the estate."

Betty has been housebound for weeks and is enjoying herself. "I miss taking my early morning walks. It gives me time to put my day together."

They continue walking and Max is lost in thought. "I stopped my walks after my wife and daughter died, but it feels good to get out again."

She can only imagine the pain that their deaths must have caused him, and they quietly walk along the horse trail enjoying the sunny morning. Apollo runs ahead following the scent of some unknown forest creature, then he returns to Betty's side.

Soon they approach an old wooden bench at the top of the knoll, and Max motions to her. "Have a seat," and he looks out over the meadow. "This is one of my favorite spots to come and think."

Betty surveys the colorful pastoral scene in front of her. "It's beautiful here, and you're right, the view is just incredible!"

"I never tire of looking at the countryside from here. Every month it changes dramatically." He points toward a group of buildings. "That's the winery, and beyond it is the vineyard."

A short distance away from them is a large stock pond, rimmed with cattails. Apollo wades carefully into the water, freezes for a moment, then splashes after something in the shallows. They sit for a few minutes admiring their surroundings, then Betty breaks the silence. "Max, I'm sorry about your family. I can't imagine how difficult it must have been for you."

"Yes, I was devastated. They never found their bodies so there were no goodbye's, no funeral, and no closure."

"I'm sorry about wearing your wife's clothes. Something changed in the way you look at me."

"It wasn't you. I suddenly realized that I've been living in the past for too long, and I need to get on with my life. This war won't last forever, and someday our lives will return to normal. We should focus on good thoughts for the future." He stretches his legs out in front of him and takes a deep breath. "Ready to head back?"

"Yes and thank you for the walk."

He calls to Apollo. "Let's go, big boy!" and he immediately splashes out of the pond and heads their way, stopping several times to shake the water from his long coat. Max offers her his hand. "Here, let me help you," and she slowly stands.

"Thanks. I'm still a little stiff."

As they walk, he continues to hold her hand, but Apollo walks between them, and it falls from his grip. On the way back they come to a rocky section of the trail. Max goes first, then reaches out to help her. "Careful, it's slippery here."

She takes his hand, and steps carefully, but Apollo brushes by her and she loses her balance. However, Max is quick to prevent her fall and pulls her close to him. For a moment they stare into each other's eyes, but she quickly regains her composure.

"I'm sorry, Apollo bumped into me just as I took a step."

As they approach the barn, they see a blue tractor pulling a hay wagon parked in the driveway. Helga and the driver are walking down the rear stairs and they wave to them. "That's Jannik, Helga's husband and our winemaker. They live nearby."

Max closes the pasture gate, and as they walk toward them, Jannik's two dogs run playfully to greet Apollo. "Good morning. Jannik, this is my friend Elizabeth."

Jannik is friendly, and about the same age as Max. He has a receding hair line, piercing dark eyes, and a weathered face from years of working outside. He extends his hand. "Very nice to meet you. Helga speaks highly of you."

Betty shakes his hand. "Thank you for your kind words."

Max pats him on the shoulder and looks over at the tractor. "I see you brought us a load of hay."

"Yes, and I also traded some of our wine for sausage and cheese."

"You're quite the barterer. How do the grapes look?"

"It's going to be an excellent year for us. The boys are off fighting in the war, but some of the village women are helping, and they're doing a great job."

"That's good to hear. We'll stop by later in the week. I want to show Elizabeth around."

Jannik looks at Betty. "It was nice meeting you."

"Thank you. I'm looking forward to touring your winery."

CHAPTER 14

FORBIDDEN LOVE

IT'S THE END OF A LONG, ARDUOUS DAY AND BETTY AND Max are working in their makeshift laboratory in the estate's great room when Helga enters, carrying a tray of food. "Sorry to interrupt, but you two can't miss dinner," and she sets down a platter of sandwiches.

Max looks up. "Thanks, Helga. I guess we lost track of time," and he asks Betty, "Would you like a glass of our Riesling?"

"Yes, I would."

"The wine cellar is just down the hall." They walk down the wide hallway, and he swings open a heavy wooden door.

Betty looks around the room. "Max! Your library is impressive!"

"Both my parents were avid readers, and so am I. Do you enjoy reading?"

"Yes. I think I spent most of my youth in the library."

"Well, we seem to have something in common then. You're welcome to use it any time you like."

He walks over to an arched alcove with an oil painting of their vineyard hanging on the back wall, presses a hidden latch, and the back of the alcove swings open, revealing a dark stairway. The mysterious secret passageway surprises Betty. "Where does this go?"

"It's fairly common for old buildings like this to have hidden rooms to hide valuables in, or tunnels used to escape invaders."

The passageway is carved into solid rock and winds full circle, revealing a large, well-lit room with polished tile floors. Metal racks containing hundreds of wine bottles line the walls and are interspersed with beautiful oil paintings of their vineyard.

Attached to the rock wall at the back of the cave is a huge six-foot diameter cover from a large wine barrel. Cut deeply into the wood is the outline of a heraldic shield with a winged dragon at the center. Its highly polished oak surface makes it a glistening focal piece.

The elegance of the décor impresses Betty. "Max, this is stunning!" She walks down an aisle of wine racks, then stops at a large oil painting. "This artwork is gorgeous. Who is the artist?"

"My mother. She was a well-known painter in this area."

"What a talent! I love this. It looks so real."

"Yes, it does, and it's a favorite of mine, too."

She asks, "Were you close to your mother?"

"I was close to both of my parents and growing up was an exciting and wonderful time for me."

Betty reflects for a moment. "I was close to my parents, but they died when I was young. My uncle Karl raised me, and we are close."

"I'm sorry. I can't imagine how difficult that must have been," and he wanders down the racks of wine bottles.

Betty follows him. "What are you looking for?"

"Something special," and he removes a bottle. "Ah, here it is!" and wipes the dust off the label. "I store some of our best years down here. Come, let's sit outside and watch the sunset."

"After all this excitement, I can't wait to try it!"

The sun sinks into the horizon as they walk out onto the terrace. Max works at building a fire and fans the smoldering kindling until it bursts into flames. They sit in comfortable chairs, enjoying the heat from the bonfire as darkness closes in around them and he fills their wineglasses. "To the smartest student that I ever had!" and they touch their glasses.

"That's because you make it fun and interesting, but as a student, I have a question. In reviewing my mathematical models, I discovered that it's much more energy efficient to switch from your dipole antenna array to a parabolic dish. Have you thought about that?"

"No, I haven't, but it's an interesting idea. Where do you suggest we mount it?"

"We could enclose it in a fiberglass dome under the fuselage."

Max thinks about it. "Interesting! What made you think of it?"

"When you described how wave propagation works, I realized that a parabolic dish, and one of the new cavity magnetrons, might strengthen the output signal."

"It's an interesting idea, and I think we should try it." He puts another log on the fire. "What do you say we take a break and do something fun tomorrow?"

"What should we do? A drive in the country, a walk on the beach?"

He smiles at her. "If you're up for it, let's take the horses and I'll show you around. There's the vineyard to explore, and maybe a walk along the river. And, depending on how you feel, we could tour the winery. What do you say?"

"I'd like that very much," and she takes a sip from her wineglass.

"What do you think of the wine?"

"This is exquisite. Now I know what the Greeks meant when they called it the nectar of the Gods."

Max smiles. "According to Dionysus, wine has magical properties that will confer immortality on anyone who has the luck to drink it."

Betty laughs. "It's fun to think of it like that."

They sit by the roaring fire enjoying themselves and talk late into the evening.

The next day, Max is in the kitchen and already has the coffee made when Betty enters. He looks up at her. "Good morning!"

She's wearing a white blouse and tan riding breeches tucked into tall boots. "I'm looking forward to our adventure today."

"Good! Breakfast is on the terrace."

After eating, they walk to the barn with Apollo leading the way and saddle their horses. As they ride out into the sunny meadow, he asks her, "How are your ribs feeling?"

"It's been seven weeks since our accident, and I feel a lot better, thanks." She leans forward and strokes Arabella's neck. "If I take my time and don't re-injure myself, I'll be alright."

"Are you comfortable riding her?"

"Yes, but she moves like a leopard that's ready to spring on its prey."

"You're feeling the stride of a powerful animal, and she's absolutely explosive on the show course. Let me know if you want to try jumping someday."

"That sounds exciting!"

"Elke lives nearby, and she's an excellent teacher."

"Thanks for the offer. I'd like to meet her."

They ride their horse's side-by-side, chatting and enjoying the beautiful morning. Soon, they arrive at the end of the meadow and tie their horses to a wooden fence. Max holds her hand as they approach a large rock outcrop that juts out of the hillside. A single tree shades them as they enjoy an eagle's view of the blue Mosel River.

They stand together, admiring the fantastic scenery, and their eyes meet. Max holds her in his arms and pulls her close to him. She presses her body tightly into his, and their kiss is long and passionate, but she pushes him back and whispers softly into his shoulder. "I'm sorry, Max. I'm married."

Just then, a rabbit bursts from a nearby bush, and Apollo charges after it. The moment is broken, and they separate. Max yells after him. "Apollo, come back here!" but he ignores him and races down the gorge's steep slope. Max turns to Betty. "I'm sorry, but we better see if we can find him."

"How do we get down to the river?"

He motions toward a narrow trail that zigzags down through the rows of vines. "The path is over there but be careful. It's very steep."

They mount their horses and carefully maneuver their way down the slope, as Max explains. "These are Riesling grapevines. They're known as the king of the white grapes, and they like our cool climate and sandy soil."

"Growing grapes on such a steep incline must be harder than the vineyards that grow them on flat ground."

"Yes. And it's about five times more costly."

"So why do it?"

"Ahh, because it makes the flavor more intense. We have little topsoil, limited water, and a lot of sunlight. It stresses the plants, and they produce a much more flavorful grape than on the flatland, and our wine becomes more desirable."

Soon they reach the end of the trail and arrive at the riverbank. Ahead of them, and lying under a large shady tree, is Apollo, who seems surprised to see them. Max is happy to have found him. "Apollo! Are you coming with us?" He jumps to his feet and joins them as they ride along the shoreline.

The beauty of the river surprises Betty. "The Mosel is impressive! It doesn't look this big from above."

"At times there can be a lot of traffic, mostly barges and passenger ferries."

They stop, dismount, and walk along the river's edge. Max asks her, "Are you enjoying the ride?"

"Yes, and it feels good to be out of the house."

"Have you ever been to a vineyard before?"

"No. I haven't."

"Well then, let me show you around." He reaches into the heavy undergrowth of wide green leaves and reveals a cluster of greenish-yellow Riesling grapes. "These still have some time to go before they're ready to harvest."

Betty picks a grape and tastes it. "Hmm. They're a little sour."

"Yes. The sugar content won't raise until just before harvest time."

"When is that?"

"It depends on the year, but usually somewhere in September."

They walk alongside the river and come to a creek that seeps out of the hillside, forming a large pool that overflows into the Mosel. A small ferry works its way upriver and several passengers on the stern wave to them. Max puts his arm around Betty's waist, and they wave back. "Are you up to touring the winery?"

"Yes! I've been looking forward to it. I always wanted to know how wine is made."

The large winery building is constructed with heavy stone blocks and massive wooden beams. They enter a cool room filled with stainless-steel tanks, and a row of barrel presses line the adjacent wall. Max explains. "We gently press the grapes to avoid crushing the skin, which would release tannins, making the wine harsh. Then we pump the juice into these refrigerated fermentation tanks for about three weeks. After that, we filter and bottle it."

"You don't have to age it?"

"Most whites are not oaked, but because of the war, we store it in oak barrels rather than waste it. Unlike reds, whites can be aged twenty years or more because of their high acidity content. After we bottle the wine, we cellar it and keep it at a cool, stable temperature."

Betty wonders about his dragon story. "Where are the caves that you talked about?"

He points to a nearby wrought-iron gate. "This leads to them," and he turns on the lights, revealing a dark tunnel. After thirty feet, it opens into a large, well-lit cavern, with irregular tunnels leading off to the side. The smooth stone walls are heavily coated with a tan-colored mineral and beautiful dragons are painted on them.

"These are beautiful! I was expecting to see crude petroglyphs," and she walks slowly along the wall, transfixed by the paintings.

"Many years ago, my father invited an archeologist here from the university to assess them. The professor said they were an extraordinary find, and estimated they were painted at the end of the Upper Paleolithic era about twelve thousand years ago."

Betty admires each one as she slowly walks past them. "I wasn't expecting to see them in color. How did they do that?"

"The professor told my father that the various colors come from naturally occurring mineral pigments. They combined the pigments with animal fat to create a type of paint. These paintings are unusual because not only are they outlined, but many are painted solid, and include shadowing to give them a three-dimensional appearance."

Intrigued by the paintings, Betty stops at a large, golden-winged dragon poised on a rock ledge, ready to take flight. "What do you think artists living twelve thousand years ago saw that encouraged them to create such beautiful creatures?"

"Maybe they just painted what they saw."

She is surprised at his comment. "Do you think dragons actually lived here?"

"According to legend, they did. I guess you will have to let your imagination be your guide."

Betty peers into a darkened side tunnel filled with barrels. "This is a lot of wine. Don't you sell it?"

"Not since the war started. Distribution is dangerous, and the average person can't afford it."

They walk down an aisle between long rows of large barrels stacked on top of each other, and he explains. "The caves are ideal for us. They're dry and cool, which is perfect for storing wine. There's not much demand for it now, but when the war is over, we will start selling it again."

The room is cool, and Betty rubs her hands together. "It's a little chilly in here."

"Come. I'll show you the rest of the winery," and she follows him into the processing area. The extensive facility impresses her. "You make it sound pretty easy, but I'm sure it's not."

"Every component in the growing and finishing process can be very technical. Winemaking is an interesting mixture of science and artistry."

As they walk, she notices a large copper-domed kettle sitting on top of an oven made of yellow-colored fire bricks. Next to it are several other vessels with interconnecting copper tubing. "Is this a still?"

"Yes, it's a hobby of mine. Our grapes are similar to the grape used in making cognac so, I decided I would try to make brandy for our own use."

Betty is fascinated. "Were you successful?"

"Yes, but I don't sell it commercially."

She walks closer to inspect it. "I'd like to taste it sometime."

"Perhaps after dinner tonight," and they walk toward a heavy wooden door at the end of the building. "Our tasting room is just ahead."

"I bet you have some real treasures stored in there."

"Yes, I always keep wine from our best years."

Max opens the door, switches on the lights, and they enter a rocky cavern. In the center is a heavy wooden table surrounded by chairs. Metal wine racks filled with dusty bottles line the walls. Betty is surprised. "This room is wonderful!" She walks down an aisle and removes a bottle. "I like the dragon on this label. I think I saw it in the cave."

"You did. It was a favorite of my grandfathers."

He motions toward a wooden table. "Have a seat. What would you like to try?"

"I don't know. What do you recommend?"

"Since we are celebrating the completion of your physics class, I recommend a rare 1920 semi-sweet Riesling." He dusts off a bottle, uncorks it, and pours some into a glass. "See what you think of this?"

She swirls it around and holds it up to the light, revealing its amber color. "This is delicious! I've never tasted a wine this old before." She sniffs the aroma. "Hmm, it smells fruity, with a hint of apple," and takes another sip. "And I can taste a little lime and something earthy."

"That's correct, and I see you know your wines."

"Yes, a little. I joined a wine tasting club when I was studying at the university, but I never had time to tour a winery."

"I'm impressed!" and he changes the subject. "Do you like music?"

"Very much so."

Max walks over to a record player and searches through a rack of albums. "Are you familiar with Tàrrega?"

"No. I'm not."

"He was a Spanish classical guitarist around 1880."

"Do you play the guitar?"

"Yes. My mother taught me when I was young, but lately I haven't had the time to play."

"You surprise me, Max. What type of music do you like?"

"My favorite is Spanish classical." He returns to his chair and raises his glass. "Prost!" and they touch wineglasses.

The sound of romantic guitar music fills the room, and they sit quietly, enjoying the moment while sipping their wine. When the song finishes, Betty opens her eyes. "That was beautiful. What do you call that genre?"

"It's a fusion of Brazilian samba and Spanish classical."

"I felt like I was walking on a sunny beach in a distant land."

Max smiles at her. "Well, it seems we have another passion in common."

In the distance, they hear the crack and roll of an approaching thunderstorm, and she looks over at the doorway. "Is it supposed to rain today?"

"I don't think so. That sounded like it was far away, but we should probably head back, just in case."

He calls to Apollo, who is laying down. "Let's go, big boy!" and he springs to his feet. They mount their horses as the sun slips behind towering storm clouds and Max looks at her. "We took it pretty easy getting here, but we should probably pick up the pace on the way back. Are you comfortable with that?"

The highly adventurous Betty grins. "Yes! I'd love to."

Max taps his stallion lightly in the ribs with his heels, and Gunnar immediately moves forward at a steady canter. The trail skirts a wooded tree line, then drops to a long meadow and Betty and Arabella easily keep abreast of him. A loud clap of thunder rolls through the clouds above them, and Max calls to her. "Can you handle a little more speed?"

She leans forward in her saddle and nods her head. "Yes, I'll follow you."

A powerful gust of wind sweeps across the grassy meadow, and he slackens his reins as Gunnar picks up the pace. Betty and Arabella stay by his side with her hair blowing in the breeze. Max looks over at her and sees that she's easily keeping up. "Let's have some fun!" and he relaxes the pressure on Gunnar's reins.

The big stallion throws his head back, lunges forward, and explodes into a gallop. Arabella is quick to pick up the pace and stays beside him as they race flat out down the twisting dirt trail. At the far end of the meadow, they slow down and disappear into a wooded glen. Their horses slide down a steep embankment and trot out into the deep grass at the bottom of a ravine. Max helps her dismount, and they let the horses walk out into a shallow stream to drink.

Betty is exhilarated. "That was an incredible experience! Thank you!"

Max is impressed. "You're an excellent rider! Arabella can be a lot to handle."

She bubbles over with excitement. "I've never ridden a horse that could run that fast!" Suddenly, Apollo bursts from a dense thicket of brush and runs to her, panting heavily. She bends down and strokes his head. "He's amazing . . . and fast!"

Max pats his shoulder affectionately. "He's used to running with the horses and can usually beat us home because he knows all the shortcuts." He walks toward a large fallen log on the other side of the shallow creek. "Let's rest here for a minute," and holds out his hand to Betty. "Be careful. The rocks are wet."

She carefully crosses the stream but slips, and Max is quick to stop her fall. He pulls her close to him, and for a moment they embrace tenderly. "Are you alright?"

"Yes, thank you."

Betty realizes she has fallen in love with Max, and she knows he feels the same way about her. She desperately wants to be with him, but if she were discovered to be a spy, it would endanger his life, and above all else, she needs to protect him. Suddenly, a loud crash of thunder interrupts them, and scattered drops of rain fall from the dark clouds overhead. Betty flinches as they land on her shoulders. "Brrr! That is cold!"

Max looks up at the threatening sky. "We'd better get back to the house before we get soaked."

They hold hands, splash across the shallow creek, and quickly collect their horses. Arabella is a tall horse, and Max helps Betty swing up into the saddle. She pulls on the reins to back Arabella up slightly, but she is eager to leave and paws at the ground. She snorts loudly and tosses her head while lurching nervously to the side, but Betty expertly keeps her under control.

Max mounts Gunnar. "Let's make a run for the barn while we can!"

Apollo is laying down in the middle of the shallow creek, and Max calls to him. "Apollo! Home!" and he leaps to his feet and dashes into the brush.

Betty struggles to hold Arabella back. "I'll follow your lead!"

With a slight tap in his ribs, Gunnar explodes up the steep trail as chunks of mud and rocks fly in all directions. Instantly, Arabella launches, and charges after him in hot pursuit. Betty expertly leans forward in the saddle as she blasts up the embankment.

As the storm front closes in, a stiff breeze whips at the trees and tears at the meadow grass. A gray wind-swept wall of rain approaches them as they gallop side-by-side down the long, winding dirt trail. Betty crouches down close to Arabella's neck as she runs flat out. Halfway back, the rain catches up to them, but it only encourages the horses to run even faster. Suddenly, Apollo blasts out of the tall grass and joins them as they race toward home.

They arrive at the barn soaking wet and shivering, and Betty is ecstatic. "Wow! What a ride!"

Max helps her dismount. "I'm impressed! Where did you learn how to ride like that?"

"I spent several summers at a girlfriend's farm, and we rode every day."

They remove their saddles and walk their horses to their stalls. Betty takes an apple from a basket and puts it into her pocket, but Arabella is quick to smell it and nuzzles her, looking for it. She laughs at her antics and feeds it to her. "Good girl!" and hugs her neck.

Apollo is muddy and soaking wet. Max struggles to dry him with a large towel, but he is full of energy and makes a game of it by weaving through his legs playfully. Suddenly, he pulls the towel away from him and runs toward the house, dragging it across the rain-soaked ground.

Max watches him bound away, and smiles. "So much for that! He's headed for the warmth of the fireplace, and so should we."

He takes Betty's hand, and they dash through the downpour to the house and burst into the kitchen. A surprised Helga, who is standing at the stove, exclaims. "Oh, my. Look at the two of you!"

Max pushes his wet hair back with both of his hands and wipes the rain from his face. "Hi, Helga. We were returning from the winery when the storm caught up to us."

"Well, it looks like you had fun. You better warm up. I'll have a meal ready for you when you get back."

Drenched and shivering, they depart for a hot shower and a change of clothes. An hour later, they enter the cavernous kitchen and sit down at the table. Apollo is already dry and laying by the wood-burning stove. Helga looks at Betty. "Did you get to see the river?"

"Yes. It's impressive!"

Max is complimentary. "It turns out that our city girl is an excellent rider."

"Good for you. This is a beautiful place to ride."

He asks Helga, "How did it go with the troops? Did they deliver our equipment?"

"Yes, they left an hour ago." She picks up her umbrella. "It's been a long day for me, and I'm headed home. Dinner is in the oven."

They say goodnight to her and sit down to eat. As they finish eating, Max looks over at Betty. "Ready for a brandy out on the terrace?"

"I am but let me change into something warmer first."

A half hour later, the sun has set, and Max has a roaring fire going. A bottle of brandy and two glasses sit on a small table next to their chairs. Betty walks toward him and looks up at the clearing sky. "It looks like the rain has passed."

"Yes. It's typical of our summer weather, but the fire's hot and the brandy will warm your soul."

"I like your romantic side, Max."

He pushes a burning log with a long metal poker, and a shower of sparks dance in front of him. "I've been too focused on this project, but I seem to have a new outlook with you around." He walks over to Betty, pours a small amount of brandy into a snifter, and hands it to her.

She takes the glass and sips the amber liquid. "Oh, that's very smooth."

"Thanks, it's over twenty years old."

Max sits down next to her, and they sip their brandy, quietly enjoying the last rays of a beautiful sunset, and he asks, "What are you thinking about?"

Betty stares at the fire, lost in thought. "I've spent most of my life living in the city. I never realized how extraordinarily beautiful the country can be."

"Yes, but even this is developed. We should ride our horses to the alpine lake above the house. The trail winds its way through a breathtakingly beautiful forest. It takes an hour to get there, but you can experience nature at its best; wild and untamed."

His offer sounds adventurous to her. "I would love to see it, Max. When could we go there?"

"I have meetings tomorrow. If you think you are up to it, we could leave the following day. My grandfather built a cabin alongside the lake. It was one of my favorite places to visit when I was growing up. We'll pack a lunch and get an early start." He gazes at the fire as the fading sun slips behind the horizon. "If there wasn't a war, where would you like to be?"

Betty brushes her long auburn hair to the side and relaxes in her chair. "I love to travel, and I've always wanted to spend some time in a romantic city like Paris or Rome. And you?"

"My dream is to visit Spain and take lessons from a famous guitarist."

"Speaking of guitars. Are you going to play something for me tonight?"

"Yes, if you like."

He disappears into the shadows, and reappears moments later, holding a glistening guitar with mother-of-pearl inlays in the neck. He sits down in a chair next to her and plays a soft, romantic melody. Betty relaxes and closes her eyes. When he finishes, there's a long silence. "Max, that was beautiful! I loved it!"

"Thanks. An unknown composer wrote it more than a hundred years ago."

"It has a dreamy quality about it."

He picks up his guitar and softly strums the strings. "This is a love song written by a gaucho to his sweetheart who lives in a distant village."

Reflections from the flames dance across his face as he plays. His music drifts out into the shadowy night, and Betty sinks into her chair and closes her eyes. When he stops playing, there is a long silence between them, and she sits motionless. "That was delightful. I didn't want it to end."

"I thought you might like it." He stands, sets his guitar down, and walks over to a nearby record player. Romantic music soon fills the air, and a silvery moon slowly rises above the towering Swiss Alps. He extends his hand. "Would you like to dance?"

"Yes. I'd love to."

He holds her close to him as they quietly sway to the music. The evening is warm, and flickering stars fill the sky . . . and Betty is in heaven.

Two days later, they are up early and walk to the barn. They saddle their horses and ride them to a fence that runs along the edge of the tree line. Max opens a gate, and they follow a seldom used trail just wide enough for a tractor. It winds its way deep into the shadowy forest. Tall trees filter the sunlight, exposing large boulders surrounded by lush green ferns. They ride side-by-side, and the natural beauty of the forest is enchanting. The trail is steep and, as they crest a ridge, they surprise a herd of wild boar. The piglets squeal and quickly vanish into the dark shadows. As they continue climbing, Max tells her about a local legend.

"My grandfather used to tell me stories about the moss people that live here."

"Were they like fairies?"

"Yes, but the size of small children with long unkempt hair and clad in moss."

She smiles at him. "Did you ever see one?"

"Of course. I had a vivid imagination, and I could see them dart about."

Betty laughs. "Were they kind, or fearsome?"

He pretends to be very serious. "They were kind, but they could be troublesome if you angered them. My grandfather said they would sometimes ask him for food, so he always brought bread for them. He told me they were generous and would repay him with good advice, but I also heard stories of them stealing small children, so I was cautious and remembered to bring them a treat," and he winks at her.

Betty reflects on memories of her childhood. "I remember my mother reading me bedtime stories about fairies and elves. Those were wonderful days."

They ride silently, enjoying the forest. Up ahead of them, sunlight streams to the ground and they see part of a meadow filled with green grass and wildflowers. Max calls softly to Apollo. "Apollo! Come here," and he returns to his side. Betty stops. "What's the matter?" He holds a finger to his lips and whispers. "There's something up ahead I'd like to show you."

They dismount and quietly approach the shadows at the edge of the forest. In front of them is a sunny meadow with a herd of deer grazing in the center. The males are large and have colossal antlers, while the females are much smaller. Betty is amazed. "I've never seen deer in the wild before. They're beautiful!"

"I don't allow hunting here, so they know they are safe. I thought you would like to see them."

She peeks through the low-hanging tree limbs. "They're magnificent, but I don't want to frighten them."

"We won't. Our trail skirts the meadow."

They watch them for a while before slipping back into the shadows. A short time later, the forest thins out and they enter an alpine valley. In the center is a beautiful lake surrounded by green grass and wildflowers. Near the shoreline is a cabin made of heavy masonry blocks. It has a covered front porch, a large stone chimney, and a slate roof. Max points to it. "That's grandfather's cabin. Jannik and Helga were up here last year so everything should be in order."

Betty looks around at the wild untamed valley and admires its beauty. "This is absolutely breathtaking! It would be wonderful to spend some time here."

The snow-covered Swiss Alps tower above them, and far below is the winding Mosel River. They unsaddle their horses and Max puts a leather hobble on Gunnar's front legs, and another one on Arabella. "They're going to be hungry after a walk like that, and the hobbles will keep them from wandering off."

Betty is worried. "Are you sure they'll be safe? Aren't there dangerous animals in the woods?"

"There are no bears or wolves, and the wild boar won't bother them."

The cabin has a covered porch with a table and chairs that overlook the lake. They enter a large room with a massive stone fireplace at the far end, and a tall pile of wood is stacked next to it. A sunny kitchen window overlooks the shoreline, and there are several beds placed along the walls. An upside-down canoe lies on top of a heavy wooden table, and Betty slides her hand over it. "This looks like fun. Can we take it out?"

"Of course. Are you hungry?"

"You bet! My tummy is grumbling!"

He picks up the saddle bag that contains their lunch and he hands it to her. "There's a sunny table on the porch with a spectacular view of the lake. I'm going to look for something to drink."

"That sounds perfect!"

She spreads out their sandwiches, and Max joins her. "Look at what I found!" and holds out a bottle of wine.

After eating they walk to the edge of the shimmering lake, and Betty asks, "Are there any fish out there?"

"Yes. Brown trout, and they are delicious. Do you want to try your hand at fishing?"

Betty, the city girl, is instantly interested. "I'd love to. Can you teach me?"

"Sure. In my youth I spent many days fishing here with my father."

Max calls to Apollo who is wading in the shallow water, and he dashes out of the lake and joins them. "I'm going to leave Apollo in the cabin. He can take a nap while we're gone."

"This is so exciting! I've never been fishing before."

They carry the canoe down to the shallow water, and Max walks back to the cabin. Moments later, he returns with two poles and glances down at Betty's heavy riding boots. "I suggest you go barefoot. Those boots will be uncomfortable."

She reaches down, takes them off, and wades into the lake. Max guides the canoe through the shallows and holds it steady while she sits down in the front. "Be careful, it's very tippy. Don't make any quick moves until you get the hang of it." He shoves it into deeper water and steps into the back. "We're headed for that shady cove across the lake. That was always my favorite fishing hole."

The canoe slips through the clear water with ease, and they paddle silently enjoying the tranquil morning. The sun is high overhead and there's not a cloud in the sky. When they arrive at the cove, he hands her a fishing pole with a large worm wiggling on the hook. "The fish can't resist one of these worms. Just throw it out as far as you can and sit quietly."

She follows his advice, and they wait in silence enjoying nature and the beautiful scenery that surrounds them. The canoe slowly drifts in the light breeze when suddenly Betty gets a big strike, and the tip of her rod jerks violently toward the surface of the lake. She cries out excitedly. "Oh, my gosh!"

Max looks over the side of the canoe into the deep crystal-clear water. "You've caught a nice one. Don't panic. Just reel him in slowly."

As the fish nears the surface, it jumps several times before Max can slip a net under it. "She's a beauty! We can have it for supper tonight."

Betty watches intently as he lifts it into the canoe. Its brassy-green body is covered with large black spots, and its white underbelly shimmers in the bright sunlight. "That's the first fish that I ever caught!"

Max compliments her. "And it's a nice one. Now that we have dinner, let's explore the rest of the lake."

With their fishing over they silently paddle along the shoreline admiring the birds and wildlife. By the time they return to the cabin it's late afternoon, and Max looks up at the darkening sky. "A summer storm is coming this way. We'd better get inside."

As they walk up the path, he has a suggestion. "If you like, we could spend the night here and return in the morning. The heavens up here are extraordinarily beautiful."

Betty is having the time of her life, and she surprises him once again. "Let's do it! I don't want this day to end!"

A bright silver bolt of lightning flashes through the dark clouds above them, and moments later a loud crack echoes through the valley as a curtain of rain moves toward them. Betty carries her fish, and Max follows with their fishing poles. He opens the cabin door and Apollo races to her side wagging his tail. She scratches his head, and he runs to the lake to take a drink.

As they carry the canoe, a powerful gust of wind sweeps across the lake. Apollo is standing in the shallow water, and Max calls to him. "Apollo! Come here!" and he charges out of the water, only stopping occasionally to shake his thick coat. The wall of rain crosses the lake and slams into them just as they enter the cabin. Safely inside Betty asks, "What can I do?"

"If you wouldn't mind, there might be something in the cupboard we could cook for dinner."

For Betty this is high adventure, and she looks through the cabinets while Max cleans her trout in the sink. Afterword, he goes to the fireplace and starts a fire, which quickly warms the cabin.

Betty looks over at him. "I love your fire. I can feel the warmth from it."

"Thanks. It gets chilly in the evening at this altitude."

Strong winds buffet the cabin and sheets of rain hammer against the windows. Max rummages through a wall locker, finds a candle lamp, and places it on the table. Its bright flame fills the room in a warm glow. He walks to the sink, puts his arms around Betty and nuzzles the back of her neck. "I came to steal your fish."

She pretends to push him away, and hands him the fish. "Here, it's ready to cook."

Max picks up the trout and puts it in a large cast-iron frying pan. "This is the only way to cook brown trout," and he holds it over the flames.

Betty hands him a pot of vegetables, which he places on the hot coals. Apollo is curled up near the roaring fire watching Max fry his fish, and Betty smiles. "It looks like Apollo is going to eat with us tonight. He'll like that."

By the time they finish dinner the storm has stopped, and the air is pungent with the sweet smell of rain. Max puts their horses in the corral for the night, then lights a bonfire by the edge of the lake. The evening is cool, and he and Betty sit together in comfortable chairs sharing a warm blanket across their laps. As the sun sets in the distance, darkness engulfs the valley, and the heavens fill with shining stars. A full moon rises above the black silhouette of rugged mountain peaks, and they sip brandy from metal coffee cups.

Betty looks up at the darkening sky. "The moon is beautiful tonight."

"Yes, and if we're lucky, we might see something quite extraordinary."

As it climbs high into the sky, it changes from a bright silver to a light blue, and it astonishes Betty. "What makes it change color like that?"

"It's because of an extremely unusual weather condition caused by the fire-bombing of our cities. The firestorm releases particles that preferentially scatter the red light, and it creates a blue cast."

She watches it intently. "I've heard of a blue moon, but I didn't know it was real!"

As the moon climbs into the evening sky, it slowly turns into a beautiful iridescent blue and Max points to it. "See, it's happening now."

"That's magical!"

They bundle up in front of the roaring fire, and he puts his arm around her. She pulls the blanket up to her chin and cuddles close to him, spellbound by the spectacular event unfolding in the heavens.

The following morning finds them laying on the floor in front of the fireplace on a makeshift bed of blankets and old pillows. A shaft of sunlight streams through the kitchen window, and Betty slowly wakens. Max is sleeping next to her, and she rolls onto her side, staring at him as he sleeps. She reaches out, brushes his blonde hair to the side, and kisses his forehead tenderly. He slowly opens his eyes and smiles at her. "Good morning, beautiful. Did you sleep well?"

"Yes, it was like sleeping on a cloud," and she dreamily inspects a gold medallion that Max is wearing around his neck. "This is beautiful."

"It's a symbol of our family's heritage. Lotar and I were each gifted one on our twenty-first birthday."

Max caresses her cheek, pulls her toward him, and they kiss passionately. He whispers in her ear. "I'm so happy that you are in my life, mien leibling."

She nuzzles close to him. "I love being with you, Max," and she runs her fingers through his hair. "I'd like to watch the sunrise. Do you want to go with me?"

"I think I'll stay here. I'll have the coffee on by the time you get back," and he buries his head into a pillow.

Betty gets out of bed, puts on her clothes, and opens the front door. She looks at Apollo and whispers. "Apollo, come," and he immediately jumps up and follows her outside. The sun peaks over the distant Alps, and they walk along the sandy shoreline. The morning air is chilly and a light mist hovers above the lake. Here and there fish swirl at the lake's glassy surface in search of something to eat.

They follow a narrow animal trail that winds its way along the edge of the lake. Ahead of them a fish splashes after a frog in the shallow water, and Apollo carefully approaches it.

The trail stops at a rock ledge that juts out into the lake. Betty steps onto its flat surface, walks to the end, and sits down with her legs dangling over the edge. Apollo follows, laying down next to her, and she places her arm over his shoulders.

A pair of loons call to each other from across the lake, and a flight of colorful green-headed Mallard ducks fly toward them. They set their wings, lower their feet, and settle into the nearby water.

They both sit silently for a while, and Betty stares at her wedding ring, lost in thought. Then she removes the ring and throws it out into the deep water. It flashes in the bright sunlight as it slowly sinks into the depths.

After a while she stands, and they walk back to the cabin. Smoke rises from the chimney, and the distinct odor of fresh coffee fills the air. She enters, and Max removes the blackened pot from the hot coals. "Ready for coffee?"

"Yes, and it smells fabulous!"

He pours two steaming cups and hands one to her. When she takes it from his hand, he notices that her wedding ring is missing, and smiles to himself. "I moved a couple of chairs to the beach. Let's have our coffee lakeside," and they leave the cabin.

The sun climbs into the sky, and its golden rays fill the valley. A light breeze sweeps away the morning mist, and the countryside is ablaze in the vibrant colors of late summer. Betty relaxes in a chair and takes a sip of coffee. "Yum, that's just what I needed." She admires her surroundings. "Max, it's so beautiful here."

"Yes. This is a special place for me, too."

She looks at him lovingly. "Yesterday was a magical day, and one that I will cherish forever."

They drink their coffee in silence while admiring the beauty of the hidden valley. After a while, Max reaches over and holds her hand. "I would love to stay longer, but we should get back to the farm. We have a lot of work to do."

CHAPTER 15

BUILDING THE DISRUPTOR

IT'S THE FOLLOWING DAY, AND BETTY AND MAX ARE WORK-
ing in their impromptu laboratory. Stacked along the walls are boxes of vacuum
tubes, circuit boards, and equipment cases. Max watches a dancing waveform
on the screen of an oscilloscope as Betty slowly turns one of several dials on a
complicated-looking instrument. "Slowly. Slowly. You've almost got it. A little
more . . . more . . . stop! That's the strongest reading we've ever seen."

Suddenly, Apollo barks and Betty looks over at him. "I think someone
is here," and walks to a window. "It's the major," and she greets him at the front
door. "Major Krüger, what a pleasant surprise. Come in."

"It's time I checked in on the wounded. How are you feeling?"

"Much better. The doctor said I'm doing fine. Only two more weeks and
I'll be as good as new."

"And Max?"

"He's doing well. Fortunately, the shrapnel missed his femoral artery, but
it did a lot of tissue and bone damage. Come in. He's in the lab."

"You have a lab here?"

"Yes. We needed a large area to work in, so he converted the great room."

Major Krüger enters and is taken aback by all the electronic equipment.

"Hello, Max. What is all this?"

"We're testing a new antenna design, and it's producing twice the signal output!" He points to several cases stacked against the wall. "That's the upgraded disrupter system that we'll be installing."

The major stares at it approvingly. "This looks very complicated. Does it have more range?"

"Yes, quite a bit."

He turns to Max. "By the way, the Heinkel bomber that you requested arrived yesterday."

"That's good news, Major. We're about ready to test this system under combat conditions."

"Excellent," and he turns to Betty. "Oh, by the way. Do you know of a Dr. Müller?"

"No. I don't think so."

"He's the director of advanced technologies at Peenemünde and has become interested in our project. He will be here soon with his staff for a demonstration."

The thought of being discovered terrifies her, but she conceals her fear. "Thank you, Major. I'm looking forward to meeting him."

He's in a hurry and walks to the door. "Sorry to rush off. I just wanted to see how you were doing."

After he leaves, Max excitedly congratulates her. "Thanks to you, all of our hard work will soon be recognized."

"Max, you're the genius behind all of this."

"I couldn't have done it without your help," and he hugs her.

Unfortunately for Betty, this is the worst possible news. She's caught in an excruciatingly difficult position, and her world is closing in on her. In order to avoid discovery, she needs to return to England immediately, but she has few options. If she leaves, she could lose Max forever, and if she stays, she could be exposed by Dr. Müller, and shot as a spy. Gerta becomes her only chance to escape, but she hadn't seen her for almost five months. Somehow, she'll have to get a message to her, and quickly, but it won't be easy because she is always with Max or confined to the underground hangar. The only other possibility would be through the forest at night, but she was a city girl and would easily become lost in the darkness.

Max is elated by the major's news, as their future looks bright. "This never would have happened without you!"

Betty is nervous. "Thanks, Max."

He picks up a notebook. "We're going to need a few more supplies to finish," and he rips out a page and hands it to her. "We need to pick up these parts right away."

She reviews his list and looks up. "When do you want to go?"

"It's still early. We should leave now."

A half hour later, they are dressed in their military uniforms and drive off in Max's black Mercedes, headed to the supply depot near Cologne. Apollo rides in the back seat with his head sticking out the side window, as usual. Max has a worried look on his face. "We never discussed this before, but how long can you stay?"

The dramatic changes have caught Betty off-guard, and she hasn't had a chance to develop a plan to avoid Dr. Müller. "Max, I've already stayed longer than I should have. This was supposed to have been a short-term assignment. I need to return to Peenemünde."

"That's too dangerous! The Allies have been bombing it for months, and the roads leading there are attacked daily."

"Then I'll figure out another way to get there."

"Elizabeth, I don't want you to leave. We will be fully operational soon, and you have a fantastic future here."

She struggles to avoid a commitment. "There's nothing I can do about it. We can put our lives back together after the war ends."

"It doesn't have to be that way. I'm going to ask Dr. Müller to transfer you so we can finish this project. What we are doing here is important!"

They drive in silence for a while, then Max slows the car and turns onto a narrow country road. "There's a little café about a half hour from here. We can talk more there."

"Another one of your famous hidden cafés?"

"Yes," and he takes her hand. "I don't want to argue. Let's enjoy this beautiful morning."

After a while, they turn off the main highway and drive along a winding country road before arriving at a quiet village. Max stops at a vine-covered, open-air café, and they enter through a wooden gate that leads to a secluded terrace overlooking a slow-moving river.

The owner sees them approaching. "Hello, Max. Thank you for stopping to see me," and she hugs him.

"Adele, this is my friend Elizabeth."

Betty shakes her hand. "Nice to meet you."

"Max has been coming here since he was a young boy," and she bends down and gives Apollo a hug. "My, he seems to get bigger every time I see him. Well, what will you two have?"

Max looks at her display case. "I think we'll try your plum cakes and coffee."

"Very good. Please, have a seat. I'll be right back."

They make themselves comfortable at a small table, and Apollo finds a sunny spot to stretch out on. Betty is happy to be out in the sun and fresh air and takes off her Gestapo officer's jacket.

Max reaches over and holds her hand. "Please don't leave. I need your help."

She nervously lies to him. "I'm sorry, Max. We're at war, and it's not my choice to make."

Adele returns with their coffee and pastries. "Enjoy."

Max looks up at her. "Thank you, Adele."

Betty takes a sip of her coffee and smiles. "I'm going to miss your secret cafés."

He sits back in his chair, and after a few moments, he surprises her. "There's something that I haven't told you." He leans forward and lowers his voice. "In the process of developing the navigation disrupter, I accidentally discovered a new technology that could give Germany a massive edge in aerial warfare, and I need you to help me develop it."

Betty sets down her coffee. "What are you talking about?"

"As you know, the navigation disrupter will be defeated at some point and forgotten, but not this new technology. Basically, it hides an attacking plane from the enemy's radar screen by creating multiple false images on their CRT monitors and there is no defense against it. The enemy would be completely blind in a combat situation."

Betty is shocked. "How far along are you?"

"I finished the prototype a while back. With your help, I believe we could downsize it so that it could fit into any airplane."

"That's incredible! It would change the face of modern warfare!"

"Yes, and it shows tremendous promise."

"Does Major Krüger know about this?"

"No! I want to create a full-scale unit before I show it to anyone. Our priority is to finish testing the navigation disrupter."

The unexpected and terrifying revelation of a deadly new weapon has caught Betty off-guard. Her loyalty is to the Allies, but just warning them won't be enough, because there is nothing that they can do about it. Her only option is to work with Max and discover its secrets. Somehow, she will have to figure out a way to deal with Dr. Müller. She makes a bold move. "All right, I'll stay and help you develop it," and lies. "I'll call my husband's father. He can tell Peenemünde to wait a little longer."

Just then, Adel approaches their table. "Well, where are you two off to this morning?"

"To the supply depot."

"Be careful going that way. It's not safe. The Allies have bombed Cologne over fifty times. Thousands of people are homeless and starving."

"Really?"

She frowns. "The newspapers don't tell us the truth anymore. Did you know Hitler just surrendered Paris to the Allies? And now they're coming this way!"

Max is shocked. "What! That's impossible! Paris is only three hundred miles from here!"

Adele disappears into the kitchen for a moment, then returns with a French newspaper and hands it to him. Neither of them can read French, but from the photos they see enormous crowds cheering the return of General de Gaulle. Max looks through the pages and passes it to Betty. "What do you think?"

She glances through the paper and shakes her head. "She's right. The Nazi army has withdrawn."

Max can't believe it. "How could this be? Goebbels is always telling us about German victories."

Adele leans close to him and whispers. "They lie about everything!"

This is not good news, and it unnerves Max. "I appreciate your honesty," and he hands the newspaper back to her. "Thank you, but we had better get going."

They walk to their car, and he opens the door for Betty. "Lotar was right about the impossibility of this war. Hitler has lost, and it's time to think about our survival!"

"What should we do?"

"The Allies will soon cross the Rhine, and then they will be in our backyard. We should move anything of value into the wine caves and seal it off."

Betty wonders. "And our project?"

"We need to finish the disruptor. It may not help the war effort, but at least we can prove it works."

"And what about the radar scrambler?"

"We should test it as soon as possible. If the Allies win, it could be a powerful negotiating chip for us."

"If you are right, then time is of the essence."

Max opens the door to his Mercedes and sits down. "Let's pick up the parts that we need and finish our disruptor project."

On their way back from the supply depot, they decide to stop at the underground hangar. They drive down the ramp and park their car near the new Heinkel bomber. Captain Rolf Klein, the disruptor pilot, approaches them. "This is an impressive plane! We're almost finished with the modifications, and our first high-altitude test flight is scheduled for tomorrow night."

Max appreciates his hard work. "Thanks, Rolf. You've done a great job overseeing the modifications."

They walk to the front of the plane, and Betty inspects the fiberglass dome attached to the underside of the fuselage. "Is the parabolic reflector installed?"

"Yes, and the positioning motors are functional as well."

She walks with him back to their car. "Thanks for your help, Rolf. We finished our work on the disruptor, and we'll install it tomorrow night."

As they drive away, Max is lost in thought, and not much is said on their trip back to the farm. When they arrive, they walk up the steps to the front door in silence. Betty is worried and takes his hand as they enter. "I'm glad to be home. Let's have an early dinner and enjoy the evening."

"Good idea. We need to plan this next phase very carefully," and he puts his arm around her as they walk onto the terrace.

Betty asks, "Where is the radar scrambler?"

"It's hidden," and he explains. "While I was testing the disruptor, I accidentally made a startling discovery. During a test flight, I noticed we were being scanned by one of our radar units. The screen showed inbound radar waves hitting us, but when I increased the output, they destabilized, and even disappeared from our screen. I suddenly realized that when the waves collided, they neutralized each other."

"Theoretically, it's possible, but how did you do it?"

"It was a completely unexpected discovery, so I immediately built a radar signal generator, and used my navigation disruptor to see if it could modulate the incoming waves and it worked!

"I call it a scrambler because it confuses the contact images on the receiving screen. We should test it along with the disruptor tomorrow night because I need real-world data to validate it. We'll use your moveable parabolic dish, so we can scan a much wider area." He cautions her. "Remember, secrecy is of paramount importance. If the wrong people found out about this, we could be in great danger."

The following day, they spend the morning boxing up their disruptor notes and specialized test equipment. Max picks up a box. "Our research needs to go into storage, where it's safe."

"Where are you going to hide it?"

"If you wouldn't mind carrying those notebooks, I'll show you."

They walk down to the library and open the secret door in the alcove. At the bottom of the stairs, Max reaches behind a tall wine rack. "There's a hidden lever here," and presses it. Then he walks over to the large wooden barrel cover that's built into the far wall and pushes against the lid. It swings inward, revealing a secret room. He steps inside, then holds out his hand to Betty. "Let me help you," and she enters. The secret vault is filled with electronic test instruments, books, and some unusual looking equipment. "This is the research that I've been doing over the last couple of years."

Betty surveys the shelves of equipment. "This is amazing!"

He takes a large electronic component off the shelf. It has a myriad of switches and dials on the front panel and hands it to her. "This is the transceiver module for the radar scrambler. Be careful, it's heavy."

"This looks very sophisticated! Is it working?"

"Yes. We'll test it tomorrow night, and when we return, we'll remove it along with the other equipment. I'll tell them we need to make a few adjustments to the disruptor, and we can return it here."

It's mid-day, and they are on the terrace waiting for Jannik to arrive. Betty is worried. "I like Jannik, but are you sure you can trust him?"

"We've worked together for years. I would trust him with my life."

Jannik's blue tractor arrives, and he steps out of the cab. Max waves to him. "Come on up."

Moments later, he walks out onto the terrace. "You sounded worried. What's happening?"

Max motions to a nearby chair. "Please, sit down. We're having a brandy. Will you join us?"

"Thank you," and he hands him a snifter. "We made a trip to the supply depot near Cologne this morning and on the way, we stopped by to visit a long-time friend. She showed us a copy of a recent French newspaper that had photos of the Allies entering Paris."

"No. That can't be!"

"That's what I said, but it's true. There are no German victories. We are in what they call a fighting retreat, and the Allied army will be here in a month or two."

The news shocks Jannik. "Did you know they bombed Koblenz last night?"

Betty is stunned. "That's only sixty miles away!"

Max is in deep thought and taps his fingers on the arm of his chair. "This is happening quicker than I expected. There could be fighting here, and we need to prepare for that. We should remove anything of value from the house, store it in the wine caves, and then seal the entrance to hide it."

"Yes. I agree," but Betty still worries. "What about our horses? We can't just leave them here!"

Jannik has an idea. "We can turn them out in the high meadow. They will be safe there."

"Are you sure?"

"Positive. I love those horses, too," and he turns to Max. "And the wine?"

"Leave a lot out for them. Otherwise, they'll tear the house down looking for it."

"When do you want to start?"

"Come back after lunch and bring your trailer."

That afternoon, Jannik helps them remove their valuables from the house, and they hide them in the caves. All that remains to be done is to get the horses to safety. Betty and Max mount their horses, gather up the rest of the herd, and start their long journey. Jannik follows them in his tractor, and Apollo rides in the trailer.

An hour later, they reach the high meadow and the horses spread out into the deep green grass. Betty brought Arabella's favorite treat with her and feeds her an apple. As she eats it, she strokes her head and whispers to her. "I'm going to miss you, Arabella. I promise I'll return as soon as it's safe," and she puts her arms around her neck and holds her tightly.

Max walks toward the tractor and calls to her. "Elizabeth! We'd better get going."

She kisses Arabella's nose and stares at her longingly. "I love you. I promise I'll be back!" Tears fill her eyes, and she quickly turns away, unable to watch her standing there alone.

CHAPTER 16

ESCAPE FROM GERMANY

THE FOLLOWING EVENING, THEY ARRIVE AT THE UNDER ground hangar and unload their disruptor, including the secret radar scrambler, from the trunk of Max's Mercedes. Rolf exits the bomber and walks down the steps to greet them. "Good evening! Do you need a hand with that?"

He's a highly experienced pilot and Betty has taken a liking to him. "Yes. Thank you, Rolf," and she walks toward the open trunk.

He picks up a case and asks, "How long will it take to get every- thing working?"

"I just need to interconnect the modules."

"Good. The Allied bombers should be up there somewhere tonight."

Later that night, Rolf hangs up the phone, and calls to Max. "It's time to go. They're crossing the Channel now."

"Thanks. We'll be right there."

Max has a serious look on his face and takes Betty's hand. "I'd like to talk to you in private," and they walk to the rear of the hangar where no one can hear them.

"What's wrong?"

Max is worried. "I think you should stay here. We are about to fly into combat, and it could become extremely dangerous."

"I understand, but this is something that we need to do together. I want to be with you no matter what happens."

He realizes that she's not going to change her mind and gets down on one knee. "Elizabeth, I love you deeply. When this is all over, will you marry me?"

Tears fill her eyes. "Max, please don't do this to me."

"I know you're married, but that can change."

"But there are things you don't know about!"

"I don't care, and I know you feel the same way about me."

He takes her hand and slips an engagement ring onto her finger. It's a simple band with small diamonds and alternating rubies. "This was my grand-mother's wedding ring."

Betty is astonished. "Oh Max, it's beautiful!"

It's urgent that they leave if they are to catch up with the Allied bombers and Rolf calls to them. "Max! It's time to go!"

He calls to him from the back of the hangar. "Okay! We'll be right there!"

Betty knows that if she doesn't explain her situation, she could lose him forever, so she follows her heart. "I love you, and I promise to explain everything when we return from this mission."

Rolf starts the bomber's engines and yells to them from the cockpit window. "If we don't leave now, I won't be able to catch up to them!"

"Okay. We're coming," and they hug one last time.

Betty wipes the tears from her eyes, and they walk hurriedly to the bomber. They are wearing gray military jump suits that cover their uniforms. Max calls to Apollo. "Apollo, come here!" and he dashes across the hangar.

Betty is surprised. "Are you taking Apollo with us?"

"Yes. He likes to fly."

Apollo clamors up the stairs, and they follow him inside. They sit down at their control stations in the rear cabin, and Apollo curls up on the floor behind them. Max turns on the disruptor's main power switch, then flips a bank of toggle switches to the "on" position, and the oscilloscopes light up.

Rolf slowly taxis up the ramp, then rolls out onto the paved road. The night is moonless, and he reaches over and turns on the cockpit's interior lights, which bathes him in an eerie red glow. The bomber's powerful landing lights illuminate the airstrip as it quickly gains speed. Nearing the end of the runway, he gently pulls back on the control yoke, and they lift out of the dense forest and begin an easy climb to altitude.

Soon they approach the cloud base at three thousand feet and pass through a rough section of turbulent air. Their plane buffets as they fly deep into the clouds, and a short time later, they enter a clear valley between two towering columns of dark thunderheads. At nine thousand feet, they pass through the cloud tops and climb steadily into the indigo sky. Below them, and shrouded in darkness, is a sea of puffy white clouds for as far as the eye can see. Rolf calls to Max on the intercom. "We should intercept them in an hour."

"We're ready back here. Let me know when you see them."

An hour later, they catch up with a huge flight of eight hundred Allied bombers flying at twenty-five thousand feet. Rolf levels off at ten thousand feet, the maximum height that they can safely fly without oxygen; however, they are still within the range of their navigation disruptor.

Betty and Max stand behind Rolf, staring up at the long formation that stretches out for several miles, and she is spellbound. "That's a frightening sight, isn't it?"

"Yes. It's unbelievable to see so many of them!"

Rolf looks at the formation. "They have a fighter escort, so we'll have to keep our distance."

Max is confident. "That's alright. Our signal strength is much stronger with this new unit."

They return to their seats in the rear cabin, and he works at his control panel. "Watch this," and he points at a wavelike signal on the oscilloscope's green screen. "We're coming up on their navigation beam now."

Betty stares at the monitor. "Are we close enough?"

"Yes, this new system is very powerful! I just need to determine which beam they're riding and get a lock on it."

The oscilloscope shows a fluttering sine wave, then it settles down into a straight line. Max turns a control wheel, flips a switch, and a second line appears on his screen. He works a large black dial back and forth until the navigation beam begins to bend.

"This will send them east of Berlin. There's nothing there but cows. See if you can get a visual from the dorsal gun turret."

Rolf had the heavy machine gun removed to reduce weight, and Betty sits down in the gunner's seat looking up at the huge formation through the clear plastic bubble. As she watches, the lead bomber makes a navigation correction, and the others follow.

"Max! They're changing course now."

"I don't know what to say! It has never worked this well."

Rolf shadows the flight of bombers for another half hour until it becomes apparent that they can't find their target. Betty watches them closely. "They're breaking up the formation and turning back."

The bombers set a course back to England, and the sky is soon empty of planes. Rolf calls to Max. "It's still early. I'd like to test these engines at altitude."

"What are you thinking?"

Rolf looks back at him. "Let's see how they perform at twenty-five thousand feet."

Max scans his monitor, searching for any aircraft in their area. "Go ahead, there's nothing around us." Then he turns to Betty. "This is a perfect time to test the radar scrambler."

"What do you want me to do?"

"Why don't you operate the dish? I'm interested to see if we can detect any ground-based radar stations that might be tracking us."

Rolf calls to them. "It's going to be cold up there. How is your cabin heat?"

"We're warm back here, and I'm switching to oxygen."

They plug in their masks, and Max attaches a muzzle to Apollo that he adapted into an oxygen mask. Rolf pulls gently on his steering yoke, and the bomber increases its rate of climb effortlessly to twenty-five thousand feet. They take a break and stand behind him in awe of the stunning view. The distant horizon reveals the vastness of the dark sky, and twinkling stars fill the heavens.

Betty is captivated by the unexpected sight. "It's beautiful up here, isn't it? What a wonderful experience!"

Rolf scribbles down a few notes. "This plane is the perfect platform to test your technology!"

Max agrees. "Yes, it is, and our results tonight have been truly impressive!"

They return to their cabin, and he looks at his radar screen to see if the area near them is clear of planes. "Rolf! Let's take her up to her rated ceiling. I'd like to see how the disruptor works at altitude."

As they climb higher, the features of the land below become lost in the darkness, and they continue climbing with ease to thirty-five thousand feet before leveling off. This is the highest that Betty has ever flown, and the breath-taking beauty astounds her.

In the distance, a thin band of iridescent blue hovers above the earth's pitch-black curved horizon, then fades into the crystal-clear indigo sky. The Milky Way, with its densely packed stars, looks like a narrow, vertical, multicolored cloud that seems to touch the earth in front of them.

Betty is stunned. "What an amazing sight!"

Max explains. "It appears as a band like that because it's a vast spiral disk, and we are looking at it on its edge."

Rolf is worried. "I wish we could stay longer, but we better return to base before the sun rises. I don't want to be caught out here in the daylight."

The bomber's supercharged engines continue to run perfectly, and after a few minutes, he makes a wide 180-degree turn and begins their return leg by following their own white contrails. He expertly retraces their course using his compass, and times each leg of their flight with his watch. It wasn't a perfect method, but an experienced pilot could become quite adept at finding their way home.

A PHONE CALL WAKENS MAJOR KRÜGER FROM HIS SLEEP. "This is Field Marshal von Meyer. Are you requesting another engineer?"

He answers him nervously. "Yes, sir. My temporary engineer is returning to Peenemünde soon."

The general is furious. "I never sent you a temporary engineer! You idiot! I've had word of this woman. She must be a spy!"

Major Krüger jumps out of bed. "What!"

"Where is she now?"

"They're testing the latest prototype near Berlin."

"That technology cannot fall into enemy hands. Send fighters after them! If she escapes, I'll have you shot!" and he slams down the phone.

Major Krüger bolts out of bed and quickly calls his fighter command center. "This is Major Krüger. We have an emergency. Our disruptor plane must be forced to return immediately!"

Captain Hofmann, the sleepy squadron leader, jumps to his feet. "Understood! Do you know their location?"

"They followed the Allied bomber formation to Berlin, but they may try to escape to England. You are ordered to shoot to kill," and hangs up.

Captain Hofmann alerts his fighter squadron, and moments later, a siren wails in the distance. Several pilots burst from a building and run through the darkness toward their fighters. Then he calls the base's radar station. "This is Captain Hofmann. I'm looking for our Heinkel bomber. It should be returning from Berlin. Do you have anything on your screen?"

The operators work at their controls. "We're scanning for it now, sir," and the massive three-story antenna slowly sweeps the dark night for the missing plane.

THE EARLY MORNING SKY IS CLOUDY, AND ROLF IS HOME-ward bound. A light rain beats against the windshield as the sun peaks over the distant clouds. Max stares intently at his oscilloscope as his radar scrambler scans the sky ahead of them. Suddenly, he sees blips on his screen and calls to Rolf. "I'm picking up two planes twenty-five miles out. They just crossed the English Channel and are headed in our direction."

Rolf searches for them. "They're probably British fighters going out on patrol." He takes evasive action, and they quickly vanish into the clouds.

Minutes later, a bright blip appears on Max's monitor, and he looks over at Betty. "We are being scanned by the radar station at our base. Something's not right."

She worries they may have discovered her and, thinking fast, she makes a quick suggestion. "Maybe you should test your radar scrambler on it."

"Good idea. If we can defeat it, we will have proven our technology. See if you can focus your parabolic reflector on it."

Betty works at her controls, and her radar dish searches the darkness underneath them. Max turns several dials when suddenly, a dozen flashing blips appear on his screen. "Elizabeth! Come and look at this!"

She walks to his station and stares at it. "Can they see us?"

"No. We're completely masked by these false contacts." Suddenly, the adjacent screen flashes with two new contacts high above the approaching RAF fighters, and Max calls to Rolf. "I'm picking up two more planes diving on the British!"

Minutes later, the Spitfires are jumped by two of Major Krüger's fighters. One of the British planes is hit and goes down in flames, but the second one makes a tight turn and attacks one of the German planes. He tries to throw him off, but a thick trail of smoke streams from his engine, and it bursts into flames as it spirals toward the ground. The lone Spitfire chases after the remaining German fighter, but he avoids him by flying directly into a cloud and vanishes from sight.

Unfortunately, Rolf's luck runs out, and they unexpectedly fly out of the clouds into a wide, sun-drenched valley between two massive cloud banks. The British pilot sees them emerge and dives after them. Rolf yells. "He saw us! Hang on!" and shoves his throttles forward to full power in an attempt to cross the valley to the safety of a distant cloud, but it's too late. The Spitfire closes in on them in a high-speed dive, and attacks with his guns blazing. He scores a direct hit and rakes the side of the bomber with machine gun fire. The cockpit windshield explodes, and the plane shutters from the impact. Large sections of the fuselage rip away, and Betty screams in terror as the bullets rip through the cabin. From the corner of her eye, she sees Max hit in the chest, and he flies off his stool and slams against the rear bulkhead.

Seconds later, they cross the sunlit valley and disappear into the dense clouds. Betty struggles through the rubble, trying to reach Max, but the high voltage feeding their shot-up equipment showers the cabin with sparks, and thick smoke from electrical fires fills the air, making it difficult to see anything.

Betty looks toward the cockpit and calls out. "Rolf! Are you alright?" but there is no response. The dense smoke slowly dissipates through the shot-out windows, and she sees Max lying motionless on the cabin floor in a pool of blood. She pushes a rack of equipment out of the way, rushes to his side, and carefully opens his flight jacket. He struggles to breathe, and pink foam bubbles out of his open chest wound. Acting quickly, she takes off her scarf, presses it against his chest, and his breathing stabilizes.

"Max, can you hear me?" and she wipes spatters of blood from his face.

Barely conscious, he mutters softly. "Yes."

"Hold on! I'm going to get you to a hospital."

But before she can leave, he pulls her toward him and whispers. "If anything happens to me, will you take care of Apollo?"

"Yes, yes, of course," and she takes his hand and places it on Apollo, who is unhurt and lying next to him. "Apollo is right by your side. I've got to help Rolf."

His lips tremble, and he mutters softly. "Throw the scrambler overboard!"

Tears stream from Betty's eyes. "I will."

She leans forward, kisses his forehead, then forces her way back through the tangle of broken electrical wires. They arc against the metal equipment racks and shower her with sparks as she pushes past them. She pulls a pair of wire cutters out of a tool kit and frantically cuts the connecting wires to the scrambler. As she works, she calls out again. "Rolf! Can you hear me?" but there is no answer, only the sound of the wind roaring through the shattered windows as the stricken bomber slowly spirals down through the clouds.

Moments later, she cuts the scrambler free, pulls it out of the rack, and tosses it out a shattered window. She forces her way through the debris to the cockpit and struggles to open the door. An icy blast of wind from the blown-out windshield slams into her as she drops into the copilot's seat. Rolf is sitting upright with his arms by his side, and she shakes his shoulder. "Are you alright?" He slumps forward into the instrument panel, revealing the back of his blood-soaked jacket.

"Oh, no!"

The heavily damaged plane shakes violently, and the gusting wind blasts through the shattered windshield, pressing Betty into her seat. She struggles with all her might to regain control and slowly flies out of the flat spin and into bright sunlight. Below her is the wind-torn North Sea, an icy grave for many pilots. If something were to happen, and she had to crash land at sea, she would die of hypothermia long before anyone could rescue her.

She knows Max needs immediate medical attention, and the quickest way to get help is at Kenley Field, which isn't that far away. It's only a twenty-minute flight across the English Channel to safety; however, her airspeed continues to drop because of the heavy battle damage, and she begins to lose altitude. Engine failure is now a real possibility, but if that happened, and she's close enough to England, she might be able to glide to one of the coastal beaches.

Betty's immediate concern is that Major Krüger most likely sent fighters to search for her, and she slowly turns the dial on her radio. Suddenly she hears cryptic chatter between two German fighters. From the clarity of their voices, she knows they are not far away, and is paralyzed in fear. "Damn it!"

High above the English Channel, two Messerschmitt Bf 109 fighters fly side-by-side above a layer of broken cloud cover. Far below them, the low coastal cloud's part and they see Betty's Heinkel bomber. The lead fighter dips its wing steeply to one side, and dives, which allows him to keep her plane in his sight.

All Betty needs is a few more minutes, and she'll be across the North Sea to safety, but until then, she's in mortal danger. She worriedly searches the sky in front of her, then glances up at her rearview mirror, and sees a flash of sunlight reflect off one of the diving fighters. Immediately, she breaks radio silence and calls for help. "Kenley Tower, come in. Kenley Tower, come in."

"This is Kenley Tower. We read you. Who is this?"

"Lt. Bauer. I'm returning in a stolen Heinkel bomber. Request immediate fighter cover! I repeat. Request immediate fighter cover!"

"We have fighters in your area. Stand by."

Suddenly, her radio crackles with a familiar voice. "Betty, this is Andy. Where are you?"

"I'm off the coast of Ipswich. Two German fighters are closing in on me from above."

"Hang on. I'm not far away."

A few moments later, the radio crackles again with another familiar voice.

"Betty! It's Charlie. I'm directly ahead of you with Andy."

"Boy, am I ever glad to see you guys!"

She watches as the pair of high-performance Supermarine Spitfires approach her at nearly four hundred miles an hour. These are the latest versions and are outfitted with four twenty mm cannons, and a new supercharged Rolls-Royce Griffin engine, making it a much-feared plane. They fly at her head-on, then split up and pass on each side of her. As they flash by, she can see straight into Andy's cockpit. He's wearing a white scarf and raises one hand slightly as he blasts by her in hot pursuit of the approaching fighters.

The German pilots see them, and immediately bank steeply to the side and return to Germany. The end of the war is close, and they don't want anything to do with the new Spitfires. Andy lets them go, and circles back to help Betty. He and Charlie fly next to her and are shocked to see the amount of damage to her plane. Fuel from her shot-up wing tanks streams across her bomber's wings and large sections of the plane's fuselage are missing. Andy is surprised to see Betty flying the bomber.

"Where the bloody hell did you steal that from?"

Her controls rattle and shake violently, and the wind howls through the shot-out windows. "It's a long story."

"Are you wounded?"

"I'm okay, but the pilot is dead, and I have a badly injured passenger. Can you call ahead for medical help?"

"Affirmative!"

She scans the gauges on her instrument panel. "I'm losing fuel, coolant is low, and my oil pressure is dropping." The wind blowing through the shot-out windshield is deafening, and she yells into her microphone. "I don't think I can keep it together much longer."

Andy's voice is calm and reassuring. "Kenley Field is dead ahead. You are only minutes away."

The howling wind distorts her vision. "I think I see it!" She is flying low over the frigid North Sea and her situation is very serious. The minutes pass slowly, and she successfully crosses the wave-tossed English Channel. Below her are the green fields of England, and safety.

Andy continues to advise her with a calm voice as she approaches Kenley airfield. "That's good. You're lined up perfectly. Only a few miles to go."

She struggles with her poorly responding controls. "I've got red lights on the landing gear, and my oil pressure just dropped to zero! I'm not going to make it!"

Andy is highly experienced at making emergency landings and warns her. "I need you to trust me on this. I want you to switch off your engines."

"Do what!"

"Switch off your engines! You're soaked in fuel. One spark from your exhaust and you'll explode. You want them cold when you belly in."

Betty immediately pulls back on the throttle levers, switches off her engines, and an eerie silence fills the cockpit with only the sound of the wind, and flapping shreds of metal banging against the fuselage. Andy's voice is reassuring. "Okay, that's good. Keep up your air speed the best you can. Wait until the last minute, then lift your nose, and stall it just before you hit the ground."

She yells into her microphone. "I'm losing control!" Betty is still way short of the runway and struggles with the controls, but there is nothing she can do, and the bomber slowly sinks toward the ground.

One of her wheels is down, and Andy warns her. "Betty! Wheels up! I repeat, wheels up!"

She looks at her instrument panel. The "Wheels Up" light is red, indicating that a wheel is down. She flips the switch several times, but there is no response, and she is out of time. The ground rushes toward her, and she braces for impact. The huge bomber belly lands in the tall grass at speed, and the landing gear rips off, lurching it violently to the side. It bounces into the air a few feet, then slams into a cluster of small trees shearing off half of the right wing.

Dirt and pieces of the plane fly in all directions as it plows across the deep grass of a large field. It bursts through an old wooden fence, then skids sideways before coming to a smoldering stop in an enormous cloud of dust and smoke.

Andy and Charlie fly low over the wreckage to check on her, but they can't see anything because of the smoke, and circle back to the airfield. They taxi at speed, jump out of their planes, and run through the tall grass toward her. The sound of sirens wailing in the distance pierces the quiet countryside as emergency vehicles race to the crash site. Chunks of debris rain to the ground and an enormous cloud of dust settles onto the smoldering bomber.

Betty is unconscious and slumped over the controls, but after a few minutes, she begins to move. The air is filled with the pungent smell of aviation fuel, and the acrid stench of burning electrical wires. Dense smoke fills the cockpit, and she slowly realizes where she is. Ever since she watched her B-17 catch fire and explode, she's had nightmares of being burned to death, and she's terrified.

Her instinct to escape is strong, and she struggles to untangle herself from the jumble of debris that surrounds her. At last, she is free and staggers into the darkened rear cabin just as Andy and Charlie force their way in through a side door. Exhausted, she leans against the bulkhead as they rush to her side.

Andy asks her, "Are you alright?"

"I'm okay, but I've got a wounded passenger in the back. Can you help him?"

Charlie warns Andy. "I'll check on him. Better get her out of here. There's avgas everywhere."

The interior is dark except for sunlight streaming through bullet holes along the walls and ceiling. Attached to the wall next to the open door is a flashlight. Charlie removes it and walks toward the back of the cabin. He pushes past a maze of smoking electronic equipment and carefully works his way through the rubble.

Suddenly, Apollo's low, guttural growl warns him not to come any closer, and he stops dead in his tracks. His flashlight probes the darkness, and he sees a body covered in blood with an enormous dog standing guard directly over him. He takes a step forward and tries to calm him. "It's okay, big fella. Good dog."

And with that, Apollo's growl turns into a toothy snarl, and he crouches down, ready to attack. The hair on his back bristles as Charlie takes another step closer, and he can see that the dog's next move will be a full-on charge. He carefully steps back and calls to Andy. "There's a huge attack dog back here."

Andy turns to Betty. "Charlie says there's an attack dog back there, and he can't get past him."

"Oh my gosh. I forgot about Apollo." She steps into the dimly lit cabin and calls to him in German. "Apollo, come here!"

Apollo immediately stops growling and charges past Charlie, knocking him against the fuselage, and bounds through the rubble to Betty, excitedly wagging his tail. She bends down, grabs his collar, and calls to Charlie. "I've got the dog. How is the professor?"

He struggles through the rubble. "I can't tell. I'm going to need help to get him out of here."

Betty and Andy enter the cabin and rush to Max's side. Charlie looks up at them as they approach. "Be careful. He's got a nasty chest wound!"

Andy bends down to help, and they struggle to move him. "I've got his arms. See if you can lift his feet."

They carry him through the darkened cabin, exit through the side door, and lay him down in the grass, away from the wreckage. A military ambulance arrives, and Mattie and her medics run toward his lifeless body. She carefully opens his shirt and removes the scarf that was plugging the hole in his chest. Blood spurts into the air, and she quickly covers his wound with a large bandage. His breathing stabilizes, but it is very shallow. The severity of his wounds horrifies them, and Betty asks her, "Is he going to make it?"

"It's hard to tell. He's having difficulty breathing, and he's lost a lot of blood, but I've seen worse pull through."

Max is unconscious, and Betty tenderly cradles him in her arms. She whispers to him in German. "We made it, darling. You are only minutes from the hospital," and she kisses his forehead. "I love you, Max. You are the love of my life!"

The medics arrive carrying a gurney. "I'm sorry, mam, but we need to move him."

Mattie helps them lift his body onto a stretcher, and they load him into the ambulance. It pulls away with its siren screaming, and races toward the hospital. Betty watches it leave as tears stream down her cheeks.

Mattie tries to comfort her. "He's in good hands now," and she looks at the wrecked bomber. "What about the pilot?"

Betty shakes her head. "He was hit by cannon fire. He's gone."

Andy notices several broken electrical cables sparking against the fuselage and warns them. "Get back! This thing could blow at any minute," and they quickly distance themselves from the wreckage. A small spark-induced flame licks up the side of an engine cowling, and a sheet of low blue flames fans out across the top of the wing. Andy sees it, and yells. "It's going to explode!" and everyone starts running. Moments later, the flames reach the fuel tank, and the bomber explodes violently, sending a huge orangish-red fireball hundreds of feet into the air. A towering black column of thick smoke rises into the clear sky, and the three of them stare silently at the burning wreckage.

Andy looks at Betty. "It's incredible to see that you are still alive. When we lost contact with you, we assumed you were dead."

"Well, it's a long story."

He laughs. "It's always a long story with you!"

"My original contact was killed before I got there. I stayed a few days to familiarize myself with the technology, but I was badly wounded in a strafing attack and spent months recovering." She pauses for a moment. "I'm exhausted. Let's sit down somewhere, and I'll tell you the whole story."

Andy looks at her worriedly. "You look pretty shaken up. Are you okay?"

"Yes, but I need to get out of this flight suit," and she unzips the dirty jump suit, which reveals her Gestapo officer's uniform.

Charlie stares at it. "Wow! Where did you get that uniform?"

"It's another long story!"

He laughs. "I'll bet! I think a good stiff drink would help right now!"

Betty puts her arms around them. "You're reading my mind!" and they walk away.

Andy pulls up in front of the Red Lion, their squadron's favorite pub, and they enter. A large group of pilots are singing loudly at the piano and Betty, still dressed in her Gestapo uniform, follows Andy and Charlie with Apollo at her side. Charlie is wearing Betty's Gestapo hat, and he goose-steps forward and yells loudly. "Sieg Heil!"

The shocked airmen stop singing and turn in amazement. Charlie clicks his heals together, raises his arm in a Nazi salute, and places his finger under his nose mimicking Hitler's mustache. Using his fake German accent, he threatens them. "You are all under arrest! The Führer can't sleep with all this ruckus! You're to be shot at dawn!" and the room breaks into laughter.

A friend of Charlie's approaches and slaps him on the back. "Bloody hell, mate. You really had us going for a while."

Charlie laughs. "I wish I had a camera. You should have seen the look on your faces!"

Another airman approaches and stares admiringly at Betty. "Where did you get that uniform?" and then he notices Apollo. "And that dog! Where did you find a fantastic animal like that?"

"Well, I . . ."

Andy interrupts him. "We'll tell you all about it later. Right now, the lady needs a drink." The pilots return to their piano, and the good times continue. He motions toward the back of the room. "There's a quiet table over there," and orders a round of drinks.

Charlie is full of questions. "Did you ever figure out how the disruptor works?"

Betty thinks quickly and decides it would be best to keep her story simple and not reveal anything about the radar scrambler. "The professor explained the general theory to me, but the original plane, and disruptor equipment, had a lot of technical issues, and only worked intermittently."

"But you were gone for five months."

"Believe me, I know! Early on, an American fighter strafed the car I was riding in, and it rolled down a mountain. I ended up in a German field hospital, and spent ten weeks recovering from my injuries."

Andy is shocked. "Are you okay now?"

She takes a long sip from her drink. "Yes. Completely."

"Did you get the film?"

Betty laughs and shakes her head. "There was no film. Our intel boys have been watching too many Hollywood movies. It's never that easy!"

"So, where is the information?"

"You were standing in it."

Andy is confused. "What do you mean?"

"The bomber. That's the disruptor, and the professor invented it."

"Will he help rebuild it?"

"Yes, of course. He's on our side."

Charlie looks over at Apollo. "Bloody hell! Where did you find that dog? He's fantastic!"

"His name is Apollo, and he's the professor's attack dog."

Andy continues to question her. "We assumed that you were killed. What happened over there?"

"Well, I'm lucky to be alive. Nothing happened according to plan."

He sighs. "I tried to tell you . . ."

"Yes, I know. War is unpredictable."

"So, what does all this mean?"

Betty explains. "Their disrupter technology is very impressive, and incredibly dangerous, but it was poorly engineered and barely functioned. I decided to stay and help them so I could develop a counter measure. Initially, it kept catching on fire, and it took a total redesign to strengthen the signal and stabilize the high voltage current required to operate it. Their laboratory was underground and there was no way to escape. It just took longer than I expected."

Charlie questions her. "How did you end up with that plane?"

"My chance to escape came last night when we flight-tested the new disruptor system for the first time. After we left, they somehow found out I was a spy and sent fighters to shoot us down. We were late returning to our base, and a Spitfire spotted our plane and strafed us, killing our pilot and wounding the professor.

"We were spinning down through the clouds, but I was able to regain control. I lost the Spitfire in the clouds and headed for England. While I was crossing the English Channel, German fighters spotted me, and you know the rest."

Andy takes a sip of his drink and sets his glass down. "I told you it would be dangerous. I'm shocked that you remained undetected for so long."

"Yes, but as always, a lot of it is just plain luck."

Charlie can't believe what he's hearing. "What a story! We bombed several airbases in that area. You were lucky they didn't kill you!"

"They hit us hard, but I was a mile away in an underground bomb-proof hangar."

"That's pretty clever of them. No wonder we couldn't get to it!"

Betty explains. "The Nazis had thought of everything, but our bombing campaign totally collapsed their supply chain and communication networks. I only survived because the phone lines were always out, and it was difficult to contact Berlin."

"What about the plans? Did you get a copy?"

"That was impossible. Each schematic was on a sheet of drafting paper two feet by three feet and there were more than a hundred sheets."

"So where are they?"

"They're back at the underground base in my office. The initial plans were just a jumble of mark-outs and redlines, and I had to redesign the entire system."

"Does it really work?"

"Oh, yes. We tested the new version and shadowed a night bomber formation to Berlin. It worked perfectly, and we diverted them off their target."

Andy looks relieved. "Well, at least they don't have their weapon anymore, and we have you and the professor."

Betty sets down her drink. "Fortunately, the bomber was a prototype, and there isn't another one."

"Do you know how it works?"

"Yes, and I know exactly how to defeat it."

Andy is excited. "I think you've discovered something that might help bring this war to an early conclusion. Good job, Lt. Bauer!" and pats her on the back.

Charlie can't believe what she went through. "What a story! I'm glad you made it back in one piece," and he raises his glass in a salute to her.

"Thanks, guys, Max and I would have been dead if you didn't show up when you did!" and they touch their glasses in a toast.

Andy sets his beer down. "I hate to tell you this, but your unit declared you missing in action and presumed dead. You should call your uncle Karl. They probably sent him one of those *Killed in Action* telegrams."

Betty is shocked. "Oh, no! I'll try to get a call in to him tomorrow."

"Also, the Army Air Force recently disbanded your unit. I guess there are enough male pilots now. It looks like you're a civilian again."

She is stunned. "I don't know what to say! So much has changed!"

Andy sees that she's exhausted. "It's getting late, and you've had a big day. Why don't we drop you off at Matties? I'm sure she will be excited to see you. We can go over the details later."

"Thanks, guys. I really appreciate your help today!"

Andy's staff car stops across the street from the nurse's barracks, and Betty and Apollo get out. She stands at the passenger window. "Thanks for the lift."

He smiles at her. "Better rest up. We'll stop by tomorrow and see how you're doing."

Betty waves goodbye, and they drive off. She walks toward the nurse's barracks, worrying about her uncle Karl. He's the only family member that she has, and she knows that he loves her dearly. She called him the night before leaving for England, and they talked for a long time. After arriving in Britain, they had written each other often, but that was five months ago. Exhausted, she decides to wait until the following day to call him.

She climbs the steps and stands in the open doorway. The surprised nurses stare at her Gestapo uniform and attack dog, not knowing what to do. Suddenly, Dottie recognizes her and runs to greet her. "Betty! Where have you been? They told us you were dead!"

"Well, it's a long story!"

"And your dog! He's beautiful!" She reaches out to pet him but stops. "Will he bite?"

"No. He's a good boy."

The rest of the nurse's surround her, and she looks around the room. "Where's Mattie?"

"She's still at work, but she should be here soon," and they walk with her to the back of the barracks. All the attention overwhelms Apollo, but he seems to love every minute. She hangs up her Gestapo uniform and slips into a robe.

Minutes later Mattie walks into the room and runs to greet her. "I couldn't believe my eyes when I saw you. We thought you were dead! What happened?"

Betty laughs. "It's a story better told over a cold drink!" She has been extremely worried about Max and asks, "How is the professor?"

Mattie shakes her head negatively. "I'm sorry, Betty, but he didn't make it. He lost too much blood. The doctors worked on him for more than an hour, but there wasn't anything they could do."

Betty is caught off guard, and tears fill her eyes. Mattie's news is devastating, and she struggles to hide her emotions. "Oh, no!"

"Was he a friend of yours?"

"Yes. We worked together for a while."

"I'm sorry, but in war bad things can happen to good people."

"What did they do with his body?"

"Because he was wearing a Nazi uniform, they took him to the military morgue. His body will be returned to Germany after the war."

"I understand. Thanks, Mattie," and she slumps to her bed. She knew Max's wound was bad, but she can't believe that he's gone. He was the greatest love that she'd ever known, and they had made so many plans for the future. It had been an extremely emotional day, and she needs to be alone. She picks up her towel and asks Mattie, "Could you watch Apollo for me. I'm going to take a long, hot shower."

The following morning Betty is dressed in her nurse's uniform helping in post-op as before. Mattie enters and walks over to her. "Thanks for your help, but you should rest up after your ordeal."

"I'd rather keep busy, and we've got a lot of wounded this morning."

"Yes, bomber crews. They were badly shot up on a raid over Schweinfurt."

Betty looks around the crowded hallway. "I haven't seen Dr. Hunter. Is he on shift today?"

Mattie has a sad look on her face. "Oh, that's right, you don't know. He took his boat out one day and never returned. They think he might have hit a sea mine."

It's another crushing blow to her. "Oh, no! He was such a great guy, and always doing something crazy."

"I know, we all miss him."

The deaths of two very special people in her life were too much for her, and she sinks into a chair and cries. Mattie puts her hand on her shoulder and tries to console her. "I'm so sorry, Betty."

DAYS LATER, SHE AND APOLLO ARE UP AT DAWN FOR THEIR usual morning walk, and Betty is enjoying her favorite time of the day. Ever since Max's death, she and Apollo have become inseparable friends, and at times, she took him to visit her patients. He is always a big hit as he lifts the spirits of the wounded boys.

Their walk takes them along a remote security fence, and Betty likes to relax at a stone bench on a low ridge that overlooks the rolling hills of the English countryside. Someone, maybe a century ago, built it and it's now their favorite place to stop and rest.

Betty is completely devastated by the loss of Max and Blake. She had put on a brave face, but her emotions finally catch up with her, and she sits down and cries for a long time. Max, the love of her life had been killed, and so had her good friend Blake. Her body trembles, and her hands quiver uncontrollably as fear and depression finally set in. Apollo sits quietly staring up at her with his big brown eyes, and she leans forward and hugs him with both arms. She sobs for several minutes, then kisses him on his forehead. "I love you, Apollo. Promise me you'll never leave me."

What happened in Germany had changed her life forever. She had discovered a connection to her heritage that she had suppressed for decades, and for the first time she felt a powerful need to belong to Germany. Her thoughts about going home began with her long talks with Max, and they had become a pivotal turning point in her life, but now she would have to wait until the end of the war to implement her dreams.

Andy had asked her what she was going to do after the war, and it weighs heavily on her mind. If she returned to America, there would be continued gender discrimination, and poor job opportunities for women. As for Britain, she had no ties there at all. Then there was Germany. Hitler's reign of terror would end someday soon, and the massive reconstruction phase would begin. Andy was right, there could be many business opportunities for them. It would be a struggle at first, but the future could be bright, and the quality of life would be worth her early sacrifices.

Apollo stares quietly at her, and she runs her hands through his long fur. As she strokes his neck, she notices the large medallion hanging from the heavy chain. On the front is an Iron Cross and on the back is Apollo's military identification. She unhooks the medallion and flings it into the brush. "Apollo, you are now officially retired from the German army . . . and your new name is going to be Wolfie. Do you like that?"

He remains motionless, and quietly stares at her as she ponders her next move. Surely there would be a debriefing, and she needed to be careful with what she told the investigators, or they could construe her actions as helping the enemy. She had helped to develop an enemy's advanced weapon system, and it was something that could have changed the outcome of the war in Germany's favor. If they misunderstood her position, the penalty could be death or imprisonment, so she decides to tell them as little as possible. Above all she needs to protect the radar scrambler. Her intimate knowledge of Max's advanced technologies might become useful after the war.

Tears run down her cheeks, and she stares at her shaking hands. She notices her engagement ring and slips it off her finger. Overwhelmed with sadness, she slides it on a finger on her other hand. Wolfie tries to comfort her and lays his enormous head in her lap. Betty strokes him lovingly, "I love you," and kisses him. Feeling a little better she stands and wipes away her tears. "Okay, big boy. Let's go!"

Wolfie knows what that means and bolts off down the trail.

Later in the day, she and Wolfie are walking across the lawn in front of the Headquarters building. Andy sees them, and he runs to catch up. "Good afternoon! Where are you going?"

Betty is irritated. "To the dentist."

"The dentist? What's wrong?"

"I want to get this damn implant out of my mouth. Every time I eat something, I think I'm going to die!"

"What are you talking about?"

"The resistance insisted that I have a cyanide pill implanted in my molar. It's just a minor item that our intel boys forgot to tell me about."

"Bloody hell!"

She hands him the leash. "Would you watch Wolfie for me? This won't take long."

"You changed his name to Wolfie?"

"Yes, he's a civilian now."

She enters the dentist's office, and Wolfie sits motionless staring at the door that she just went through. Andy, who knows nothing about dogs, tugs lightly on his leash. "Okay, Wolfie. Let's go," but he continues to stare at the door that Betty disappeared into and doesn't move an inch. Andy pulls on his leash once again. "Come on, Wolfie. Good doggy."

He slowly turns his enormous head and gives Andy a toothy snarl. A half hour later, Betty exits the dentist's office and sees that Andy and Wolfie are right where she left them. "Oh, you're so sweet, but you didn't have to wait for me."

"Is everything okay?"

"Yes. It was easier than I thought," and speaks to Wolfie in doggy talk. "Were you a good little boy?"

Andy looks down at him and sighs. "Oh, yeah. We got along famously."

CHAPTER 17

VICTORY DAY IN EUROPE

IT'S MAY 8, 1945, AND A BEAUTIFUL DAY. BETTY'S SHIFT JUST ended, and she's enjoying her walk back to the nurse's barracks. A flock of birds chirp in the nearby trees, and the typically busy airfield is unusually quiet. The ringing of a distant church bell echoes across the farmlands, and a warm breeze filled with the scent of spring fills the air.

Curiously, church bells from the surrounding villages also begin to ring. Of course, there had been air raid warnings in the past, but today seems somehow different. Ahead of her is the squadron's headquarters building, so she decides to drop by to see if someone there knows what's happening. As she approaches, she hears the muffled sounds of excited voices coming from inside. Suddenly, the front door flies open, and several people rush out and run past her.

One of them is Charlie. "Ah, there you are! I've been looking all over for you! Winston Churchill just announced to the world that Hitler surrendered! The war is over!"

Betty is stunned. "I can't believe it!"

He gives her an enormous hug. "Time to celebrate!" and grabs her hand. "Come on, let's find Andy."

They dash up the stairs and run through an excited throng of people exiting the building. The crowded main corridor is filled with people shaking hands and hugging each other as excitement fills the air. Betty sees Andy talking to someone, and she runs to him, almost knocking him down with a flying hug.

"We made it! Let's head down to our watering hole one last time!"

They enter their favorite pub, and it's already packed with excited pilots noisily celebrating and toasting their friends. Some are in tears with emotion, while others are reflective, knowing that the war is finally over, and somehow, they had made it out alive. Flying in combat was very dangerous work, and the long years of war had taken many lives. It could be mechanical trouble, being jumped by an enemy fighter when you least expected it, or foul weather. Some had parachuted to safety, only to be taken prisoner, and others just vanished, never to be heard from again.

As they weave their way toward the crowded bar, they occasionally stop to shake hands with friends. Some were new replacements that they had only known for a little while, but all of them were brothers-in-arms. War was a shared experience that would bond many of them together for a lifetime.

Andy is the first to the bar and orders a bottle of champagne. He calls to Betty. "Grab that table. I'll be right there."

He returns a few minutes later with their drinks and sits down. Charlie holds up his glass. "How about a toast to the three of us? How we made it this far is a miracle!" and they touch glasses.

Betty makes the next toast. "May we never forget our time together!"

Andy looks up from his drink. "Through it all, there were some good times." He has a big grin on his face and smiles at Betty. "I'll always remember you dressed in that Nazi uniform, and Charlie pretending he was Hitler!"

Charlie laughs. "We really had the boys going with that one! By the way, where's Wolfie? He was a big part of that night, too."

"He stays with the girls when I'm at work. They adore him, and he loves all the attention."

"Are you bringing him back to America?"

"Yes, for sure. We shared a lifetime of adventure together, and with Max gone, he helped me through some pretty tough times." She pauses for a moment. "I should have told you, but over the months of working together, he and I became close. We planned to marry after the war."

"Andy and I guessed there was more to your story," and he puts his hand on her arm. "I'm truly sorry, Betty."

"Thanks, Charlie. I should have said something, but it was too painful to talk about." She picks up her beer mug. "Well, what are you guys going to do now?"

Andy smiles. "I need to spend some quality time with Olivia and get reacquainted with my family. My girls are growing up way too fast, and I don't want to miss out on that."

Betty asks Charlie, "What are your plans?"

"Well, tonight I'm going to ask Shelagh to marry me."

"That's wonderful! I really like her and you two make a great couple."

Andy extends his hand. "You're a lucky guy, and she's a great girl. I wish you two the best." He turns to Betty and asks, "What's next for you?"

"I guess I'll go back to California. I have a job waiting for me at my uncle's company."

"Well, before you decide on that, Charlie and I have a proposition for you." A large group of celebrating pilots sing loudly, and Andy looks back at the boisterous crowd. "It's a little noisy here. Let's go somewhere more private."

"Sure. Where do you suggest?"

"How about the King and Country Inn?"

Betty is excited. "Wow. I've never been there. That's a pretty fancy place!"

Andy pushes his chair back. "It's time to celebrate, and I'm buying."

They soon arrive at the exclusive King and Country Inn and the friendly manager shows them to a table overlooking the River Thames. All the mystery has Betty curious. "Well, I'm dying to find out what this is about. I can't imagine what you two are up to."

Andy lays out their plan. "Charlie and I have an idea about the future, and it involves the three of us. Now that the war is over, the reconstruction phase will start, and it has to happen quickly. The massive destruction of Germany has created vast business opportunities, and there's going to be a tremendous period of rebuilding that will last for decades. What I'm suggesting is that we combine our talents, and our love of flying, and be part of it."

Betty is shocked that they would ask her to join them. "I'm interested, but what kind of business opportunities are you talking about?"

He continues. "My family owns a large factory here in London that manufactures war material. My father wants to me to modernize our plant and take over the business so he can retire."

Charlie lays out the logistics. "Just out of curiosity, Andy and I drove over to one of the military surplus yards to look for equipment that his factory could use. They were auctioning off a mountain of supplies, including hundreds of airplanes, and they're selling them for the price of scrap metal.

"It gave me an idea. Why not purchase a couple of cargo planes and start an air freight company? Andy's father talked to his government contacts and was told that they have an urgent need to transport supplies into the British Occupation Zone.

"Millions of people are homeless, jobless, and without food. The Soviets control half of Germany, and the remaining half is split into thirds, with Britain, France, and America responsible for the administration and reconstruction of their sectors. We could purchase a couple of cargo planes and get going right away. It would be hard work and long hours, but good money.

"I know your passion is electrical engineering, but this would provide you with an immediate income. Later on, you would have the capital to develop that construction company that you've always talked about. So, what do you think?"

Betty loves their idea, as flying is dear to her heart. She had thought about the possibility of starting an electrical construction company in Germany, but didn't have the money, or the connections, to get started. "Yes, of course. I want to be part of it!"

Andy continues. "Modernizing our factory is going to take up most of my time, but I could indemnify the startup financing, and I'm pretty sure I can get us government contracts. You and Charlie would run the company."

Charlie is overflowing with enthusiasm and has everything planned out. "Shelagh just graduated from business school, and she can handle the office. You and I would do the flying until we could afford to hire some help. We'll pick up freight from the channel ports like Southampton, Le Havre, Rotterdam, and so on, and fly it to inland cities. We would base our operations somewhere around London for now."

"That sounds exciting!"

Andy looks at her. "So, we're all in agreement?"

"Yes. Count me in. What's first on the agenda?"

"I think we might have found one plane. We just have to make a bid on it. As for the other one, they're scattered all over the country, so it could take a couple of weeks."

Charlie interjects. "I found a small hangar that we can use for now, but it will take time to find something that's big enough to handle our cargo planes."

Andy asks her, "Have you wrapped up things at the hospital?"

"Yes. I just need to find a cottage to rent and buy a car."

"Do you need any help?"

"Thanks, but you guys have plenty to do."

Andy suggests. "Check out the surplus yards. They're practically giving away staff cars. You can find something better later on."

"Okay. Give me a couple of days and I'll check back with you."

The following day, Betty and Wolfie take a taxi to one of the largest surplus yards. She wanted to buy a small British car, but Wolfie was too big to fit in the back. The taxi drops them off in front of a sprawling salvage yard, and she approaches the guard at the entrance gate. After explaining her situation, he points her to a long row of staff cars. She walks over to them, but they are big and ugly, so she continues looking. Parked next to them are military ambulances, but they are too large for her purpose.

Betty is getting discouraged when she notices something at the far end of the row. It's a white 1940 Ford ambulance with a chrome siren mounted on the roof, and a large red cross painted on the side. She opens the rear door and Wolfie jumps in. There's plenty of head room for him, and lots of space. She sits down, turns the ignition key, and the engine starts immediately.

An hour later, they are driving down a country road near the airbase looking for a cottage to rent, but with no luck. Ahead of her, a tractor stops, and the farmer opens a gate to a large field. She pulls over and asks if he knows of a rental in the area. He tells her they are hard to find, but that he has something she might be interested in, so she follows him to his farm.

On a knoll overlooking the rolling farmland is a small cottage with a thatched-roof, limestone walls, and a fenced-in garden. She walks through the rooms, then looks at Wolfie. "Well, big boy. Do you want to live here?" He goes from room to room, checking on things, then hears something and dashes out the back door. A startled cat runs across the backyard and claws its way up a wooden fence. Betty turns to the farmer. "This is delightful. I'll take it."

Later that day, she moves into her cottage, and after dinner, celebrates her new future with a glass of champagne. A violent storm rages outside and sheets of rain whip at her little bungalow as she and Wolfie warm themselves in front of a roaring fire. That night, her reoccurring nightmare once again interrupts her sleep. It never changes. The Hitler Youth walks out of a huge orange-red fireball with a hangman's noose over his shoulder. She cowers in the shadows, immobilized in fear, and he reaches out to grab her.

Suddenly, she wakes up, her heart pounds, and perspiration drips from her face. She bolts upright in bed, only to realize it was just a dream. Afraid to go back to sleep, she pulls the duvet off her bed and picks up her pillow. Wolfie is sleeping by the fireplace, and his massive body is stretched out full length. She lays down next to him, places her pillow by his head, and covers up with her duvet. Placing her arm across his wide shoulders, she falls back to sleep.

The following morning is sunny, as Betty and Wolfie arrive at their new hangar. Andy and Charlie are inside perusing navigation maps and, upon hearing them approach, Charlie looks up and laughs. "Well, it looks like you've been to the surplus yard!"

"Wolfie loves it and with all that glass, he can see what's happening around him."

"It's a great idea. Did you find a rental?"

"I asked a farmer if he knew of anything in the area. Turns out he had a cute cottage with a thatched roof, so I rented it."

Charlie is curious. "What did you think of the salvage yard? They've got everything under the sun there."

"I'm a little embarrassed, but I bought something else as well."

Andy looks at her and grins. "Oh, no. I've seen that look before!"

Charlie pushes his baseball cap back and laughs. "Ok. What did you buy?"

She pauses for a moment, then sheepishly admits. "An airplane."

He can't stop laughing. "Oh, no! Which one?"

"I've never seen anything like it, and it was love at first sight."

"So, how much did you pay for this mystery plane?"

"Sixty quid."

Charlie laughs. "Well, at least it didn't cost that much."

Paddy is nearby and overheard her. "So, what is it?"

She gives him a sheepish look. "It's a German Stork."

"A Stork! That's a beautiful plane! I've worked on several of them."

Betty is astonished that he is familiar with it. "Really!"

"Sure. General Rommel used one in North Africa, and Field Marshal Montgomery had one as his personal aircraft. During the war, the Allies captured quite a few. Even the Soviets copied the design. What condition is it in?"

"It looks pretty new. They were going to scrap it, and it was too beautiful to be crushed."

Talk of the unusual plane captures Charlie's interest. "Did you try to start it?"

"The battery was dead, and there wasn't an easy way to fly it out, so I'm not sure how to get it out of there."

Paddy asks her, "Do you have paperwork on it?"

"Yes." She reaches into the ambulance and hands him an envelope. "Here's the Bill of Sale."

He flips through the documents. "Hmm. It looks like you bought the latest version. If it's alright with you, I'll go get it tomorrow."

Betty is surprised. "Really? I didn't know you were a pilot."

Paddy gives her a mischievous smile. "I'm not. The wings fold against the fuselage. I'll just put the tail in the back of my truck and pull it here."

Andy laughs and shakes his head. "It sounds like you bought a great plane, Betty. It will be a fun addition to our little air force."

As they walk back to the hangar, she asks Paddy, "We've got some time before our first C-47 arrives. Can I help you clean her up?"

"Sure. All it takes is soap, hot water, and a lot of hard work. I'll go through the engine and give her a complete tune-up."

"Thanks, Paddy. She's beautiful, and I can't tell you how excited I am to get her flying again."

The next morning, Andy and Charlie leave to look for their cargo plane, and Betty and Paddy drive to the salvage yard to pick up her Stork. It was easy to get it ready, and Paddy pulled it backwards in his pickup truck, creating quite a stir with the locals. They arrived at their hangar a few hours later without incident. She helped him unfold the wings and then they went to work and removed the trash and spare parts from the plane's cabin. Dirt and grime covered the Stork, but, as usual, Betty was up for the challenge and washed her new plane.

Both the Nazis and the Allied forces valued the Stork as a tandem seat reconnaissance plane. Its fuselage is forest green, and the belly and the underside of the wings are painted sky-blue, making it an attractive camouflage scheme. The reason that the Germans called it the Stork was because of the long length of the landing gear, which allowed it to land on rough terrain. However, the most unusual feature was the plexiglass cabin enclosure. It began low on the fuselage and angled up at forty-five-degrees for a foot, then sloped back to a narrow roofline, providing an extraordinary view, both straight down and outward, for both the pilot and the passenger.

After two days of hard work, she had her plane looking factory fresh. Paddy finished his engine tune-up, and it started right up and ran beautifully. The next step was the fun part. It was time for her flight-test, and it didn't disappoint her when it lifted off the ground for the first time. After an hour, Betty returned to the hangar and picked up Paddy. She wanted to treat him to something special and, as a surprise, she flew him to a coastal fishing village overlooking the English Channel for lunch. They landed on a deserted country road and taxied to a small restaurant. The owner, who was surprised to see a plane parked in front, greets them with a friendly smile. "That's a beautiful airplane."

Betty appreciates his compliment. "Thanks. We've heard about your fabulous seafood, so we had to stop."

"Would you like to look at a menu?"

She smiles at Paddy. "If you like seafood, I've got a couple of suggestions."

Paddy is a highly experienced mechanic, having spent his entire career working on airplanes. He's slightly balding, stocky, and speaks with a heavy Irish brogue. "I love seafood, lass. I'm from Dublin and grew up on it."

"Great!" and she orders for them. "I think we'd like to try your jellied eel and mash, and we'll share a side order of smoked kippers." Then she asks Paddy, "What would you like to drink?"

He looks up at the owner. "Smithwick's Red Ale, if you have it."

"I do, and you miss?"

"Coffee please."

Betty is thrilled to be flying again. "I appreciate your help, Paddy. This is on me."

"Thank you. Now that you've flown her, what do you think?"

"I love the plane, and it was more fun than I expected, but I'm a little disappointed by its slow speed."

"That's because its great war time capabilities are not useful in peace time. You don't need a plane that can land on rough terrain and stop in forty feet."

"Is it possible to modernize it?"

Paddy is very knowledgeable about the Stork. "Of course. I've upgraded several of them."

"What would it take?"

"Well, I'd swap out the engine with a more powerful, and reliable, radial. And I'd switch out those extra-wide wings and replace them with shorter, narrower ones."

"I like that. Any other ideas?"

"You don't need that long landing gear either, so I'd convert it to something more conventional."

"What would I gain from those modifications?"

"It would be faster, more agile, and a lot more fun to fly. Best of all, it wouldn't cost anything to make the upgrades. My mate works at a large salvage yard, and we could just exchange the parts. The good news is that I have little to do until our C-47 arrives. If you wanted to help, the work would go that much quicker."

"I'd love to help. Let's do it!"

"Today is Friday and my mate won't be there until Monday, so why don't you fly it this weekend and have some fun?"

Early the next day, Betty and Wolfie arrive at the hangar. She rolls the Stork out and puts a small overnight bag into the back, along with dog food. After hearing Paddy's stories about Ireland, she decided it would be a fun place for them to explore. She still hadn't gotten over the shock of Max's death and struggles with depression from time to time. Now, she has something fun to do, and it becomes the start of her road to recovery.

Betty hadn't thought about it, but she soon discovered that getting Wolfie into the back of her plane was going to be difficult. However, with the help of a short stepladder, she was successful, and he easily fit into the roomy cabin. He loved to fly, and the two of them left in search of high adventure.

Their first stop was Liverpool, three hours to the north to refuel, and to have lunch. After that, they crossed the Irish Sea, arriving in Dublin, Ireland, an hour later. They spent the rest of the afternoon exploring the city, and that night they stayed at a small country inn near the airport. The next day, they left early and flew the length of the southern coast. Betty loved flying her Stork because she could land just about anywhere, whether it was on a secluded beach, or in a mountain meadow, and she and Wolfie had the time of their lives. It had been an exhilarating adventure for her, but she was excited to return home and get to work modifying her plane.

On Monday morning, Betty and Paddy drove his truck to the salvage yard and met with his friend, Tommy. He agreed with Paddy's modification ideas and told them that exchanging the parts wouldn't be a problem. They looked through several enormous warehouses filled with aircraft parts from every conceivable type of plane.

Paddy picked out a new radial engine still in its shipping crate, then they went through a long row of neatly stacked wings of every imaginable size and shape. After an hour of hard work, they had what they were looking for. As for the landing gear, he only needed wheels and brakes as he planned to fabricate an undercarriage of his own design. They tied the wings to the truck's lumber racks and piled the rest of their parts into the back.

When they arrived at their hangar, Paddy's eighteen-year-old son, Finn, was there to help them with the conversion. It was hard work, and Betty got her first lesson in hands-on mechanics. As usual, she threw herself into the modifications with great gusto, and by the end of the day, she was as dirty as the rest of the crew. Several days later, her work was nearly complete, and her Stork had new landing gear, shorter wings, and a much more powerful radial engine.

Suddenly, the loud sound of an approaching plane surprises them, and they look up to see their first C-47 land and taxi to a stop outside their hangar. Charlie waves to them from the cockpit and shuts down his engines. Betty runs to greet him, and he excitedly points out all the details regarding their new purchase. He also explained that Andy was driving back in his car and would meet up with them the following morning. He notices the re-engineered Stork parked in the shadows and stares at it. To Betty's surprise, he's unexpectedly interested in it and wants to know every detail, so she eagerly explains the modifications that were done to it.

The following morning, Andy arrives and drives up to the hangar. He is also impressed with the work that they did on the Stork. However, they need to clean up their C-47 and get it ready. He has exciting news and tells them he has their first contract with the British military, and they are only days away from making a run into Germany. Paddy, Finn, and two part time mechanics immediately go to work on the cargo plane and strip the olive-green paint to bare metal, service the relatively new engines, and remove the interior bench seating used by paratroopers, so that they can carry more freight.

With their refurbishing underway, they turn their attention back to Betty's Stork. Andy and Charlie didn't realize that Betty had yet to test her newly modified plane, so with a little help from Paddy, she takes off on her maiden flight and is shocked at its performance. It had much more power, and her airspeed increased from seventy to one hundred thirty miles an hour, and the shorter metal wings made it highly maneuverable and a lot of fun to fly.

Charlie and Andy then flipped a coin to see who would fly it next, and Charlie won. He was so excited that he disappeared for an hour. Then it was Andy's turn, and he was just as exhilarated. With everyone so interested in the Stork, Betty declared it would become a company plane for all of them to use.

Over time, Andy flew his family in it many times. His girls were quick to catch the flying bug, so Paddy suggested they convert it into a trainer. He installed a second instrument panel in the back cabin along with stick and rudder controls, and they had a perfect two-seat trainer. Much to Andy's delight, his girls spent many happy hours learning how to fly. As for Betty, she and Wolfie used it quite often to explore northern England, Scotland, and Wales.

A WEEK LATER, BETTY RETURNED FROM A LATE AFTERNOON flight in her Stork and notices Charlie standing in front of the hangar, waving to her. After she lands, he excitedly motions her toward their newly refurbished plane, and points to the large black lettering painted over the plane's cabin windows that reads, "*Dakota Air Cargo*".

Charlie asks, "Do you like the name?"

"Yes. Was that your idea?"

"Not exactly. She's an American DC-3, which the military calls the C-47. However, the Brits nicknamed them Dakotas. It's an acronym from its ID plate; Douglas Aircraft Company Transport Aircraft and she's a real workhorse. With twelve hundred horsepower engines, she can carry three tons of cargo, cruises at 160 miles an hour, and has a range of 1,600 miles. Perfect for what we need."

Andy joins them. "Charlie and I reorganized our hangar. Want to take a tour?"

"Sure, I'd love to see what you've done."

She walks with him, and he proudly points out their new shop layout. "All this is temporary. I'll find us a larger place to work out of later. You and Shelagh have offices in the back, and that side is Paddy's workshop."

"I'm impressed!" She turns to Andy, "How are the government contracts coming along?"

"Very well. I just took it to the bank, and we're fully funded with enough capital to get us going, and then some."

Charlie asks Andy, "Did you tell her about the surprise?"

"No. I was waiting for you."

Betty loves surprises and grins. "Okay, guys. What's up now?"

Andy opens a manila envelope and hands her an official-looking document. "This is our first purchase order. We're going to fly sick and wounded POWs out of camps to hospitals in Britain."

"This is exciting, Charlie! When do we leave?"

"Tomorrow morning. You and I are flying, and Andy is going to look for our next plane, and don't worry about Wolfie. Shelagh will take good care of him until you return."

"Thanks. That takes a big load off my mind."

The following morning, the two of them walk around the plane and go through their usual pre-flight routine. He explains. "I'm already checked out on her. Why don't you take the left seat for the first leg, and I'll fill you in on the rest when we're airborne."

Betty is thrilled to be working again. "Thanks, Charlie. We've both flown high-performance aircraft before, but there's something exciting about flying one of these."

He laughs. "Yeah, everything changes when you're the owner."

They spend the next week picking up prisoners of war from all over the Allied-occupied zones. Configured as an aerial ambulance, their transport plane can carry eighteen stretcher cases in tiers of three cots and has room for two nurses who are needed to attend to the sick and wounded during their return flight to Britain. A few days later, Betty and Charlie leave to pick up critically ill prisoners from Dachau, a notorious Nazi concentration camp near the city of Munich in southern Germany. The American army had recently liberated it and they need to fly the worst cases to England for treatment.

They land in a field next to the camp and exit their plane to oversee the loading of sick and injured prisoners. Many of the POWs are in critical condition and can only be treated by a modern medical facility. It saddens her to see the extent of their injuries; some from combat, and others because of mistreatment by the prison guards. Starving and skeletal looking, they have an unfocused stare like zombies in a horror movie. From her experience working in the hospital, she knows some won't live much longer. Sadly, many will never fully recover from their wounds, and will carry the scars of war with them for the rest of their lives.

The Army medics load stretchers containing the gaunt and haggard POWs into their plane, and they lay motionless, covered in olive drab blankets. A weeping man clutches his hands together in prayer as they lift him into the cargo bay. Others are too weak to keep their eyes open, making it difficult to tell if they are dead or alive. Betty's parents died in a prison camp like this, and it sickens her knowing the horror that they must have endured. A nurse standing with them shakes her head in disbelief. "This is the lowest that humanity can go."

When all the patients are loaded, they board through the rear cargo door. Charlie makes his way forward to the cockpit, and Betty follows him. As she walks past the stretchers, she hears a faint voice call out her name. "Sparky!"

She looks to see who called to her but recognizes no one. As she walks away, a patient lying on the floor reaches out and touches her foot with his dirty hand. She glances down and sees an emaciated elderly man. He has a heavy beard, wears filthy gray pajamas with wide black stripes, and is in terrible shape. She kneels next to his side and smiles at him. "How do you know my name?"

His face is dirty, and his lips are cracked. He tries to speak, but can only whisper, and she leans closer to hear what he's trying to say. "Betty, it's me. Blake."

Betty recoils in shock and looks like she's just seen a ghost. "Oh, my! We were told you were dead! What are you doing here?"

He struggles to speak but can't.

"Don't talk. We can visit later at the hospital. I'm flying this plane, but I won't leave you," and he slowly nods his head. She turns to the nurse standing next to her. "We have a special patient with us today. He's an Allied doctor."

Blake's body convulses with fever, and he shivers uncontrollably. The nurse bends down, pulls his blanket up to his chin, and smiles. "I'll take good care of him."

Betty had to fly cargo runs for the next three weeks, but on her first day off, she went to the hospital in London to visit Blake. She finds him resting peacefully, and he smiles, happy to see her. She bends down over his bed and gives him a long hug.

"How are you feeling?"

"Much better, thanks." She lays a bouquet down on the nightstand, and he smiles at her. "Thanks for the flowers, Sparky!"

Betty pulls up a chair and sits next to his bed. "It was the shock of my life to find you at that prison. How are you doing?"

"My fever is gone, so I'm past the most dangerous stage. I need to build up my strength, but it's still hard to keep anything down. The good news is that I'm on the mend."

"When you didn't come back to work, everyone was incredibly worried about you. They thought you probably hit a sea mine and were killed."

Blake pauses a moment, thinking about that fateful day. "I sailed to the cove that we stopped at and anchored there for the night. Early the next morning, I awoke to find a German commando standing over me with a knife at my throat. A small group of them had been ashore on a reconnaissance mission as part of Hitler's plan to invade England, and they couldn't take a chance that I had seen them. They were going to kill me until one of them noticed my medical bag. When they realized I was a doctor, they scuttled my boat and forced me to go with them.

"After we got ashore, I discovered that there were a lot of sick and wounded soldiers, and they didn't have a doctor to care for them. I worked there for several months, but because of the unrelenting Allied advance, we were in a constant retreat as the fighting raged on. One day, a powerful artillery attack surprised us, and many of them were killed. Unfortunately, shell fragments hit me, and I was knocked unconscious. When I came to, I had severe leg wounds, and I couldn't walk. In a short time, my wounds became infected, and a fever set in.

"When they retreated past the concentration camp at Dachau, they left me there. Jewish prisoners cared for me and saved my life. The guards fed us meager rations, and we were starving, but incredibly, the prisoners shared what little they had with me and attended to my wounds as best they could. I was delirious for weeks and almost died many times.

"One of them was a doctor, and he used maggots from a dead man to eat the putrid flesh from my leg wounds. That was enough to keep me alive, but they had no way of surgically removing the shrapnel from my legs. Weeks later, the Americans overran the camp and freed us, but my time had come, and I could feel myself slipping away. When I was lying on the floor of your cargo plane, a beautiful, winged angel arrived to show me the way. When you found me, she was standing right next to you."

Betty is in tears. "Blake, I'm so sorry. You saved hundreds of lives. It's not fair to let you die on a dirty floor like that."

"But I didn't die, and I'm going to make a full recovery. Who knows why things happen? I'm just grateful that you found me."

A nurse walks over to Betty and touches her shoulder. "I'm sorry, but our doctor needs his rest."

"I understand." She stands and looks down at him. "I'll come and visit you next time I have a day off," and kisses his cheek.

Another week passes, and it's late in the evening when Betty and Charlie finish their last flight. They taxi up to their hangar and shut down their engines. They are exhausted, and he complements her. "Nice work, Betty. You made those long flights pass quickly and being able to speak German on the other end was really helpful. I'll see you tomorrow."

They exit through the rear cargo door and walk down the boarding steps. Wolfie runs out of the hangar to greet her, and she bends down, wraps her arms around him, and hugs him tightly. "Hi, big boy. Did you miss me?"

Paddy approaches them, wiping grease from his hands, and asks Charlie, "How did it go?"

"It was a smooth flight. A little rain in the morning, then it cleared up for the rest of the day. We're beat and headed home for a hot meal and a good night's sleep."

They continue to make flights deep into Germany over the following weeks. On their last flight, they stop at Zürich, Switzerland, for lunch and to treat themselves to a quick tour of the city. Betty notices a chocolatier shop, and they go to investigate it. Because of the many years of war, chocolate was impossible to buy in Britain, but the store had a small selection of their famous milk chocolates. Later in the day, they returned to London, tired and exhausted, but happy to discover they have two days off to recuperate.

The next morning, she and Wolfie drive to the hospital to visit Blake. She knocks on the door to his room and sticks her head inside. "Is anybody home?"

A cheerful Blake invites her in. "Yes! Come in, Betty."

She gives him an affectionate hug. "They must be treating you well. You look like a completely new person!"

"Thanks," and he looks at Wolfie. "And who is this?"

"His name is Wolfie."

Blake holds out his hand. "He's gorgeous . . . and big!"

"He's a good boy. How are you feeling?"

"I'm doing well. They operated on me a week ago, so I'm able to get around a bit."

She walks to a nearby wheelchair and rolls it over to his bed. "It's a beautiful spring morning, and you need some sun. Let's take a stroll."

"Thanks, I'd like that."

Betty helps him into his wheelchair. "Any idea of when they'll discharge you?"

"I've been here six weeks and I've got two more weeks of physical therapy. If all goes well, they will release me soon, and I can go home."

"Where exactly is home?"

He smiles at her. "It's directly under your feet, Melbourne, Australia."

She laughs. "I'm going to miss your humor, doc!"

"Sparky, if you ever tire of the rain and cold, come down and visit me. I can promise you sunny days and warm beaches."

Betty rubs his shoulder affectionately as she pushes his wheelchair. "You never know, doc. I might just do that!"

She wheels him out of the building and down a path toward a flowering garden. They cross a well-manicured lawn, stop at a large fountain, and she sits down on a bench next to him. Blake looks up at the sunny sky. "I'd forgotten what a warm sun feels like." He reaches out and touches Betty's hand. "And it's always bloody great to see you!"

Betty smiles. "I brought you a little present," and hands him a gift-wrapped box.

"This is for me? Thank you," and he unwraps it. "Chocolate! Where did you find this?"

"Charlie and I stopped for lunch in Zürich, and there was a chocolatier near the café."

"Thank you, Betty," and they embrace warmly.

She straightens up, reaches into her other pocket, and produces a second box of chocolate. "I also remember how much you appreciate your nurses. I thought you would like to treat them to something special."

He's taken back by her thoughtfulness. "Thank you, Betty. Only you would fly to Switzerland and return with chocolates!"

Knowing that he will soon leave for home puts her in a melancholy mood. "Let me know when you're leaving. I want to take you to the airport."

"Thanks, but I'm not flying anywhere. I've had a dream for a long time, and with the war over, I'd like to treat myself to something fun."

"Really! What's that?"

"Well, I love sailing. I want to buy a blue water sailboat and sail it back to Melbourne."

"That sounds like a trip of a lifetime!"

"It's about fourteen thousand miles, and I'm going to take my time getting there. The six-month voyage will take me through the Mediterranean, down the Suez Canal, and across the Indian Ocean to Australia." He looks at her lovingly. "And I'd like you to come with me."

Betty is surprised by his offer. "Blake, I'd love to, but I've got commitments here for the next year or two. I hope you understand."

"Well at least consider sailing back from Sweden with me."

"Why Sweden?"

"There are several famous blue water boat builders in Stockholm, and we could sail it back to London together. It would be a fabulous experience."

Although Betty is on the road to recovery, she occasionally sinks into depression thinking about Max. Blake's offer is exciting, and she is suddenly thrilled at the thought of it. "That sounds like a trip of a lifetime, and I'm pretty sure Charlie would cover for me."

"Great! I promise that it will be quite an adventure."

"How long will it take us?"

"We should be back in two weeks." He reaches over and scratches Wolfie's head. "And this guy would be lots of fun to travel with."

CHAPTER 18

THE SWEDISH ARCHIPELAGO

IT'S SEVERAL WEEKS LATER. BLAKE HAS COMPLETELY RECOV-
ered and stands in front of a London pub waiting for Betty. She exits a taxi, runs
to him, and they kiss passionately. He whispers in her ear. "I missed you."

She holds him tightly. "I missed you, too."

They walk toward the pub, and he asks, "Are you hungry?"

"Yes, I am!"

They enter, and a waitress ushers them to a quiet booth. "Do you need
a menu?"

Blake looks at her. "Do you like fish and chips?"

"Sure, that sounds great!"

He orders for them, and the waitress disappears into the crowd. Betty
has been looking forward to his report on their upcoming trip. "So, you found
a couple of boats to look at?"

"Yes. I have a flight to Stockholm tomorrow morning, and if all goes well,
I'll purchase one of them. It will take a little time to get used to handling it, but
I'll stay in touch with you. You should plan on meeting me there three weeks
from today."

"This is so exciting! Charlie said that he would be happy to cover for me.
Tell me more about the trip!"

"Well, it's about thirteen hundred miles, and it should take us about two weeks. We'll take our time and only sail during daylight hours."

Betty is excited at the thought of a new adventure. "What's a typical day going to be like?"

"There are a lot of fun places to visit along the way. We'll get an early start, but we can stop to explore whenever we want to. In the late afternoon, we'll anchor in a secluded cove, or tie up at a dock in some quaint fishing village. Best of all, we can treat ourselves to romantic dinners at out-of-the-way restaurants.

"From Stockholm, we'll sail through the archipelago islands to the Baltic Sea, then follow the coastline to Denmark. After Copenhagen, we'll cross the North Sea to England, which will be our only overnight passage."

"Do you think the motion of the boat will bother Wolfie?"

"He'll be fine, and there's plenty of wildlife for him to watch along the way."

"What should I wear?"

"Nothing special. We're going to do some exploring, so bring comfortable walking shoes. I have storm gear for you, but the weather should be great this time of the year. We can pick up dog food for Wolfie on the way, so figure on traveling light."

In a few days, Blake calls her with good news. He purchased the boat of his dreams and tells her to fly to Stockholm in two weeks. This is the news that Betty has been waiting for, and she's excited at the thought of taking a break from work.

Two weeks later, she arrives at Stockholm's Arlanda Airport and Blake is there to meet her. He works his way through the crowd, and greets her with a hug and a kiss, and then they walk to the air freight terminal to pick up Wolfie. When she opens the door to his shipping kennel, he rushes out and showers her with affection.

Blake hails a taxi that takes them to the center of town, and during the ride, he brings her up to speed on his latest adventures. It drops them off at the waterfront, and they walk hand-in-hand, watching the colorful sailboats tacking across the breezy bay. Betty admires her surroundings. "I can't believe how beautiful this city is!"

"Yes. It survived the war with only minor bomb damage." A brisk afternoon breeze blows across the harbor and Blake puts his arm around her. "Ready for lunch?"

"Yes, I've been so excited I forgot to eat!"

"I discovered a small bistro that specializes in Swedish meatballs. The food is great and best of all, it's dog friendly."

"Yum, I love them!"

After a tasty meal, they spend the rest of the afternoon walking around the city and visiting local tourist attractions with Wolfie. As they walk, Betty squeezes Blake's hand. "I'd love to see your boat. Is it far away?"

"No, it's in the next marina," and he motions toward a nearby motor launch that's boarding people. "We can take that water taxi. She's only about ten minutes from here."

They board the launch, and after several stops, arrive at the marina. Blake holds her hand as they walk along the edge of the bay and after a few minutes, he points at a large sailboat tied to a slip in front of them. The white fifty-four-foot ketch was specially built for extended offshore cruising. Across the stern, and written in gold letters, are the words, "*Oceanus*", and below it, "*Melbourne, Australia*", his home port.

"Oh, Blake. She's beautiful! I wasn't expecting it to be so big!"

He laughs. "She'll get a lot smaller when we're out in the middle of the ocean!"

"Is it new?"

"She's only a year old, and exactly what I was looking for. Let me show you around."

They go below deck and she's shocked to see how much room there is. It has two spacious staterooms, a kitchen with a large refrigerator, a built-in freezer, and a four-burner stove. Initially, Wolfie had trouble going down the stairs into the cabin, but Blake patiently showed him how to climb and descend, and he was quick to catch on.

He asks Betty, "Ready to take her for a spin?"

"Sure. Let's go!"

Blake starts the inboard diesel engine, and she helps to cast off the mooring lines. As they motor out into the harbor, he sets the sails and the big ketch cuts through the calm water with ease. The warm sun and fresh sea air are invigorating, but most of all, Betty loves the ocean breeze in her hair, and the smell of the salty spray. While apprehensive at first, Wolfie quickly got used to the rocking motion of the boat.

As the sun sets in the west, they turn around and head back to the marina. The late afternoon is warm and as darkness falls, they have cocktails on deck and watch the lights of the city. Betty cooks them a fantastic meal, and they spend their first night on the sailboat.

The following day, they purchase a few more provisions, and by early evening, return to their boat to relax. A man standing on the deck of a much larger two-masted schooner waves to them as they board their sailboat. Blake had met the owners earlier in the week and discovered that they were also from Australia, and were sailing around the world with another couple.

At sunset, they board their dinghy and motor out to the schooner to have cocktails with them. Getting out and meeting new people was just the therapy Betty needed, and it was fun for her to socialize with them. They invited them to stay for dinner, but Blake had planned a special evening, and as they leave, he puts his arm around her. "I have a surprise for you tonight."

"Really? I love surprises!"

"We're going to a fantastic Swedish restaurant overlooking the harbor, and dancing afterward. Apparently, that's incredibly popular here."

"I love to dance!"

"Yes, I know. I saw you and Charlie put on an incredible performance at the Officer's Club."

"Oh? I didn't realize you were there."

"I was, and you were unbelievable! Where did you learn to dance like that?"

"I went to dance school for several years, and I danced in college productions after that."

"Well, it shows! I love to dance, but I just never had the time when I was going to med school."

"Don't worry, I'm a great teacher. We'll have lots of fun!"

He hands her a warm jacket. "If you're ready, let's go."

They have a light dinner at a romantic restaurant overlooking the lights of the harbor and afterword, they take a taxi across town and stop in front of a large building.

"I was told they have an enormous dance floor here, and it's packed every night."

"Do you know what's popular here?"

"I knew you would ask, so I checked around. They call it the Swedish Bugg. It's fast paced, but not acrobatic, and incorporates some Latin flavors like jive, but its roots are based on the Lindy Hop."

"Awesome! I can't wait to try it!"

They enter the building and stare at the enormous dance floor. The room is filling up quickly and the excited crowd waits impatiently while the band tunes their instruments. They find a table, order drinks, and a short time later, the announcer introduces four pairs of professional dancers in colorful costumes. Betty asks a young couple sitting next to them what he's saying, and the woman explains that they always start the evening by showing the audience new routines, so that they can try them if they feel like it.

The band plays a fast-paced rhythm, and the dancers put on a fantastic show. As they finish, the crowd applauds, and they wave to them as they leave. Shortly afterward, the music starts again, and couples from the audience walk onto the dance floor. Betty has fun showing Blake a few routines, and he's quick to learn. They spend the next hour having a great time dancing together, and when the band takes a break, they return to their table for a cold drink. After twenty minutes, the band returns along with the professional dancers, but this time they dance to a much more complicated routine. After they finish, they split up and each of them picks someone from the audience for their next number.

A handsome man with blonde hair, and dressed in a glittering white and gold costume, walks over to Betty, and invites her to dance. She takes his hand, and the crowd applauds wildly as the eight couples spread out across the floor. This time the music is much faster, and they dance much more complicated routines. Betty puts on a spectacular show with her sexy dance style and the audience goes wild with applause. When the music stops, her partner thanks her, and walks her back to her table. Blake stands and claps his hands excitedly as they approach. They continue dancing for several hours, but he plans to leave in the morning, so at midnight, they return to his boat.

The next day, they set sail and begin the first leg of their trip through a beautiful inland passage that leads to the Baltic Sea and the famous Archipelago Islands. Later in the afternoon, they stop at a fishing village and walk into town for dinner before returning to their sailboat for the evening.

Early the next morning, they motor out of their protected harbor and sail through the islands. Blake's ketch has a tall main mast with a shorter mizzen mast just ahead of the helm, and it's a fast boat on light winds. He releases the colorful spinnaker, and it billows out in the warm breeze. They spend the next few days sailing through the thousands of lightly inhabited archipelago islands, and occasionally stop at one of the small, brightly colored fishing villages to explore the settlement. Betty is a passionate coffee drinker, and she loves the Swedish custom of fika, a steaming hot cup of coffee, accompanied by a sweet pastry.

They continue sailing through the rugged granite islands of the archipelago and finally enter the deep blue Baltic Sea. Their next destination is the island of Gotland, a hundred and twenty miles to the west. Once out in the open water, they sail past a pod of killer whales traveling north and later in the day, they are joined by a group of bottlenose dolphins. Wolfie loves to stand at the bow and watch them surf just below him.

That afternoon, they arrive at the Swedish island of Gotland and decide to spend the following day exploring. In the morning, they hike to the famous Blue Lagoon and change into their swimming suits. Blake dives in and swims out into the warm turquoise water, and Wolfie splashes after him. He calls to Betty, and she dives in and catches up to them. Blake brought a piece of wood with him, and they have fun playing fetch with Wolfie, who never tires of chasing after the stick. After an enjoyable time together, they swim back to their sunny beach to picnic and sunbathe.

The following day, they continue sailing toward England. They are nearly alone on the open sea and Blake sets the autopilot, a self-steering device. Wolfie is standing at the bow watching the boat slice through the waves and they join him. Blake wraps his arms around Betty, and she snuggles close to him. The sun is warm, and a strong breeze blows on their faces. Later in the afternoon, they stop at a small, out of the way village for dinner and a walk, before settling in for the night. In the morning, they visit a local bakery and buy freshly baked bread, churned butter, and Lingonberry jam.

The next day is sunny and warm, and they continue sailing toward Copenhagen. That afternoon, they anchor in the sheltered cove of an uninhabited island and try their luck fishing for sea trout. For Betty, it's a thrill to catch them, and she quickly becomes quite skilled at it. After cleaning them, she flame-broils them on a small grill that swings out over the boat's stern.

A gorgeous sunset floods their private cove with a beautiful golden light. It's a special time of the day for Betty, and they relax with a champagne cocktail, talking about the day's events. The evening is warm and as darkness falls, they listen to music. Unexpectedly, the voice of Frank Sinatra singing *I'll Never Smile*

Again fills the air, and she smiles at Blake. "That's my favorite song. Remember when we danced to it on your other boat?"

"Yes, I do," and he holds out his hand. "Shall we dance?"

A silver moon climbs into the eastern sky, and small swells gently rock their boat as the heavens fill with twinkling stars. Blake holds her in his arms, and they dance slowly to the romantic music. After a while, a cool breeze drifts across the Baltic, and they retire below deck to their warm cabin.

A few days later, they sail into Danish waters, and tie-up at a marina in Copenhagen. They spend two days exploring the beautiful city, but they are eager to continue, and the following morning they work their way through a group of large islands that lead to the infamous North Sea. The weather in the Baltic had been sunny and calm, and the winds were steady, but the North Sea is icy cold, and swept by unrelenting, powerful winds. However, the big ketch was built for rough weather, and it becomes a fun adventure. Ahead of them is England, but first they must cross three hundred and fifty miles of open water.

The morning is cloudy and large white-caped waves, slammed by powerful gusts of wind, create long spindrifts of spray that drift far behind them. Because of the enormous waves, Blake protected Wolfie with a specially made life jacket should he be accidentally washed overboard. By the evening of the first day, the winds settle down and rolling swells rhythmically sweep past them, creating high crests and deep troughs.

Their bow cuts deeply into the crest of a wave, then hangs in midair for a moment, before crashing to the bottom of the trough. It submerges, then rises steeply as the wave sweeps under them. Green sea water rushes from the bow, and surges across the deck to the stern, and the violent cycle is repeated with each passing swell. This will be Betty's first overnight sailing experience and she'll have to handle the big ketch alone during her four-hour shift. Blake is confident that she's learned enough to safely sail the boat, but if something unusual were to happen, she can always call to him for help.

Fortunately, it's a full moon. The evening is clear, and the winds are steady as the sun sets behind a cold gray fog bank. A white fiberglass top and a large windshield partially enclose the helm station, which protects them from most of the foul weather and their heavy storm jackets keep them warm and dry. That night, they stay up laughing and talking until Blake's shift, which starts at 10 pm, and Betty and Wolfie go below to sleep. At 2 am, he wakes her, and she starts her shift, which will last until dawn.

The full moon reflects off the water as large rolling swells sweep under the boat from the starboard side. Betty arrives at the helm with a thermos of hot coffee and safely secures it. Blake gives her last-minute instructions, and double checks their course on the compass. He pets Wolfie, gives her a hug, then goes below deck to sleep. The sea breeze is chilly, and she pulls the hood of her storm jacket over her head. She reefs down hard on the boom, and the ketch heels over on its side, surging forward as it cuts into the rolling swells. Wolfie sits next to her, gazing at the horizon intently. She gives him a hug and a dog biscuit, and they settle in for the long passage ahead of them.

The night ends as the first rays of dawn peak over low clouds in the east, and lights from several large ships twinkle in the early morning mist. A sleepy Blake arrives with hot coffee and a Danish pastry, and she excitedly relates her nighttime experiences on the open sea. He hugs her, then she and Wolfie go below deck for a brief nap. By dusk, they reach the foggy English coast and sail up the nearby Tyne River. In the fleeting twilight, the lonely sound of bells ringing on the river's navigation buoys guides them safely to a well-protected marina.

A thick fog bank cloaks the town of Newcastle, nearly obscuring the orange glow of its streetlights. A single car drives slowly along the waterfront, and its taillights disappear into the mist. They idle into port under diesel power, and dock at the commercial wharf. The following morning is sunny and clear, and Blake is below deck searching through a large storage locker. He surprises Betty with two bicycles he had stowed away, and they peddle down the wharf and disappear into one of the town's narrow streets. Wolfie follows them, and they spend the day riding through the desolate, windswept farmlands.

In the afternoon, they bicycle along a wind-blown road that overlooks the English Channel and as dusk approaches, they stop for a meal of freshly caught brown crab and a cold beer at a popular pub. The following day, they get an early start and sail south down the coast toward London. Just after dark, they arrive at the great estuary that connects the River Thames with the North Sea.

After finding a sheltered cove, they drop anchor for the night. Blake turns on their mooring lights, and the ketch gently sways in the light swells. Betty cooks them a special dinner, and they spend their last evening together, celebrating their adventures in their toasty cabin.

The next day, they have a leisurely breakfast topside, and enjoy the scenic view as large ships come and go from all parts of the globe. Blake goes below to check on their diesel engine, and Betty relaxes in a deck chair. She is in a melancholy mood as she realizes her trip of a lifetime will soon end. The long journey to Melbourne would be a fantastic experience, but she made unbreakable commitments to Andy and Charlie, and they are depending on her.

The morning fog hangs close to the water, but the rising sun soon burns it off. Blake walks to the bow, brings in the anchor, then returns to the cockpit and starts the boat's diesel engine. This will make it safer for him to navigate amongst the massive ships that are coming and going from the Port of London.

They motor up the River Thames for another thirty miles before stopping near London's Big Ben Tower where they disembark. Blake bends down next to Wolfie and gives him a long hug. "Goodbye, big boy!" then holds Betty in his arms. "Are you sure I can't talk you into sailing to Melbourne with me?"

Tears fill her eyes. "I would love to, but I have commitments here that I can't break. I'm sorry, but it's just bad timing for us."

Their kiss is passionate, and they embrace tenderly for a long time. Blake brushes her hair to the side of her face. "We've gone through a lot together, Betty. I'm going to miss you. You'll always have a home waiting for you in Australia."

"Thank you, Blake. I promise to keep in touch." She hugs him for a long time. "It's hard to say goodbye, Doc."

He is emotional as well, and they embrace for the last time. "The tide is changing. I'd better leave while I can," and he boards his boat and starts the diesel engine. The powerful sailboat slowly backs away from the dock and enters the main channel. Blake waves goodbye. "I'll always remember you, Sparky."

She returns his wave, and her heart is filled with sadness. Tears glisten in her eyes as he disappears into the busy river traffic. It would have been a trip of a lifetime, and with someone that she deeply cared about, but Andy and Charlie were depending on her, and it was a promise that she could not break.

CHAPTER 19
A GHOST FROM THE PAST

AFTER RETURNING FROM HER TRIP TO SWEDEN, BETTY AND Charlie put in a grueling three weeks flying cargo into the British Occupation Zone. Andy continues to work hard to find them a second C-47, but he keeps getting outbid at the last minute. As a result, they have to scramble to fulfill their orders with only one plane. It had been an unusually long day, and they land in London after dark. Exhausted, they disembark and lock up their hangar just as Andy pulls up in his Jaguar sedan.

Charlie walks up to the passenger window carrying a heavy flight bag over his shoulder. "Hi, Andy. What brings you out this time of night?"

"I know you two have been putting in incredibly long days, and I'd like to treat you to dinner."

"Thanks for the offer, but I'm knackered," and he turns to Betty. "It's your call. Are you hungry?"

She looks in the passenger window at him. "Hi. Sure, as long as I can get to bed early."

"Good. Hop in. I promise to get you home on time."

They drive off into the night, and Andy turns onto a country road. Betty sits in the back seat and closes her eyes for a brief nap. Charlie looks out the window at the unfamiliar countryside. "Where are we going?"

"If you don't mind, I would like your opinion on a plane that I'm bidding on tomorrow. It will just take a minute."

"Sure. I'd be glad to."

Andy turns off the road, drives into an abandoned RAF airbase, and pulls up to an enormous hangar. They exit the car and enter the pitch-dark building. Betty looks up at the moonlit skylights high above them. "Wow! This place is immense!"

"Yeah, it is. Let me turn on some lights."

He disappears into the darkness, and they hear him switching on the overhead lights. As they slowly warm up, Betty is surprised to see a small group of their friends standing behind a table decorated with colorful balloons and a large cake on it. They call out in unison. "Surprise!"

As the lights brighten, she sees their second C-47 parked behind them. Its olive drab paint has been removed, and its highly polished aluminum fuselage shimmers under the lights. Above the windows are the words, "*Dakota Air Cargo*" painted in black lettering.

Betty is shocked. "Andy, I can't believe it!"

Shelagh walks toward them. "Welcome to our new home!" and she gives Charlie a hug. "Surprise, honey. We've been working day and night on this for the last two weeks!"

He's amazed. "What a beauty!"

Paddy joins them. "What do you think of her?"

Charlie grins. "I'm impressed! You did a great job cleaning her up."

A man with a camera hung around his neck approaches, and Andy makes the introductions. "This is Roger Westley with the London newspaper, *The Sunday Times*."

Betty shakes his hand. "It's a pleasure to meet you."

"Thank you, miss."

Andy explains. "Roger was kind enough to do an article about our new company."

"This is a great human-interest story. If you wouldn't mind, I'd like to take a photo of everyone standing by your plane."

Charlie, the consummate promoter, ushers them over to the C-47. "How is this?"

Roger adjusts his camera's focus and looks up. "Perfect," and the flash from his camera lights up the entire hangar. "Thank you. Your story will appear in our paper next week."

Andy walks with Betty. "I know you're exhausted, but before you leave, I'd like to point out a couple of things. She's in perfect condition, and the engines are new. Paddy removed the interior jump seats to make room for more cargo, and he also installed a bathroom in the tail section. This one will be yours, and I've hired more pilots to fly the other plane."

Betty is excited, as they are now fully staffed, and she smiles at him. "We're starting to look like a real company. I can't wait to take her up!"

IT'S BETTY'S DAY OFF, AND A SUNNY MORNING SEVERAL weeks later. Paddy is temporarily short staffed, and she volunteered to lend a hand. While she waits for him to arrive, she sits in the cockpit of her C-47 organizing the many navigation charts that they use to fly into Germany. Lost in thought, she reflects on her dangerous spy mission and her two horrific plane crashes. Charlie and Andy had talked about it many times. Sometimes, whether you live or die, comes down to just plain luck.

Paddy soon arrives, parks his truck in front, and enters the hangar. He waves to Betty as she exits the plane and catches up to him wearing bib overalls, a baseball cap, and a ponytail.

"Good morning, Betty. I appreciate your help."

"Sure thing, Paddy. What can I do?"

"Your C-47 needs an oil change. She's scheduled to make a run after lunch, so we need to get right on it."

"Okay. Just show me what to do."

The plane's engines are high off the ground, but Paddy already had a platform rolled under them. As they climb the stairs, he explains. "I'll work with you on this engine, and you should be able to handle the second one by yourself."

"Thanks, Paddy. It's fun learning how to work on our planes."

Paddy spends the next half hour changing the oil with her, and they push the rolling platform to the second engine. After he leaves, she climbs up the stairs, removes the engine cowling, and crawls under the radial engine to remove the drain plug.

Betty is laying on her back and struggles to remove the plug, but it won't budge. She hears Paddy coming up the stairs and calls out to him from under the engine.

"Hey, Paddy. The drain plug is stuck. Could you hand me the other wrench?" and extends an oily hand. Something is placed on the palm of her hand, and she asks, "What's this?"

She pulls her hand back and stares at a small bouquet of iridescent blue wildflowers. Startled, she bumps her head as she slides out from under the engine.

Standing there is a handsome blonde man looking down at her and says, "At last, I found you, mine leibling."

"Oh my gosh! Max!"

She runs to him, jumps into his arms, and kisses him excitedly. He speaks to her in English. "Elizabeth! I can't believe it's you!"

She pushes him back. "You speak English?"

"Yes," and grins. "It's a long story."

"How can this be? I thought you were dead?"

"I almost died several times that day."

Wolfie is in the office with Charlie and Shelagh and begins to bark loudly. Alerted by the commotion, they rush out of the office as Wolfie blasts past them. They call to Betty. "What's happening?"

Wolfie jumps up on Max placing both paws on his shoulders, and excitedly showers him with dog kisses. Max hugs him tightly in a bear hug and nuzzles his neck. "I love you, big boy!"

Tearfully, Betty turns and calls to Charlie and Shelagh. "This is Max!"

She takes Max's hand, and they walk down the platform's steps. "These are two of my best friends, Charlie Barclay and his wife, Shelagh."

Max extends his hand. "It's nice to meet you."

Charlie is amazed. "I helped pull you out of that wreck. You were in pretty bad shape. What happened?"

Max explains. "I had lost a great deal of blood and was already in a coma when they rushed me into the emergency room. The doctors were excellent, but my heartbeat was so shallow they couldn't detect it. Apparently, they worked on me for quite a while before pronouncing me dead. Because I was wearing a Luftwaffe uniform, they took me to a military morgue. Prior to injecting me with embalming fluid, they cut the femoral artery in my groin to drain my blood, and when they did, blood spurted out, and they knew I was alive.

"They rushed me to a nearby hospital, and the doctors saved my life. When I arrived, I was naked, so they didn't see my Nazi uniform. Later, when they interviewed me, I told them I was a university professor and defected in a stolen plane. We had heavy battle damage and crash landed, killing everyone but me. They believed me, and I avoided being sent to a POW camp. Unfortunately, I was severely wounded, and it took me many months to recover."

Max looks around the hangar. "How long have you been here?"

Betty explains. "Only a couple of weeks. Charlie and I, and another friend, own this air cargo company. We have a contract to fly freight into the British Occupation Zone."

Max's friendly demeanor impresses Charlie, and he comes up with a suggestion. "What do you say we continue this over dinner tonight? I'm sure our partner will want to meet you. How about eight o'clock at the King and Country? It's one of Betty's favorite restaurants."

Betty is wildly excited. "Thanks, Charlie. We'll be there."

He shakes hands with Max. "I'm glad to see that you pulled through okay."

"Thank you."

They say goodbye and she gives Max another hug and kisses him. "I love you, sweetheart."

Max brushes her hair away from her face and holds her tightly. "I love you, too, my darling. You are the love of my life!"

Betty squeezes his hand. "Let's go. I live in a cute little cottage nearby."

She parks in front of her cottage, and they walk up the garden path, followed by Wolfie. Max puts his arm around her. "I spent many sleepless nights thinking I would never see you again."

She smiles at him and winks. "Then we better make up for lost time!"

An icy wind buffets the outside of her cottage, and a light rain streams rivulets of water across the windows. They're lying in bed, and a roaring fire burns brightly in the fireplace. Betty runs her fingers through his long blonde hair and looks at him lovingly.

"What are you thinking?"

"I thought about this moment many times. My recovery was very difficult, and remembering our life together was the only thing that kept me going." He kisses her hand. "I see you are still wearing your engagement ring."

"Yes. I thought you had died, so I put it on my other hand. It reminds me of all the wonderful times that we had together."

He pulls her close to him and they kiss. "I love you, Elizabeth."

She snuggles into his arms and whispers. "I love you, too. I cried myself to sleep many nights, thinking I had lost you forever. If it wasn't for Apollo, I wouldn't have survived. The nights were cold and lonely, and I cuddled with him in front of the fireplace, wishing you were here with us." She runs her hand across his chest and stares at his scars. "Are you fully recovered?"

"Yes. The doctors told me to exercise daily, and my strength will return to normal."

Betty is curious. "How did you find me?"

"I saw your picture in a newspaper at the hospital, and the article said where you were."

"It's so strange to hear you speaking English."

"Well, I studied it in grade school, and during my time in the hospital, it slowly came back to me."

"There's so much to tell you I don't know where to begin. Do you remember anything after we were attacked?"

"No. I was shot and fell to the floor. Apollo was standing over me, licking my face, and then I passed out."

"That fighter tore us up pretty badly. Rolf was killed, and I took over the controls."

"Ah . . . I see. I thought you said you didn't know how to fly?"

"Oh boy! I have a lot of explaining to do. Do you remember the night when I promised to explain everything to you?"

"Yes. I do."

"My real name is Betty Bauer, and I was born in Berlin. When I was fourteen, Nazi death squads roamed the streets killing Jews, and I barely escaped. My parents sent me to live in America, and they were to follow, but the day after I left, the Gestapo arrested them, and I never heard from them again."

"Betty, I'm so sorry. I wish you had told me."

She tries to simplify her story, but it's complicated. "I received my engineering degree from Stanford University in California. After that, I joined the military and transported planes from aircraft factories to the coasts for shipment to the war.

"I was part of an experimental group of women pilots that volunteered to fly B-17s to England. Bad weather forced us off course and into Germany. I was shot down and my aircrew was killed. A British pilot landed near my crash site and rescued me, and that's how I got to London.

"The Brits knew the Nazis were developing a navigation disruptor, and they needed someone to find out what they were doing. I spoke German and had a technical background, so I volunteered. Late one night, I parachuted into a field near your airbase, and a resistance group smuggled me inside. My orders were to retrieve a roll of film and return in a day or two, not five months later.

"And you know the rest. If I hadn't volunteered for that mission, I would have never met you. As for the aeronautical part, I'm a highly experienced pilot. I've flown almost every plane in the American inventory, including all of their advanced fighters."

"Ah . . . I see. The pieces are beginning to make sense. I have to say, you were very convincing, and you certainly made Major Krüger nervous!"

Betty laughs at the thought of him. "He must have discovered I wasn't who I said I was. I guess they either shot him, or else he's back to raising pigs."

"You're probably right," and he holds her hand. "And what about your husband?"

"I never had a husband. The world was at war, and I was living a secret life. The German resistance insisted that I wear a wedding ring to protect me from unwanted attention. Later on, I desperately wanted to tell you who I was, but I couldn't because it could have endangered you. If I was discovered to be a spy, they would have killed you, too."

Tears well in her eyes. "I had to sacrifice my love to protect you, and it broke my heart. Had we returned to our base that night, I would have been arrested and executed." She gives him a long hug and apologizes. "I'm so sorry that I'm not the person you thought I was."

Max is emotional and wipes the tears from her cheeks and kisses her gently. "Betty, I love you more than ever. I can't imagine how difficult that must have been for you. I once asked you to marry me, and that hasn't changed." He pulls her close to him and holds her tightly. "Will you marry me?"

She whispers. "Yes, darling. I love you with all my heart, and I want to spend the rest of my life with you."

They kiss passionately and Max reflects. "Life might be difficult for a while. Our beautiful country has been destroyed, and I don't even know if our house is still standing."

She hugs him. "I will be forever grateful that we found each other. When I was very young, I lost everything. My family and relatives were murdered. I had lost my home, my language, and my country, and it was a terrifying experience for a young child.

"But we have much to be thankful for. We're together now, and my company is expanding rapidly. It's been my dream to return to Germany, and in time we can still do that. I'm sure our future will be filled with exciting possibilities."

"That's my dream too. I don't know how, but I want to be part of rebuilding our country. Our farm is a wonderful place to raise a family, and we can have a good life there. I never want our children to know the horrors of war that we lived with for so many years."

Later that afternoon, Betty parks in front of the King and Country Inn, a stately three-story brick hotel overlooking the River Thames, and she and Max walk up the steps with Wolfie. She holds his hand. "I'm glad we decided to treat ourselves to a night here."

"Yes, something fun after all that we've been through!"

They walk through the luxurious lobby and check in. A bellman picks up their luggage, and they follow him to a room overlooking the river. Betty takes off Wolfie's leash. "There you go, big boy."

Max removes his jacket, sits on the edge of the bed, and Wolfie returns to his side. He runs his hands through his long fur and gives him a hug. "I missed you, Apollo."

Betty smiles and looks at the two of them. "I hope you don't mind, but I changed his name to Wolfie. He's a civilian now."

Max is surprised. "Wolfie? Well, I like it."

Later that evening, they walk into the elegant hotel dining room, and approach their table. Betty makes the introductions. "This is Andy McQueen, the fighter pilot that saved me when I crash landed in Germany, and his wife Olivia. And you already met Charlie and Shelagh."

Max smiles and greets them. "Hello everyone," and they sit down.

The waiter appears at their table and Andy asks Betty, "We're drinking champagne. What would you like?"

Betty grins. "This is a very special night. I think Max and I will have French 75s."

Andy laughs. "That's what I figured!" and looks at Max. "That's Betty's favorite drink to celebrate with!"

Max is confused. "What is it?"

He explains. "It's gin and champagne with a twist of lemon and shaken in ice. They say it feels like you're being shelled by a French 75 mm field cannon."

Max looks at Betty and laughs. "This is a daring side of you that I've never seen."

Andy is serious. "I'm glad we're all together tonight, and it's especially good to have you with us, Max."

"Thank you. I'm very grateful to be here."

"Do you have any plans for the future?"

"No, not yet, and there's not much to return to in Germany."

Andy continues. "Now that the war is over, there are a lot of business opportunities here, which is why we started this air freight company. My father wants to retire and hand over the management of our manufacturing plant to me, which leaves us shorthanded. Would you be interested in working with us? We're going to need all the help we can get," and he looks at Charlie. "Tell them what your idea is."

"You and Betty would be perfect for running the operation on the German side. I know it's not science, but in time you could become a full partner. It might take a year or two for us to get established, and you could save up some cash. Then, if you wanted to do something on your own, you could."

Max is surprised. "Thank you . . . I . . . I appreciate your offer. I have several friends, if they are still alive, that were well connected and could be very helpful."

Betty is overjoyed. "Thank you so much, Andy. That's a wonderful idea, and it will really help us!"

Charlie raises his glass. "All right then. I propose a toast to our new partnership," and they touch glasses in agreement.

Later that evening, Betty and Max are lying in bed talking about Andy's offer to include him in their company and she snuggles close to him. "I can't believe that we'll be working together. Only a few hours ago, we were worried about what we were going to do with our lives, and now we have a chance to build a future for ourselves. What we do is important, and our dreams of helping Germany to recover are starting to come true!"

Max is overwhelmed by Andy's generous offer. "I like your friends, and for the first time, I feel like we have some direction in our lives."

"Charlie is right, it's not science, but it is a chance for us to make a difference," and she pauses. "I have a secret to tell you."

"What do you mean?"

"When I was a child and crossing America by train, I was terrified and worried about what was going to happen to me. It was very late at night, and I was fast asleep. A beautiful angel appeared in my dream and told me I was going to a safe place, and I would be starting a new life. Since then, she has comforted me many times, and I know she's always with me."

Max holds her tightly and kisses her. "That's a wonderful story, and I'm so happy for you." He pauses for a moment, then confides to her. "I have a secret, too. When I was recovering in the hospital, I was weak, in terrible pain, and lingered on the edge of death for weeks. One evening, a tunnel of bright light with shadowy people inside it appeared. I couldn't see their faces, but I recognized their voices, and they called for me to join them. If it wasn't for my thoughts of you, I would have gone with them. Over time, I slowly recovered my health, but I struggled with fear and depression for months. Then I saw your picture in the newspaper, and my heart was filled with hope."

Betty has tears in her eyes and holds him close to her. "I'm so sorry for your pain, Max. I want you to know that I will never leave your side. You are my soulmate, and I love you deeply. We live in a beautiful cottage, and Wolfie is safe with us. We are on the very edge of having a wonderful life together."

A week later, Betty and Max are having a late lunch at their favorite bistro. A radio is playing music in the background when a special bulletin interrupts the broadcast. The reporter describes horrifying stories of the Soviet Army terrorizing East Germany. Stalin is in a desperate rush to find Hitler's advanced weapons before they fall into Allied hands. A great deal of equipment and people have been shipped back to Russia as war reparations, including many of the scientists and technicians that worked on them.

Betty gives Max a worried look. "That sounds scary."

"Yes, but if they discover our project, they will come looking for me."

She squeezes his hand. "At least you're here and in a safe place."

Just then, Charlie enters. He notices them sitting at a table in the back of the room and joins them. "Well, well. Fancy meeting you two here."

Max pulls out a chair. "Hi, Charlie. Please join us."

"I hope I'm not interrupting. You looked like you were in a deep conversation."

"We just heard on the news that the Soviets are scouring the countryside looking for German vengeance weapons, and the scientists that created them."

"Yes, I was listening to the same broadcast on my way over, but it's not only the Soviets. The Americans and Brits are searching for them too. Wernher von Braun, the director of the Nazi V-2 rocket program, and hundreds of his top scientists were just relocated to the States."

Max is nervous and looks at Betty. "Remember, my research notes are at the house, and my lab still contains a sizable amount of extremely sensitive information. When they discover my name, they will go to my home and tear it down, looking for anything that might be hidden there. That would put Jannik and Helga in great danger."

Betty is worried and looks at Charlie. "He's right. If they find that information, they will come looking for Max!"

Max is very uncomfortable. "I'm sorry, but I need to get back to the air-base before someone discovers its secrets."

Travel in post-war Germany was very dangerous for many reasons and Betty is worried. "No, Max. You can't do that!"

Charlie thinks for a minute and comes up with an idea. "Maybe I can help. We could fly you in. It's only two hours away."

Betty thinks about it for a moment. "Charlie's right. At least it's not in the Soviet Zone, and the underground hangar is only thirty miles inside the French Zone. We could be in and out before anyone knew it. We're a licensed British carrier, and I don't think the French would make a big deal out of it if they did stop us."

Charlie likes the simplicity of the plan. "Let's leave tomorrow morning at first light. You can leave Wolfie here with Shelagh if you like."

Wolfie is lying at her feet, and she bends down and rubs his head. "Do you want to go with us?" He barks excitedly, and she laughs. "I think he wants to go home, too."

The following morning, they meet Charlie at the hangar. He kisses Shelagh goodbye, and they enter the C-47. Betty follows him and they walk to the cockpit and sit down at the controls. Max sits in the navigator's seat behind them and Wolfie wanders through the plane, checking out all the smells, before laying down at Max's feet. Charlie calls out the side window. "Clear One!" and starts the engines.

While they warm up, Betty radios the tower for instructions, then turns to him. "We're cleared to taxi."

He waves to Shelagh, and they slowly roll out onto the taxiway. The early morning traffic is light, and he pushes the throttles forward as they speed down the runway. Betty reviews her navigation charts, then reaches out and sets their compass heading. "It's only 350 miles, so we should be there in a little over two hours. Max's place is on the Mosel River, close to the British Zone. We can land on a long meadow next to his house. It won't take much time to retrieve his files."

Several hours later, they approach the border of the French Zone and Betty takes over the flight controls, descending rapidly to five hundred feet. Max's estate soon comes into view, and they make a low pass over it. She stares down at the house. "It looks pretty quiet down there."

Max looks out the windshield. "That's a good sign. At least the house is still standing."

She banks steeply, returns to the meadow, and lands. As they exit the plane, Max points at the tree line. "Look at that!" Hidden in the trees under a dense canopy of branches is a German Focke-Wulf 190 fighter. "Did the army leave it there, or is someone at the house?"

Betty is nervous. "I don't like it."

Charlie unzips his flight jacket and reveals a shoulder holster holding a large forty-five caliber pistol. She stares at him nervously. "Is that necessary?"

"You never know. The Soviets might be here."

A blustery breeze whips at the surrounding trees and buffets their parked plane. Suddenly, they see a man leaving the house about a hundred yards away. He wears a crumpled hat pulled down to his ears, a heavy sweater, and leans into the cold wind as he walks toward them. They freeze, not knowing what's about to happen.

Betty stares at him. "He's carrying something!"

Charlie is uncomfortable and releases the safety strap on his shoulder holster. "Yeah. It looks like a weapon!"

She reaches down and grabs Wolfie's collar. He senses they are nervous and immediately goes into alert mode. His ears twitch back and forth nervously, and his hackles raise up. He strains hard against his collar and stares intently at the approaching stranger. The man quickens his stride, and suddenly Wolfie charges, nearly dragging Betty to the ground. He races across the field, and she screams after him. "No! No! Wolfie! Come back here!"

The man sees the charging attack dog and stops just as Wolfie collides violently with him, knocking him to the ground. For a hundred-and-fifty-pound dog, he is extremely agile and charges back at him. The man struggles to his feet just as Wolfie flies into him again, hitting him full force in the chest and throwing him backwards to the ground. The man grabs him by the neck with both hands and they roll over, as dirt and grass fly in all directions. Wolfie bites into his heavy sweater and shakes him violently. Finally, the man gives up and lies on the ground, exhausted. Wolfie releases his grip and stands behind him.

By this time, the group has caught up with them and they arrive panting and short of breath. Betty is astonished and speaks in German. "Lotar! What are you doing here? We thought you were a Russian!"

He sits up and brushes the dirt and grass off his thick sweater. "Well, I was going to surprise you."

"Why were you carrying a gun?"

"A gun? I had a bottle of brandy for us to celebrate the end of the war with."

Lotar is sitting on the ground and takes off his hat. Wolfie immediately recognizes him and towers over him, showering him with affection, much to Betty's amusement. "He didn't recognize you with that hat pulled down to your ears, and neither did we!"

"Well, the wind was gusting, and it's freezing cold." He stands and pats Wolfie's shoulder lovingly. "I'm glad that we're buddies, big boy!"

Betty laughs. "Well, you like to play rough. See what happens!"

He scratches Wolfie's head affectionately. "I'm going to have nightmares remembering that charge!"

Max greets him with an enormous bear hug. "Ah, little brother. We've been worried sick about you!"

"I'm fine, and I can't tell you how happy I am to see that you're still alive, big brother."

Then he turns to Betty. He gives her a warm hug and speaks in English. "And how is my favorite engineer? I see you've learned to fly. You're a woman of many talents!"

She is astonished. "Where did you learn to speak English?"

"From my Swedish girlfriend."

She laughs. "I should have known it would be something like that," and gives him a long hug. "Welcome home, Lotar. It's wonderful that we're all together again. Are you alright?"

"Yes, except for a couple pieces of shrapnel in my backside!"

"Just enough to show the ladies, huh?"

He gives her a big smile. "Ah, you know me too well!"

Betty is curious. "How did you get here?"

"I was stationed outside of Berlin. The Americans surrounded our airbase and our general surrendered without a fight. There were at least five hundred of us, and they herded us into a cow pasture. We formed into a long line and were told to throw our weapons into a pile.

"Then we sat down, and they fed us hot soup. The Soviets were fighting in Berlin and the Americans didn't seem too concerned. A cook left his military jacket hanging on a fence post, so I grabbed it. Later that evening, I put it on, walked over to a plane, and took off." He nods toward the parked fighter. "That's my 190 over there. I hid it in case they came looking for me, but they didn't care. Everyone knew the war was over."

Betty shakes her head. "Only you would try a crazy stunt like that."

He laughs and ushers them toward the house. "Come inside. I found some food and wine. I want to hear all about what you've been doing."

As they walk, Jannik pulls into the cul-de-sac, driving his blue tractor and Lotar calls to him. "Look who I found!"

Jannik approaches Max and embraces him. "Max, my friend! We thought you had been killed!"

"I have a lot to tell you. You remember Elizabeth?"

"Yes, it's good to have you back."

"Thanks, Jannik. What happened here?"

"Several units of the German army retreated through this area. They stayed in the house and drank a lot of wine before they left. Then, a couple of days later, the Americans arrived and did the same thing. I heard there was bitter fighting fifty miles from here."

Max looks around at the property. "Well, the house is a little rundown, but at least it's still in one piece."

Betty gives Jannik a worried look. "How are the horses? I didn't see them anywhere."

"They're still in the high meadow. There's no reason for anyone to go up there, so I'm pretty sure they are safe."

Suddenly, the noise of an approaching vehicle catches everyone's attention, and they turn to see a French military police car. It approaches with its red rooftop emergency lights flashing ominously, then stops in the cul-de-sac. Two officers get out and approach their group. The senior officer addresses them in French and points to the cargo plane. Lotar is the only one that knows a little French, but he has great difficulty understanding what they are saying, and they struggle to understand each other. Max tugs at Lotar's arm. "What do they want?"

He shakes his head. "I'm not sure. He seems to be upset about the plane."

Charlie tries to help. "Tell them we had engine trouble."

Lotar explains in broken French and hand signs, but to no avail. A heated discussion ensues in three languages, with everyone wanting to say something at the same time. While all this is going on, and unnoticed by them, a third officer exits the police car and walks over to the plane. He stops at the open cargo door and looks inside the empty bay. As he leaves, he notices the Focke-Wulf 190 fighter parked under the trees. Unseen by the arguing group, he walks up behind them.

Betty turns to see who is standing behind her and exclaims in German. "Adrian! Is that you?"

The group stops arguing, and stares at them in stunned silence as he greets her in German. "Ah, Nurse Bauer. What a pleasant surprise!"

She is shocked to see him and gives him a hug. "It's so good to see you, but please call me Betty. I'm so sorry I missed saying goodbye. When I arrived at work, I was told they had moved you to a POW camp."

"I appreciate everything that you did for me. And thank you for mailing my letter. My wife said she will be forever grateful for your kindness."

Adrian is about the same age as Betty. He has an athletic build and is very attractive with angular features, medium length light-brown hair streaked with blonde, and a very short beard. He looks at the bewildered group and speaks in English. "What's going on here?"

Betty is surprised. "You speak English?"

"Yes. I'm sorry, but when I came out of surgery, I was groggy, and it was so pleasant speaking to you in German, that I left it that way."

"I understand," and she takes his hand. "Please let me introduce you. This is Charlie Barclay, and this is Lotar von Hirschel, a Luftwaffe fighter pilot like yourself," and they exchange pleasantries.

Adrian stares at Betty's flight jacket. "You're a pilot?"

"Yes, but it's a long story," and she introduces him to Max. "This is my fiancée, Max von Hirschel, and this is his farm."

Adrian shakes his hand. "It's a pleasure to meet you. Your farm is quite beautiful."

"Thank you."

Betty is excited to see him. "Why don't you stay for lunch? We'd be happy to fly you back, and I would love to hear what you are up to."

"I appreciate your generous offer. I'd like that." He turns to the police officers and, speaking in French, tells them they are old friends, and that they will fly him back.

Betty takes him by his arm, and they walk toward the house. "It's so wonderful to see you! Come. Let me show you around."

Adrian notices the horse barn. "Ah, you raise horses here?"

"Yes. Do you ride?"

"It's a great passion of mine. That's quite a nice horse barn. Can we look at it?"

"Certainly, but unfortunately, the horses are in the high meadow."

As they approach the barn, Adrian stops to admire the large red battle shield. "I've seen this before," and thinks for a moment. "You raise dragon horses here?"

Max doesn't understand what he's talking about. "I'm not sure what you mean?"

"Sorry, but your horses are well known in France. I recognize the dragon on your coat of arms."

"Really! I didn't realize there were any in France."

"Oh, yes. Only a few, and they are fantastic competitors. I'd love to see your horses. Is that possible?"

"Of course. However, it's an hour ride by tractor to reach them."

"My wife is on the French equestrian team. I can't tell you how excited she will be when I tell her about this."

Max makes a suggestion. "Well then, we'll bring saddles with us and make a day of it."

"It would be a dream of a lifetime, my friend."

Betty suggests. "This will take some time. Would you like to spend the night? I can fly you back in the morning."

"Excellent. I'd like that very much."

Max asks her, "Would you mind explaining this to Charlie and Lotar?"

"No, not at all."

She goes over to them, fills them in on what just happened, and returns a few minutes later. "Charlie is going to stay here with Lotar, who has promised to show him the fighter."

"Good. Let's get underway then." Max looks at Jannik. "Do you mind if we borrow your tractor? We'd like to check on the horses."

"No, not at all. Enjoy yourselves."

The tractor has an enclosed cab with large windows and pulls a utility trailer. Max drives and Betty and Adrian sit in the back. As they drive away, Wolfie chases after them, and when they stop, he jumps onto the trailer.

Betty smiles. "Well, it seems that we've picked up a passenger."

Adrian turns to see what she's looking at. "What a magnificent animal! I've never seen a German Shepherd that large before."

"Actually, he's an Alsatian Wolf Dog from the Black Forest. Max felt he needed protection when he was traveling back and forth to his project, so he bought an attack dog."

Adrian asks her, "What project was that?"

"We both worked on one of Hitler's wonder weapons. We can talk about it at dinner if you like."

They leave the barn and follow the faint outline of a trail that leads into the dense forest. Its narrow path winds its way to the high alpine meadows an hour away.

Charlie and Lotar cross the meadow and head toward the parked Focke-Wulf fighter. The sleek plane impresses him. "Thanks for offering me a tour of your 190. They were a much admired, and feared, fighter with the British pilots. To tell you the truth, I've never been this close to one."

Lotar jokes with him. "Maybe that's a good thing!"

Charlie laughs. "Yeah, you're right about that!" and they walk around it. "This is quite a machine. What variant is it?"

"It's the latest version, a G model, but it differs slightly from most." He points to the underside of the wing. "Besides the twenty mm cannon in the nose, they fitted it with additional cannon pods under each wing, and the combination is deadly."

"I'll say. Only a couple of hits from those cannons and down you go!"

Charlie continues to admire the plane and Lotar asks him, "Would you like to fly it?"

"You bet! You must be reading my mind."

"Well, get in and I'll talk you through it. Of course, everything is marked in German, but it's pretty obvious what the functions are. Personally, I prefer the 190. Unfortunately, the wheels are close together on the 109, and it can become quite uncontrollable if the ground is uneven. Regrettably, we lost a lot of inexperienced pilots because of it."

"I didn't know that, but I can see what you mean."

"Come. I'll show you how to pre-flight it," and Lotar takes him through the routine. They finish and he asks him, "Well, are you ready to get in?"

"You bet!"

They walk across the wing and Charlie steps into the cockpit. Lotar finishes explaining how to work the controls. "Check out the rate of climb. It's far superior to any Allied fighter."

"Thanks, I will."

He warns him. "She's fully armed, so be careful. Just keep the lockout on the red firing button in the covered position."

Charlie nods. "Got it."

Lotar closes the cockpit enclosure for him and jumps to the ground. Charlie starts the engine, taxis out into the meadow, and idles down to the end of the field. He rotates the fighter 180-degrees into a light breeze, brings it to full power, and the plane races down the grass airstrip and climbs steeply into the morning sky. After a while, he drops in over the trees, makes a perfect landing, and taxis toward Lotar. He shuts down the engine and exits. "What an experience! Thank you."

"You're quite welcome."

"And you're right, the rate of climb was unbelievable. I'm glad I never had to face one of these. An experienced pilot can have a bag full of tricks, but if you can't run away, you're a dead duck."

Lotar nods his head in agreement. "Fortunately, those days are behind us."

BETTY, MAX, AND ADRIAN ARRIVE AT THE HIGH MEADOW. IN the center is a group of twenty horses standing in deep green grass. Adrian watches them intently. "It's an unbelievable sight to see so many! They're beautiful, and your stallion is powerful looking!"

"Thanks. His name is Gunnar. The black mare standing next to him is Betty's horse, Arabella."

Upon seeing the tractor, the horse's race across the field, knowing that they have hay for them. Arabella sees Betty and runs to greet her. Their reunion is tearful, and she throws her arms around her neck and hugs her tightly. Betty reaches into her pocket and offers her an apple, which she is quick to consume, then strokes her head and kisses her cheek lovingly. "I missed you every day."

Max spreads out the hay amongst the horses. Standing at the edge of the group is a tall, powerful looking young stallion. He puts a bridle over his head and hands the reins to Adrian. "You'll like this horse; his name is Warrior, and he's the son of Gunnar and Arabella."

"He's magnificent. I can't wait to ride him."

Max continues. "I call him Warrior because he loves to jump, and he's very aggressive on the course. A highly competitive nature like that is a sure sign of a future champion."

Betty finishes adjusting her saddle and says to Adrian. "There's a pristine alpine lake above us and it's a beautiful ride. Would you like to see it?"

"Yes. I certainly would!"

They mount up and follow a well-worn horse trail. Ahead of them are rugged mountain peaks draped in snow, and far below is the deep blue Mosel River. The trail crosses the meadow, then winds through the forest toward the alpine lake high above them. Wolfie follows them at a casual pace, stopping from time to time to smell the scent of some wild animal. Soon they come to a long, winding section that weaves its way through a thinly wooded area where several large logs lay across the trail. They ride side-by-side and Max asks Adrian, "Can you handle these low jumps?"

"Yes, I'll follow you two."

Max nudges his powerful stallion, and Gunnar leaps forward. Betty follows him in hot pursuit, and Adrian charges after them at full speed. They race down the twisting trail, gallop across the meadow, then sprint to the fallen logs and easily clear them.

Ahead of them, a mountain stream cascades down a shallow gully lined with grass. Their horses slow, slide down the embankment, and jump the fast-running water. Clumps of mud from their hooves fly high into the air as they explode up the opposite bank and, one by one, they gallop into the dense forest and disappear.

The trail climbs higher and higher up the rugged mountainside, and they soon enter a hidden valley. A clear alpine lake runs the length of it, and it's surrounded by meadows filled with wildflowers. They dismount at the shore and let their horses stroll out into the water for a long drink.

Betty walks over to Adrian. "That was fun! I see you are a very accomplished rider."

"Thank you. I love riding. I just never dreamed that I would ride a horse of this caliber. Warrior is absolutely stunning, and what a jumper!"

"He hasn't been ridden for quite a while, so you haven't seen him at his best." She walks toward a massive rock ledge that overlooks the lake. "Here's a good place to sit."

The clear mountain air is intoxicating and the three of them sit down to enjoy the spectacular view. "We love coming up here," and she points down the lake. "Max's grandfather built that stone cabin."

Adrian admires the valley. "The scenery here is absolutely gorgeous!"

Betty is curious about his past. "Tell us about yourself. How did you get released from the POW camp so early? The Brits just started repatriating their prisoners."

"I'm married to the daughter of a French general who works closely with General de Gaulle. When my wife received your letter, they knew where I was. The general's staff contacted the British military, and I was repatriated as soon as the war ended."

"So, what's your position with them now?"

"I am the Director General of their Economic Reconstruction Program, but so much about me. What are you doing here?"

"We own an air cargo company and have a military contract to fly freight into the British Occupation Zone. We stopped here so Max could check on his property."

"That's very interesting. We desperately need that same service. Would you consider working with us as well?"

"I'd love to, but I wouldn't know how to navigate the French bureaucracy, and then there's the language barrier."

Adrian thinks about it for a moment. "There might be a way we could do this. I would be interested in being a silent partner. I could finance it, set up the corporation, handle the politics, and secure the contracts on the condition that you would run the company."

Betty is excited by his offer and looks at Max. "What do you think, darling? I'd love to, but you have a say in this too."

He nods his head in agreement. "I like the idea."

Betty extends her hand to Adrian, and they shake on it. "I'll talk with Charlie when we get back to the house. He can easily handle our British contracts. Where would we be based?"

"Paris, the City of Light."

"Wow! I've always wanted to spend time there!"

"Well, now's your chance. The war damage is minimal. No traffic jams and smog like London, and it's a simpler life. Most people get around by bicycle, or the Metro, and it has several internationally acclaimed universities. The food and wine are fantastic, and the opera and symphony are fabulous. Need I say more?"

Just then, Wolfie arrives at Betty's side. She reaches down, pets him, and he wanders over to the lake and plops down in the shallow water to cool off. Betty turns to Adrian. "This is really exciting! Let's talk more after dinner tonight."

"Good. I look forward to it."

It's late afternoon and Max turns to Adrian. "It will be dark soon. Do you mind if we head back?"

"No, not at all. And thank you again for this astonishing day."

They saddle up and ride along the shoreline, following the trail into the tall trees. After a while, they cross the lower meadow and arrive at the tractor. They dismount, unsaddle their horses, and load their riding gear into the trailer.

As they prepare to leave, Betty calls to Wolfie. "Wolfie! Load up!" He races back to them and jumps onto the trailer.

The ride had been quite an exciting experience for Adrian. "Your young stallion is an extraordinary animal."

"Yes, he has the heart of a champion."

"Would you consider selling him?"

Max laughs. "I'm afraid you've fallen in love with a very expensive horse."

The tractor lurches and bumps its way down the steep incline, and he smiles. "It's a bad habit of mine, and it's gotten me into trouble many times!"

"I'll bet! Was it worth it?"

"Well, nice things do come at a price. Renée's birthday is at the end of the month, and I'd like to surprise her."

Max looks back at him and smiles. "Well then, he's yours."

"Thank you. She's going to be absolutely thrilled!"

Betty is delighted to see that they are passionate about horses. "Why don't you bring your wife here and stay with us? I'll have our trainer work with her. We have a challenging cross-country course that I'm sure she would like."

"Thanks, Betty. That's a fantastic idea!"

It's late afternoon and everyone has gathered in the great room. A roaring fire in the massive fireplace warms the cool evening air. Off to one side, Betty is talking to Charlie. "Adrian made us a fantastic offer. It seems the French also need help to distribute aid to their sector, and he wants to partner with us in servicing that market."

"Really? Is he able to set that up?"

"Yes, but he would be a silent partner to avoid any conflict of interest. He would handle the finances and supply us with contracts. I'd like to do it, but I don't want to leave you stranded with our British commitments."

"Don't worry about that. I like the idea. When does he want to start?"

"Right away, before the government contracts with someone else."

"Which plane is he considering?"

"He only wants the four-engine Skymaster. They cost more, but they also carry four times as much cargo, and they load level because of their tricycle landing gear."

"I agree with him on that. Our C-47s are slow to load. I think we should upgrade our planes as well. I'm certain that Andy will like your idea. Why don't you confirm it with him?"

"Thanks, Charlie. I'm really excited about this!"

Betty goes over to Adrian, who is warming his back against the fireplace. "I just went over your offer with Charlie, and he likes it. He could have two Skymasters ready in a week or two."

After a bit, Charlie joins them and shakes Adrian's hand. "Well, my friend, I'm looking forward to working with you."

"Thank you. It's a good chance for us to help our countries, and we can make some money at the same time."

"I agree," and Charlie looks over at Betty. "Well, you better start practicing your French!"

Adrian turns to her. "About that. You're going to need someone who knows how to navigate our bureaucracy. I know of a highly qualified woman pilot, and she can also teach you French during those long flights."

Betty is excited and quickly accepts his offer. "Thank you. That would be perfect!"

"Her name is Charlotte Escoffier. She's going to be thrilled when I tell her."

Max smiles and pats his shoulder. "You're making one of Betty's dreams come true."

"It's my turn to thank you and Betty for such an unbelievable afternoon, and your horses are fantastic!"

Just then, Helga enters wearing a white apron. "Dinner is served."

The group follows her into the dining room, where a massive oak table is overflowing with food. In the center is an arrangement of flowers, and a colorful porcelain tureen. Betty watches as she enters with a large bowl. "Everything looks wonderful, Helga. What have you prepared for us?"

"We have vegetable soup, homemade bread, potato salad, and the entrée is one of Max's favorites; fire-grilled lake trout."

Max motions to the group. "Please, sit wherever you like." He walks around the table, filling everyone's wineglass. "This is a 1938 semi-dry Riesling, one of our better years."

Adrian tastes the wine. "This is excellent!" and he raises his glass. "I propose a toast to our future business," and they touch glasses.

Helga returns from the kitchen, pushing a serving cart, and places a dinner plate in front of each guest. "Jannik caught these trout from our alpine lake this morning."

She serves Lotar, and he smiles approvingly. "Ahh, this is one of my favorites! Thank you, Helga."

"Welcome home," and she pats his shoulder.

After dinner, she clears the table and returns with small wineglasses which she places in front of each guest. Max gets up from his chair. "Excuse me. I have a little surprise for everyone," and he disappears into the kitchen, only to reappear minutes later with a chilled bottle of dessert wine. "This is ice wine from our vineyard. Please enjoy it while it's cold."

Adrian stares at the icy glass, then takes a sip. "This is delicious! I've heard of ice wine, but it's impossible to find."

"It's fairly rare for us to have it. It requires an early hard freeze at just the right temperature. If the freeze does not come quickly enough, the grapes can rot, and the crop is lost. If the freeze is too severe, the juice can't be extracted. And the longer the harvest is delayed, the more fruit is dropped, or lost to the birds.

"But when the temperature is just right, we pick them late at night, and press the grapes before they thaw out. The sugars and dissolved solids do not freeze, but the water does, allowing for a more concentrated flavor to develop."

Adrian takes another sip. "Do you have enough of this to be sold commercially?"

"Yes, I suppose so. What are you thinking?"

"This would be highly sought after in Paris, along with your Rieslings. Who do you sell to now?"

"The war stopped all of our commercial sales, but through the lean years, we continued to grow, and store our wine."

"Then you have a lot of it?"

"Yes. Why do you ask?"

"I would like to partner with you and distribute your wines in France. It would be highly profitable for both of us."

"I'm interested. Let's talk about it later."

That evening, the group is sitting on the terrace enjoying a roaring fire. The golden-tinted clouds of a fading sunset mark the end of a beautiful summer day, and the indigo-blue eastern sky closes in on them. Max appears with a bottle and approaches Adrian. "Are you a brandy drinker?"

"Yes, when I can find it."

"Well, I have one more surprise." He pours a small amount into several snifters and passes them around. "Perhaps we should toast to you and Warrior."

Betty raises her glass. "And to many more days of riding together."

Adrian takes a sip and swirls the amber liquid. "I haven't tasted a brandy this good since the war started. What is it?"

Max explains. "It's made from Riesling grapes. They're similar to the grape that the French use in making cognac."

"This is excellent. Do you have much of it?"

"I make a few barrels of it every year. I suppose we've got at least twenty years of brandy in the caves."

"Really! That's fantastic! We could sell this in Paris, and for a very good price. Because of the war, there's nothing on the market right now, and we'd be sold out in a month. Let's put your label on it and we'll call it Dragon Brandy."

Max touches glasses with Adrian. "You have a deal, my friend. And we certainly could use some cash."

"Your Rieslings are extraordinary, and they will be in high demand as well. How much survived the war?"

"A great deal. We sealed the entrance to our storage caves before the invasion and it's still hidden there. Then there's this year's crop. It will be ready in the fall." Adrian is excited and already has a plan. "I have a friend who has a wine shop on the Champs-Élysées that I could partner with. There would be a rush for your brandy, and we could expose your other wines to the public. I assume you can fly some of it to Paris?"

Betty interjects. "Of course. We could make a flight a day for a week. That should give you plenty to start with."

Adrian holds up his glass. "Well then, a toast to our newest venture!" and they touch glasses again.

It's getting late and Betty apologizes. "I'm sorry to break this up, but it's been a long day. We'll see you at breakfast."

They enter the master bedroom, and she prepares the bed. The evening is warm and Max leaves the glass doors to the balcony open. The light from a full moon fills the room as they get into bed. "It's good to be home. So much has changed since last week," and she kisses him. "Now you're a partner in our company, and we are here enjoying our beautiful home. It was the shock of my life to see Adrian, and now we've expanded our company into France!"

He kisses her and hugs her for a long time. "I can't believe so much could happen so quickly. I was worried about our home, but it survived the war. Jannik and Helga are safe, and now Lotar is here. It feels like we've been given a second chance to pull our lives together."

Betty snuggles close to him. "Yes, we have much to be thankful for and I'm excited about living in Paris; it's a dream come true." She thinks for a moment. "Why don't you start working on your radar scrambler? It's something that you love to do, and it could be extremely valuable. We're going to be very busy with the new French company, but we can work on it together in our spare time."

He passionately kisses her. "Thanks for your support, and yes, it is something that I love to do."

Betty and Max are up at dawn preparing breakfast in the kitchen, when Charlie and Lotar enter, followed by Adrian a few minutes later. Betty greets them as they wander in. "Good morning, everyone. There's coffee on the stove and pastries in the oven."

Lotar stretches and yawns. "Hmm, that's just what I need." He looks over at Max. "What needs to be moved out of your vault?"

"Not much. Only a few boxes and some electronic test equipment. It won't take long. Jannik should be here with his tractor any minute."

Adrian asks them. "Will you have room on the plane for a barrel or two of your brandy?"

"Yes, of course."

The sound of Jannik's diesel tractor announces his arrival, and minutes later, he enters the kitchen. "Good morning! I picked up a pallet of wine on the way over."

"Thanks, Jannik. If you wouldn't mind giving us a hand, we have a few more boxes to load before we can leave." Max finishes his coffee. "If everyone's finished, let's get under way."

They follow him down the hall to the hidden door in the library and descend to the wine cellar. At the bottom of the stone stairway, he trips a secret lever.

Adrian admires the racks of wine bottles. "What an exquisite collection! Now I understand all the secrecy."

Max looks at him and smiles. "Next time you're here, we can enjoy a bottle if you like." He walks over to the enormous wine lid embedded in the far wall, and presses against it. It slowly swings open, and he steps into the concealed room. Adrian is surprised. "Ah, Max. You never cease to amaze me! What have you got hidden back there? Some of that legendary dragon's gold?"

"Nothing that exotic! Just research for my radar scrambler."

"What's that?"

"It's a completely new technology that scrambles radar waves by modifying the Doppler shift of the transmitted signal."

"Are you saying that you would be invisible?"

"In a way. It produces multiple false images that hide your location."

"Where are you going to set up your research facility?"

"I'm not sure. Germany is too unstable right now, and who knows what the Soviets might do if they found out about it?"

Betty interjects. "England is always a possibility, but it's too cold and rainy for me."

Adrian comes up with a suggestion. "What about Paris? Some of the best universities in the world are there, so there's plenty of talent to draw on. Actually, my father-in-law is a high-ranking general. The French government might be interested in it."

Max likes his idea. "Can you arrange that?"

"Let me talk to him and I'll get back to you."

Charlie checks his watch. "We'd better get going. We've still got a lot of flying to do."

Max hands out several boxes, and they carry them up the stairs and out to the tractor. It doesn't take long, and they are soon finished. They return to the kitchen and Betty unfolds her navigation charts. Adrian pours himself a cup of coffee and points at the map. "It's only a two-and-a-half-hour flight to Le Havre. If you don't mind making a quick trip to my office, I'll prepare a contract for your partners to look at."

Betty looks up at him. "Thanks, Adrian. That would be great!"

Max points at the map. "Our project is here at this abandoned airfield. It's urgent that we remove our equipment as soon as possible."

She looks at the group. "If everybody's ready, let's get underway."

They finish their coffee and exit through the back door. As they walk toward their plane, Adrian catches up with Lotar. "What are you going to do with your 190?"

"Nothing. The war is over."

"Well, this one's over, but I have an Israeli military friend that would pay a handsome price for it."

"Really?"

"If you follow us to Le Havre, I'll take it from there."

Lotar holds out his hand. "You've got a deal, my friend."

CHAPTER 20

RETURN TO
STARLIGHT FOREST

THEY FINISH LOADING THEIR PLANE WITH MAX'S RESEARCH boxes, then roll the wine and brandy barrels aboard, and secure everything to the floor with cargo nets. Charlie starts his engines, and they taxi down the meadow. He rotates into the wind and immediately roars down the grass runway. Lotar is next to take off in his Focke-Wulf 190 and, once airborne, he quickly catches up with the slower cargo plane and they fly side-by-side into the clear morning sky.

Soon, the secret airbase appears in front of them, and Adrian can't believe the extensive destruction caused by the bombing raid. "It looks like the Allies were serious about trying to stop your project."

Max stares at it. "Yes. Early testing showed the disruptor to be quite effective."

Suddenly, Betty spots something moving on the ground. "What is that! There are people looking through the bombed-out buildings."

Adrian is quick to recognize them. "It's the Soviet Army! They're not supposed to be in this sector."

Betty watches them worriedly. "I'll bet they're searching for the disruptor! I hope they don't know about the underground hangar!"

Max shakes his head. "It's only a matter of time before they find it."

Charlie asks, "Where is it?"

Betty points to the forest ahead of them. "It's a mile in front of us. Follow the dirt road, then turn to the right and land on the paved road. The entrance is at the far end."

They approach the runway, and Charlie banks steeply to line up with it. He stares at the dense forest surrounding them as they touch down. "No wonder we missed bombing it. There's nothing here!"

Lotar lands in his fighter, and together they taxi to the end of the road. Charlie looks at the forest and is confused. "Where's the hangar?"

Betty points to the side. "It's hidden in the trees over there!" She gets up from her seat, runs to the back of the plane, and jumps out the cargo door. Wolfie and Max follow her, and they disappear into the woods. Moments later, the huge camouflage screen slowly opens, revealing a wide concrete ramp leading underground.

Charlie taxis into the cavernous hangar, muttering to himself. "Well, I'll be dammed!" and stares in amazement at the Heinkel bomber parked inside.

Betty runs to the bomber, enters through the rear passenger door, then calls to Max. "This plane is still armed, and they've already installed another disruptor!"

He mutters to himself. "Damn, they are way ahead of schedule! Do you know how to fly it?"

"Yes. It's the same plane I flew to England."

Max runs to his office and calls to Adrian. "My research papers are in here. Just throw them inside the bomber!"

Suddenly, loud sounds of hammering against steel echo throughout the hangar, and Max yells to Betty. "They're trying to break into the emergency escape door! See if it will start, and let's get the hell out of here!"

Betty sits down in the pilot's seat, throws a few switches, and her engines burst into life. Charlie runs to his cargo plane, starts it, and taxis toward the sloping entrance ramp. Adrian and Max finish loading his research boxes into the bomber just as an enormous explosion detonates in the rear of the hangar.

Max yells to Adrian. "They just blasted open the emergency escape door! They'll be here any minute!"

Adrian throws the last of Max's secret records into the plane and slams the door shut. Betty pushes on her throttles, and the bomber slowly moves forward. Suddenly, Soviet soldiers enter from the back and run out into the hangar, firing at them. The sharp staccato sound of machine gun fire echoes loudly, followed by the shrill scream of bullets ricocheting off the thick concrete walls.

He calls to Max. "See if that dorsal gun works. Just slide the cocking mechanism toward you and pull the trigger! I'll check the belly gun!"

Max climbs into the dorsal bubble, cocks the heavy machine gun, and squeezes the trigger. It fires rapidly in loud bursts and sprays the invading soldiers with deadly fire. Seconds later, Adrian's twin machine guns burst into life, and his bullets chew up equipment along the walls and shatter windows. The Soviets fire back, but the withering gunfire from their heavy machine guns pins them down. The floor is littered with bodies, as the Soviets return fire from concealed positions.

Charlie taxis out of the hangar and rolls out onto the runway. He is fully loaded with cases of wine, and barrels of brandy, and his engines scream at full power as he struggles to become airborne. Lotar's fighter is parked on the edge of the airstrip, and he runs to it, starts his engine, and chases after him.

Betty is the last one out of the hangar. She follows Lotar and they take off together in a long line. At the far end, several large Soviet trucks drive onto the airstrip and attempt to block their escape. From the safety of their trucks, the soldiers shoot at the approaching planes, trying to stop them. Charlie is heavily loaded, and struggles to gain altitude, but it won't be enough to clear the vehicles parked on the runway ahead of him.

Lotar, who is flying behind him, is quick to make a move to save Charlie. He drops to only a few feet above the ground and unleashes a torrent of fire from his three twenty mm cannons. He skillfully slides his fighter from side-to-side as his cannons tear into the blockade, literally ripping apart the Soviet trucks, and they explode violently into flames. Bodies, parts of vehicles, and chunks of asphalt fly in all directions as he lays waste to everything in sight. Charlie and Lotar fly through the dense black smoke and climb to altitude.

Betty follows them as more soldiers run toward the runway, firing their weapons at her. Max and Adrian see them approaching and lay down a lethal barrage of heavy machine gun fire, leaving the ground covered with dead and wounded soldiers. Their powerful bomber roars past the horrific scene of destruction, and they climb safely into the clouds. Betty is worried, and radios Max. "Is everyone alright back there?"

"I'm good and Adrian was just firing, so he should be okay."

"Thank goodness, we all made it out safely!"

She flies alongside Charlie, and sets course for Le Havre, France. Hours later, they approach the huge shipping port, and Betty descends steeply toward the airport. A battered Renault pickup truck with a large orange and white checkered flag mounted in the back meets them. They follow it to a remote parking area, where a dozen French military police cars are waiting with their lights flashing. The heavily armed men stand near their vehicles, but do not have their weapons drawn. Adrian is the first to leave the plane, and he walks over to them. Speaking in French, he identifies himself and explains the situation. Charlie and Lotar park next to Betty, shut down their engines, and exit.

Adrian approaches them. "I've taken care of everything. They will guard your planes until you return," and points to one of the parked military police cars. "My office is close by. We can take this car."

The Allies heavily bombed the port during the Nazi occupation, and the French are working around the clock to repair it. They soon arrive at a large building and Adrian leads them through a busy room, before ushering them into his private office. "Please, take a seat."

He sits at his desk, signs several documents, and hands them to Betty. "These are clearance papers allowing you to use French airspace. You'll need to show them to the people at the airport. When you come back next week, I'll have the freight contract ready for you and, hopefully, you can start right away."

"Great, this is so exciting!"

Adrian goes over to a large safe, works at the combination, and the heavy door swings open. He shuffles through his files, then turns and approaches Charlie with a sizable amount of cash in banded bundles. "This is a retainer for my share of the new cargo company. I'll have the rest ready for you next week."

"Thank you," and he approaches Betty. "And for my favorite nurse, a down payment on the purchase of your bomber."

"Oh, no Adrian. I wasn't expecting anything!"

"Nonsense. It's worth a lot of money, and you risked your life to fly it out."

Next, he hands Max a healthy stack of bills. "And this is for that beautiful horse of yours. I'll always remember the day I met Warrior, and the wonderful afternoon we spent riding together."

Max stares at the cash. "Adrian, this is too much."

"No, it's a fair exchange, and Renée is going to be ecstatic when she sees her present!"

He goes over to Lotar and hands him several stacks of bills. "Lotar, my friend, thanks for getting us out of trouble back there. This is for that beautiful 190. It was incredible to watch you handle a fighter like that."

"Thanks. I'm sure you would have done the same for me."

Adrian winks at Betty. "Do you think you could talk Lotar into working for us? I like the way he handles himself."

She smiles. "I think I might be able to sway him to our side!"

Lotar shakes his head. "I'd love to, but my French is not that great."

Adrian laughs and slaps him on the shoulder. "That's alright, my friend. I'm sure I can find a pretty tutor for you," and he smiles at Betty. "Let's meet here next Friday, and I'll have the paperwork ready for our new air cargo company."

She gives him a hug. "Thanks, Adrian. We'll offload your brandy and wine before we leave, and I'm looking forward to meeting your wife."

He is clearly excited about his purchase of Warrior. "It's going to be a fun weekend, and it will be a huge surprise for her." He hands Betty another envelope. "Give this to the military police guarding the plane. It allows you to remove your disruptor equipment."

"I appreciate your help. Thanks."

Lotar is the last to leave, and he and Adrian walk together out to the car. "If you come across any more fighters in good shape, let me know."

"Why? Everyone is developing jets. Piston planes are a thing of the past."

"That's true, but the Israelis need something to defend their country with."

"How many planes are you talking about?"

"Well, they're rebuilding their air force. At least a few, I would imagine."

"Actually, I might know where a couple are. I'll keep an eye out for them."

They get into their car, and Betty questions Lotar. "Adrian seems to have taken a liking to you. Would you be interested in developing the French air cargo company with me?"

"Interested! I'd jump at the chance. Flying by day and surrounded by beautiful French women at night! It's a bachelor's dream job!"

"Great! I like your positive attitude."

They arrive at their London hangar later that afternoon and exit their plane. Betty questions Max. "What do you want to do with your lab equipment?"

"Let's lock it up in one of your storage rooms. It should be safe there."

They quickly unload the plane, and Lotar takes off his gloves. "I'm ready for a beer. How far away is your cottage?"

She smiles at him. "It's close by, and there's plenty of cold Guinness."

Back at her cottage, they sit around the kitchen table having a drink and Lotar asks, "Did you hear what Adrian was talking about?"

"No. I was talking to Max."

"He said he'll buy any fighters that we find, and the money is very good."

Betty says, "I like the idea, but how can I help?"

"You're perfect for the job. You and Adrian have history together, and he trusts you. I'll locate the planes, and you can handle the sales with him. There's probably not a lot of them in flyable condition, but I'm sure I could find a couple. It would be fun, and we could make some quick cash doing it."

"Is it legal to sell them?"

"I'm not sure, but for the moment, the Allies have far more important things to worry about. If we are discrete, it shouldn't be a problem."

It's mid-afternoon the following day, and the three of them are having a late lunch at their favorite pub in London. Charlie arrives, and Lotar pulls out a chair for him. "Hi. Please, join us."

"Thanks. Well, my friend, what's your opinion of England now that you've seen it from the ground?"

"I like it here. The people are polite, and your Irish beer is great." He raises his eyebrows and grins. "But I don't think I'm ever going to try your famous haggis!"

A few minutes later, Andy enters the pub, and Charlie waves him over to their table. "Sorry I'm late. I got hung up at the office. It sounded like you had quite an adventure over there."

Charlie pushes back his baseball cap. "Yeah. We had to shoot our way out! Silly me, I thought the war was over!" and he makes the introductions. "This is Lotar, Max's younger brother, and an ex-Luftwaffe fighter pilot."

Andy extends his hand to him. "It's always a pleasure to meet a fellow fighter pilot."

"It's nice meeting you," and shakes his hand. He continues. "Betty told me a lot about you. You have quite an impressive record."

"Well, I've heard many stories about you and Charlie."

After pouring himself a beer from the pitcher, Andy takes a long sip and looks over at Betty. "We're considering upgrading our fleet to four-engine Skymasters. What's your vote?"

"Count me in on that. There's going to be a lot of cargo to transport, and the C-47s are too slow and hard to load."

"Good, then we're all in agreement."

Charlie looks at Lotar. "I'd like to propose a toast to our newest pilot," and they clink their beer glasses together.

Andy turns to Lotar. "Charlie and I are making a bid on a plane tomorrow. Can you fly with Betty?"

"Are you kidding? I'd love to."

"Great!" and he looks at Betty. "Where's the Wolf?"

"He's sacked out in the ambulance," and she stands. "Sorry, but I've got an appointment with the vet for his annual checkup."

Max gives her a hug. "See you at home."

She works her way through the crowded pub and walks out the front door. Now that she's left the room, Max can talk in private. "I didn't want to mention this while Betty was here, but she's gone through a lot. Now that I have a little cash, I'd like to surprise her with a plane of her own. Are there any surplus planes I could buy for her? Maybe something that's fast and different."

Andy shakes his head. "Not really. Mostly Mustangs and Spitfires. If you're looking for all out speed, most fighters wouldn't qualify because they're overdesigned to carry a heavy weapon load."

Lotar is in deep thought and taps his fingers on the table. "You know, there might be something. The Luftwaffe developed an experimental high-speed fighter called the Dornier 335 Arrow, but the war ended before it saw combat."

Charlie frowns. "I've never heard of it," and turns to Andy. "Have you?"

"No, that's new to me. What does it look like?"

Lotar explains. "They only made a few dozen for testing. It's a big plane with a unique push-pull configuration; a conventional V-12 engine in the front, and another one behind the tail. The major advantage of that type of design is its high speed."

Charlie has always been interested in unusual planes. "That sounds exotic. How fast is it?"

"The pilot that I talked to said he flew it to 470 mph, and it had excellent handling characteristics."

"That's faster than our Spitfires! Do you think you could find one?"

"Maybe. They were secretly testing one at a little used emergency landing strip just north of Cologne, in the British Zone, so it would be easy for us to check it out. My mechanic introduced me to the brothers that worked on it. They lived on a small farm nearby, and if it's still there, I'm sure they would jump at the chance to earn some cash."

Charlie is always up for an adventure. "Hmm, that's only a couple of hours away in our C-47," and grins. "Let's see if we can find it."

Andy likes Max's idea of giving Betty a fun plane. "Don't worry. If it's not there, we'll find something else for you."

Charlie slaps the table. "Alright then! The weekend is coming up. Let's go check out this mystery plane of yours!"

It's early morning the following day. They load a borrowed motorcycle into their C-47 and leave for Cologne. Soon, they arrive at a sleepy municipal airport ten miles south of the city and offload their motorcycle. A half hour later, they leave the main road and drive across the rolling hills of farm country. After a bit, Lotar turns off and continues down a dusty farm road. Several miles later, they come to a small dairy farm and approach the front of a run-down farmhouse.

Charlie looks around at the cow pastures and dilapidated buildings. "Are you sure this is the spot? I wouldn't expect to see a secret plane out here with the cows."

"That's right, and that's exactly why they put it out here. Let's check out the barn. The brothers might be in there."

They walk over to an old barn and open the front door. In the shadows at the back of the building, they see the brother's milking cows, and Lotar waves to them. "Hi, do you remember me? I'm Klaus's friend."

The brothers stare at him for a moment. "Ahh, yes. The fighter pilot," and they approach and shake hands. "I remember you. I'm Jürgen, and this is my brother, Otis. What brings you this way?"

"I'm interested in that 335. Is it still here?"

"Yes, it is. When the war ended, they closed the hangar doors and disappeared. No one ever came back."

"What would it take to get it into running condition?"

"Well, it's new, so everything should work. We'd have to check out the fuel system, things like that."

"I'll pay you five hundred dollars American if you can get it ready to fly this weekend."

Jürgen looks over at his brother, who nods in agreement. "We would be happy to do that."

"By the way, do you know of any 109 or 190 fighters abandoned around here?"

Otis thinks for a moment. "There's probably quite a few tucked away all over the countryside. Some are in good condition, but most are in need of repair."

"I can pay you five hundred dollars for everyone you deliver to my farm near Koblenz. Are you interested?"

"Yes! That would be an enormous amount of money for us. How many would you be looking to buy?"

"At least a dozen," and Lotar pauses. "As I remember, your brother is a pilot."

Otis sets down the pail of milk that he is holding. "I am."

"Good. We've got an airstrip at our farm, and it's only a hundred miles from here. I would need you to drop them off there."

"That's not a problem and thank you." Jürgen extends his hand. "You have a deal, my friend!"

Lotar pulls a map out of his jacket, presses it against the wall, and marks on it with his pen. "This is my place. My caretaker's name is Jannik, and he will pay you for each one that you deliver. Just buzz the main house, and he'll meet you at the airstrip."

Lotar turns to Charlie, who doesn't speak German, and explains the situation. "The Arrow is nearby, and they are happy to get it ready."

"Great! I'm dying to see this thing!"

The brother's step into their beat-up Kübelwagen, and Lotar and Charlie follow on their motorcycle. They cut cross their pasture and enter the adjoining woods. Ten minutes later, they drive out of the dense forest, and down a narrow grass runway overgrown with weeds. At the far end is a camouflaged hangar hidden amongst the trees and out of sight from the air.

Jürgen opens the doors and parked in the dark shadows is an intact Dornier 335 Arrow. It's painted in camouflage colors of green and light gray and is very impressive. The Arrow's twin-engine design gives it an extremely unusual looking appearance. One engine is in front, the other is behind the tail, and it has a tall tricycle landing gear that leaves the fuselage high off the ground.

Charlie approaches the fighter and stares at it. "This baby is a monster! Why is it sitting so high up?"

Lotar explains. "To keep the rear propeller from hitting the ground on take-off."

Otis rolls a tall boarding stairway toward the cockpit, and the four of them walk up the stairs. He tilts the plane's canopy to the side and explains the control layout.

"There's one unique feature on this plane that you should know about," and he points to a red lever next to the pilot's seat. "This is the world's first rocket powered ejection seat. Because the rear engine is directly behind the pilot, they had to come up with a way for the pilot to eject without getting hit by that huge rear propeller. When you pull on the ejection lever, explosive charges detonate and separate the rear engine from the airframe. Then the canopy blows off, and the rockets fire to eject the pilot."

Lotar is amazed. "That would be an unbelievable ride!"

He turns to Charlie and translates how it works. He can only shake his head. "Leave it up to the Germans to invent something like that!"

Otis laughs. "Obviously, you want to be careful, and don't accidentally pull that lever," and jokes. "The mechanics hate it when that happens!"

They set about to ready the Arrow for flight and Jürgen pulls a large battery charger over to it. He plugs it into a socket in the fuselage, then starts a small gasoline-powered engine. With the batteries charging, they climb a scaffolding, remove the metal cowlings covering the engines, and by early evening, they finish checking out the plane.

Lotar sits down in the pilot's seat, and Otis shows him how to start it. The engines crank over a few times, then roar into life. He lets them idle for a few minutes, then shuts them down. Jürgen joins them. "It's getting late. Why don't you stay the night and leave tomorrow morning?"

"Thanks. I'm so excited I probably won't get any sleep tonight, anyway!"

The crowing of a rooster wakens them the following morning. Lotar and Charlie walk downstairs to the kitchen where Otis already has breakfast waiting for them. Jürgen sits at the table drinking coffee and welcomes them. "It's a beautiful day. You're going to have a nice flight back to London."

Lotar slides a stack of money across the table to Jürgen. "I appreciate your hard work."

"Thank you! This will really help us."

After breakfast, Lotar and Charlie leave the house and walk to their motorcycle parked in the front yard. Charlie puts on his goggles and zips up his leather jacket. "I wish I was going with you." He straddles his motorcycle, throws his weight on the starting crank, and the engine bursts into life. "Have fun with that beast! I'm jealous!"

Lotar slaps him on his shoulder. "Don't worry, my friend. You will be the next to fly it."

Charlie nods his head, guns his motorcycle, and roars off down the dusty farm road. The brothers pull up alongside Lotar in their Kübelwagen, and he gets in. They drive to the hangar, and Otis slides the huge doors open. Lotar stands in front of the plane, admiring the sleek fighter. "I can't wait to see what this baby can do!" He climbs the boarding stairs and steps into the cockpit.

Otis cautions him. "The engines are new, so don't push them too hard." He goes over the pre-flight instructions one last time and stays with him while they start. They burst into life, and after a few minutes, Lotar gives him the thumbs up, and closes the heavy bulletproof canopy.

The big fighter rolls out into the bright morning sunlight and taxis to the end of the grass airstrip. After checking his instruments one last time, he revs his engines, blasts down the runway, and in a short distance, the Arrow is airborne. He quickly climbs to ten thousand feet to avoid visual detection by anyone on the ground, and heads for England, three hundred miles away. An hour later, Lotar crosses the coastline of Belgium and flies out over the English Channel. Their airport comes into view, and he lands the sleek fighter.

As he taxis up to their hangar, Paddy and the other mechanics come out to greet him. He shuts down his engines, opens his canopy, and looks down at them. "Well, are you going to help me out of this damn thing or not?"

With that, Paddy gets some help, and they roll the boarding stairs up to the cockpit. "Where the bloody hell did you find this? It's enormous!"

Lotar walks down the stairs and pats him on the back. "She's Max's surprise birthday present to Betty! Do you think you can clean her up?"

"Sure. We'll remove the military hardware and strip her down to bare metal. What color do you want to paint her?"

"Good question? I know Betty likes the colors on the dragon shield."

Paddy agrees. "That's a great idea."

Shelagh appears and walks over to him. "What a fantastic plane! But what have you done with my husband?"

Lotar laughs, and jokes with her. "He couldn't keep up with his motorbike, but he should be here in a couple of hours." Then he asks Paddy, "Where can we park this thing? We need to keep it hidden for a while."

"There's an empty hangar a few spaces down the line. We can hide it there."

Several days later, Betty, Max, and Lotar pull up in their ambulance and park in front of their hangar. Wolfie jumps out the back door and follows them.

Betty greets Charlie. "Good morning. We're off to meet Adrian in Le Havre. Which plane should I take?"

"Take the best of the two C-47s. We need to look as professional as possible."

"I agree."

Lotar walks with her to the plane. "I'll pre-flight it while you get ready."

Max and Wolfie follow them, and in a few minutes, they head for Le Havre, France, an hour away. Betty is flying, and it's a beautiful day. They soon approach the airport, land, and taxi to the air freight terminal. Adrian is standing in front, and waves to them.

They exit the plane, and Betty greets him with her usual hug. "Good morning, Adrian!"

"Good morning, my friend! How was your flight?"

"Wonderful! and it's a beautiful day."

They enter the coffee shop and sit down. Adrian orders for them, then produces an envelope, and hands it to Max. "This is the paperwork to incorporate our wine company. Please sign them, and I'll file it with the government."

Then he gives Betty a thick envelope. "And these are the incorporation papers for our French air cargo company."

She scans the paperwork, then puts them in her flight bag. "Thanks, Adrian. I'll have Andy and Charlie sign them. I can't wait to spend some time in Paris."

He smiles at her. "It's beautiful this time of the year. We'll have lunch at one of my favorite restaurants overlooking the Seine."

"I can't thank you enough, Adrian. This is a dream come true. I'm so excited!"

"Good. I'll meet you at the airport at noon tomorrow."

Three hours later, Lotar is flying, and Betty is enjoying the view. Below them are the snow-covered Swiss Alps, and the wide Rhine River. As usual, he flies low to let Jannik know they are about to land, then circles back and lands in the long meadow next to the house. By the time he shuts down the engines and they exit the plane, Jannik arrives in his blue tractor and Max waves to him. "Hi, Jannik!"

He has an anxious look on his face. "Did you pick up the rest of your research equipment?"

"Yes, but the Soviets were sacking the base, and we had to shoot our way out!"

"What!"

Max pats him on his shoulder as they walk toward the house. "It's been a long day, my friend. I'll fill you in later. Let's get together tonight."

That evening they are relaxing on the terrace having a drink and watching the sun go down. Jannik takes a sip of brandy. "So, what's the plan, Max?"

"We're going to make a flight a day for a week. That should give Adrian enough product to prepare for his grand opening. He's found a store on one of the main avenues in Paris to sell our wines."

Jannik is pleased. "It feels good to be back in business again. I already moved enough wine for a plane load and stacked it under the trees."

"Thanks for your help."

The next morning finds them busy loading wine, and they secure a heavy cargo net over it. Max puts his arm around Betty. "You're not going to need me for anything. I think Wolfie and I will stay here."

She gives him a kiss. "That's fine. Lotar and I can take it from here."

Max exits the plane, and he and Jannik swing the cargo doors shut. Betty waves goodbye as they taxi down the meadow. She turns the cargo plane around and speeds down the runway. Max waves at her as they pass by, and they soon disappear into the morning sky.

Hours later, they approach Paris, and Lotar looks down from his side window. "There's the Eiffel Tower, and that must be the Seine winding its way through the city. What a beautiful sight!"

Visiting Paris someday was one of Betty's lifelong dreams, and she's excited. "Yes, and I can't wait to explore the city."

They land and taxi to the freight terminal. Standing in front of the hangar, and waiting to greet them, is Adrian and a pretty woman. They park their plane, and Betty greets him with a hug. "It's always so good to see you."

He hugs her back. "How was the flight?"

"The weather was clear all the way."

Adrian introduces the young woman standing next to him. "This is Charlotte Escoffier, the pilot I told you about."

"Hi, I'm Betty," and she extends her hand.

"My pleasure, but my friends call me Chara."

Lotar introduces himself. "Hi. I'm Lotar."

She smiles at him. "Very nice to meet you as well."

Chara is very attractive with long jet-black hair and piercing blue eyes. As she looks at Lotar, it's easy to see there's an immediate attraction between the two of them. Adrian is eager to show them Paris, and they walk toward his car.

"The terminal people can unload the plane. What do you say we have some lunch?"

Betty's hungry as usual. "Great. How about you Lotar?"

"I am too, and we're both excited to explore your city."

Betty asks Chara, "Will you join us?"

She answers with a distinctly French accent. "Thank you, I'd like that."

Adrian points to a maroon four-door Citroën sedan with a black roof. "This is my car. I want to take you to one of my favorite cafés for lunch."

He drives them through the city, parks near the Seine, and points to a small café overlooking the river. "It's over there with the colorful umbrellas."

As they walk along the sidewalk, Chara asks Lotar, "Have you been to Paris before?"

"No. This is my first time. Betty said you were quite an accomplished pilot. What have you been flying?"

"I flew cargo planes during the war. And you?"

"I was a fighter pilot and flew on the Eastern Front."

They enter the café, and the waiter seats them on a sunny deck overlooking the river. Adrian orders coffee and has a suggestion. "I highly recommend their steak-frites."

Lotar is curious. "What are steak-frites?"

Chara explains. "It's a steak paired with French fries, and it's very popular here."

"Well, I'm eager to try your recommendation!"

The waitress returns with their coffee, takes their order, and leaves. Adrian looks at Betty. "I told Chara that you're fluent in English and German, but now you need to speak French."

Chara smiles at her. "It sounds like you're probably good with languages. We'll have fun with it and I'm sure you'll catch on quickly."

Betty takes an immediate liking to her. "Thank you. I'm looking forward to working with you."

Chara asks Lotar, "Do you speak French?"

He smiles at her. "Just enough to get me into trouble, but I would like to become fluent someday."

Adrian digs into his briefcase and hands Betty a large envelope. "Here's a copy of our incorporation papers. You'll need to sign them, and by the way, I'll need a copy of your passports to register our company."

"I don't have a passport, and it would take time to apply for it. And I don't think Lotar has one either."

Lotar is apologetic. "Sorry. And who knows where I would go to get one."

Adrian thinks about it for a minute. "I think I can get French passports for both of you. I just need your military identification cards. You will need a passport to enter French airports."

The waitress arrives with their lunch, and Lotar stares at his plate. "This looks delicious!" His steak is covered with a golden sauce, and he asks, "What is this?"

Chara explains in her sexy French accent. "It's called Café de Paris. It's a fusion of thyme flowers, fresh cream, white Dijon mustard, and butter."

He slices off a piece of steak and dips it into the golden liquid. "This is really tasty!"

"The French take their food and wine seriously, so you need to know what you're eating if you are going to live here."

Betty speaks to her. "How soon could you come to work?"

"I'm available whenever you need me."

"Good. We're flying cargo between Koblenz and Paris for a week. It would be great if you could start right away."

"I'm ready. What should I wear?"

"You know, that's a good question. We need to look more professional. Is there a military surplus store nearby?"

"Yes, just down the street."

After lunch, Betty looks at Adrian. "If you boys don't mind, Chara and I will return shortly." As they walk away, she explains. "I'm tired of walking around the hangar looking like someone's lost girlfriend!"

They exit the restaurant, and forty-five minutes later, they re-emerge dressed in black shoes, dark blue pants, a white short-sleeved blouse, and dark blue ties. They're wearing black leather Luftwaffe flight jackets, with a pair of wings sewn on the front pocket, and dark green pilot's glasses. It's a stunning combination, and they walk back to the café.

Adrian is the first to notice them. "Well, well. What a transformation!"

"Thanks to Chara, and her excellent taste in fashion, we created a very professional look," and the guys all agree.

After lunch, Adrian checks his watch. "It's getting late, and you probably need to start back."

They leave the café and walk toward his car. Betty asks him, "It's your wife's birthday this weekend. Are you still planning to pick up Warrior?"

"Yes, and I've been counting the days. This is the biggest surprise that I've ever given her, and I can't wait."

"Great! Then we'll make it a very special time for her."

As they walk, Lotar talks with Adrian. "Remember when you asked if we could find some fighters? I talked to a couple of mechanic friends about it, and they said there were probably quite a few abandoned in the area. I told them we would pay five hundred dollars American for anything flyable, and in good condition."

"That's great news! I'll mention it to my contact."

They drive back to the airport, pull up to the freight terminal, and thank Adrian for lunch. As they walk to their plane, Betty chats with Chara. "This would be a good time for you to get checked out on our C-47."

"Thanks. I'd like that."

Then she turns to Lotar. "Would you mind flying with Chara on this leg? I need to go over the paperwork that Adrian gave me."

"Sure, no problem." He smiles at Chara and tries to be cute. "Ready for a lesson on the C-47?"

However, she is not a woman that is easily intimidated. "The French have them too. I have eight hundred hours flying them. How many hours do you have?"

The always confident Lotar now has a sheepish look on his face. "Ahh, I just started flying them."

"Well, maybe I can teach you a thing or two," and she motions him toward the cockpit. "After you."

Lotar has never been around a woman like Chara. He's used to having the upper hand, but she is very different, and he secretly admires her confidence. He enters the cockpit and sits down in the copilot's seat. "Okay, professor. I'm all ears."

She smiles at him. "I'm sure you are an expert in many things, but when it comes to flying C-47s, and learning French, it looks like you are going to be the student!"

He responds confidently. "Touché!"

She answers in French. "Attachez votre centure, mon gars. Partons!

"What?"

"I said. 'Buckle up, big boy. We're leaving!'"

Several hours later, they cross the Mosel River and approach their estate. Chara looks over at Lotar. "Now it's your turn to show me something. Why don't you take us on in?"

He straightens up in his seat and takes over the controls. "Thanks. That's our place up ahead." He descends to five hundred feet, buzzes the house, then circles back to the grass airstrip, and makes a soft landing.

Chara is impressed with his flying skills. "That was very nice. You have quite a talent."

Max and Wolfie greet them. "How did it go?"

Betty bubbles over with excitement. "Paris was beautiful, and I've got a lot to tell you. This is Chara Escoffier, the pilot that Adrian spoke of."

"Hi, I'm Max. Very nice to meet you," and offer's his hand.

She smiles at him. "I'm pleased to meet you."

Max takes a step back to admire Betty's uniform. "Your new look is very professional!"

"Thanks."

Wolfie walks over to Chara, and she pets him. Betty looks at them. "It seems you have a new admirer."

"I love dogs, and he's beautiful." She stands and looks at the horses in the meadow. "And your horses are gorgeous! Do you raise them here?"

"Yes, Max does. Do you ride?"

"No. Living in the city I never had a chance, but I'd love to learn someday."

"These are Hanoverian show jumpers. They're a little too much for a beginner, but I'll find something suitable for you if you're interested."

"I would enjoy learning very much."

Betty asks Lotar, "Why don't you show Chara the property?"

He gives her a wink. "Sure, I'm happy to give you the full tour," and they head off toward the horse barn.

Betty can see that they are both highly competitive, and Chara is slowly warming up to him, especially now that they have something in common to talk about. As they stroll back to the house she asks Max, "Do you think you could find a horse for Chara to begin on?"

"Yes. I think so. Elke knows everybody in the valley. I'll give her a call," and wonders for a moment. "What do you know about Chara?"

"She's a graduate of a prestigious business school in Paris and has an advanced degree in finance. Adrian told me she lost her parents in the war, and life has been a struggle for her."

"Lotar seems to be quite taken by her. How are they getting along?"

"He said that she's very different from other women he's known."

"What do you think of her?"

"I had an immediate connection with her. She confided to me that she caught her last boyfriend with another woman, and it was a devastating experience. Now she's slow to trust anyone and is very cautious about getting involved. I don't think she is going to fall under his spell too easily."

"She's certainly pretty, and well educated. I think Lotar needs someone like that to challenge him."

Betty agrees. "I found her to be an experienced pilot and fun to be with. I'm always surrounded by men, so it's nice to have a woman around that I can talk to."

Later that evening, the group is sitting by a roaring fire having drinks on the terrace and Betty asks Chara, "How did your day go?"

"Lotar showed me your beautiful horses, and I learned a lot about what you do here. You have an impressive vineyard, and your Riesling wine is extraordinary. No wonder Adrian is so excited about it."

Max interjects. "Speaking of wine, I have something special to show you," and he disappears into the night, only to return moments later. "I'd like you to try the brandy that we make here," and he pours some into a snifter and passes it to her.

"Thank you." She holds the glass in both hands for a few minutes to bring it to room temperature. "How old is this?"

"This bottle is about twenty years old."

She sniffs the brandy, and smells it for hints of flowers or fruit, then takes another sniff looking for stronger aromas. Finally, she takes a small sip. "This is exquisite! It rivals the very best of French cognacs. Is this what we're shipping to Paris?"

"Yes. I see you know your brandies. Do you think we'll be successful selling it?"

"I think you will be wildly successful. Because of the war, it's extremely difficult to find anything of quality." She stands and sets her brandy snifter down. "I have a small gift for you. Please excuse me, I'll be right back."

She enters the house, and a few minutes later, returns with three gift wrapped packages and hands one to each of them. "This is just a little something to show my appreciation for your hospitality." They open their presents and discover that she has given them a beginner's language book, and everyone thanks her. "I hope this will help demystify French for you."

Chara checks with Betty. "What time are we leaving tomorrow?"

"The plane should be ready by nine o'clock, but you have to be back by dark, because our airstrip isn't lighted. If you don't mind, I need to stay here and go over this paperwork with Max. Can the two of you handle it?"

"Yes, of course," and she asks Lotar, "Are you okay with that?"

He's happy to be alone with Chara. "That will give us plenty of time to practice French, Oui?"

"That's the spirit!"

It had been a long day, and Betty and Max excuse themselves. "It's getting late, and tomorrow will be another busy day. We'll see you at breakfast."

Chara and Lotar call after them. "Good night."

A gentle breeze sweeps the clouds away, and the heavens above them are filled with glittering stars. They remain on the terrace warming themselves in front of a roaring fire, while sipping brandy and chat into the night.

The next morning, Betty is up early and already has breakfast prepared. Chara and Lotar enter the kitchen, followed by Max and Wolfie.

She looks up from the stove. "Breakfast is out on the terrace. Please sit and help yourself."

As they sit down, Jannik pulls up in his tractor, and Max waves at him. "Come and join us for coffee."

He walks up the rear steps to the terrace. "Thanks, and good morning, everyone!"

Betty makes the introductions. "This is Chara, our newest pilot."

"I'm Jannik. Very nice to meet you," and he sits down next to Lotar. "I stacked the wine near the plane, so we can load up quickly."

A few minutes later, a truck pulling a horse trailer pulls up behind Jannik's tractor and stops. The woman waves to them, then walks to the rear of the trailer. She lowers the ramp and disappears inside. Slowly the rump of a tall horse backs out and into the sunlight. Its body is a stunning chestnut color, with a long flaxen mane and tail. Chara is surprised. "That's the most beautiful horse I've ever seen. What breed is it?"

"He's a Black Forest horse . . . and he's yours."

"What?"

"He's a present from all of us."

Tears begin to flow. "Thank you, no one has ever done such a nice thing for me."

They walk down the rear stairs, and Betty makes the introductions. "Elke, this is Chara."

Elke holds out her hand. "It's nice to meet you."

But Chara gives her a hug instead. "He's magnificent!"

"Let me introduce you. He's an eight-year-old gelding, very gentle, and quite rare. An older couple owned him and needed to find a good home for him."

Chara rubs his neck in astonishment. "What's his name?"

"That's for you to decide. He's smart, and he'll soon figure it out."

She strokes his mane and looks at him admiringly. "I think I'll call him Cyrano because of his long nose!"

Betty laughs. "That's very cute," and turns to Lotar. "Can you find a place for him in the barn?"

"Sure, we have plenty of room."

It had been an overwhelming experience for a city girl, and Chara is thrilled. Her horse walks quietly next to her, and she and Lotar disappear down the path leading to the barn.

CHAPTER 21

CENTRE EQUESTRE DRAGON INVITATION À NOTRE CONCOURS COMPLET

FINALLY, THE LONG-AWAITED WEEKEND ARRIVES, AND Betty is filled with anticipation and excitement. Adrian and Renée arrive from Paris late in the afternoon and park their truck and trailer near the barn. Wolfie barks, alerting them of their arrival, and Betty walks outside to greet them. She cheek kisses Adrian, and he introduces his wife, Renée. She is tall and pretty, with an athletic build, and cheek kisses Betty. "It's so nice to meet you. Adrian has told me many exciting stories about you."

Betty feels an immediate connection to her. "Thanks. This is my fiancée, Max, and our dog, Wolfie."

They exchange pleasantries, and she bends down and pets Wolfie. "Your dog is extraordinary! I've never seen such a large dog before."

Betty smiles at her. "He has a long and interesting history with us. I'll tell you more about him at dinner."

Several mares and their colts graze in the adjacent meadow, and Renée stares at them intently. "Your farm is gorgeous! I can't tell you how excited I am to meet Warrior."

Betty motions toward the horse barn. "Well, let's introduce you then. Adrian said that you are on the French equestrian team. How long have you been riding?"

"My father bought me riding lessons for my sixteenth birthday, and I've been passionate about it ever since."

Betty is impressed. "You've got quite a background! Tomorrow, I'll show you the rest of our horses, and then we'll ride the entire complex. Besides the cross-country course, we also have a large vineyard, and a winery to visit."

"Would it be possible to see your dragon paintings? Adrian said that they are unbelievable."

"Yes. Of course."

They reach the barn's entrance doors and enter the shaded interior. Most of the horses are outside except for Warrior, Arabella, and Gunnar, who are in their stalls. As they walk up to Arabella's stall, she sticks her head out of her open Dutch door. "This is Warrior's mother, Arabella. She's a German National Champion and my personal horse. I ride her almost every day."

"Oh, Betty. She's beautiful!" and they continue walking. "This is Gunnar, our stallion, and Warrior's sire. He's the holder of many national championships, and his bloodline is well-known in the horse community."

Renée looks at him intently. "He's a powerful-looking animal, and taller than I was expecting."

Betty explains. "Yes, all of our horses are part thoroughbred."

Then they walk over to Warrior's stall. He is jet-black like his mother, and his ears tip forward as he watches them approach.

"This is Warrior. He is almost four years old and is in peak condition. Our trainer works with him nearly every day, and she knows him very well."

Renée is immediately taken by him and strokes his neck. "What a fantastic looking animal!"

Betty continues. "He's tall and powerful like his father and has the coloration and courage of his mother. Best of all, he has all of their outstanding traits."

After dinner, the group retires to the terrace. The evening is cool, and they sit around the crackling fire reminiscing about the war. Renée thanks Betty for mailing Adrian's letter, and they chat over her story of how she met him in the hospital.

The following morning, Betty and Max are in the kitchen making breakfast when Adrian and Renée enter. She's wearing white riding britches and a dark blue polo shirt with an embroidered logo of her club on it. Adrian approaches Betty, who is standing in front of the stove. "Is there anything we can do to help?"

"No but thank you. Breakfast is on the table out on the terrace."

Just then, Elke arrives and steps out of her truck, dressed in her riding outfit. She's attractive, about thirty-five, medium height, and slender. She's been riding ever since she was a little girl and has been working for Max for the last ten years. Betty introduces her. "This is Elke, our trainer. She's going to work with you and Warrior today," then asks her, "Have you had breakfast?"

"Yes, but a cup of coffee sounds good." Elke complements Renée. "Betty told me you were a very accomplished rider and a member of the French equestrian team. Congratulations!"

"Thank you. Betty introduced me to Warrior yesterday, and he's fantastic! Can you tell me more about him?"

"Certainly. I started working with him two years ago with low impact riding, swimming, and dressage. A horse must be in top condition before I move on to the jumps. Warrior has proven to be powerful and aggressive, and he likes me to be closely connected to him when we ride. He handles voice commands for encouragement, or warning, extremely well, and he is very sure footed. He has a big heart, and will give you everything you ask for, and then some."

"Does he have any issues I should know about?"

"Yes, and I've been working with him on that. If he shies at a fence, I always encourage him verbally, and he recovers his confidence quickly. Also, and depending on the lighting, he sometimes has trouble reading brown fences, but knowing that, you can usually help by adjusting his approach."

Renée asks her, "What do you have planned for this morning?"

"We'll start with dressage, and you can see his strengths and weaknesses, but overall, he's getting quite good. Then we'll go over to the arena and go through the show jumps there. Warrior has been over the course many times, and he is very familiar with it.

"As for the cross-country section, it's about three miles long. It begins in the upper meadow with six obstacles, then it transitions to a downhill section that weaves through the forest to the river. There are twelve obstacles there, and then it returns uphill with sixteen more. We use a wide variety of fences that the horses might encounter in competition, so there are several types of tables, chevrons, and angled houses. Nature provides us with two creek crossings, a shallow pond, ditches, and, of course, long uphill and downhill sections."

Renée has been looking forward to this day for some time. "I can't tell you how excited I am to work with him."

"You are going to be impressed, but first we'll walk the course."

The girls stand, say goodbye to the men, and leave the terrace. They walk the course with Wolfie and inspect the many obstacles. After a bit, they enter the forest and walk the downhill section as it winds its way through the trees to the river. Midway, they stop at the chicane, a long downhill 'S' curve with two log jumps.

After that, the trail weaves through the trees before crossing a large, shallow pond. As they walk, they stop to look at each fence and end up at the Mosel River. The canyon ends just before the river on a wide bench, and in the center is a long swimming pool formed naturally in a rock formation.

Elke explains its purpose. "I use this quite a lot, especially in the summer when it's hot. And of course, it's also an excellent way to exercise a horse that is recovering from a leg injury. The pool is about one hundred and fifty feet long and is fed by that creek coming out of the canyon. There are sandy ramps at each end that allow the horses to approach the deep water gradually. The rider simply walks on the bank alongside the horse, holding the lead rope."

Renée stares at it with interest. "I've never used one before, but it looks like a wonderful way to exercise them."

They continue their tour with Wolfie, and walk the uphill section, passing a creek crossing and the rest of the obstacles. After walking the entire course, they approach the barn, and Elke asks Renée, "Well, what do you think?"

"It's beautifully laid out, and it exposes the horses to many of the challenges that they will face on the circuit. You should be very proud of it."

In a short time, they are tacked up, and ride back to the course. Elke rides Gunnar, Betty follows her on Arabella, and Renée rides Warrior. They cross the meadow to the dressage arena, and Elke takes Renée and Warrior through their paces to familiarize her with his capabilities.

After that, they enter the arena that is set up with show jumps. Renée is feeling at ease with Warrior, and he easily clears the fences. Elke follows her on the ground, advising her of his unique approaches, while Betty sits on a nearby bench, petting Wolfie as she watches them.

Afterword, the girls regroup and canter their horses across the meadow, warming them up prior to starting the strenuous cross-country course. There will be no easy way for Elke to talk Renée through the fast event they are about to begin; however, this is still about training, and time is not that important. Elke explains that she will go first, followed by Renée, so she can see where she is going. Betty, who has been on the course many times, will follow her.

Elke quietly enters the starting box and waits for a few moments. Then, at her command, Gunnar explodes out of the box at a full gallop. Clumps of dirt and grass fly in all directions as he thunders down the trail. Seconds later Renée enters the starting box, and at her command, Warrior blasts after them in hot pursuit. She is a highly experienced rider, and leans forward, whispering encouragement to him. He immediately connects with her, and they gallop at full speed down the narrow curving path as it winds through the tall trees to their first obstacle, a large brush-lined table. He makes the long jump with ease, then increases his stride toward the next obstacle. The rhythmic cadence of his hoofs hitting the hard ground echoes through the forest. She sees that he's approaching a sharp bend too fast, and whispers to him.

"Easy... easy!"

Warrior slows slightly, then gallops forward, jumps a large log, followed by a complex set of two chevrons. He bounds down a steep bank on the back side of the last chevron, splashes across a shallow pond, and easily clears a tall fence in the center of the pond. Renée leans forward, close to his neck, as he gallops toward the next obstacle a hundred yards away. He's running flat out, and she encourages him in a soft voice.

"Good boy. Good boy."

Soon they are at the bottom of the downhill run. He gallops past the exercise pool, and she lines him up for the next obstacle, a tall fence. The jump begins in the sunlight and ends in the shadows of the forest, testing the horse's courage and skill as the landing point is difficult to see. When Renée reaches the upper meadow at the end of the course, Elke is ahead of her and is already cooling down Gunnar. She slows Warrior to a canter and catches up with her. Betty is right behind her, and the three of them ride side-by-side.

Renée is excited. "That was the most incredible ride of my life! We connected almost right away. I've never ridden a horse that was that confident and brave."

Betty complements her. "You're the impressive one! I've never seen anyone new to the course do so well!"

They walk toward the barn, cooling down their horses, and Elke looks at Renée. "I've got work to do, but we can make another run at the end of the day if you like."

"Thanks, Elke. I appreciate all your help. It's going to make a gigantic difference in getting to know Warrior."

"You're welcome. It was a pleasure working with you."

Elke rides back to the barn, and Betty and Renée trot their horses to the rock outcropping that overlooks the Mosel River valley. They dismount, walk out to the lone tree, and Renée is stunned by the view. "You're right. The scenery here is unbelievable!"

Betty points out the landmarks. "Our vines are terraced all the way to the Mosel River. The mountains you see in the far distance are the northern side of the Swiss Alps." They stand and admire the spectacular view for a few minutes, then Betty asks her, "Would you like to see the dragons?"

"Oh, yes. I'd love to. I've never seen Adrian so excited about anything!"

"Well, they are quite extraordinary." She motions toward the building just ahead of them. "The caves are inside the winery. Afterword, I thought you might enjoy riding up to our alpine lake. The forest is bewitching, and the lake is a jewel of nature."

"That sounds like fun. I'm looking forward to it."

They leave their horses in the coral and walk into the winery. Max and Adrian are working on one of the wine presses, and Max looks up from his work. "How is your day going?"

"We're having fun, and Renée is dying to see the dragons. Why don't you boys take a break and join us?"

The four of them enter the tunnel and walk to the central cavern. Max turns on the lights, and the dragons on the far wall emerge out of the darkness. The sight of so many of them astounds Renée. "These paintings are amazing!"

She takes her time, and slowly walks past them, admiring each one as she passes by. "This is hard to believe. They look so real!"

Betty explains. "We were told it's a style far more advanced than any other paintings of that era."

Renée stops at a large painting of a golden-winged dragon standing on a ledge with its wings outstretched. "This is my favorite."

Betty asks her, "Do you think they ever existed?"

"I do. Stories about them appear in too many cultures for it to be a coincidence."

Adrian jokes with Max. "All this talk of dragons makes me thirsty. Do you have anything cool to drink here?"

"Sure, follow me."

They sit at a large wooden table in the center of the tasting room, and Max serves them a glass of chilled wine, while Betty sets a plate of cheese and crackers on the table. They relax, and Renée fills Adrian in on their morning adventures, and how thrilling it was to ride Warrior. After a while, the men go back to work, and Betty and Renée leave for their long ride to the alpine lake.

An hour later, they arrive, unsaddle their horses, and let them graze by the lakeside. Seated in comfortable porch chairs, they admire the lake and have a light lunch. Soon they begin their long descent back to the farm.

When they arrive at the farm, Elke is just finishing her work, and they return to the cross-country course for one more run. Afterword, they cool down their horses, and take their time returning. It was a perfect run for Renée, and she was even more thrilled than her first ride.

As they ride up the shady driveway, their C-47 approaches low over the trees. It lowers its landing gear, touches down in the adjacent meadow, and taxis up to the house. Lotar and Chara wave at them from inside the cockpit as they trot past the plane.

The women dismount in front of the barn, and Elke volunteers to put their horses away, so they can get back to their friends. They walk up the side steps to the terrace and find Max and Adrian already relaxing with a cool glass of iced tea. Minutes later, Lotar and Chara join them, and Adrian introduces Renée. She and Chara take an instant liking to each other and chatter away, drifting in and out of French and English.

After a pleasant dinner, they retire to the terrace to watch the sunset as it sinks below the horizon and darkness envelopes the valley. Max lights a roaring fire, and Lotar passes a snifter of brandy to everyone. The men talk about their wine business, and the three women chat amongst themselves.

Renée asks Chara, "Are you a horse woman?"

"I love to ride, but I'm a beginner. I work with Elke whenever I can, but lately I've been very busy flying and setting up our new air cargo company."

Betty sets down her snifter. "Chara has a stunning eight-year-old Black Forest gelding." Then she unexpectedly makes her an unusual offer. "Max and I know you're passionate about becoming a cross-country rider, and now would be the perfect time for you to start working with a young horse. We want to give you a colt of your choice. Which one would you like?"

Her generosity shocks Chara, and she is at a loss for words. "Oh no, I can't let you do that. They are so expensive!"

"We're going to be working together for a long time, and we want you to have a horse that you can be proud of, like we are of our horses."

"Thank you so much. I'm speechless!"

"Well? Which one has caught your eye?"

Chara smiles at her bashfully. "I've already fallen in love with one of them! He's one of the two-year-old colts, and I bring him a carrot every day."

"Hmm, I'm not sure which one you're talking about."

"I don't know his name, but I heard Max call him Baby."

"Baby!" and Betty laughs. "You've chosen well. His name is Marco, his name is derived from the Roman word for Mars, the God of War, and he is the descendent of several national champions. Max named him wisely, considering his breeding, and he's destined for greatness."

"I'm sorry. I didn't know he was so special!"

"He's a superb choice. Elke can start with you this weekend. You have a couple of years of hard work ahead of you, but it will be an extraordinary experience."

Renée has a suggestion. "Both of you should think about joining my riding club in Paris. It would be a great way for Chara to learn, plus the three of us could have a lot of fun together."

"That sounds like fun! Thank you so much," and Betty turns to Chara. "Do you want to join?"

"Yes, of course. I'm going to need all the help that I can get!"

Chara asks Renée, "What do you think of Warrior?"

"He's fantastic! We connected almost immediately and flew through the course without a fault. He's going to be my special boy for many years to come."

Betty is excited and comes up with an idea. "Since we're all training together, let's plan on meeting here every year for a week of practice and fun."

Just then, Lotar arrives with a bottle of brandy. "Excuse me, ladies. Would you like a refill?"

They thank him, and he adds a small amount to their snifters. Chara looks up at him affectionately. "Merci, mon cheri."

Eventing is the equestrian version of a triathlon, where a single horse and rider compete against the clock in dressage, show jumping, and cross-country racing.

Betty is excited about the idea. "Why don't we have a yearly event here? Max held events here before the war, and he said they were a lot of fun."

Chara turns to Renée. "Who do you suggest we invite?"

"I know several national equestrian teams that would love to attend. We should make it by invitation only."

Betty agrees. "They could keep their horses here, and there are plenty of places to stay in town."

Chara, the extrovert, loves the idea. "And in the evening, we could have a barbecue and get to know everyone. It could become the social event of the year! What do you think we should call it?"

Renée has competed in many events and comes up with a suggestion. "Maybe something exclusive, like Centre Equestre Dragon Invitation à notre Concours Complet?"

Betty is excited. "Wonderful! Let's have the first one this summer. Chara and I can take care of the logistics, and you can handle the invitations," and they touch glasses in a toast.

The following morning, Adrian loads Warrior into his trailer, and Renée waves goodbye to them, as they leave for Paris, three hundred miles away.

CHAPTER 22

FLIGHT OF THE ARROW

IT'S LATE AFTERNOON, AND A STORMY DAY OFF THE COAST of England. Intermittent showers restrict their visibility as Charlie and AJ Bennett, a newly hired pilot, struggle at the controls of their C-47. They are returning to London after an all-day flight deep into Germany. As they cross the English Channel, a strong turbulence shakes the plane violently.

Charlie looks over at AJ. "It's pretty bad out here. I'll be glad to get this baby back on the ground."

AJ puts away the navigation chart that he had been looking at. "Yeah, and that delay in Berlin threw us way off schedule." He looks out the windshield as they approach their airport. "That's a welcoming sight."

"Better let them know we're coming in."

"Wilco," and he radios the tower.

They land, and Charlie shuts down the engines. Parked inside the hangar is a huge four-engine Skymaster and AJ looks at it with a smile. "Now that's a real cargo plane! What a beauty!"

"Yeah. We're replacing our C-47s with them. That one is going to France."

AJ pulls up the collar on his jacket and steps out into the rain. "I'll see you next week sometime," and heads toward his car.

Charlie waves goodbye and enters the hangar. At the far end, Paddy looks up from behind an engine. "Hi, Charlie. How did it go?"

"We had a long delay in Berlin, and rough weather on the return flight, but all is well. How are you coming with the Arrow?"

"Great! Do you want to take a look at it?"

"Sure, if you're not too busy."

"Now's a good time." He grabs a heavy jacket and puts it on. It's cold and rainy outside, and they walk down the flight line. Paddy unlocks the door, and they enter the darkened hangar. He throws a switch, and the large overhead lights slowly build to full strength. In the center is Betty's newly painted Arrow.

Charlie is stunned by the work that Paddy and his crew did. "That paint job is fantastic! She looks like a completely different plane, and I love the golden dragon on the tail."

"It shocked me, too. She's going to be a real showstopper. I checked out her engines, and everything looks to be in perfect working order. Your German mechanics did a great job."

Charlie is curious. "What all have you done to her?"

"We lightened her up considerably by removing the cannons and armor, and we replaced the heavy bullet proof canopy with a sleek plexiglass one. She's going to be a very fast plane!" He walks toward a pile of aircraft parts laying on the floor. "Let me show you something. Besides the two twenty mm cannons on her wings, they equipped her with a huge thirty mm cannon that fired through the propeller hub."

Charlie stares at the weapons. "I wouldn't want to be on the wrong end of that thing. It could do some real damage!" He continues to admire the plane. "Has Max or Lotar seen her?"

"Nope. You're the first one."

He shakes his head. "They're really going to be shocked when they see this baby!"

The following Monday, Charlie arrives at work and checks out their new Skymaster. It's painted olive drab, with RAF markings on it and sits level on its tricycle landing gear. It dwarfs the other aircraft parked nearby and is almost twice as large as a C-47.

Paddy pulls up in his pickup, and Charlie greets him. "Good morning. How long will it take before we can put this baby into service?"

"She's nearly new, so I just need to go over the engines and strip the paint off."

"That's perfect timing. Betty will be here next week to pick it up."

It's a beautiful morning one week later. Betty and Chara are flying their C-47 from their farm in Germany to their company's home base near London and are transiting high above the English Channel. Lotar is napping in a jump seat in the cargo bay, and Betty looks over at Chara. "There's something that I've been wanting to ask you."

"Of course. What is it?"

"Max found a secure building in the Latin Quarter in Paris. It's a perfect place for him to set up his lab. I promised to consult with him when I can, but I've made a serious commitment to make this company a success. To do that, I'm going to need your help. Adrian told me you have advanced degrees in business and finance. I think you would make a great chief financial officer for our company. Are you interested in the position?"

Betty's offer surprises her. "Interested! I would be thrilled!"

"I was hoping you'd say that. You and I can run the business side, and Lotar is a natural born leader. He can handle the marketing and the flight crews." Betty flashes her a smile. "As an officer of the company, your compensation will be significantly higher, and in time, you would become a full partner."

"I'm stunned! I don't know what to say!"

"We're small now, but with a little hard work, our potential is unlimited."

"Thank you, Betty. I appreciate your offer, and I'm thrilled to be part of it."

They hit a pocket of rough air, and it lurches the plane about. Moments later, Lotar enters the cockpit and stands behind them. "Is everything alright?"

Betty glances up at him. "Just some turbulence. I was talking to Chara about the future of this company. We're growing quickly, and I can't do this by myself anymore. She agreed to be our chief financial officer, and she and I will run the business side. Would you be interested in handling the operations and marketing?"

Her offer surprises him. "Yes, I'd like that very much."

"You have an exceptional talent for making business deals. We wouldn't have gotten that contract with the French postal service if it wasn't for you. At the rate we're expanding, we'll need to move into management soon, and let others do the day-to-day flying. As I just told Chara, your compensation would be significantly higher, and in time, you would become a full partner."

"What an offer! Thank you!"

"I think we make a winning team, and I'm thrilled that we'll be working together."

The turbulence shakes the plane and Lotar braces himself in the doorway. "I talked to Adrian yesterday. He's sending a lot more work our way, and when that happens, we're going to need more planes."

That's good news, and Betty is excited. "Great! We can talk to Charlie about that later in the day."

Lotar looks at Chara. "We'll be landing soon. Have you been to England before?"

"No, but I'm looking forward to it."

"Well, I'm a great tour guide. We can check out a couple of those famous English pubs, and maybe I'll introduce you to haggis."

"Who's haggis?"

"Not who. It's the national dish of Scotland, and it's delicious!" He looks over at Betty, and she just smiles and shakes her head. An hour later, they land in London, and Charlie opens the cargo door to greet them. "Welcome home!"

"It's good to see you, Charlie!" and Betty introduces him. "This is our newest hire, Chara Escoffier."

"Hi, I'm Charlie."

"Nice to meet you. Betty has told me many incredible stories about you and Andy."

"Thankfully, those days are over!" He turns to Betty. "I like your new outfits. You look very professional."

"Thanks, Charlie."

"Where's Max?"

"He found a high-security building for his research lab, and he's trying to close on it."

Lotar catches up with them, and Charlie is happy to see him. "Ah, Lotar, my friend. How are you?"

"Hi, Charlie. You and Shelagh will have to come and visit our new facility."

"Only if you promise to show us around Paris."

"Well, I've discovered a couple of great restaurants, but they don't have anything that compares to your haggis!"

Charlie grins. "You got me there, mate! Do you want to look at your new plane?"

"You bet!"

Paddy and his crew worked long hours to prepare their Skymaster, and they did a beautiful job. The olive drab paint has been removed, and the shiny aluminum plane glistens in the sun. Charlie motions toward it. "Well, I'm sure you're eager to get checked out on this beauty."

Betty has been looking forward to flying it and is excited. "We can't wait, Charlie. This is a big day for us," and she stares at it in amazement. "She looks like one of those fancy commercial airliners."

"Thanks, but Paddy and the boys deserve all the credit." They walk to the boarding stairs, and Charlie bows and sweeps his arms toward the stairs. "After you."

Betty enters the cavernous cargo bay of the Skymaster. "This interior is enormous!"

"Yup. We removed the jump seats and installed six rows of first-class passenger seats up front. If you don't need them, they're easy to remove."

She runs her hand over the top of a luxurious leather seat. "Boy! These are nice. When are you going to upgrade our planes?"

"Andy is already looking at a couple of Skymasters, so that day is not far off. I talked to Adrian, and he's got buyers for our C-47s. That guy has amazing contacts."

Betty laughs. "I know, and thanks to Lotar, we're picking up more business with the French postal service. We're going to need two more planes pretty soon." She enters the cockpit and looks around. "This is a really nice layout!"

"Thanks. Andy wants to celebrate tonight. We're going to fly her up to Edinburgh to some seafood restaurant that he's crazy about. That will give us plenty of time to get everyone checked out."

Betty is excited at the thought of flying it and starts to leave. "That sounds like fun! We'll be back shortly. I want to show Chara a little of London before it gets dark."

"Great idea, but before you go, I have something you need to see."

"Can I look at it after we get back?"

"Oh, this will just take a minute. Come on."

They follow Charlie over to the main hangar. The enormous doors are closed because of the cold weather, so they enter from a side door. The inside is brightly lit, and there's a ten-foot-high black curtain stretched across the entire width of the hangar. In the middle of the empty section are four chairs facing forward.

Betty stops dead in her tracks. "What is this?"

Charlie plays dumb. "Gee, I don't know."

She turns to Lotar. "Are you in on this?"

He fakes his reaction. "No. I'm as surprised as you are!"

Charlie pulls out a chair for her, and the others seat themselves. Moments later, the lights dim until it's pitch black, and then ethereal music plays softly. Betty leans over to him and whispers. "This is all very dramatic!"

He just nods his head and smiles. In total darkness, she hears the rustling sound of the curtains being pulled back. Moments later, flood lights illuminate the hangar, and the shimmering outline of a large aircraft sitting fifty feet in front of her emerges from the shadows. As the lights increase in brightness, they reveal the stunning sight of the Arrow. Its high-gloss black paint shimmers under the bright lights. A checkered red and gold pattern circles the nose, and a golden-winged dragon is painted on the tail. The huge propellers are highly polished and shine brightly, reflecting light in all directions.

Betty is in complete shock. Never in her wildest dreams could she have envisioned a plane like it. Charlie explains. "She's your birthday present from Max. The guys have been working on her for a month."

She is speechless and cradles her face. "I've never seen a plane like this. What is it?"

"It's a Dornier 335 Arrow. It was the fastest propeller-driven fighter of the war, except it came out late, and never saw combat. They only made a few of them for testing. You have Lotar to thank. He's the one that found it."

Betty slowly approaches the plane. "She's incredible, Lotar."

"It wasn't just me; they're all in on it."

She wipes tears from her eyes. "What do you mean 'they'?"

He points to the darkness behind the plane. With all the excitement, she hadn't noticed the people standing in the shadows. Max approaches her with Wolfie at his side, and she runs to him. "Oh, Max. She's beautiful! Thank you so much!"

"Happy birthday, darling!"

"What a surprise!"

"You spend long hours flying our cargo planes. I wanted to give you something a little more exciting to have fun with."

"Thank you! How did you get here? I thought you were in Paris?"

"Adrian chartered a plane. We were only a few minutes behind you."

Adrian and Renée emerge from the shadows, and Renée hugs her. "What a beautiful plane! I'm dying to see you fly it."

Betty asks Max, "Is it flyable?"

"You bet. The boys went through everything."

Paddy arrives with a tug and pulls the Arrow out in front of the hangar. Lotar and Betty follow, and he explains its operational features. They walk up the boarding stairs to the cockpit, and he goes over the layout of the controls.

"There is one thing unusual about this plane," and he points to the red handle. "It has a rocket propelled ejection seat. So be careful with that lever."

"Why did they do that?"

"If you have to eject, you'll need it to clear that huge rear propeller."

"Oh my gosh! That would be breathtaking!"

Betty steps into the cockpit and straps herself in, as Lotar continues explaining the plane's unique features. He stays with her as she starts the engines. "It will take time for you to get used to her, so don't push her too hard. She's quick, but easy to handle. Just be extra careful on the first couple of flights."

She nods her head in acknowledgement and gives him a thumbs up. He pats her on the shoulder, then walks down the boarding stairs. She increases her rpm, and the massive plane creeps forward and rolls out into the bright sunlight. The control tower gives her permission to take off, and the huge fighter rotates out onto the runway and turns into the wind. She points it down the long strip of concrete and checks her gauges one last time.

Satisfied that all is well, she closes her canopy, pushes the throttles forward, and the Arrow shudders as the propellers slash at the air. The roar of the powerful engines pierces the silence of the morning, and it screams down the tarmac. She climbs steeply and disappears into the clouds. A few minutes later, she returns and makes a high-speed pass above the runway. Spectators cover their ears and watch in amazement as she vanishes from view. Andy looks at Max and shakes his head in disbelief. "She's truly an incredible pilot!"

A short time later, Betty returns to the airport and comes to a stop in front of their hangar. She tilts her canopy to the side, and Max runs up the stairs to congratulate her. "You looked great out there! How did she handle?"

"Smooth as silk. That was really fun!"

He helps her out of the cockpit, and as they walk down the boarding stairs, he comes up with a suggestion. "Charlie is exhibiting our new Skymaster at the Paris Airshow. Why don't you take the Arrow and go with him? It would help draw attention to our cargo business."

"That's a great idea!" As they walk away, Betty puts her arm around him. "Thank you for my present, darling. It was the surprise of my life, and I'm thrilled!"

Andy catches up with them. "What do you say we leave for Edinburgh, and we'll have a little celebration tonight?"

Renée approaches. "I'm sorry, Betty, but we can't go with you. Adrian has an early morning meeting, and we need to get back."

Betty hugs her. "I'll miss you. Let's have lunch next week," and she cheek kisses Adrian goodbye.

Everyone is excited about flying to Edinburgh, so they board the Skymaster and sit down in the first-class passenger seats. Charlie and Betty enter the cockpit and make themselves comfortable at the controls.

He looks over at her. "Ready to take her up?"

"Yes! This is exciting!"

Lotar is sitting in one of the comfortable passenger seats in the rear cabin, and glances over at Andy. "So, tell us about this fantastic seafood restaurant of yours? What do you recommend?"

"Well, it's all delicious."

Max laughs. "That's what you said about haggis!"

A few minutes later, they are airborne and head to Edinburgh, Scotland. An hour passes, and they land, flag down a couple of taxis, and drive to a restaurant known as Nessie's Fish House, named after the famous sea monster that lives in Loch Ness. The hostess leads them to a private room overlooking the rocky shoreline, and they excitedly talk amongst themselves as they sit down.

Andy looks across the table at Betty. "So, what do you think of your new Skymaster?"

"She's a beautiful plane! Paddy and the guys did a fantastic job getting her ready. Chara and I named her, *La Ville Lumière*, or the *City of Light*."

"Why did you call her the *City of Light*?"

Chara explains. "During the Age of Enlightenment, Paris was the center of intellectual and philosophical movements that dominated the world of ideas."

"Well, it's a perfect homage to a beautiful city!" The waiter arrives and asks Andy, "Are you ready to order, sir?"

"Yes. We're all having lobster," and he motions toward Chara. "Except this lady who wants to try your haggis."

But Chara is quick to speak up. "Oh, no! No sheep's pluck for me," and she looks over at Lotar, who can't stop laughing. "Since you like haggis so much, you are going to love my andouillette."

He abruptly stops laughing. "What's that?"

"More or less the same thing except it's cooked in the colon of a pig."

Lotar is speechless, and the group bursts out in laughter. Max stands and taps on his water glass with a fork. "My friends, I have an announcement to make. Betty and I are getting married after the Paris Airshow, and you are all invited to join us." Everyone excitedly claps their hands. "I know it's taken us a while, but we're going to take a week off and honeymoon on the French Riviera."

Charlie claps the loudest. "Good for you! Where are you getting married?"

"We haven't decided yet, but we're excited to share our marriage celebration with the ones that we love!"

Andy proposes a toast. "To the soon to be newlyweds! May you live a long and happy life together!"

The waiters appear with their lobster dinners, and they talk excitedly amongst themselves, enjoying each other's company. After dinner, they exit the restaurant. A light rain falls, as Max and Charlie stand on the wet sidewalk trying to flag down a taxi.

Betty hugs Andy. "Thank you for the wonderful evening."

He smiles at her. "It was my pleasure, and I wish you and Max the very best."

"Thanks, Andy. If you don't mind, I have a special favor to ask you."

"Sure. What can I do?"

"The French do things a bit differently. Technically, we were married when we signed our marriage license. We don't belong to any specific religion, so we'd like to ask if you would officiate for us at our wedding ceremony."

"Of course. I'm honored that you asked me."

The next morning, Betty and Max are having breakfast at a small sidewalk café near their hotel. She sets down her coffee cup. "I talked to Uncle Karl late last night. He would love to be here for the wedding, but he's swamped with military construction contracts. I told him not to worry, but as soon as his work slows down, he promises to spend a few weeks with us."

Max is disappointed. "I'm sorry, Betty. I know you were looking forward to seeing him."

"Well, I can't blame him. It's a long way to travel for an afternoon party."

"What's on your schedule for today?"

"I'm meeting a reporter from *Le Figaro* for lunch. She heard about the Arrow and wants to interview me. And you?"

"Hopefully, I'll be able to negotiate a lease for the laboratory. It's time for me to build a full-scale prototype and prove its commercial viability."

Betty smiles. "I have more good news. Lotar and Chara agreed to help me manage our French cargo company. I can still work with you, but Andy and Adrian are depending on me, and I don't want to let them down.

"Darling, I understand completely, and you have my full support."

CHAPTER 23

LA GROTTE DU DRAGON

IT'S A BEAUTIFUL SPRING MORNING IN PARIS, AND THE grand opening of Adrian's long awaited wine shop on the Avenue des Champs-Élysées, famous for its luxury shops and sidewalk cafés. It starts at the massive Arc de Triomphe, and its wide tree-lined sidewalks that extend for nearly a mile.

Adrian named his store, *"La Grotte du Dragon"*, or Dragon Cave, because of the large amount of wine and brandy that comes from Max's vineyards, but he also carries a wide selection of local boutique wines. Today there will be wine tasting that includes paring various wines with food.

Betty and Max, along with Chara and Lotar, enter the shop. Adrian's grand opening was well publicized, and, although it's still early in the afternoon, he is very busy. Betty looks around and is surprised. "I didn't expect to see so many people! I'll bet he's happy about that!"

Max agrees. "Yes, and they seem to be excited about our Rieslings, and even more so with our brandy!"

A door to the back room opens, and Adrian appears with a case of brandy. He hands it to a customer, then waves, and works his way through the crowd to greet them. "Ah, there you are! Thank you for coming."

Betty cheek kisses him. "Your store is stunning, and everyone seems to be enjoying themselves."

Adrian is excited. "Your brandy and wine are the talk of the town!" He shakes hands with Lotar, then cheek kisses Chara. "I'm so happy that you could come."

The store is very crowded, and he motions toward a side door. "Let's talk out on the patio." They follow him outside, and he hands each of them a glass of wine. He's very excited at the positive turn-out.

"What do you think, Max? I told you that your wine would be a big hit."

"All I can say is that you are amazing, as usual!"

Just then, the patio door opens, and a distinguished gentleman and an attractive woman approaches Adrian. He waves to them, and grabs Lotar by the arm. "If you will excuse us, I would like to introduce Lotar to someone."

As they walk away, Lotar questions him. "Who are we meeting?"

"This is my Israeli military contact. The one that is looking to purchase our fighters."

They work their way through the crowd, and Adrian greets them warmly. "Ah, Colonel Ben-Ami. What a pleasant surprise!" and he cheek kisses his wife. "It's always nice to see you, Dalia."

She has long blonde hair streaked with light brown tones, dark eyes, and speaks English with an accent. "Thank you, Adrian. It's wonderful to see you. We've been looking forward to your grand opening."

"I'm glad that you were able to attend. By the way, I'd like to introduce you to my associate, Lotar von Hirschel," and they exchange pleasantries. He continues. "Lotar was a high-scoring fighter ace in the Luftwaffe."

Colonel Ben-Ami is impressed. "I see! So, you must know these fighters very well then."

"I had to. My life depended on them."

Just then, a dignified gentleman walks into the shop, and Adrian notices him. "Ah, the Mayor is here, and I need to talk to him. Would you excuse me for a moment?"

"Of course, Lotar and I have a lot to discuss," and Colonel Ben-Ami continues. "My government is interested in purchasing fighters. Do you have any for sale?"

"A few. I specialize in 109s and 190s. My mechanics go through them completely before we sell them."

"Do you have any other planes for sale?"

"Yes. We have a new twin-engine Heinkel He 111 fast attack bomber," and he thinks for a moment. "Would you be interested in any C-47 cargo planes?"

"Yes, why do you ask?"

"We're upgrading our fleet, and we have a dozen or so for sale."

"Let's talk about that. I'm definitely interested. What is your professional opinion of the fighters?"

"They are very good planes, but if you're building up your air force, I recommend you stock up on parts. They are well engineered, but over time, everything wears out."

"Do you have parts for them?"

"Yes. I can locate whatever you need."

"I really appreciate your help, Lotar. What else would you recommend?"

"I might be able to find a few highly qualified mechanics to train your people. That would reduce your learning curve and probably save a few lives as well."

"That would be very helpful. We hope to convert to jets, but that's a couple of years away. In the interim, your planes would be quite valuable in a defensive role, and especially as trainers."

"When you upgrade to jets, you could easily sell them to third world countries, so it wouldn't be a lost investment. I believe Adrian can help you with that as well."

"I appreciate your advice, and my negotiations with him are almost complete. Do you have any planes ready to sell?"

"I have seven or eight that are refurbished, and I'll have another three or four finished in a week or two."

"We are definitely interested," and the colonel takes a sip of his brandy. "This is excellent. Adrian said it comes from your vineyard in Germany."

"Yes, but that's my brother's world. Why don't you join us for a drink?"

"Thank you, I'd like that," and they walk over to their group.

Lotar makes the introductions. "This is my brother, Max, his fiancée, Betty, and this is my friend, Chara."

The general asks Max, "Are all of you involved in the wine business?"

"Just me, but I have a vintner that handles the day-to-day operations. We operate an air cargo company that keeps us pretty busy."

The colonel is curious. "I see. What is the range of your planes?"

"We fly four-engine Skymasters with a range of four thousand miles."

"That's interesting. I'd also like to discuss contracting with you to transport freight from France to Israel."

Just then Adrian arrives and rejoins the group. "Sorry, that was important. Well, what have I missed?"

The colonel summarizes their discussion. "Lotar has been very helpful. As you know, we're looking for fighters, but we'd also be interested in your Heinkel bomber, and a few of your C-47s as well. And I've come to a tentative agreement with Lotar to supply us with mechanics and all the parts that we're going to need."

"Very good." Adrian turns to Lotar. "How do you recommend we proceed?"

Lotar explains. "I've been thinking about the logistics. Israel is two thousand miles away, which is a long flight for a used fighter. After we refurbish them, we could truck them to Marseille, and then transport them in ocean shipping containers. When they arrive, our mechanics could easily reassemble them."

The colonel agrees. "I like that idea. We have cargo ships that could pick them up," and he turns to Adrian. "Perhaps we could complete our agreement in Israel. My wife and I would take great pleasure in showing you our country."

Lotar is surprised by his offer. "Thank you. We'd be happy to accept your kind invitation."

Dalia turns to Betty and Chara. "I would love to entertain you while the men work out the details. There is much to see and do."

Betty is excited at the thought of seeing a country that she had only heard her parents talk about, and she graciously accepts. "Chara and I would be thrilled to visit you!"

The colonel looks at his watch. "I'm sorry, but we need to be on our way. I have an important conference to attend. It was a pleasure meeting you."

Betty makes a suggestion to Dalia. "Why don't you stay with us? Chara and I would love to show you Paris!"

She turns to her husband. "Is that alright with you?"

"Yes, of course. This could take a while."

She hugs him, and he disappears into the crowd. Chara smiles at Lotar. "If you boys don't mind, Betty and I would like to take Dalia out to lunch." She winks at him. "And maybe we'll do a little shopping."

It's a week later. Betty, Max, and Wolfie board Betty's plane, followed by Lotar and Chara. In a few hours, they buzz the main house and return to land. As they roll to a stop, Betty notices something strange. Parked under the large trees next to their airstrip are six German fighters, and she laughs. "It looks like Lotar and Adrian have started their own air force!"

Max can't stop laughing. "Those two make a dangerous pair. They're totally unpredictable!"

As they exit their plane, Jannik arrives in his tractor and Lotar greets him with a handshake. "Hello, my friend. It's good to see you."

"Thank you," and he stares at the fighters and smiles. "It looks like you're getting ready to start another war!"

Lotar takes his joke in stride and laughs. "Yeah, I guess it does look like that."

Betty looks over at Max. "If you don't mind, Chara and I are dying to ride our horses. We'll see you at dinner tonight." She gives him a kiss, and they walk down the path toward the horse barn. As they saddle up, Chara asks Betty, "Where are we going?"

"I'd like to show you our alpine lake, but it's an hour ride. Are you up for that much riding?"

"Yes, I would love to! Lotar said the forest trail is like being in an enchanted fairyland!"

"It's gorgeous! And the pristine lake remains untouched by the passage of time."

They walk their horses to the fence that borders the forest and pass through the gate. Then they mount up and enter the woods, riding side-by-side and chatting. The beauty of the shadowy landscape intrigues Chara. "This is like something out of a child's fairy tale."

Betty smiles. "Max remembers riding to the lake with his father, who told him stories about the moss people that lived in the forest."

"I'll bet that was fun for him. Did he ever see any of them?"

"Oh, yes. He said they were peering around rocks and hiding behind trees."

"Are you planning to have any children?"

"In a few years, but first, I need to get this company off the ground, and you and Lotar are going to be a big part of making that happen."

They continue to ride, talking about life and their shared experiences. Soon they reach the lake, and its natural beauty captivates Chara. They dismount, remove their saddles, and let their horses walk out into the shallow water for a drink.

Betty points to the old stone cabin. "Their grandfather built that cabin a long time ago, and Max and I spent an incredibly romantic weekend there.

We canoed around the lake, watched a gorgeous sunset, and enjoyed a blazing bonfire until late at night.

"How did you and Max meet?"

"Oh, gosh. That's a long story. It happened during the war. British intelligence sent me to infiltrate a Nazi airbase that was developing a secret weapon, and Max was the project director. At first, we couldn't stand each other because we each thought the other person was a Nazi fanatic.

"He was brilliant, handsome, and charismatic, but all I wanted was to get the information that they sent me to retrieve and leave as soon as possible. Unfortunately, a short time later, an American fighter strafed us, and we were both seriously wounded. When we left the hospital, we came here to recuperate.

"The German underground insisted that I wear a wedding ring, and Max was still wearing his wedding ring three years after his wife died. It took months for us to straighten that out. During that time, we had to take care of each other, and as the days passed, we slowly fell in love."

"What a romantic story! I caught my last boyfriend with another woman, and it was a devastating experience. Even now, it's hard for me to talk about it."

"I know how terrible that can be. I was engaged to someone in college, but he was killed early in the war. It was a crushing blow to me, and I swore I would never trust my heart to anyone ever again."

"So, what changed your mind with Max?"

"Well, I struggled to keep our love from happening. I even tried to deceive him and told him I was married, but that didn't work either."

Chara smiles at her. "You've renewed my faith in finding true love."

"Bad things can happen to anybody, but if you don't trust your heart to someone, you will never have truly lived. You must be doing something right. I've never seen Lotar so happy."

"I'm crazy about him. For me, he's a dream come true. Underneath his playful spirt is someone who cares deeply about his family and friends. He's affectionate and showers me with unexpected presents."

"Max is that way, too. I'm thrilled for you both."

"Thanks, Betty."

"It's taking a lot of effort to get our company up and running and at times, it can be very stressful, so remember to take time to relax and enjoy life."

"Actually, we've been talking about taking a long weekend and visiting Madrid."

"That sounds like fun. When were you planning to go?"

"Lotar has another fighter arriving in a day or two, and then we'll leave."

"That's wonderful. And don't worry about the company. I'm happy to cover for you."

CHAPTER 24

A PARISIAN WEDDING

THE HIGH SECURITY COMPLEX THAT MAX IS INTERESTED IN is on the Left Bank. As he walks toward the building, he sees Adrian standing in front. Waiting with him is an older man in a military uniform, someone that he's never seen before. "Good morning. I'd like to introduce you to General Bellefleur, Renee's father, and the commander of the French Air Force."

Max offers his hand. "I'm honored to meet you, sir."

"It's my pleasure, Doctor. I hope you don't mind, but Adrian told me you've invented a new technology that scrambles radar transmissions."

"That's correct. I plan to set up my lab in this building and continue developing it."

"I asked my people if they knew what a radar scrambler was, and they didn't know what I was talking about. Have you tested your system?"

"Yes. It was one of Hitler's secret wonder weapons. I built a prototype and tested it extensively during the war."

"Where is it now?"

"It's in storage. You are among the few that know it exists. The Soviets were after it, and Adrian helped me fly it out of Germany."

The general is concerned. "If our enemies got ahold of technology like that, France could be in great danger. As Adrian explained, we would be completely blind in a combat situation. We are prepared to pay you handsomely for exclusive rights to it, but this building will never do. You would have to work with our scientists at our high security complex outside of Paris. Would you be amenable to that?"

"Yes, of course."

"When could you start?"

"I'm leaving on my honeymoon in a few days. After that, I'll be available."

"I will explain all this to General de Gaulle today and get back to you. Keep me informed of any changes." He extends his hand. "Doctor, it was my pleasure. I look forward to a long and successful relationship with you."

He drives off in an unmarked chauffeured car and disappears into traffic. Max continues talking with Adrian. "Thank you for the introduction. I'm happy to work with the French government, and it saves me a lot of time and money renovating this building."

"Yes, I think it's the best of all possibilities for you."

Max thinks for a moment. "I would like your opinion on something. Now that I have a little extra cash, I want to give Betty something special for a wedding present, and I need your help."

"Of course. What can I do for you?"

"We would like to spend more time at our horse farm in Germany, but it's too far to drive. I'm thinking about buying a commuter plane, but I know very little about planes, and you do. What do you suggest?"

"My suggestion is to look at all the latest models at the airshow and buy one of them. All the manufacturers will have their planes on display."

"Thanks, Adrian. That's a great idea."

BETTY AND LOTAR ARE AT THE CONTROLS OF THEIR C-47, and Max and Chara relax in the cabin. They're flying from their farm to their

London office to get ready for the Paris Airshow. When they arrive, they find Charlie at work on their new Skymaster.

Betty asks him, "You look busy. What can we do?"

He is excited and filled with energy. "This is going to be a fun weekend. We're almost finished detailing this plane, and Paddy has the Arrow ready to go. You can leave now if you want. We'll be right behind you."

"Thanks, Charlie. I'll see you there."

Paddy already has it warmed up, and he goes over the flight plan with her. "Be sure to keep her under 300 mph, as the engines still need to be broken in, and don't forget to pre-oil them before you start. Okay?"

Betty is very familiar with the Arrow and is comfortable flying it. "Got it, and thanks for everything. Will you be there?"

"Yes. Charlie is treating all of us to a day at the show."

She steps into the cockpit and goes through her checklist. Then she gives Paddy a thumbs up and pulls away from the hangar. In a few minutes, she streaks down the runway and disappears into the clouds. Betty had been waiting for this day for quite a while and she wasn't disappointed. The weather is clear and sunny, as she flies out over the English Channel on her way to Paris.

Forty-five minutes later, Betty lands at Orly Airport. She turns onto a taxiway and follows a pickup truck with a large orange and white checkered flag attached to the back that reads, *FOLLOW ME*. An aircraft marshaller, dressed in an orange jacket, waves a red baton, and guides her into a reserved space. She walks down the boarding stairs and is met by two friendly Romanian pilots, who have their Yak-9 fighters parked nearby. They introduce themselves and are curious about her plane.

An hour later, Charlie lands their new four-engine Skymaster and parks across from the Arrow. They disembark, work their way through the crowd, and enter the huge exposition hall. That evening, Betty meets Max in the massive lobby, and they depart to the lounge for a drink and to discuss their day. He wants to surprise her and lets her think the negotiations on his lease are going better than expected, and she excitedly relates her story of flying to Paris.

The following day, the airshow opens to the public. The Arrow draws a lot of attention, and Betty has fun talking to spectators and answering their questions. Chara and Lotar are there early and take visitors on tours through the interior of the Skymaster, while Charlie fields questions from prospective clients.

Later in the day, Max, with the help of Lotar and Adrian, wanders through the aircraft displays looking for a plane that will fit his needs. They work their way through the enormous crowd, stopping occasionally to look at some of the exhibits. On the second day, they are about to leave the show when they pass the Beechcraft display booth. They stop to pick up brochures and a sales agent approaches them. He tells Max that a plane just arrived that might interest him, and they follow him out to the parking apron.

Parked in front is a shiny, twin-engine Beechcraft 18. It seats six passengers in luxury, or eleven as a commercial airliner. The sales agent proudly points out the interior, which was custom made for the show. Four luxurious brown leather seats face a highly polished mahogany conference table that folds away when not in use. There are two forward seats that are extra wide and recline for sleeping in flight.

Max thanks him and they retire to one of the busy lounges for a drink. The plane impressed him as it's perfect for what he needs. It cruises at 210 mph, has a range of 1,200 miles, and it has upgraded 450 hp radial engines which are economical to run, and extremely reliable. He told them he'd like to think about it, but Adrian warns him they will probably sell it during the airshow and cautions him not to wait too long if he's interested. As they walk away, Max asks Lotar. "Did you make the reservations?"

"Yes. The wedding ceremony is on Sunday at 3 o'clock, dinner is at 8, and you leave for the Riviera the following morning."

Suddenly, the loudspeaker announces that a group of World War II fighters will make a flyby in just a few minutes, and Max motions toward the viewing area. "Betty is with that group. Let's watch from over there."

They pick up their drinks and walk to the balcony to watch the show. Below them, she is already sitting in the cockpit of her plane as a North American P-51 fighter idles past her. Betty signals to her crew chief that she is about to start her engines, and the large three-bladed prop on the front engine slowly turns over. After a couple of revolutions, it sputters and coughs, then bursts into life in a thunderous roar that reverberates into the grandstands. A minute later, the rear propeller slowly turns, then starts in a cloud of gray exhaust smoke. The noise from her engines deafens the crowd, and the announcer excitedly gives the audience details of her powerful fighter.

She pulls the Arrow forward, turns out onto the taxiway, and follows the other planes as her prop wash blows debris in all directions. The first plane, a Messerschmitt Bf-109, takes off and the others follow. Now it's Betty's turn, and she blasts down the runway, chasing after them. The fighters regroup at altitude before making a low pass in front of the grandstands. They return at speed and peel off in a victory roll before landing. Betty is the last to land, and she idles back to her exhibit area. She steps out of the cockpit and waves to the crowd.

It's late in the day on Sunday, the show is winding down, and many of the planes that were on display have already left. Max and Lotar walk over to Chara and Charlie, who are standing next to their Skymaster, and Max asks them, "Well, how did it go?"

Charlie is excited. "The interest in this plane has been overwhelming, and I've got a stack of business cards to reply to when we get back."

Betty shakes hands with the last spectator and joins them. "That was fun, but I'm exhausted. The only thing that kept me going was daydreaming about laying on a sunny beach in the south of France."

As they walk away, Lotar pats Max on the back. "Brother, it's time to shift gears and slip into party mode. You'll have plenty of time to relax when you get to the Riviera. And don't worry about Wolfie, he loves hanging out with us."

It's midmorning, and Chara arrives at their apartment to pick up Betty. She dreamed of her wedding day ever since she was a little girl, and she's having fun getting ready. Earlier in the week, Chara helped her shop for a few fun things to wear on her honeymoon, but today is going to be very special because they are about to pick up her wedding dress.

A close friend of Chara's owns a bridal boutique and a week earlier Betty picked out a beautiful, ankle-length, strapless dress, with an open-neck lace bolero. She looks stunning in it and is thrilled to have found it. Finding the perfect wedding dress was especially important to Betty because she wants to pass it on to her children someday.

Then all too soon, it's their wedding day. Lotar sticks his head into Max's apartment door. "Are you ready, big brother?"

Max just finished dressing and calls to him. "Come in. Have you seen Betty?"

"Yes, but she's superstitious about you seeing the bride before the wedding ceremony, so she and Chara are staying out of sight."

Lotar looks in the mirror at the two of them, dressed in tuxedos. "Don't we look great!" and he slaps Max on the back. "This is going to be a fun afternoon!"

With that, they leave and take a taxi to the Musée Rodin. When they arrive, the beauty of the massive building and the surrounding flower gardens astonishes Max.

"This is beautiful! Chara wanted this to be a surprise and didn't tell us where our wedding was going to be held until yesterday. Betty must be thrilled!"

Lotar laughs. "Wait until you see the rest of it! Chara said this is one of the most romantic places in Paris. Many of Rodin's famous statues like *The Thinker* and *The Kiss* are on exhibition here."

They follow a stone path as it winds its way through islands of colorful rose bushes, surrounded by well-manicured lawns. In a secluded alcove is a large wrought-iron arched altar covered with yellow and white roses. Nearby, a classical guitarist quietly plays music composed by Francisco Tárrega, Max's favorite composer.

The men are wearing black tuxedos with tails, and the women wear ankle length formal gowns. As they approach, Jannik and Helga wave and she greets Max with a hug. "Congratulations. We're so happy for you both!"

He is shocked to see them dressed up. "Helga, you look incredible! I've never seen either of you dressed in anything but work clothes!"

Jannik laughs. "To tell you the truth, I didn't want to do this, but I kind of like it. Especially on a day like today. Betty is a wonderful girl, and we're very happy for both of you."

Colonel Ben-Ami and his wife Dalia approach, and she cheek kisses Max. "We're so excited to be here, and to share such an important day with you. Thank you for inviting us."

"I want you to know we're thrilled that you could make it."

Andy and Olivia join them, and she gives Max a hug. "Andy and I wish the two of you the very best."

"Thank you," and he shakes Andy's hand. "You are like family to Betty, and we appreciate your help in officiating our celebration today."

"It's my pleasure. I'm delighted that you asked me."

Max looks around. "I don't see Charlie. Is he here?"

"Oh, yes. He and Shelagh are with Betty."

Adrian and Renée arrive and walk up the stone path. She cheek kisses Max. "I'm so excited for you, and it's a beautiful day for a wedding."

Adrian shakes his hand. "Congratulations, my friend."

"Thank you. As you might have guessed, Betty is thrilled beyond belief."

He laughs. "I'll bet she is!"

Bells ring from a nearby tower, marking the hour, and the guests seat themselves in white chairs on the lawn. Andy and Max stand at the altar, and the guitarist plays *Canon in D* by Johann Pachelbel. Moments later Chara, escorted by Lotar, appears wearing a flowing yellow chiffon dress, and holds a matching bouquet of yellow roses. They join Max at the altar and face the audience.

After a brief pause, the guitarist plays *The Wedding March* by Felix Mendelssohn. Betty is standing with Charlie preparing to walk to the altar, when her uncle Karl, who was hiding nearby, approaches her. She is taken by compete surprise and throws her arms around him. Max had called Karl weeks ago, and they secretly planned to surprise her. As the music plays, he takes her arm, and they begin a slow walk to the altar. Betty is radiant in her winter-white wedding dress. Her hair is down to her shoulders, and she holds a bouquet of red roses. She is beaming with happiness as they approach the altar.

When they arrive, she takes Max's hand and stands beside him. Andy welcomes everyone and thanks them for bearing witness to their union. Then he addresses the couple and talks about the responsibilities of marriage and the sanctity of the vows that they are about to take. It's an emotional moment when Betty and Max exchange their personal vows.

Andy asks for the wedding rings, and Lotar steps forward, presenting a ring to each of them. Betty thought they were going to exchange gold wedding bands, but Max surprises her again. He had the diamonds from his mother's wedding ring reset into a modern design, and he slides it onto her finger. Lotar hands Betty a gold band that Max's father wore for nearly fifty years, and she slips it onto Max's finger.

Andy smiles at them. "You may now kiss the bride!"

It's a tender kiss, and he introduces them for the first time as Mr. and Mrs. von Hirschel and as they leave the altar, everyone wishes them a long and prosperous life together. They rejoin their friends, and Adrian takes pictures of the wedding party. Charlie and Shelagh brought the champagne, and they fill everyone's glass for a toast to the newlyweds.

Chara escorts an attractive woman, and they approach Betty, who is talking to her uncle Karl. She stares at them for a moment, then runs to embrace the woman and speaks excitedly to her in German. "Gerta! It's so wonderful to see you!"

Gerta has tears in her eyes. "I was shocked when I found out you were still alive. When you missed our rendezvous, I assumed that the Nazis had executed you."

"I have much to explain," and Betty asks her, "How did you find me?"

"You told Chara stories about what happened during the war, and she spent months tracking me down."

Chara explains. "I had very little information on her whereabouts, and it took several trips into the area before I found someone who knew about her war time deliveries."

Betty hugs her. "It's so good to see you! How is your father?"

Sadness fills Gerta's face. "He was transporting weapons to the underground when the Nazis stopped him at a roadblock. There was a shootout, and he was killed, along with Fritz and Bruno."

"Ohh, I'm so sorry, Gerta. He was a true hero."

"Thank you," and they hug for a long time.

"Where do you live now?"

"Do you remember Klaus, the baker?"

"Yes, of course. I liked him."

"After the war ended, I unexpectedly met him in a store, and we were married a short time later. We have a son and own a bakery in a nearby village."

Betty holds her hand. "I'm so happy for you, and there's much to tell you. Can you stay for dinner?"

"I'm sorry, I can't stay. Chara arranged for someone to fly me back to Germany, but she has my address. Please come and visit us. I know Klaus would love to see you, too."

"I'd like that very much. I'll call soon, and we'll set something up," and she hugs her goodbye.

The afternoon is warm and sunny, and Betty and Max spend the next hour laughing and talking with their friends. As the sun begins to set, they leave the rose garden and arrive at L'Escargot, an exclusive rooftop restaurant. It has a fantastic view overlooking the Seine River, and in the background is the Eiffel Tower. Their private party is screened off from the rest of the rooftop dining area, and the maitre d' seats them at a large table. Renée taps on her wineglass and proposes a toast. "Let us raise our glasses to the newlyweds!" and the group touches their glasses together.

Charlie asks Betty, "What is your wish for the two of you?"

"When Max first asked me to marry him, he said that he would make all my dreams come true, and that we would honeymoon on a sunny beach without a care in the world. And tomorrow we'll be there!"

Everyone claps, and Max pulls out a small, gift-wrapped box. "Speaking of sun-drenched beaches, I have something for you," and he hands her a present.

"Oh. Thank you. I can't imagine what this is."

Betty pulls at the ribbon and removes the wrapping, but before opening the lid, she glances around at the group and grins. "This is really heavy!" She opens the box, then laughs out loud. "Well, it looks like I've gotten part of the beach, anyway!" She scoops up a small portion of sand and lets it fall back, and everyone chuckles at Max's cleverness. "How sweet of you. Thank you, darling!"

"Actually, there's more to it."

"What do you mean?"

"There's something hidden in the sand."

She runs her fingers through it. "I think I've found something," and holds up a key. "What is this for?"

"You need to read what it says."

It's dark, and she pulls a candle toward her. "It says . . . Beechcraft 18!"

"Oh, no Max. You didn't!"

"You work hard, and now we can spend more time at the farm like you always wanted to."

She reaches over and kisses him. "Thank you, darling," then whispers. "I thought we were tight on money. What happened?"

Max has a sheepish grin on his face. "It's a long story."

She looks at her guests. "Oh, no. Not another long story!" and everyone laughs.

"I'll explain everything when we're sitting on a sandy beach with our feet in the water and a cold drink in our hands."

After dinner, the waiters return with a small wedding cake, which they divide up and serve to everyone. When they're finished with dessert, Betty looks at Max.

"Where are we going after this?"

He has a big smile on his face. "It's a surprise!"

He motions to the head waiter, and they remove the privacy screen surrounding their table. Max had rented the entire restaurant for the evening, and all the tables and chairs on the rooftop have been removed, creating a large dance floor. To the side is a small orchestra, dressed in formal wear.

Betty is speechless. "Max! What have you done?"

"I know you love to dance," and he extends his hand to her. As she stands, the orchestra begins playing the *Vienna Waltz*, the traditional first dance at a German wedding. Betty is in shock. "Do you know this dance?"

He smiles at her. "We've all been taking waltz lessons," and he starts dancing with her. The waltz takes up a lot of space, and they glide across the dance floor, elegantly flowing to the beautiful music. Below them brightly lit tour boats silently cruise the Seine, and in the distance the Eiffel tower is outlined in golden lights. When the music ends, their guests clap their hands, and the small orchestra plays the *Blue Danube* composed by Johann Strauss. It's Betty's all-time favorite romantic dance, and tears come to her eyes. "Max, you remembered!"

"Yes, and now it's my favorite as well!"

She watches in amazement as their guests flow to the rhythm of the music, and glide by them effortlessly in a magical circular pattern. She and Max join them, and they spend the evening dancing with their friends. When the orchestra takes a break, she and Max sit at a table with Karl and Sylvia, a special friend that he had been seeing in Palo Alto. Betty thanks him. "It was the surprise of my life to see you here! My wedding wouldn't have been complete without you giving me away," and she hugs him. "I love you, Uncle Karl!"

He winks at her. "I love you, too. Max and I decided to surprise you, and I couldn't wait to see you!" The orchestra begins to play, and he offers her his hand.

"May I have this dance?"

It's well after midnight when they finally stop dancing. It had been an exciting day, but the newlyweds have a long flight ahead of them, and their hearts are filled with joyous memories as they say goodbye to their guests.

The following morning, they are up early and walk a short distance to their favorite sidewalk café. Lotar and Chara are already seated at a table, and she stands and gives Betty a hug. "Good morning Mrs. von Hirschel! That was a lovely ceremony. I'm so happy for both of you."

"Thank you, Chara."

Lotar shakes Max's hand. "Congratulations, big brother!"

They sit down, and the waiter brings them coffee. Betty is beaming and full of energy. "I'm so excited. We haven't had a chance to play for a long time, and I can't wait to see my present!"

Max smiles at her. "Lotar is familiar with the plane, so he can go over it with you when we get to the airport."

Lotar is as excited as Betty. "You're going to love it. She's a high-performance executive commuter with all the latest avionics. And wait until you see the luxurious leather interior!"

Betty is impressed. "It sounds gorgeous!"

He explains. "The factory went all out on this one, and it has every imaginable option! I put the navigation charts that you'll need in the cockpit, and I left a briefcase with the ownership paperwork in the back locker."

"Thank you, Lotar. You've thought of everything."

An hour later, they arrive at the airport and walk to her new Beechcraft, and Betty is beside herself with happiness. "Oh, Max. She's beautiful!" Lotar unlocks the cabin door, and she steps inside and looks around. "You're right! This interior is luxurious!" then works her way to the cockpit. "What a layout!"

He motions to her. "Take a seat. I'll get you checked out when we're airborne." Then he calls to Max. "We'll be right back."

The engines turn over and burst into life, and Lotar goes over the flight checklist with her. After a few minutes, the plane moves forward and idles out onto the taxiway. They return a half hour later, and Max and Chara go out to meet them. Lotar helps load their suitcases into the plane's storage compartment and pats Max on his shoulder.

"Have fun, big brother."

"Thanks. We definitely will!"

Betty bends down and hugs Wolfie. "I love you, big boy," and he licks her face.

Chara takes his leash. "Don't worry about the Wolf. We'll have fun with him."

"Thanks. I'm going to miss him terribly."

Betty enters the plane and Max follows her. They work their way to the cockpit, and he sits down in the copilot's seat. She spends a couple of minutes reviewing her navigation charts before putting them away. "This is going to be quite an adventure!" and she reaches toward the instrument panel to adjust the radio. "Have you ever thought about learning to fly?"

"Yes, but there never was a good time to learn."

"Our lives are stabilizing now, and it would be easy for you to take a short ground school course. You already know the physics of flight from working on your radar projects."

"Hmm. I guess you're right. It would be fun to learn at some point."

DRAGON

"Well, there's no time like the present, and we've got a lot of flying to do on this trip. Do you want to try?"

"Sure. What's the first thing I need to do?"

"You can get a feel for the controls once we're at altitude, and we'll pick up a flight computer for you at the airport in Nice. It's a circular slide rule used to calculate time and distance, and you'll need a logbook to record your flights."

"That's all?"

"Not exactly, but it's a great start. We can practice takeoff and landings on the way, and you can take the wheel for as long as you like. I'm a certified instructor, so I can sign you off, and your hours will count when you apply for your license."

They fly south, passing close to Geneva, Switzerland. After a while, Betty turns control of the plane over to Max, and he practices touch and go landings at several uncontrolled airstrips. He's a quick learner, and under Betty's expert guidance, he is soon very comfortable flying the big twin.

Hours later, they approach Nice and land at Côte d'Azur Airport, on the edge of the Mediterranean. The sun is hot, and a gentle breeze blows off the sea as they exit the plane. They are only a few miles away from famous beaches, and the fabulous night life and gambling at Monte Carlo.

A brief taxi ride brings them to the well-known Hôtel de Paris, and they check in. Their room overlooks a beautiful marina filled with expensive super yachts and, after a brief rest, they set out on a walking tour to explore the many fabulous sights that Monte Carlo has to offer.

In the late afternoon, they walk along the marina arm-in-arm and discover a small French restaurant. Their table overlooks the yacht harbor, and they order champagne and hors d'oeuvres, followed by a delicious gourmet dinner. When they finish, Max takes Betty's hand, and places a dragon-embossed gold medallion in her palm exactly like the one that he wears.

"Oh my, Max. Is this for me?"

"Yes. The medallion is a symbol of our heritage, and I am so proud that you are now a part of our family. When Lotar marries, his wife will also receive one."

Afterword, they stroll in the moonlight through the narrow city streets, quietly enjoying a warm onshore breeze. At the hotel, they change into something more formal and walk down to the palatial casino. Max isn't much of a gambler, but Betty loves to play baccarat, and she sits in on a few hands while he wanders through the crowd, people-watching. At midnight, they stop at a quiet piano lounge and enjoy the rest of the evening dancing together.

This had been the most romantic and happiest day of Betty's life, and as they dance, she reflects on her long struggle to find happiness. She barely avoided death at the hands of the Hitler Youth and faced enormous challenges while growing up in California. Incredibly, she and Max had narrowly escaped the cauldron of war while living in Nazi Germany, and she was nearly killed in two horrific plane crashes. The lowest point in her life was when Max was shot, and she held him in her arms, thinking he was dying. Her journey had always been difficult, but now they were together, and she would be forever grateful. As they dance, she holds him close to her. "I love you, Max. I want you to know that this is the happiest day of my life."

He nuzzles her cheek. "You are the love of my life, and I can't imagine life without you." He holds her tightly and kisses her. "I would like to start a family someday, and I know you would be a fabulous mother."

Betty is overjoyed with happiness. "I would love that, Max. It's one of my lifelong dreams."

"Let's enjoy life for a while, and then we can make plans."

The following morning is sunny and warm, and a light summer breeze billows the curtains in their open balcony doors. Betty is still asleep, but Max is up early and orders breakfast.

He lays down next to her and whispers. "Time to get up, beautiful!"

She rolls over and hugs him sleepily. "Good morning, darling."

"Room service will be here soon with our breakfast."

"Thank you! I'd better put something on."

She gets out of bed and slips on a bathrobe. There's a light knock on their door, and Max goes to answer it. He returns, pushing a cart with their breakfast, and wheels it out onto their sunny balcony overlooking the marina. A heavy stone breakwater protects the harbor, and beyond it is the blue Mediterranean Sea.

Betty sets down her coffee cup and stares at their surroundings. "What a stunning day!" and she places her hand on Max's arm. "Only a couple of months ago I thought you were dead, and I had lost you forever."

He smiles at her. "I've got a little surprise for you today."

"Another surprise?"

"Yes, but you better bring your swimsuit for this one!"

They leave the hotel and walk along the marina, admiring a row of glistening sailboats as they pass by them. Max stops at a small charter kiosk and opens the door for her. "Here we are."

"Are we taking a tour somewhere?"

"Sort of." He walks up to the counter and introduces himself to the man at the desk. "Good morning. I'm Max von Hirschel. I reserved a charter for today."

The man smiles and shakes his hand. "My name is Sébastien, and I've been expecting you. If you'll follow me, I'll show you to your boat."

They walk with him down a wooden ramp that leads to a floating walkway, and they pass by a long row of impressive yachts. Betty squeezes his hand. "This is exciting!"

They stop at a sleek twenty-five-foot cabin cruiser, and Sébastien invites them aboard. "You said you are familiar with the operation of the boat?"

"Yes. I've owned several boats."

"Good," and he hands Max the keys. "If you have any questions, I'll be at the kiosk. Enjoy yourselves!" and he waves goodbye.

Betty is excited. "I love your surprises! Where are we going?"

"I thought it would be fun to just go exploring," and he starts the engine.

He skillfully idles out of the marina, then opens up the throttle, and the powerful speed boat cuts through the warm, blue water with ease. A half hour later, they've traveled several miles up the rocky coastline. He slows down, stops the engines, and they quietly drift with no one in sight. The sky is blue, and the sun shines warmly on them. Betty removes her white cotton beach pants and a loose-fitting blouse, revealing a black bikini.

Her body is sleek and Max whistles at her. "I like that bikini!" and points to the rear of the boat. "There's a swim platform in the back."

Betty walks over to the transom and steps down onto the platform. She dips her foot into the seawater and stares at the multi-colored coral scattered across the rocky sea floor below her. "Oh, Max! The water is warm and crystal clear!"

"Great! I'll be right there."

He slips out of his shirt and trousers, revealing his muscular body and a skintight swimsuit. To Max's surprise, Betty takes off her bikini and dives into the emerald-green water, swimming below the surface for a few yards, then pops up. She pushes her hair back from her face with both hands and teases him. "I seem to have lost something!"

Max removes his swimming suit, dives into the sea, and swims out to her. They embrace and he kisses her tenderly. As they tread water, she looks down at the seafloor. "Look at that! I can see fish swimming at the bottom!"

He stares into the rocky depths below them, then takes a deep breath and dives. She watches as he descends to the rock-strewn seabed. He picks up something, returns to the surface, and hands her a large piece of broken pottery with a long handle. "Look at what I found!"

Betty examines it. "This is extraordinary! What do you think it is?"

"It's part of an amphora container, probably from the Bronze Age."

She turns it over and carefully examines it. "How old is that?"

He brushes his wet hair back while treading water. "Maybe three or four thousand years ago."

"That's amazing! Let's go back to the boat. I want to look at it more closely."

Betty climbs up the boarding ladder. She's topless with a towel wrapped around her waist and carefully wipes down the broken terracotta fragment. "It's incredible to think that no one has touched this for thousands of years. How do you think it got there?"

"Maybe it's from Atlantis."

"Really! The lost city of Atlantis?"

"Plato wrote that it was located beyond the Pillars of Hercules, but no one has ever found it."

"What a romantic story!"

"Even if Atlantis never existed, it's still a stunning piece of antiquity."

She carefully wraps it in a towel. "Thank you, Max. I love it. Let's sun ourselves on the forward deck."

They lay their towels out on the white fiberglass bow and stretch out beside each other. Max is laying on his side, and Betty is lying next to him. "What a beautiful day." They kiss, and she snuggles close to him. "You promised to tell me about your lab. What happened?"

"It was something quite extraordinary. I met Adrian at the secure building, and he brought along his father-in-law, General Bellefleur. He confided to him about our radar jamming technology, and the general offered us a lot of money for the rights to it. I also agreed to work with his scientists at a high security facility outside of Paris. How would you like to live in the country for a while?"

"I'd love to do that. Let's find something with a little acreage so we can bring our horses with us."

"You're reading my mind."

He picks up a bottle of sunscreen and pours some of the lotion onto the palm of his hand. "You better put some of this on," and he rubs it on her naked body.

Betty does the same thing to him, and it's an erotic experience for them both. She whispers in his ear. "I wonder if there is anything cold to drink?"

"A little bird told me that there's something in the refrigerator."

They retire to the shade of the cabin, and he opens a chilled bottle of champagne. Later that afternoon, they return their boat just as the sun sets, and walk back to their hotel. As darkness falls, the air is warm, and they stroll together in the twilight to a small Italian restaurant that overlooks the marina. After finishing dinner, Betty has a surprise for him.

"Do you remember when I was interviewed by that reporter from *Le Figaro*?"

"Yes, I do."

"We talked for quite a while about the Arrow. I told her how fast it was, and how exciting it was to fly, and she suggested I challenge the world speed record with it. It currently stands at 492 mph, and I've already flown close to that. No piston powered plane has ever broken 500 mph in level flight."

"Are you sure you want to try that? It sounds dangerous."

"I have confidence in myself, and my plane. I know I could do it."

Max knows that he can't talk her out of it and decides to be as supportive as possible. "Well, you should probably talk to Charlie. He's pretty knowledge-able when it comes to high-performance planes."

Betty reaches across the table and squeezes his hand. "I promise!"

The next morning, they are having brunch at a hillside café overlooking Monte Carlo and Betty asks Max, "What would you like to do today?"

"Well, there is something, but because of the war, it was never possible."

"Darling, what are you talking about?"

"I've always wanted to go to the world famous La Scala opera house in Milan. It was badly damaged during the war, but I heard that it's been completely restored and was recently reopened."

Betty, the city girl, is instantly interested. "Milan is only an hour from here by air. I'd love to go, but we didn't bring any formal wear."

"We're flush with money from selling the radar scrambler. I always wanted to own an expensive Italian tuxedo, and there are plenty of famous fashion designers in Milan for you to choose from."

"Let's check out of the hotel and fly there this afternoon. Do you know what's playing?"

"Yes. Puccini's *Turandot*, and the conductor is Arturo Toscanini!"

"Oh, I love that opera, and he's world-famous!"

After lunch, they leave for Milan, one hundred and fifty miles away in northern Italy, and an hour later, they land at the airport. They ask their taxi driver if he could recommend a place to stay near the La Scala opera house, and he drops them off at a nearby hotel. They purchase their tickets, and afterword they explore the fashion district looking for formal wear and they have a fun time trying on the many possibilities.

Max found an expensive Italian tuxedo that he always wanted, and Betty purchased an elegant black cocktail dress. By the time they finished shopping for all their accessories the day was ending, and they felt like celebrating, so they treated themselves to a delicious dinner at a famous two-star Michelin restaurant. Afterward, they returned to their hotel, and spent the evening dancing at the rooftop lounge that overlooks the city.

The following day, they catch a taxi to the fashion district, and pick up their formal wear. Later that evening, a limousine pulls up in front of the La Scala opera house and Betty and Max exit. She is stunning in her cocktail dress, and he is handsome in his new tuxedo. When they arrive, a large crowd has gathered at the famous arched front doors, and they enter the lobby and work their way to a winding staircase that leads to the balcony.

From there, they walk down to their luxurious, gilded private box, with red carpet and velvet wallpaper. It overlooks the stage, and they have a commanding view of the performers and the orchestra pit. *Turandot* was an unbelievingly exciting performance, and afterward they take a limousine to one of Milan's most exclusive night clubs and dance the night away.

Their romantic honeymoon is drawing to a close, and the following morning, they load their luggage into Betty's new plane. Max takes her into his arms. "It's been wonderful to get away and have fun together. We have a lot of work ahead of us, but let's promise ourselves to take time off and enjoy life when we can."

"I'd love to do that, and there are many beautiful places for us to visit."

Max opens the cabin door for her. "Where shall we go next time?"

Betty thinks for a moment. "I like this sunny Mediterranean weather. Maybe somewhere in the Greek Islands?"

He winks at her. "I'm already looking forward to it!"

They leave for Paris, and Max flies all the way back. Betty was extremely proud of him and thrilled that she could now share her love of flying with him. When they land, Lotar and Chara are waiting to greet them. Wolfie sees Betty, sprints to her, and she hugs him. "I missed you every day, big boy!"

Max loads their suitcases into Lotar's four-door Mercedes sedan, and they drive to a favorite café to have lunch. When they arrive, Betty clips a leash onto Wolfie, and he walks with them. Lotar can't get over Max's new look. "I've never seen you so relaxed, and that suntan looks great on you."

"Thanks. We had a really wonderful time."

Wolfie lays down under the table by Betty's feet, and she beams with excitement. "I have an announcement to make," and she holds Max's hand. "We have a new pilot amongst us. Max flew most of the way down, and all the way back!"

Lotar is surprised. "It's about time, big brother! Congratulations!"

Chara asks him, "That's great, Max! What made you decide to start flying?"

"Well, I had this gorgeous instructor to show me the way, and it was an exciting experience that I'll never forget. So, what's new here?"

Lotar relates all the highlights. "The big news is that the Soviets just sealed off all land and water access to Berlin, and the Allies are getting ready to start a massive airlift to save three million people from starving to death. Andy is already talking to the British government about us joining the effort. He said they can break away two of their Skymasters, and we can give him a couple of ours as well."

Max shakes his head. "That's unbelievable!" and turns to Betty. "What do you think?"

"I definitely want to help. What caused the Soviets to do that?"

"The Allies replaced the failing Reichsmark with their newly created Deutsche Mark without telling them. In retaliation, they sealed off all access to Berlin except for a couple of narrow air corridors leading in from the Allied side. They are planning to fly in coal for heating, and enough food to feed three million people, but they will have to fly twenty-four hours a day, seven days a week, until they can work something out. Some say it's not possible, there just aren't enough planes to do that."

"How long do they expect the blockade to last?"

"For a while, I guess. Neither side wants to lose face. Right now, I'm scrambling to find pilots and mechanics that will work long hours and live away from home for what could be quite a while."

Betty is shocked by Lotar's news. "It sounds like we're doubling the size of our company!"

"Yes, and I talked with Charlie. He has more planes on the way for us."

She asks him, "What's happening with the wine business?"

"It's booming, and Adrian continues to find more customers every day."

Max puts down his coffee cup. "We have more exciting news. Betty wants to challenge the world speed record with the Arrow."

Lotar is uncomfortable. "That could be very dangerous. Anything can happen at that speed."

"Of course, that's always a possibility, but I know I can do it."

Lotar realizes she's determined. "Well, if you're certain that's what you want to do, then I want to be a part of it."

"Thanks. I really appreciate your support. Charlie suggested we repower it with the new Rolls-Royce Griffon engines that came out at the end of the war. That would boost the horsepower from thirty-nine hundred to five thousand."

Lotar is shocked. "That's very impressive!"

"I'm going to fly over next week and leave the Arrow with Charlie. The conversion will take several weeks."

Lotar continues updating them on the operation of their business. "There's another thing I wanted to talk to you about. I think it's time that we setup a regional hub in each country where we operate. Each hub would have an office manager, a logistics coordinator to handle billing and scheduling, and an operations manager to work with our air crews. Rotterdam would be a good starting point because a lot of our cargo from the United States is off-loaded there."

Betty complements him. "I like it! That's a brilliant idea!"

Lotar takes Chara's hand. "We also have good news. I asked Chara to marry me, and she accepted. We found a small apartment and moved in together."

Betty is thrilled. "Wonderful! I'm so happy for both of you."

Max congratulates them. "I wish you both much happiness. It's a time in your life that you will never forget."

Betty asks Chara, "So, when is the big day?"

"Soon. But there's a lot going on at work right now."

"Don't worry about that. Max and I can handle things while you're gone. Where are you planning to go on your honeymoon?"

"I've always wanted to visit Casablanca, and then we'll fly to the Canary Islands and find a sunny beach."

Lotar asks her. "How do you like your Beechcraft?"

"She's a genuine pleasure to fly."

"Good. The company is going to need something like it. As you know, everything's an emergency in this business."

"Well, I highly recommend it."

Chara is curious. "So much for work. We're dying to hear about your trip."

Betty is tanned and bubbles over with excitement. "We had a fabulous time, and the weather was sunny and warm. The Riviera was unbelievable, and we gambled a couple of nights at the casino in Monte Carlo.

"But the highlight of our trip was a spur-of-the-moment idea that Max had. He heard that they recently rebuilt the La Scala opera house, so we flew to Milan and spent three days there. We saw Puccini's *Turandot*, and the conductor was Arturo Toscanini!"

Chara's eyes light up. "Ahh, I love that opera! As I remember, Toscanini first performed it at the La Scala. That's so romantic!"

Betty continues. "We had an absolutely fantastic time in Milan!"

Lotar asks Max, "Sorry to change the subject, but when are you going to set up your lab?"

"Well, there's been a change. The French government purchased the rights to the radar technology, and I'm going to work for them for a year at their research center outside of Paris. We're thinking about moving to the country, and thought we'd look at property this afternoon. Why don't you join us?"

A few hours later, they drive to a quiet village outside of Paris. Betty looks at a business card General Bellefleur had given them. "Apparently this man has a restaurant here," and she points to a sign. "There it is, the Golden Rooster."

They enter and the hostess seats them. Betty asks if they could talk to the owner and a few minutes later, he appears dressed in a white chef's jacket. He's good-looking, middle-aged, and speaks French with a Swiss accent. "Hello, I'm Jean Pierre. How can I help you?"

"We're new to the area and friends of General Bellefleur. He suggested we stop by and introduce ourselves."

"Ah, yes. The General and I have known each other for a long time."

Betty motions toward their table. "Please sit down and join us. This is my husband, Max von Hirschel, his brother Lotar, and his fiancée, Chara Escoffier. We're thinking about moving out of the city, and we like this area. The general said you might know of something for sale."

"Yes, I know everyone in the valley. What is it you are looking for?"

"Somewhere quiet with acreage for our horses."

"I can think of a couple of properties that might interest you, and I would be happy to show them to you."

Betty is apologetic. "We didn't mean to inconvenience you. If you could give us the addresses, that would be fine."

"I'm sorry, but there are no addresses, and you would become hopelessly lost. The General is a good friend, and I'm happy to help you. I don't need to be here until later tonight. If you like, I could show you a couple of properties right now."

Betty appreciates his offer. "Well, yes, if you don't mind. Thank you!"

They drive around and look at a few houses, but larger pieces of land are rare, and nothing suits their taste. Lotar pulls over to the side of the road, and Jean Pierre looks over a large map that he brought with him. "That's pretty much everything," and he thinks for a moment. "There is one more place with acreage, but it's been abandoned for years. The elderly owners died prior to the war, and their daughter lives in a nursing home in Paris. Would you like to see it?"

Betty asks Max, "Are you interested?"

"Yes, let's take a look."

Jean Pierre explains. "This might be exactly what you're looking for. It has a large farmhouse, a guesthouse, a barn, and some acreage."

Betty is curious. "Why hasn't it sold?"

"It hasn't been maintained for over ten years. It's heavily overgrown, and the buildings need a little fixing up. The land is not suitable for growing grapes, and not level enough for the farmers to be interested in it. But it sounds like it would be perfect for your horses."

Lotar starts the car, and they drive off following Jean Pierre's directions. In a few miles, he points at two large stone columns and a heavy wrought-iron gate. "Pull in here. I don't have a key, but we can take that trail."

They walk around the gate, and the trail leads them to a tree-lined road that takes them to a large two-story stone house covered in ivy. It overlooks a meadow surrounded by trees and rolling hills, and nearby is a guesthouse and a barn. They stop, and Betty is stunned by the gorgeous setting. "Oh, Max. This is wonderful! It looks like something out of a children's storybook."

Jean Pierre points to the overgrowth covering the meadow and hills. "It could take a couple of weeks of pruning and cleaning up, but it would look spectacular."

Betty gazes at the house, spell bound. "Can we see inside?"

"Yes. I believe its unlocked."

They walk through every room, then cross over to the guesthouse and wander through it. The women look about while Max and Lotar walk to the barn. It's a pristine example of old-world architecture that could easily serve as a horse barn.

As they leave, they stop at the edge of the adjacent meadow, and Max looks at the heavily overgrown vegetation. "I don't know. This is going to take a lot of time and money to clean up." He thinks about it for a moment, then turns to Lotar. "This is too much work for one person, but maybe we could develop it together? I think the women are in love with it."

"I like your idea, and you're right about them liking it." He walks out into the meadow and stares at the brush and trees. "This has fantastic potential. Sure, I'll go in with you on it. Let's discuss it with the girls."

They find the women and Lotar asks Chara, "What do you think of the guesthouse?"

"I love it. Just imagine what it would look like remodeled!"

Max explains their idea to Betty. "Lotar and I thought it might be fun to develop this together."

Betty's eyes light up. "That's a great idea!" and she looks at Chara. "We could easily remodel and expand the guesthouse, and you'd have your dream home!"

Chara is in love with the cottage. "This is so cute! It looks like a Hansel and Gretel gingerbread house! It's perfect, and there's plenty of room here for our horses."

Betty asks Jean Pierre. "How do we find out how much this is worth?"

"Let's go back, and I'll make some calls."

She's excited, and hungry as usual. "Good idea, and I think we'll stay for dinner."

They return to his restaurant, and Jean Pierre gets on the phone while they order their food. He joins them as they finish eating. "I made a few calls. There have been several appraisals made on the property, so we know what the market value is. The good news is that the daughter really wants to sell and would accept any reasonable offer."

Betty looks at Chara. "Finance is your world. Whatever you decide to offer, we'll back you up one hundred percent."

"Thank you. I'll start negotiations tomorrow, and we'll see what happens."

CHAPTER 25

CHALLENGING THE WORLD SPEED RECORD

AT LAST, THE LONG-AWAITED DAY HAS ARRIVED FOR BETTY to challenge the world speed record. She will fly from Geneva, Switzerland, to Beauvais–Tillé, a small airport on the outskirts of Paris. Her attempt has been well-publicized, and there are large crowds at both airports to witness the event. Betty worked hard to prepare her plane and was extremely excited to be challenging the world record.

She wears a custom-made black leather jumpsuit. On the front is her name and the German coat of arms, a heraldic shield with an eagle set against a golden wheatfield, and on her back is a large, golden-winged dragon. She and Max enter the operations center for a short briefing, and she goes over her route with the officials. Her first stop will be Geneva to meet Paddy and Charlie, who flew there earlier in her Beechcraft 18. She will take a brief rest while they make a last-minute inspection. If there are no problems, she'll fly 255 miles back to Paris, and the return trip should take about thirty minutes.

When they leave, a large group of reporters rush toward her, and she holds Max's hand tightly as they approach. He tries to settle her nerves. "Here comes the press. They just want to meet you."

But the excited crowd overwhelms her, and she's nervous. "Max, please stay close to me."

He smiles and tries his best to keep her calm. "It seems you're somewhat of a celebrity today."

The reporters move in on them, and Max makes the first introduction. "This is Leslie Martin, with *Stars and Stripes*, the American military newspaper." They shake hands and exchange pleasantries.

She asks Betty, "I understand you went to school in California?"

"Yes, Stanford University."

"Your plane is very unusual! How much horsepower does it have?"

"The Rolls-Royce engines are rated at 5,000."

"That's quite impressive. Thank you!"

Another reporter pushes his way toward her, and Max introduces him. "This is Andrew Heston with the London paper, *The Sunday Times*."

He excitedly questions her as a sea of light bulbs from photographer's cameras flash behind him. "Can you tell us about your unusual plane?"

"Yes. It's German, and the fastest propeller driven fighter of the war."

Max continues to push Betty through the throng of reporters, and a short, pleasant-looking man approaches them. "This is Günter Meyer with *Süddeutsche Zeitung*, the largest newspaper in Germany."

"This is exciting news for our readers, and something positive to come out of the war. What country will you be representing?"

"Germany. I was born in Berlin."

"On behalf of all Germans, we wish you success in your attempt today."

"Thank you for your kind words."

The crowd surges against them, trying to hear what they are saying, and Max tries to calm them down. "Betty promises to answer whatever questions you may have later on. I've prepared a press release with all her pertinent information," and he passes out a handful of notices.

As they approach the security barrier, Betty sees her friend with the French newspaper *Le Figaro*, and waves to her. "Hi, Mélanie."

"Good luck on your attempt today."

"Thank you," and the reporters press in. Betty looks back at her. "Call me next week. We can talk more at my office."

"Thanks, I'll do that."

Andy waves from behind a security barrier. "Max, over here! The photographers are waiting!"

They enter a restricted area, and the airport security officers hold back the reporters. A photographer standing near her plane calls to her. "May we take photos of you?"

"Yes. Of course."

She looks for Wolfie, calls him to her side, and the two of them stand side-by-side to pose for the cameras. The photographers flash away for a few minutes, then Max intervenes. "I'm sorry, but that's all the time we have for now. Betty needs to prepare for her flight."

Andy and the security officers escort the photographers out of the restricted area, then he returns to help ready her plane. Betty climbs the boarding stairs, and when she reaches the top, she turns and waves at the crowd.

Lotar follows and helps her into the cockpit. "Paddy installed a methanol injection system off a Messerschmitt fighter. When you're ten miles from the finish line, push the throttles all the way forward to engage it. It allows the superchargers to run at a higher boost pressure, and it will increase your horsepower by forty percent. It's hard on the engines, so don't use it for more than a few minutes."

"Thanks, Lotar. I appreciate all the work that you and Paddy have done."

He pats her on the back. "Good luck and be safe!"

The announcer catches the crowd's attention by explaining that Betty will attempt to break the existing world speed record of 492 miles an hour. She waves to Max, blows him a kiss, then puts on her leather helmet and adjusts her goggles. Her ground crew connects the tug to the Arrow's landing gear and pulls the huge plane out of its parking space. When they arrive at the taxiway, they disconnect, and she begins her pre-flight checklist. After a few minutes, the front engine coughs into life, and its giant propeller beats the air in a loud roar. Then the rear engine goes through the same routine.

After a few minutes, she signals Andy, and he motions for her to move forward. As she idles past him, he gives her a smile and a thumbs up. By now the crowd is on their feet as the high-pitch scream of her twin supercharged Rolls-Royce engines reverberates through the grandstand. She taxis past the control tower and turns out onto the runway.

Betty reaches up and pulls her canopy closed, then lowers her flaps a few degrees. Halfway down the long runway, she lifts off the ground and rockets skyward into the clear blue sky. The stadium announcer keeps the spectators entertained by telling them about Betty's flying background, and technical facts about the Arrow.

Once airborne, she sets her compass for Geneva, and keeps her speed down to 350 mph to reduce stress on her engines. Below her are green forests, low rolling hills, and extensive areas of farming country interspersed with blue lakes and winding rivers. Forty-five minutes later, she approaches the sprawling Geneva Airport complex, and lands.

A large crowd of spectators standing behind temporary barricades cheer wildly. The big twin-engine Arrow takes all of her strength to maneuver, and Charlie guides her into a parking spot. She exits her plane, waves to the chanting crowd, then descends the stairs in her tight black leather jumpsuit. She's wearing amber pilot's glasses and her flowing auburn hair swirls in the light breeze.

He greets her. "How did the flight go?"

"Perfect! The engines never missed a beat."

Paddy walks over to her, and she's excited to see him. "Hi. Thanks for all your help."

They've been good friends ever since he helped get her Stork into flying condition. "I wouldn't have missed this for the world, lass."

"Thanks, Paddy," and she turns to Charlie. "Do you need to check the engines?"

"We'll go over them for oil leaks as soon as they cool off. I just want to be doubly sure there aren't any problems."

"I'd like to relax a bit before the return trip," and she walks toward an empty office in the restricted area.

Charlie motions toward a sizable group of bystanders waving at her. "You might want to say hello to your fans. They've been waiting there for hours to see you."

The cheering crowd makes Betty nervous, and she jokes. "Okay, but only if you'll stay near me!"

He takes all the attention in stride. "It won't take long. This is history in the making, and something they can tell their grandkids about."

Betty pulls herself together and confidently waves at them as she and Charlie head over to greet them. As they walk along the barrier, she shakes dozens of hands and signs a few autographs. Then they stop briefly to talk with a group of reporters and photographers. After a bit, Charlie thanks them, and explains that they need to prepare for her upcoming flight.

They return to the restricted area and walk over to an empty building. Charlie spreads out a navigation chart on a table and reviews it with her. "I spent some time going over your route. There are plenty of places where you can make an emergency landing if something unforeseen happens. The good news is that there are no mountainous areas to worry about."

Betty carefully examines the chart. "Thanks, Charlie. I like the course that you laid out."

"We'd have to leave the country to find anything better. Any questions?"

"I don't think so. Lotar showed me how to use the methanol injection system."

"Good, but only use it if the engines sound okay. It's extremely powerful, and will put a massive load on them, but you'll need it to break the record."

"Thank you for all your help."

He can see she needs some time by herself. "I better give Paddy a hand. We're about fifteen minutes out," and he leaves the building.

Betty nervously paces the floor, and focuses her thoughts on the upcoming return flight, as it's going to be demanding and very dangerous. She reaches into her pocket, pulls out a lock of Wolfie's long fur, and absent-mindedly runs her fingers across it, lost in thought. When she looks up, she notices Charlie standing next to the Arrow waving at her. She emerges from the building, waves at the crowd, and they go wild as she crosses the tarmac to her plane. "Thanks again. I appreciate all your hard work," and gives him a hug.

"Good luck, Betty! We'll be right behind you."

She enters the cockpit, puts on her leather helmet, adjusts her goggles, and chinches up her safety harness. Then she reaches forward and starts her front engine. Moments later, her rear engine starts, and she waits for several minutes while double-checking her instruments.

Betty is all business now. Charlie and Paddy wave to her as she idles past them, and she raises a gloved hand as she passes by. The deadly looking fighter taxis slowly to the end of the long runway, and she's immediately given clearance to take off. She revs her engines to full power, streaks down the pavement, and the clock starts!

The Arrow's twin Griffon engines are quick to respond, and their superchargers scream loudly. Ten minutes later, she glances at her airspeed indicator; it shows 498 miles an hour and is increasing! Betty doesn't waste time climbing to altitude and flies straight and level at two thousand feet. She grips the vibrating control stick with both hands, and the countryside below her is a blur.

Her plane buffets heavily as she blasts through a short section of mild turbulence. It jostles her around violently, then quickly smooths out. The day is sunny with blue skies and gentle breezes. Betty crosses the halfway point, flying at 512 mph. Her engines are running wide-open and operating flawlessly, but she worries. How long can they withstand this kind of punishment?

Minutes later, she sees the control tower at Beauvais–Tillé Airport in the distance and drops to one thousand feet in elevation. She roars directly over her ten-mile marker, shoves her throttles forward as hard as she can, and the methanol injector engages. Instantly, the Arrow surges ahead violently, pressing her back in her seat, and her engines scream as they hover at the edge of their design limits.

Betty flashes across the finish line in front of the grandstand in a deafening roar, and the excited crowd gives her a standing ovation. She is flying at a record-breaking speed, but the huge fighter is extremely difficult to control. She needs to reduce her speed and immediately disengages the methanol injection system, but she's low to the ground and pulls hard on the stick to gain altitude and climbs steeply.

Suddenly, there is a tremendous explosion in her front engine compartment, and a large piece of sheet metal covering the engine cowling flies past her cockpit. The plane shutters violently, and a cloud of black smoke trails behind it. Rivulets of hot oil streak across the windshield, reducing her vision to zero. The torque from her powerful engine rips it away from the airframe and it explodes.

Flames envelope the front of her plane, stream past her windshield, and across her wings. Betty realizes there may be only seconds before her fuel tanks explode, and immediately reaches down to the side of her seat and pulls hard on the red emergency ejection handle. Explosive charges detonate in the back of the plane and the rear engine separates from the fuselage. It spins wildly toward a farmer's nearby field and a second later, an explosive charge frees her canopy, blowing it out of sight.

Instantly, her rocket-powered ejection seat ignites, and blasts her out of the plane. She shoots straight up, and the acceleration knocks her unconscious. Her ejection seat tumbles through the sky, and she is automatically separated from it. Seconds later, her black and gold parachute deploys, but she is slumped forward, and hangs motionless in her harness. The crowd in the grandstands jumps to their feet as she slowly drifts toward the ground.

Far below, the wreckage of her plane crashes into the field, and explodes in a gigantic fireball as the spectators watch in horror. Red lights on the airport's rescue vehicles light up and their sirens deafen the crowd. Max and Andy sprint to a parked ambulance, and Andy yells at the driver. "This is her husband!"

He motions for them to get into the back, and they race across the runway to a gate in the perimeter fence. Andy points the driver toward Betty's parachute draped over the freshly plowed ground a hundred yards away. She is unconscious and lying motionless on her side, covered in black oil and bleeding from several cuts on her face. The leather gloves on her hands are fire-scorched and smoldering.

Max and Andy can only stand back and let the medics do their work. They carefully remove her gloves and wrap her hands in bandages. Then they cut her safety harness with knives and free her from her parachute. Andy and Max run to the ambulance, remove the gurney, and place it on the ground next to her. The four of them lift her limp body onto it and carry her to the back of the ambulance. Andy and the driver jump into the front, and Max and the other medic enter through the back door. The ambulance bounces across the field toward the hospital with its siren screaming and emergency lights flashing.

Black oil and dirt cover Betty, and Max carefully wipes her face as the medic works to unbutton her scorched flight suit. He removes her goggles and helmet and checks her life signs. The ambulance soon reaches the paved road, and the ride smooths out. He places a stethoscope on her chest, then looks up at Max. "She has a faint heartbeat, and her pulse is weak." He puts an oxygen mask over Betty's nose and mouth and adjusts the airflow. "This should help for now."

Betty is still unconscious, and her injuries look very serious. Max worriedly asks the medic, "Is she going to make it?"

"It's hard to say. Her vital signs are stable, but I can't tell if she has internal injuries."

The hospital is only five miles away, and they soon arrive at the emergency room. The medics rush her inside, and Max and Andy walk to the waiting room. Minutes later, Lotar and Chara enter the room and approach him worriedly. Max explains. "She's alive, but that's all I know. I should have done more to discourage her from trying to do this."

Lotar puts his arm on his brother's shoulder. "It's not your fault. This was her dream, and it wasn't your place to keep her from it."

Max asks Andy, "What do you think happened up there?"

"Hard to say, but from what I saw, I would guess that the engine mounting frame ripped away from the fuselage. The engines sounded like they were running okay."

The door to the emergency room swings open and a woman wearing a white lab coat approaches Max. "I'm Dr. Cloutier. Are you related to the patient?"

"Yes! I'm her husband."

"She's conscious now. You can visit her for a few minutes, but she's very weak."

The doctor opens the door to her private room, and Max sees her lying in a hospital bed surrounded by instrumentation. A large beeping monitor shows her vital signs, and a saline bottle drips fluid into a long tube that leads to a needle taped to her arm. Another tube feeds her oxygen through a cannula attached to her nose. She has a large bandage wrapped around her head and her eyes are black and blue. A thick yellow salve covers several blistered areas on her face, and spots of blood leak through the gauze bandages covering her hands.

Max rushes to her side. "Betty, can you hear me?" She nods her head, and he reassures her. "I'm close by. I won't leave you!"

She slowly reaches out, touches his hand, and then passes out. The doctor taps him on his shoulder. "That's enough for now. I just wanted to reassure her that you are here. She's still groggy from the pain medicine."

As they return to the waiting room, the doctor stops Max. "She needs to rest. I'll have the results from her lab work later in the day. Try to get some sleep and come back in the morning. She'll be able to talk to you by then."

"Thank you, Doctor. I appreciate all that you're doing."

He walks into the waiting room and approaches the anxious group. "She's alive, but pretty beaten up and heavily sedated. The doctor said they will know more in the morning."

Chara takes his arm. "Why don't you come home with us? We can come back tomorrow."

"Thanks, but I promised I wouldn't leave her."

Andy tries to comfort him. "She's going to be alright, Max. Now I'm worried about you."

"I'm okay, but that was the scariest moment of my life!"

Lotar gives his brother a hug. "We'll see you in the morning," and they leave.

Max settles into a chair and makes himself as comfortable as possible for the long night ahead. Hours later, he awakens to sunlight streaming through the windows. Just then, the doctor enters the room, and he greets her. "Good morning. Is my wife awake yet?"

"Yes, and she's been asking for you. Come with me, and you can see her."

Max follows her into Betty's room and finds her sitting up against several pillows. He has a smile on his face and walks to her bedside. "Good morning, beautiful. Imagine meeting you here!"

Betty holds out her bandaged hand and speaks softly. "I was so worried about you."

"Me? You're the one that was almost killed."

"I'm so sorry that I tried to do that. I know it made you worry about me. It was very selfish."

"It was your dream, and I needed to support you any way I could."

"Did they confirm my speed?"

"Yes. 536 mph. You set a new world record and broke a couple of other speed and distance records as well."

"I'm sorry about the plane. Does Charlie know what happened?"

"He thinks the methanol injector created extremely high horsepower, which caused the engine mounting frame to rip away from the fuselage."

Betty struggles to get comfortable. "I think he's probably right. There was a loud bang followed by massive vibration."

Max asks the doctor, "Do you know any more about her condition?"

"Her X-rays and lab work look normal, so we don't think she has any internal injuries. You are a very lucky lady, and you should recover fully."

Max is elated. "That's fantastic news."

She flips through Betty's lab results. "But there is one more thing."

Betty's face fills with worry. "Oh, no! What's that?"

"Do you know you are pregnant?"

She and Max exchange looks of disbelief. "What?"

The doctor smiles. "It's right here in the lab report."

Betty can't believe it. "Is the baby alright?"

"Oh, yes. You are quite early into the pregnancy."

Max bends down and carefully gives her a hug. "Congratulations, darling."

"What a way to find out you're pregnant!"

The doctor pats her on the shoulder. "Take care of yourself. When you're feeling better, I recommend you see an obstetrician . . . and no more flying for a while!"

Max gently holds her hand. "Everyone is anxiously waiting to see you."

She pulls him close to her and whispers. "I love you with all my heart."

He bends down and kisses her. "I love you both!" and he returns to the waiting room. Everyone has been waiting anxiously for news of Betty's condition, and they rush to him. "She's doing fine. Just badly bruised, and she wants to see all of you."

They enter her room, and Betty is the first to speak. "Please don't worry about me. The doctor said I will be fine, but there is one piece of good news . . .

I'm pregnant!" and she laughs. "Just a minor side effect from using the rocket-powered ejection system!"

That's the last thing any of them expected to hear, and Lotar is the first to shake Max's hand. "Congratulations, big brother!"

Andy approaches her. "I'm so happy for both of you!"

Chara hugs her. "I'm thrilled for you, Betty!"

Days later, she is released, and Max rolls her out to his car in a wheelchair. She takes a deep breath of the warm summer air. "Oh, Max! It's great to be out of the hospital. How long do I have to use this wheelchair?"

"Not long. It's just a precaution because of the extreme stress that occurred when you ejected, but no long walks for a few days."

After a short drive across town, they arrive at their apartment. As they pull up the driveway, they see Lotar and Chara getting out of their black Mercedes. Chara waves to them as they approach. "Welcome home!" and she walks over to their car. "Here, let me help you," and nods toward their front door. "There are dozens of bouquets for you."

"From whom?"

"Your friends and neighbors. Everyone in Paris knows what happened!"

Betty tries to stand and holds on to Chara's arm to steady herself. "Thanks. I'm still a little stiff."

Chara motions toward their front patio. "It's a gorgeous day. Let's sit out here for a while."

Lotar hands her a get-well card. "Everyone at work wishes you well, and a quick recovery."

"Thank you. That was sweet of them."

Chara explains. "I have more good news! The old woman accepted our offer on the property."

"Oh, my gosh, that's wonderful!" She worries. "I'm so sorry. I forgot about your wedding. Have you made any plans?"

"Yes. We'd like to get married in our cottage, with family and close friends."

"So, when is the big date?"

"As soon as you feel better. And don't worry about work, just relax and recover quickly."

Max steadies her. "Darling, if you feel well enough, it would be fun to celebrate that world record of yours."

"I'd like that very much."

And he turns to Lotar. "It's getting late. Would you and Chara like to have dinner with us?"

Lotar thanks him. "Yes. It's time to celebrate!"

They drive to Jean-Pierre's restaurant and enter the rustic building just as he walks out of the kitchen. He greets them with excitement. "Ah, my friends. What a surprise!" He bends down and cheek kisses Betty in her wheelchair. "Congratulations on breaking the record."

"Thank you."

"I heard about your terrible accident! Are you alright?"

"Yes, just a little shaken up. Do you have a minute? There's something we'd like to discuss with you."

"Of course."

They sit down at a table, and she continues. "We wanted to let you know we purchased the farm, and we will take possession in two weeks."

"That's fantastic! You are going to love it there."

"The biggest problem we face is the overgrowth on the property. Is there someone that we could pay to clear the brush and trim the trees?"

"Don't worry about that. I know a farmer that can easily take care of it, and I'm happy to oversee the work for you."

Betty is grateful. "Thank you, Jean-Pierre. We really appreciate your help."

Several weeks later, they've moved into their new home, and their horses are grazing in the pasture. A farmer and his three sons trimmed the heavy overgrowth back, and grass covers the rolling hills and wide meadows. Prior to moving into the guest house, Lotar had a contractor renovate it and doubled its size.

Betty and Chara sit on the front porch enjoying a glass of wine while watching a gorgeous sunset. Chara sets down her wineglass. "I just realized the boys won't be back until tomorrow night. Let's take the day off and go shopping. Lotar has a birthday coming up soon, and I'd like to buy him something special," and she winks. "And I'd love to show you some of the world-famous designer shops."

"That's a great idea! We deserve a girl's day off!"

The following morning, they drive into Paris. Betty parks her car at their office, and they take a taxi to the famous Avenue des Champs-Élysées. They stroll down the sunny, tree-lined sidewalk wearing stylish summer dresses. Betty's auburn hair is down to her shoulders and Chara's long jet-black hair shines in the bright sunlight. They wear dark designer sunglasses and look like two models right out of a fashion magazine.

After spending the morning shopping at some of the world's most elite clothing designers, they continue down the wide, tree-lined sidewalk carrying shopping bags with famous labels on them. Chara sees an expensive jewelry shop and grabs Betty's arm. "Let's look in here." They enter and something catches her eye. "Betty! Look at this wristwatch. I'd love to get it for Lotar. Do you think he would like it?"

"I think he would love it!"

Chara waves to a salesperson, and he approaches them. "Hello. Can I help you?"

"Yes. I'm interested in this watch. Could you tell us about it?"

"I would be happy to." He takes it out of the display case and hands it to her. "This is a solid gold Rolex, and it's one of the world's most prestigious watches." He points to the black dial. "This is a rare edition because of the green diamonds. They only produce a dozen of these a year, but I must caution you, it is very expensive."

She inspects it, then hands it back. "I like it. Let me think about it."

"Of course. Thank you for stopping by."

Chara is excited and they walk down the sunny sidewalk arm-in-arm to a café for lunch. "This is fun! We should have a girls day off more often!"

Betty is having the time of her life and laughs. "I can't remember having this much fun either! And in Paris, of all places in the world!"

They stop at a sidewalk café and relax in the sun. Men walking by give them a double take as they pass, and Chara elbows Betty. "It's an ego booster to get out like this."

"I like this side of you, Chara. And you're right, we'll have to do this more often. Life can't be all work and no play."

Chara thinks about the Rolex. "That watch is expensive, but I would love to see it on Lotar."

"You can afford it, and the boys shower us with expensive gifts all the time."

"You're right! I'm going to go back and buy it."

"Good girl! Leave your bags here. I'll watch them."

"Thank you. I'll be right back."

Soon, she returns with a gift-wrapped box. "I bought it! I'm so excited, I won't be able to sleep tonight."

Betty has a suggestion. "Their birthdays are only two months apart. Why don't we celebrate them together this year?"

"That's a great idea! It would be fun to do something special."

"I'd like to surprise Max as well," and Betty asks, "Is there a musical instrument shop nearby?"

"Yes. There's one a couple of blocks from here. Why?"

"He won't spend the money on himself, but I want to give him something for his birthday that will really surprise him. Let's see what they have."

Chara is excited at the thought of it and takes Betty by the arm. Minutes later, they enter a large music shop that specializes in professional instruments and a salesperson greets them. "Can I help you?"

Betty questions him. "I'd like to buy my husband a guitar. Could you show us what you have?"

"I'm happy to, mam. We carry an extensive selection of professional instruments. Is there something special that you were looking for?"

"He likes to play Spanish classical music. Perhaps a guitar with a history behind it."

The salesperson thinks for a moment. "I have something that might interest you."

He walks to the back of the store and disappears, only to return a few minutes later. "This is a very famous guitar, but you should know that instruments like this are quite expensive. Hermann Fischer, a well-known German luthier, built this in 1937 and it was one of Andrés Segovia's favorite concert guitars. It has a beautiful rosewood back and sides and comes with documentation and photos of him playing it. Segovia is one of the most revered guitarists of the twentieth century, and we are fortunate to have such an important instrument in our shop."

He hands the guitar to her, and she turns to Chara. "What do you think of it?"

"It's beautiful! And what a history! Max will love it!"

The salesperson stares at Betty for a moment. "Excuse me, mam, but are you the woman that just broke the world's speed record?"

As always, Betty is shy when she's in the limelight. "Yes, I am," and she holds out her hand. "My name is Betty von Hirschel, and this is my business partner, Charlotte Escoffier."

"I'm Lucien Beaulieu, and it's my great honor to meet you both."

She hands the guitar to him. "My husband is going to love it. I'll be back tomorrow to pay for it."

"That won't be necessary. It would be my honor to deliver it to you in person."

Betty hands him her business card. "Thank you. I appreciate that very much."

As they leave, Chara smiles at her. "Max is going to have the shock of his life when he sees that guitar!"

It's late afternoon a week later. Betty and Chara lock their office and enter the hangar just as Max, and Lotar are preparing to leave. Betty approaches Max. "Chara and I thought we'd celebrate your birthdays together this year, and we've planned a special evening for you two."

"Really? Well, that sounds like fun," and he glances over at Lotar who is just as surprised.

He responds with a grin. "Great idea! Where are we going?"

Chara gives him a hug. "It's a surprise!" and takes his arm. They exit the hangar, catch a waiting taxi, and a short time later they arrive at the Seine River. It's a warm summer evening, and the city lights twinkle in the darkness.

Betty ushers them down a flight of stairs to a long houseboat, tied to a narrow dock, where they are met by a cheerful captain. He introduces himself, and they follow him to a large open deck on the stern, that is lit by strings of colorful lights. At one end is a dining table set with flickering candles, and at the opposite end, their guests call out in unison. "Surprise!"

Adrian and his wife Renée greet them, followed by Jean Pierre, the owner of their favorite restaurant, and his wife, Daphné, but the real surprise was Andy and Charlie, and their wives, who flew in from London. With everyone aboard, the boat pulls out into the river, and they slowly make their way past the Notre-Dame Cathedral. Max and Lotar shake hands with their friends and excitement fills the air as they disappear into the darkness.

A bartender pops open a bottle of champagne, and waiters serve hors d'oeuvres as the party gets underway. Adrian proposes a toast. "To Max and Lotar. I wish you many more birthdays."

Everyone touches glasses, then Charlie makes a toast. "To the best of friends!"

Max smiles at them. "Thank you! Everyone here has made a huge impact on our lives, and I deeply appreciate your friendship."

Lotar holds up his glass and makes a toast. "I second that!"

A while later Betty and Max stand in the shadows at the stern railing and watch the lights of the city as they pass by them. He puts his arm around her waist. "Thank you for the birthday party! It was a total surprise to both of us."

Betty snuggles close to him. "Chara and I had fun planning it. It would be exciting to do this every year."

"I appreciate all the things that you do for me," and he holds her tightly and kisses her. "I love you."

"Max, you are everything I ever dreamed a husband would be."

An hour later, dinner is over, and they talk and laugh together as they finish desert. Betty stands and addresses them. "This has been a lot of fun and thank you for joining us." She motions to a waiter who arrives pushing a cart. "And now it's time to open the presents."

Chara hands them to Max and Lotar who proceed to open their gifts. After all the gifts have been opened Betty stands. "There's just one more thing. Chara and I have special presents for the men in our lives." Chara then disappears into the darkness. A moment later, she reappears with a colorfully wrapped gift box that she gives to Lotar. She tenderly hugs him. "I love you, darling."

He kisses her. "I love you, too, sweetheart." He opens his present and stares at the Rolex watch in amazement. "This is beautiful! I've always wanted one," and he puts his arm around her and kisses her. "Thank you, darling."

While their guests admire his new watch, Betty slips into the shadows and returns carrying a guitar case that has a large red ribbon attached to the handle. "Happy birthday, Max," and she hands it to him.

He pops open the latches, removes the guitar, and is speechless. "I don't know what to say. I've never seen a guitar of this quality before. Where did you find it?"

"It was one of Andrés Segovia's concert guitars, and it comes with quite a bit of documentation."

He reaches over and kisses Betty. "Thank you, my darling. It's stunning."

"You shower me with gifts all the time. I wanted to do something special for you."

Max plucks each string and makes a final adjustment to the tuning. Then he strums several cords while listening carefully as the notes echo into the night. Lotar watches him for a minute and asks, "Can you play something for us?"

"Yes, of course. I was just tuning it." As he plays, the guests are spellbound and listen quietly as their boat drifts downstream, and they vanish into the night.

CHARA AND LOTAR MARRIED A SHORT TIME LATER IN THEIR newly remodeled cottage. It was a small ceremony with family and friends, and afterward, they flew to Morocco for a few days before continuing to the Canary Islands to lie on the beach. Two months later, Chara was ecstatic to learn that she was pregnant.

That summer, Betty and Max were surprised, and thrilled when she gave birth to twin girls that they named Lynnetta and Natalie and three months later, Chara gave birth to a son that they named Christian. The three children would grow up together and share a bond between them that would last a lifetime.

Max and Lotar loved being with their children and spent as much time as possible with them. Even when work took them far away, they always returned home to spend weekends with their families. With the help of nannies who cared for the children during the day, Betty and Chara continued to work at their airline.

Later that year, Wolfie, their loyal companion and faithful friend, passed away in his sleep and Betty was devastated. He had helped her through some of the darkest days of her life, and she had developed an unbreakable bond of friendship with him. He loved laying in the deep grass on the rocky outcropping that overlooks the Mosel River, and they buried him there, under the large oak tree. The engraving on his granite headstone reads:

In loving memory of our faithful friend,

Wolfie

July 12, 1939 – September 23, 1954

Together, we shared the best of times.

You gave us wonderful memories,

We won't soon forget.

Wait for us, my friend,

At the Southern Cross in the heavens far beyond.

And we'll make the long journey together,

Forever friends.

CHAPTER 26
TATRA MOUNTAINS

IT'S A COLD, WINTER DAY, AND CHARLIE AND HIS CO-PILOT, AJ Bennett, leave London in one of their newest four-engine Skymasters. Flying with them, and seated comfortably in leather first-class seats, are Betty and Max, and Chara and Lotar. Betty is excited. "This is a great idea, Chara. I'm dying to spend a few days in Rome!"

"Actually, it was Charlie's suggestion. He's making a passenger run to Kraków, Poland, and that will give us a couple of days to explore the city before he returns."

Betty is happy to take a break from work. "We should do this more often. I thought about going to Kraków with Charlie, but I haven't seen the sun for months! I'm looking forward to visiting Villa d'Este in Tivoli. And you?"

"I've never been to the Sistine Chapel, and then there's dinner and dancing in the evenings. It's all so romantic!"

Five hours later, they land in sunny Rome, and after thanking Charlie, they catch a taxi to their hotel near the center of the city. While a ground crew refuels the Skymaster, they begin boarding twenty-six British intelligence officers who are going to Kraków, and they leave Rome on a seven-hundred-mile flight to Poland.

Betty and her group spend the rest of the day exploring the city, and that evening she checks in with their office in London and discovers that Charlie is overdue. She worriedly approaches Max. "Charlie never arrived in Kraków! He should have been there hours ago."

Max tries to remain positive and comforts her. "He's a highly skilled pilot, and, for whatever reason, he must have landed somewhere else for the night. He's probably at some small airport having a beer and waiting out the weather."

Betty is fearful. "But why hasn't he called?" and she worries. "I can't believe this is happening!"

Lotar has a suggestion. "Just as a precaution, we should call Andy and alert him. If we haven't heard anything by morning, we'll fly to Kraków, and work with the authorities there." He puts his hand on Betty's shoulder. "Don't worry. We'll find him."

Later that night, Andy arrives with another Skymaster and Charlie's wife, Shelagh. They go over navigation charts of his flight path, looking for airports big enough to land the large, four-engine plane. It's too late to return to the hotel, so they nap in chairs at the airport for a couple of hours.

When morning arrives, Betty checks in with their office in London, and discovers there is still no word from Charlie. Their worst fears suddenly become a reality, and they immediately switch into emergency mode. Andy contacts the British Army to let them know the plane is overdue and advises them that he and his staff are on their way to Poland. Meanwhile, Lotar calls the control tower in Kraków to notify them of the missing plane and is told that the airport is currently closed due to extreme weather conditions.

None of the news is positive, and tension builds as the reality of what might have happened to the missing plane becomes apparent. With dawn fast approaching, they board their Skymaster just before sunrise. Shelagh is distraught and crying, and Betty tries to comfort her.

Hours later, they fly over the rugged, snowcapped Tatra Mountains, the highest mountains in the Carpathian Mountain Range that borders southern Poland. The storm clouds covering them are clearing, and Betty is shocked to see the desolate mountain range covered in a deep blanket of glistening white snow.

They arrive at Rakowice-Czyżyn airbase near Kraków, and are met by Colonel Gorski, a Polish Air Force officer, and follow him to a briefing room. An air traffic controller informs them that Charlie contacted the tower yesterday, saying that they were caught in an unexpected winter storm, and were declaring an emergency. The air controller said that his transmission was garbled, but it sounded like they were having problems with the plane's de-icing system and were losing altitude. Charlie gave them rough coordinates to his position, and that was the last that they heard from him.

Due to the poor weather conditions, the Polish Air Force had not been able to send out aerial search teams, but with the weather improving, more than a dozen planes were combing the remote mountains, looking for them. The Polish Air Force gave Andy and Betty areas to search, and they immediately left to join in the effort to locate Charlie.

Several hours later, one of the search planes spots the wreckage of the Skymaster high up on a steep ridge, but they couldn't get close to it because of strong updrafts. Betty and Lotar are nearby, and their more powerful four-engine plane was able to make a low pass over the crash site. As she flies over it, they are stunned by the extent of destruction. She had hoped Charlie might have had a chance to belly in somewhere, but that was not the case. He had flown into the side of the mountain at speed and the fire-scorched wreckage was spread out over a large area . . . and there were no signs of life.

Betty is near tears. "I think he must have iced up and lost control. At least he didn't suffer," and she pauses for a moment. "He was such a dear friend. I can't believe he's gone."

Andy follows her in the second Skymaster, flying low over the crash site. He is choked up, and radios Betty. "That was hard to look at. I'll see you back at the base."

"I'm so sorry, Andy. We all loved him."

They return to the airport and disembark. Colonel Gorski greets them, and approaches Betty. "I'm terribly sorry about the accident. It's a great loss for all of us."

Tears stream down her cheeks. "Thank you."

Andy asks him, "How soon can you have someone at the crash site?"

"We have highly skilled winter search and rescue teams, and they should be onsite sometime today. If there is enough light, they will begin the process of removing the passenger's remains. How many people were aboard?"

It's difficult for Andy to speak. "A crew of three and twenty-six passengers."

Shelagh sees Betty and runs to her, crying. Betty holds her in her arms for a long time and nothing is said. Due to the stormy winter conditions, it took several more days before all the bodies were recovered and returned to the airbase.

It's sunrise on a cold, bleak morning, and time to return to England. Lead by an escort of a dozen men from the Polish Air Force Honor Guard, horse-drawn wagons carrying twenty-nine coffins slowly approach their cargo plane. The soldiers march, holding their weapons underneath their arms, facing backwards. It's a British Armed Forces tradition called "reversing arms".

The caravan comes to a stop next to their four-engine Skymaster, and an officer calls out. "Rest on your arms reversed!" and a bugler plays *Last Post*. The soldiers lower their weapons and bow their heads in a gesture of honor and respect. It's a haunting moment of prayer and sadness, and everyone is teary-eyed as the coffins are off-loaded.

Betty, Shelagh, and Chara wear black headscarves, and the men wear black armbands. They approach the side of Charlie's coffin, which is covered by a Polish flag. Betty and Chara place floral bouquets on top of it, and Betty whispers. "Goodbye, my friend."

Shelagh takes off her black leather jacket with a large, golden dragon on the back, and lays it lovingly over the front of the aluminum coffin. They bow their heads in silence as a bugler plays *The Rouse*, a traditional tune played as a final farewell.

As the coffins are loaded into the Skymaster, Max holds Betty in his arms as she sobs.

She whispers into his shoulder. "I planned on going with Charlie on that flight. I wanted to visit Kraków, but I canceled when you said you wanted to spend some time in the sun."

Max holds her tightly as a cold wind buffets against them and whispers in her cheek. "It's just wasn't our time, darling."

The flight back to London was a sad time for everyone, but they were a family and supported each other in their hour of need. Charlie was buried in an old cemetery next to the church in Kildare, Ireland, where he and Shelagh were married.

After returning to London, Shelagh held a wake for him at his favorite pub. It was a celebration of his life, and Charlie's many friends came to pay their respects. She began the ceremony and thanked everyone for attending. Then spoke of the day she first met Charlie and recalled many of their war time adventures together.

Filled with sadness, Betty spoke and recounted how important his friendship was to her, and how he had saved her life on several occasions. After she finished, Andy and many of Charlie's friends came forward with their stories and thanked him for enriching their lives. Sadly, Betty never fully recovered from the loss of Charlie, and the accident would haunt her for years to come.

CHAPTER 27

DRAGON AIR CARGO

IN 1955, AFTER NEARLY TEN YEARS OF ALLIED OCCUPATION, West Germany became self-governing, while the eastern half remained undeveloped and under Soviet control. For Dakota Air Cargo, it was the end of their lucrative government air freight contracts, and they faced an unknown future. Their fleet of aging military planes needed to be upgraded if they were to stay competitive, and it would require a significant expenditure of money. Their business had been a very successful venture for all of them, but Andy wanted to retire, and they decided to sell their company.

Betty had put her heart and soul into building up their business, and she was highly emotional when they closed their doors for the last time. She realized that after twenty years it was time to return to Germany, the country that she had left so long ago, and everyone agreed with her. They sold their estate outside of Paris and moved back to their horse farm on the Mosel River. A few months later, Max and Lotar purchased the vineyard adjoining their parent's property, and Lotar and Chara moved into its large country mansion. It was an excellent move, as it doubled their vineyard capacity.

One afternoon, Betty and Max sat down with Lotar and Chara to discuss their future. Their wine business with Adrian was booming, and even though it was a lot of work, they missed their air cargo company. Also, the massive reconstruction of Germany continued to expand, and they wanted to be part of it.

Lotar confessed that he and Chara had been discussing an idea that they might be interested in, and he suggested they think about buying a small fleet of modern cargo planes. Several weeks later, they met over dinner and drinks and Chara explained that she had been researching the air freight market, and her study showed that it was still financially feasible. The European economy was strong, and the demand for air freight was still a top priority.

As the weeks pass, they excitedly continued to rough out their new idea. One evening, they were thinking about a name to call their new company when Betty suggested calling it Dragon Air. After another round of brandy, they agreed to call it Dragon Air Cargo, and they would base their operations in Frankfort, only fifty miles away, so that they could access it quickly from their farm.

Their years of experience in the air cargo business would now pay off, as they knew exactly what needed to be done, and how to go about doing it. However, this time they would not be starting on a shoestring budget. They had made a considerable amount of money, and they immediately ordered six new four-engine Douglas DC-6 cargo planes that were specifically designed to handle freight.

The DC-6 had two large cargo doors, which decreased the loading time, and it could carry fourteen tons at 310 mph, making it the perfect size, considering the short distances between their European hubs. Their new business expanded quickly, and they now needed a fast commuter plane to check on their operations, so they bought a Grumman Gulfstream turboprop. The commercial version carried twenty-four passengers; however, they purchased the eight-passenger executive model, which was equipped with two offices, two small bedrooms, a bathroom, and a galley, and it would serve them well in the coming years.

Betty's twin girls were quite bright; already speaking French, German, and English fluently. They soon outgrew their local school, and she enrolled them in a private school for gifted children near their second home in Frankfurt. Betty formed a close bond with her twins, and she and Max brought them on many of their business trips. It was a thrilling experience for the girls, and one that would ignite a lifelong interest in flying.

Later that same year, Betty received word that her beloved Uncle Karl had passed away at his home in Florida. Years earlier, he visited Germany and spent the summer with Betty and her family. They enjoyed many evenings sitting around the terrace firepit, sipping brandy, and talking about their lives. He loved to fish and when he retired, he realized his lifelong dream and moved to Sarasota, Florida, which is well-known for sport fishing in the Gulf of Mexico.

He had been the only family that Betty had, and in his will, he requested to be buried with his father and mother in Berlin, and it was a tearful moment when they said their graveside goodbyes to him.

In less than a year, their financial risk to reenter the air cargo market paid off in a big way, and over the following years, Germany continued to make a robust economic recovery, along with the rest of Europe. Lotar and Max threw themselves into their new venture and traveled extensively to support their service centers. Soon, they had thirty-five planes operating throughout Europe, and they continued to expand over the next few years.

THE YEAR IS 1962, AND IT'S LATE AT NIGHT. MAX IS IN THE kitchen looking for a snack when he hears Betty crying out from the upstairs bedroom. He runs to find her tossing and turning in bed, fighting her phantom demon. She cries out in her sleep. "No! No! Stay away from me! Please!"

Betty is having a terrible reaction to her reoccurring nightmare, and it was one of the worst episodes she's ever had. Max rushes to her side. "Betty! Betty! Wake up!"

She bolts upright in bed, soaked in perspiration, and clutches him. He holds her close and tenderly brushes her hair away from her face. "It's alright, darling. It was only a nightmare."

Her body shakes. "Oh, my! It was so real!"

The full moon shines through the open glass doors that lead out to the upstairs deck. Max is worried. "I think you need a brandy to settle your nerves. I'll be right back."

"Thank you, darling."

He leaves and, in a few minutes, returns with two snifters, and sits next to her. They sip their brandy, and Max puts his arm around her. "Do you feel better now?"

"Yes, thank you."

He hands her a robe. "Here, put this on. Let's sit out on the deck for a while." They walk out into the moonlight, and Max pulls together two chaise lounges. "Darling, that was your worst episode. I think you should get help to conquer your demons."

"You mean a psychiatrist? I'm not crazy!"

"I'm not saying that, but this has been going on ever since I met you. It breaks my heart to see the agony that you go through. Was it the same fireball?"

She struggles to avoid telling him the truth. "Yes. I'm afraid of being trapped in a plane and burned alive."

But he shakes his head in doubt. "I think there's more to it. You called out 'No! No! Stay away from me!' What is it you're not telling me?" He holds her hand. "We can beat this thing together, like we've done so many times before."

Betty stares into the night for a long time without answering him. "There are things about my past that I haven't told you."

"What do you mean?"

She lays back on the chaise lounge. "It's about the war when I was little. I had a terrifying experience with the Hitler Youth, and they almost killed me. When I was younger, I could blank those terrifying memories out of my mind, and I was alright for many years."

She takes another sip of brandy and pauses. "My nightmares returned after I crash landed my B-17, and it was a terrifying experience. Susie, my copilot, and friend was dead, and cannon fire killed my navigator. By some miracle, I escaped before the plane exploded in a gigantic fireball right in front of me."

"But what happened when you were little?"

"I can't face it. The pain is too great. It will only make things worse."

He holds her in his arms. "Darling, the war ended a long time ago. If you went back, you would see that it no longer exists. Your imagination is just running wild."

Betty wipes the tears from her eyes. "I've thought about returning, but it's impossible."

"Where are you talking about?"

"East Berlin."

"Is that where it happened?"

"Yes, but the Soviets built a wall around the city and sealed it off from the world."

"But it's still possible to visit. There's a lot of paperwork to fill out for the visa, and the secret police interrogate everyone when they leave, but you need to face your demons, or this will never stop."

He holds her in his arms, and she is silent for a long time. She wipes the tears from her eyes. "I think you're right. Will you go with me?"

"Yes, of course."

She hugs him tightly. "I love you, Max."

A week later, they arrive at the huge Tempelhof Airport in West Berlin in her Beechcraft King Air. It's a beautiful spring day and they exit the plane. Betty is nervous. "I'm afraid. I don't want the secret police to know where we're going."

"When we leave East Berlin, they'll ask, and what will you tell them?"

Betty thinks for a moment. "Let's look at some tourist attractions before we try to find my old neighborhood."

Max tries to be as supportive as possible. "Alright, we can do that."

They exit the airport terminal and walk past a long row of taxis parked at the curb. Betty approaches an elderly driver and looks in the passenger window. "Excuse me. Do you know East Berlin?"

"Yes, mam. I was born there."

"We would like to charter you for a couple of hours. Are you available?"

"Yes, I am."

"We have day visas and would like to visit the Brandenburg Gate, Frederick the Great's summer palace, and drive around the city a bit."

"I understand."

They get into the taxi, and he pulls away from the terminal. A short time later, they drive past the massive Brandenburg Gate, and Betty stares at it as distant memories of her childhood flood into her mind. Soon they pass through an American checkpoint and enter East Berlin. The Soviet border guards stop them, check their visas, and wave them on. They spend several hours visiting the major tourist attractions and return to their taxi. The driver asks, "Would you like to look at anything else?"

"No, thank you. We've seen enough." Betty leans forward from the back seat and hands him a piece of paper. "Do you know where this is?"

He looks at the address and returns it to her. "Yes, but it's not a place where tourists go."

"I grew up in that area and I'd like to see what it looks like."

Ten minutes later, he turns off onto a side street and enters her old neighborhood. Although there are some new apartment complexes, much of the area still shows the scars of war. He pulls over to the curb and stops. "Your address is somewhere ahead of us. Do you recognize anything?"

She stares at the buildings, searching for something familiar. "No. I was a young girl when I left. Nothing looks like I remember."

Max holds her hand. "Do you want to get out and walk around?"

"No. I don't recognize anything."

The driver questions her. "When did you leave?"

"1935."

"Ah, yes. Much has changed since then."

Betty stares at the buildings, trying to find her bearings, and hoping to find something she might recognize, but sees nothing. "I went to school close to here, but I'm not sure of the direction."

"There were several schools in the area. We can look for them, but it was a long time ago, even for me."

Betty is still hopeful and asks, "Do you mind driving around? I might see something I remember."

He starts the taxi. "That's a good idea," and pulls away from the curb. They search the general area for the next hour, but with no success, and he pulls over to the curb and stops. "I'm sorry, but I've searched everywhere I can think of."

Betty has tears in her eyes and gives up looking for her past. She turns to Max. "My demons have consumed my life! Now I'll never get them out of my mind!"

Max holds her hand and tries to comfort her. "I'm sorry. I wish we could have found something."

She wipes the tears from her cheeks, leans forward in her seat, and speaks to the driver. "Thank you for looking. I appreciate your help. Can you bring us back to the airport?"

"Yes, mam."

Max tenderly comforts her. "I'm so sorry, Betty." They drive a short way down a shady treelined street. "Would you mind if we got something to eat before we fly back?"

Betty's mood perks up. "Now that you mention it, I'm hungry, too."

"I haven't had a Berlin schnitzel since my school days."

The driver overheard him. "One of the best bistros for schnitzels is up ahead. Do you want to stop?"

"Yes, please," and Max looks at Betty. "Let's get out and enjoy the sun a bit before we start back."

Betty pulls herself together. "That's a good idea."

The driver parks his taxi, and she invites him. "Please join us for lunch. We appreciate your help today."

"Thank you. I would like that."

As they walk, she turns to him. "My name is Betty, and this is my husband, Max."

He is short, rotund, and in his late sixties. "My name is Gerhard. It's nice to meet you."

They sit at a table, and he asks, "Where are you from?"

"We have a vineyard in the Mosel Valley."

"I understand it's a beautiful area."

"Yes, it truly is."

A waitress walks up to their table. "Good afternoon. Can I help you?"

Max glances at the menu and looks up at Betty. "They offer a Berlin specialty here."

"What is it?"

"Wiener schnitzel. It's breaded veal slices fried at high temperature and served with potato salad and fassbrause."

"Yum. It sounds delicious! But what is fassbrause?"

Max explains. "It's a Berlin original; a mixture of apple juice, herbs, and malt. And it's alcohol-free for us pilots." He asks Gerhard, "What would you like?"

"That's my favorite as well."

Max orders for them. "We will have wiener schnitzels and fassbrause," and the waitress disappears back into the restaurant.

The sky is blue, and the sunlight filters through tall trees that line the street. Eating at a sidewalk café is a favorite pastime of theirs, and Max questions Gerhard. "Berlin is a beautiful city. How long have you lived here?"

"All of my life, except for two years. My family fled when the Soviet army attacked the city in 1945. When we returned, my father found work on the west side. We were lucky and didn't get trapped on the east side."

Soon the waitress appears with their order. "Please enjoy."

Betty takes a bite. "This is delicious. At least the trip wasn't a complete waste of time."

Max is sentimental. "This takes me back to my college days. Money was in short supply, and this was a real treat."

Betty tries her drink. "I love the taste of this fassbrause!"

As the meal ends, she glances down the treelined street in front of them and sees something that horrifies her. "Oh, my gosh!" and the blood rushes out of her face. "That's the tree in my dreams!"

She gets up from the table and walks to the curb for a better look. Max turns to Gerhard. "I think she's found something. We'll be right back."

"I'll wait for you here."

Max rushes to her side. "Are you alright? You look like you've seen a ghost!"

She points to the park across the street. "See that large tree? That's the hanging tree in my dreams!" and she squeezes his hand. "Max, please stay close to me. This is going to be the hardest thing I've ever had to do," and her body trembles in fear. "If I'm going to face my demons, I need to go there."

They cross the street and walk toward the tree. "When I was fourteen years old, the Nazis started arresting Jews. They deported some, and lined others against a wall, and shot them. There were many public hangings of men and women; some old, some young. Then the Hitler Youth gangs began terrorizing school children. At first it was bullying, but it soon turned violent, and they were on a rampage to find Jewish children and kill them.

"That day it had been snowing, and it was freezing outside. I had been studying in the library, and it was almost dark when I started for home. As usual, I stayed to the side streets and alleys to avoid the Hitler Youth. As I neared the park, I saw two boys and a girl from my school hanging from the branches of that tree. Their bodies were frozen and covered with white frost. The girl had a crude sign hung around her neck that read, "*No One Is Safe!*".

"I stopped walking, paralyzed by the horrific sight in front of me." She points across the street. "Suddenly, a large group of Hitler Youth appeared from that alley. Some of them held blazing torches, others carried ropes with a hangman's noose, and they were dragging two young boys toward the hanging tree. They were crying and struggling to escape, but the bigger youths overpowered them.

"The leader was much older than the others and yelled for me to stop. I knew they would kill me if I did, so I dropped my books and ran as fast as I could. They were catching up to me," and points across the street, "so I ducked into that alley, only to discover that it was a blind alley with no way out.

"I was frantic, and tried to enter several doors, but they were all locked. When I tried the last one, it opened, and I burst into the building and locked the door behind me. I peeked out a crack in the old door to see what was happening in the alley. Several of the boys ran from door to door, shaking the doorknobs, and as I watched them, I held my breath, paralyzed in fear.

"Then, out of nowhere, the leader stepped in front of my door and shook the doorknob. Our faces were close, and his flickering torch illuminated his angry face. He's the one that I see in my nightmares. He walks out of a cauldron of flames, and comes toward me holding a hangman's noose, then stops only inches away from me.

"After a few minutes, the other boys began to leave the alley. They called to him and said they were returning to the hanging tree. He shook the door one more time, then cursed and hit it as hard as he could before vanishing into the night.

"I stayed there, trembling for a long time, until I was sure they had left. Then I ran home as fast as I could."

Max is shocked. "No wonder you have nightmares!"

"Later on, they were so terrible that I couldn't function. In order to survive, I learned to suppress all memories of my past life, until I crash-landed my bomber. Then they returned and haunted me for years to come.

"Luckily, I escaped to America, but I had lost everything. I was alone in the world and left with a tremendous feeling of guilt that I had survived when so many others had perished."

Betty stares at the alley that she had used to escape the Hitler Youth. "I need to find that door."

They cross the quiet street, and to her amazement, the alley was still unchanged. She walks down to the last door and stands in front of it, trembling in fear. Then she reaches out, turns the doorknob, and it swings inward, revealing a gutted building.

A surprised flock of pigeons takes to the air and flies out the open windows. Rays of sunlight shine through the burned-out roof, and the floor is piled high with rubble. Betty stares at the empty interior for several minutes and her hand shakes as she slowly closes the door. It had been a terrifying and incredibly emotional experience for her. Tears stream down her face, and she buries her head into Max's shoulder and whispers. "It's over, Max. I just want to go home."

He is stunned by her story. "I don't know how you survived such a horrific ordeal!"

Betty's heart is racing, and she takes deep breaths, trying to calm herself. Max holds her tightly and caresses her tenderly. "Are you alright?"

"Yes. You were right. The war is over, and the ghosts of my past have died with it." She squeezes his hand. "Thank you for helping me."

He nuzzles her cheek. "The next stage of our lives is just beginning. It's time to relax and enjoy life like we always said we'd do."

She looks up at him. "Thank you, Max. An enormous weight has been lifted off my shoulders, and I feel like a new person."

"I'm so sorry Betty. I can't imagine the terror that it's caused you all these years."

They walk down the deserted alley, and Betty is excited thinking about their new future. "I love our beautiful home and our horses, and I want to spend more time with you and the twins. Best of all, I love sitting around the fire in the evening, listening to you play your guitar, and watching the moon rise into the heavens."

Max squeezes her hand. "That's my favorite time of the day, too." As they leave the alley, he whispers in her ear. "I love you, my darling."

CHAPTER 28
THE MOSEL RIVER VALLEY

IT'S THE SUMMER OF 1965. THE EXCITED SHOUTS OF THE twins awaken Betty from her nap, and they call out in French. "Look! Lotar and Chara are here!"

She looks over at the airstrip as they land their Gulfstream and taxi to a stop across from her King Air. She waves to them, and they wave back from inside their cockpit. A few minutes later, they exit their plane and head toward the house. Today is Betty's forty-fifth birthday, but she looks much younger. She is wearing amber-colored sunglasses, a green silk designer blouse, and her auburn hair is shoulder length. It's a special time of the year for her, and she always looks forward to enjoying it with her family.

Every year Max tries to do something special for her birthday, and this year he had been planning her surprise for quite some time. He remembered Betty had fond memories of the fun she had flying her Stearman biplane during her college days, so he decided to surprise her with an acrobatic plane.

Six months ago, he talked to Lotar and asked for his help in locating a plane. It took him several months of research, but he finally found an American designed Pitts Special in Sweden. The Pitts is a hand-built biplane, and it had been a famous competitor in the World Aerobatic Championships for many years.

The plane was new, and the latest model; a two-seat trainer with dual controls. It was perfect for them because she and Max could have a lot of fun flying it together. It's painted bright red, with a white sunburst across the wings, and has a fixed landing gear, with sleek fairings that cover the wheels. However, its most exciting feature was the large bubble canopy that covers the tandem seats, allowing for nearly unlimited visibility.

Best of all, it's a powerful plane with a cruising speed of 180 mph and a range of 350 miles. Lotar had it flown from Sweden to his German mechanics near Cologne, and they stored it in their hangar. Today, he has it hidden out of sight at a nearby farm. Betty's party always starts in the late afternoon, and the celebration usually continues into the early evening.

Max had the terrace decorated with colorful balloons, and there is an enormous pile of presents on a table surrounded by several dozen white folding chairs. Helga made a huge double-decker birthday cake, and it sits next to a champagne fountain.

At 4 o'clock, Max calls their guests to attention. "Thank you for coming to help celebrate Betty's forty-fifth birthday. Now if I can find my wife, we'll get her to cut the cake and begin the festivities!"

A smiling Betty steps forward. "Ah, here she is."

Their guests clap their hands, and someone calls out. "Speech!"

Betty is bashful as usual and waves to them. "Oh, dear. I love you all and thank you for coming!" She walks over to the cake and picks up a large serving knife just as the loud whine of a powerful aircraft engine fills the air, and the astonished group looks up to see a bright red biplane diving low over the house. Betty is surprised by the sudden appearance of the plane and drops the knife. "Oh, my gosh!"

As Lotar passes overhead, he dips his wing to one side and drops a red parachute with a small package attached to it. Then he guns the engine and disappears into the clouds. It sways back and forth as it floats to the ground and lands in front of her. She picks it up and takes out a colorful birthday card. In the center is a sketch of the Pitts Special, and it reads, *"Happy Birthday, Darling! Your loving husband, Max."*

Betty holds it up to the crowd of stunned guests. "It's my birthday present from Max!" They clap their hands, and she puts her arm around him. "I'm speechless!" and kisses him. "I love you."

He hugs her back. "I love you, too, sweetheart. Do you want to check out your present?"

"Yes, of course! It reminds me of my old Stearman."

"I remembered it was an exciting time in your life, and there are plenty of beautiful places around here for us to explore."

Max takes her by the hand, and they walk down the back steps to their airstrip just as Lotar drops in over the tree line and taxis toward them. He shuts down the engine and tilts the bubble canopy to the side.

"Happy birthday!" and exits the plane. "You won't believe how much fun this is to fly!"

Betty gives him a hug. "Thank you, Lotar!" She admires the bright red plane, then looks inside the cockpit. "Max! She's beautiful!"

There is no fancy control yoke. Instead, the pilot controls the plane by moving a vertical stick while using floor pedals to control the rudder. It's a simple, but extremely accurate system that's needed when flying advanced aerobatics, and it is the same system that Betty used when she flew high-performance fighters during the war.

Max puts his arm around her shoulder. "Ready to take her up?"

She runs her hand along the fuselage, admiring the plane. "Yes! I'd love to, and the stick and rudder layout is super!" She looks at Lotar. "Is there anything special that I need to know?"

"No, not really. You'll be surprised at how much you miss flying our faster planes."

Betty turns to Max. "Are you coming with me? This is going to be fun!"

He grins. "Sure, let's go!"

They climb into the cockpit and Lotar hands her a short pre-flight checklist. She reviews the list for a minute, then puts it in a side pocket and buckles her safety belt. Lotar closes the bubble canopy. "Have fun! We'll continue the party while you're gone."

Betty starts her engine and lets it warm up while she familiarizes herself with the controls. She looks up, waves to everyone, and taxis to the far end of the meadow. The bright red biplane turns into the light breeze, blasts down the runway, and quickly disappears from sight. An hour later she buzzes the house, and Lotar walks out to the airstrip to meet them, followed by Chara and their children. She idles up to them and exits the aircraft. "You were right. She's a fantastic plane, and a lot of fun to fly!"

Max puts his arm around her shoulder. "When life gets a little boring, we'll just go exploring and have some fun."

"Thank you, darling. That was exhilarating!" She kisses him, and they return to the terrace.

Later on, as her birthday celebration comes to a close, Betty stands and makes a toast to her family. She is reflective, teary-eyed, and emotional. "As I think about my life, I'm grateful for every moment because it led me here to you … but my journey wasn't easy. Early in the war, I lost everyone in my family, and I witnessed terrible things that no child should ever see. Then came the years of fighting, and it was a time of great suffering. How we escaped the caldron of war alive, and in one piece, is a miracle. I love our country, and it's wonderful to be with you today."

She holds up her champagne glass. "To my dear Lotar. I still remember the day when you buzzed this house with your fighter. We've shared some exciting times together and enjoyed more than our share of success. I am honored to call you my friend."

Then she looks at Chara, who is sitting next to him. "And thank you, Chara, for being such an important part of my life. We've been flying together now for almost twenty years, and I could not have asked for a more loyal friend. You are the sister I wish I had, and a special friend that I can never replace."

She scans the crowd, looking for the twins. "And to Natalie and Lynnetta, my darling daughters. You are the children that every mother wishes for. I'm so excited to watch you discover the fantastic world that awaits you. I love you both!"

Christian is seated next to the twins. "And to my darling, Christian. You are like a son to me, and I love you dearly."

Betty looks down at Max and puts her hand on his shoulder. "And to my husband. You are the love of my life. When I needed help the most, you were always at my side. You've been my nurse, my confidant, and my best friend. Together, we've shared the highest of highs and the lowest of lows." Her eyes are filled with tears of happiness, and she hugs him tenderly. "I love you with all my heart!"

It's later in the afternoon, and Betty is standing at the terrace railing watching the sun go down and reflecting on her life. Her daughters notice her and approach.

Lynnetta puts her arm around her. "Happy birthday, Mother."

And Natalie hugs her from her other side. "We love you!"

"I love you too, my precious daughters!"

The three of them stand at the railing together, watching the last rays of the setting sun, and Betty looks at them lovingly. "I have a surprise for both of you. And it's something that's very dear to me."

Lynnetta is excited. "What are you talking about?"

"Come with me," and she walks to a nearby table. "See those two large presents? They are for you to share."

Natalie picks up one of the boxes, unties a red bow, and opens it. She removes a Gestapo officer's uniform and turns toward her mother. "Is this yours?"

"Yes. I wore it during the war when I first met your father, and I was wearing it when I was shot down and crash landed in England. He was badly wounded, and I held him in my arms, thinking he was dying. I pulled him close to me and told him I would love him forever.

"He couldn't speak, but whispered that he loved me, and then closed his eyes. I thought he had died, and it was the saddest day of my life! It has great sentimental value to me."

Lynnetta can hardly wait to open the other present. She removes the lid from the second box and takes out Betty's custom-made black leather jumpsuit. Embroidered on the front is her name and the crest of Germany, and on the back is a large golden-winged dragon. It still shows fire damage and dark oil stains from the accident. "I wore this when I set the world speed record and the next day, I discovered I was pregnant. It's astonishing to think that all three of us were together on that incredible flight!"

Lynnetta lays it down and embraces her. "Thank you so much, Mother. I don't know what to say!"

Natalie hugs her as well. "They are beautiful. We will treasure them forever."

The sun slips below the distant horizon, and the twins embrace their mother as darkness fills the valley.

CHAPTER 29

DAWN OF THE JET AGE

IN 1970, BOEING INTRODUCED THEIR MASSIVE DOUBLE-DECK 747 Jumbo Jet, the world's first wide-body airliner. It accommodated four hundred passengers, reduced fares by thirty percent, and their fuel-efficient freighter version would soon revolutionize the cargo industry.

Dragon Air Cargo's aging piston powered planes could no longer compete, and they faced a dilemma. Upgrade their fleet at a cost of $25 million a plane or sell the company. In the end, it was too much of a debt load for them to assume, so they sold out and retired. Betty and Max returned to their vineyard on the Mosel River to enjoy life and to raise their beloved Hanoverian horses. Lotar and Chara moved back to the large estate next door that they had purchased years before.

ONE SUMMER EVENING, THE TWO COUPLES ARE SITTING ON the terrace enjoying after-dinner drinks and a blazing fire. Chara confides to Betty. "I can't believe it's been five years since we sold the airline and retired for the second time. I miss the excitement of flying, and all the wonderful cities we got to explore."

Betty stares at the dancing flames. "Max and I have talked about that same thing. We're too young to just sit back in a rocking chair and grow old."

Chara refills their brandy snifters and sits down. "We feel the same way. However, Lotar has been researching an exciting new idea, and we think you might find it interesting."

Betty is instantly curious. "Really? I hope it has something to do with flying!"

Lotar laughs. "Well, it does," and he sets down his drink. "After being in the air freight business for twenty-five years, we built up a lot of industry contacts, and I still keep in touch with many of them. I'm not suggesting we start another airline and try to compete with the big boys, but there is a niche market that's in high demand and has almost no competition."

Max smiles at his brother. "Okay, Lotar. You've got our full attention. What are you talking about?"

"There's a world-wide demand for moving heavy freight, typically into remote areas, and it takes a special type of plane that can handle short takeoff and landings on unimproved airstrips. It involves transporting heavy cargo like oil exploration drill rigs, extra-large components for hydroelectric stations, and a wide variety of heavy cargo for civilian contractors, and foreign governments, and on every continent."

His idea fascinates Betty. "Wow! That's very interesting! When you say large, how big is that?"

"The plane that I'm thinking about can accommodate freight that is nine feet wide by nine feet tall by fifty feet long, and it will transport up to twenty-five tons."

Betty is shocked. "That's gigantic! Who makes a plane that can do that?"

"Lockheed. They've been making it for the military for the last ten years and they just started selling a civilian version. It's powered by four 4,500 horsepower turboprops, and they call it the L-100 Hercules. It takes two pilots, a navigator, and a flight engineer to crew it."

Lotar's description of the plane fascinates Betty. "What's its range?"

"It has a loaded range of 1,500 miles, a ferry range of 7,000 miles, and a cruising speed of 340 mph, so it can easily handle long-distance international flights."

Betty is surprised by its capabilities. "That sounds like an incredible plane!"

Lotar details his plan. "The good news is I've already found a highly experienced ex-military crew that would sign on with us. The thing that you'll really like is that there are no daily schedules to keep, no cargo hubs to maintain, and only a few employees to worry about. I'm pretty sure we can find work for one plane, but if things pick up, we can always buy a second one.

"As for potential clients, I've called around, and there is plenty of work out there. If we decide to do this, I could easily line up projects for the next two years in New Zealand, the Canadian High Arctic, Brazil, and several other South American countries."

Betty is excited. "Really! This sounds like a challenge! Where would our headquarters be?"

"Frankfurt would still be the logical choice, because it's only fifty miles away by air, and we could stay close to home."

Max likes his idea. "It seems the two of you have done your homework in planning this out," and he turns to Betty. "What do you think?"

"It sounds like a fun part-time job doing something we all love to do," and she looks at Lotar. "Tell us more about it."

Chara reaches into her purse, pulls out a brochure, and hands it to her. Betty flips through the pages and passes it to Max. "It's colossal! I can't imagine what it would be like to fly something that big and heavy."

"If we did this, we would have to pick it up at Lockheed's plant near Atlanta, Georgia, and then it's a 4,600-mile trans-Atlantic flight back to Germany. As for the cost, they're about seven million dollars."

Betty is surprised. "Really! The price of planes has gone up since we bought our first C-47!"

Lotar laughs at her comment. "Yeah, I'll say. Those were the good old days. Of course, the payload for the C-47 was three tons vs twenty-five tons for the Hercules."

Max likes what he hears and asks, "Have you thought about a name for the company?"

"Yes. Titan Heavy Lift. Do you like it?"

Betty hands the brochure back to him. "I love it! Just thinking about flying again makes me feel twenty years younger!" She looks at Chara. "Have you calculated the financial risk?"

"Yes. Assuming Lotar's projected contracts actually happen, we could sell the plane in two years, and still have a small profit, so there is a way out if it became necessary."

Betty looks at Max, who nods his head in approval. "This is exciting! Count us in. And you two?"

Chara answers her excitedly. "We're in, too! This's going to be fun, and we're thrilled to be flying again!"

Max asks Lotar, "Does Lockheed have a plane available?"

"Yes, they do, and I've been talking with them. They have one about to come off the assembly line, but we need to purchase it before someone else does."

Betty is curious. "What about a flight crew?"

Lotar explains. "I'll see if the pilot can stop by tomorrow so you can meet him."

The following day, their prospective pilot arrives for lunch, and Lotar makes the introductions. "I'd like you to meet Jacques Moulin," and he introduces himself to everyone.

Betty questions him. "How did you become interested in flying these planes?"

Jacques is tall, with a crew cut, and is physically fit. "When I was younger, I wanted to do something exciting, so I enlisted in the French Air Force. I flew jet fighters for a couple of years, then one day I heard they were looking for volunteers to join a newly formed unit flying C-130 Hercules cargo planes, or Herc's as most people call them, and I immediately joined. For me, it was a dream job, and I finished my military career by flying them. Just after I retired, I heard Lotar was looking around for a crew, and I called him."

Chara, who is concerned about the financial risk, asks, "What do you think of our idea?"

"There seems to be an enormous demand for moving heavy freight. I'm surprised that someone isn't doing it already."

Betty is curious. "What about the rest of your aircrew?"

"I keep in touch with my ex-military buddies, and they would love to fly again."

Max wonders. "Will there be a problem picking it up?"

"No. I have eight thousand hours flying them. I only need to become familiarized with the latest in avionics, and the flight characteristics of the civilian version."

Betty shakes his hand. "I think I can speak for all of us. Welcome aboard!"

The days pass quickly, and soon it's time to leave for Atlanta to pick up their plane, but Max, Lotar, and Chara need to stay behind to set up their new company and secure hangar space at Frankfurt Airport. Betty volunteers to pick up the Hercules, and she is thrilled at the thought of flying once again.

The summer is just starting, and she surprises the twins by inviting them to go with her to America. Delirious with excitement, they can hardly wait to leave. They are almost twenty-one years old, and are very attractive, with Betty's emerald-green eyes and Max's blonde hair. Lynnetta is majoring in aerospace engineering, and Natalie is studying aeronautical engineering. Both of them are avid pilots, having been flying since they were sixteen.

On the morning of their departure, Betty and the twins meet Jacques, and his aircrew, at the airport's passenger lounge. From Frankfurt they board

DRAGON

a massive Lufthansa 747 and, as a special treat, Betty bought everyone a first-class ticket.

Seventeen hours later, they arrive in Atlanta, Georgia. It's Friday afternoon, and she walks with Jacques across the massive lobby. "If you don't mind, I have some business I need to take care of. The twins and I will meet you at our hotel in Marietta on Monday."

"No problem. The guys want to explore the area, so that will work out just fine."

Betty charters a flight to Burlington, Vermont, and they take a taxi to a large mansion sitting on a cliff overlooking Lake Champlain. She asks the driver to wait for them, and they approach the house. She presses the doorbell, and a butler opens the door. "Yes, may I help you?"

"Is this Senator McAllister's residence?"

"Yes, mam, it is."

"My name is Betty von Hirschel. I flew with their daughter Susie in the war, and I have a message for them."

The butler seems surprised and excuses himself. Moments later, a pretty blonde woman in her forties appears at the door and introduces herself. "My name is Kelly. I'm Susie's younger sister. Please come in."

"Thank you. These are my daughters, Lynnetta, and Natalie."

She extends her hand to them. "Nice to meet you." Then she turns to Betty. "My parents are quite elderly, but they want to see you. Please follow me."

They enter an elegant living room overlooking the beautiful lake. Susie's mother is sitting in a comfortable chair, and her father is in a wheelchair sitting next to her. Betty introduces herself, and the twins, and they sit down on a nearby couch.

Susie's father is very appreciative. "Thank you for taking the time to see us. We never knew what happened to our daughter. We only have a telegram saying that she was killed in action."

Her mother asks, "How well did you know our daughter?"

412

Betty explains. "She was just out of flight school when we met. On our first flight together, we flew a twin-engine B-25 attack bomber from Scott Army Airfield near Houston, Texas, to New Castle Army Air Base in Wilmington, Delaware. She was an excellent pilot, loved to fly, and we had a lot of fun together. We had plenty of time to talk about our lives on those long flights, and we became close friends. She told me many stories about growing up, and how much she loved her family.

"Susie loved to dance, and we would go to the officer's club on our layovers. She was very pretty, a great dancer, and was always surrounded by handsome pilots waiting their turn to dance with her.

"I can tell you a funny story that she told me. Before I met her, she ferried fighters from various manufacturing plants to the east coast for shipment to the war zones. Of course, there is no bathroom on a fighter, and at times, the flights can be quite long. On one of those flights, nature called, and instead of wasting time to find an airport, she landed in what turned out to be a pig pasture and splattered the plane in pig poop. When she finally delivered it, she had a lot of explaining to do!"

Her mother laughs and asks, "Did you fly together very long?"

"Yes, by war standards. Perhaps a couple of months. At that time, our country was extremely short of male pilots, and we were chosen to be part of an experimental group of women pilots to fly the four-engine B-17 Flying Fortress bombers to England.

Susie and I learned to fly them at New Castle, and as soon as we completed our training, we left for the Royal Canadian Air Force station in Labrador, about 1,000 miles away. We were fogged in for two days, and then we started for England, 2,500 miles away, on a night flight.

"Late that night, we flew into a huge thunderstorm, and a powerful lightning strike hit us just in front of the windshield, causing multiple electrical fires in the cockpit. Susie was a hero and fought the fires with a fire extinguisher in one hand, and a flashlight in the other. Working alone, she kept the plane from catching on fire. After that we battled the violent storm for hours, and it took all of our strength to fly the plane. By dawn, we were tired and exhausted.

"However, the lightning bolt burned out our navigation system and we were lost. When the sun came up, Susie tried to orient us with landmarks on the ground, but at 25,000 feet, and on oxygen, that can be difficult. Our navigator finally figured out where we were using a sextant and gave us the bad news; we had overflown England and were fifty miles into Germany. I was flying and immediately made a 180-degree turn, but it was too late, and we were attacked by two German fighters."

Susie's parents wipe their tears away, and Betty stops talking. "Should I go on? The rest of her story is going to be difficult to hear."

After a few moments, her mother pulls herself together. "Please do. We want to know how our daughter died."

Betty continues with great sadness. "We didn't have a gun crew, and the fighters hit us pretty hard. We had two engines on fire, and the flight controls were not responding. On the next pass, they strafed the side of our plane, killing our navigator. Susie was sitting two feet away from me when machine gun fire hit her in the back, and she died instantly.

"Our windshield was blown out, there were fires everywhere, and we were descending rapidly. Suddenly, from out of nowhere, a British fighter appeared, and eventually shot down both of the German fighters.

"It was a cold winter's day, and I crash landed in a plowed field. We skidded to a stop in shallow water at the edge of a large lake and that put out our engine fires. There wasn't anything I could do for Susie, or my navigator, and the situation was extremely dangerous, so I jumped into the icy water and slogged my way to shore. We still had plenty of fuel aboard, and when the fire got to the gas tanks, there was a tremendous explosion, and the plane exploded into a million pieces. A German halftrack emerged out of the forest and began firing, but the British fighter landed on a nearby farm road and rescued me."

Betty has tears in her eyes. She opens her purse and takes out a map and several photos. "I'm sure Susie would want you to know where she is," and she hands them to her mother. "I've visited the crash site many times to say hello . . . and to say goodbye . . . and to tell her that I love her. She was one of my best friends, and I think of her often."

Everyone in the room is teary-eyed. "I'm so sorry to have upset you, but I made a graveside promise years ago that I would tell you what happened. We live in Germany, and this is the first time that I've been back in America since the war ended."

Her mother stands. "I know this must have been very difficult for you as well. Thank you."

Betty gives her a parting hug, then turns to her father. "I have something of Susie's, and I'm sure she would want you to have it." She reaches into her purse and removes a medallion attached to a silver necklace. "When we graduated from B-17 flight school, our instructor gave each of us a silver dollar with our wings soldered to it. Susie was very proud of hers and wore it as a necklace," and she hands it to him. "She was wearing this the day that she was killed."

Her father's hand shakes, and he reaches out slowly as tears run down his cheeks. His voice cracks. "Thank you!" and he carefully inspects it.

Betty bends down and hugs him. "I'm so sorry. I loved her too."

Susie's mother puts her arm around Betty. "Thank you so much. You are always welcome in our home."

Betty holds her hand. "Thank you. It is so nice to finally meet you," and she hugs her goodbye.

Kelly walks them to the front door. "It was a pleasure meeting you and thank you for taking the time to visit with us. Our family will be forever thankful."

Betty shakes her hand. "Thank you. By the way, you look a lot like Susie."

"I've heard that before. I wish I had known her better, but I was much younger. We've wondered all these years about how, and where, she died. You are an angel."

Betty hands her business card to her. "If you ever want to visit her gravesite, I am happy to take you there."

It's Monday morning and a Lockheed van picks them up at their hotel. When they arrive at the plant, they are met by a friendly sales manager and, after brief introductions, he escorts them outside to look at their new plane.

When Betty saw the Hercules for the first time, she was shocked. Lotar wanted to surprise everyone and hadn't mentioned that he had ordered it with a custom paint scheme, and his design was stunning. Most of the plane was painted glistening white; however, the bottom is painted dark red that continues to the rear, then sweeps up dramatically, covering the entire tail section. The company logo, a multi-colored graphic of the Earth, is centered in the huge tail, and across the length of the fuselage are the words, *"Titan Heavy Lift"*.

After recovering from her initial shock, they are taken for a brief tour of their plane. By the end of the following week, Jacques and his air crew had familiarized themselves with the fight controls and had flown it several times. For Betty, it had been nearly thirty-three years since she left the United States, and she was amazed to see the many changes that had taken place.

The twins were incredibly excited to be in America, and they begged her for a chance to see more of the country. Betty thought it would be fun to show them where she grew up and revised their return schedule. Their first stop would be Avenger Field in Texas; the place where it all started. After an exciting three-hour maiden flight in their new Hercules, they landed near the small town of Sweetwater, Texas. The once busy airbase was now a quiet municipal airport, and with the arrival of their massive cargo plane, they quickly became the center of attention. Several local news reporters came over to look at the Hercules, and Jacques and the twins patiently answered their questions.

While they were talking to the press, Betty slipped away from the group and walked across the parking apron to the long rows of shuttered desert tan army buildings. This was her home many years ago, and a wave of nostalgia sweeps over her. It was an incredible feeling knowing that she once walked on these exact pathways thirty-three years ago, talking and laughing with her girlfriends. Memories of those long-forgotten days flood through her mind, and she wondered what had happened to her friends. She thought of Sharron, her best friend from Canada, and of Cheryl, and the others. Where had their lives taken them? And where were they now?

Lynnetta and Natalie are standing under the gigantic wing of their cargo plane talking to curious bystanders when they notice Betty walking by herself across the field. They excuse themselves and join her. As they walk arm-in-arm, she feels deeply connected to the twins, and it's an emotion of warmth and love that she's never before experienced. The twins are no longer children, they're young women now, and about the same age she was when she first flew with the WASP.

As they wander amongst the abandoned buildings, she tells them about her life as a WASP ferry pilot, including exciting, and sometimes hilarious, stories about her friends. After walking around the base, they have lunch at a small coffee shop on the flight line, and then leave for San Francisco International Airport, four hours away. Betty and each of the girls, under the expert instruction of Jacques, got to spend time flying the huge Hercules, and it was a thrill of a lifetime for them.

After they land in San Francisco, Betty surprises the twins and tells them they are going to stay for a few days. They rent a car and drive south to Palo Alto, where she shows them her high school, and the house that she grew up in. Afterword, they have lunch at Stanford University, Betty's alma mater, and spend several hours touring the campus. At the end of the day, they return to San Francisco for dinner, and to explore the city after dark.

The following day is the twin's twenty-first birthday, and Betty surprises them with birthday presents, then hands each of them a small, gift-wrapped box. They thank her, and excitedly open their gifts, revealing a gold medallion and chain.

Lynnetta exclaims. "Mother, it's beautiful!"

Natalie turns it over. "What does this mean?"

"It's a family tradition that your grandfather started many years ago. The medallion is pure gold. The dragon represents our family coat of arms, and the eagle on the back is the German coat of arms. The date, 1854, is the year that your great-grandfather purchased our land.

"Your father and I have one, and Lotar and Chara have one. All family children will receive one when they turn twenty-one, and when you marry, your spouses will receive one."

The twins are thrilled and thank her profusely as they place them on each other. After breakfast, they tour Chinatown in the morning, then drive across the Golden Gate Bridge to visit Sausalito. In the afternoon, they board a sightseeing ferry for a long ride around the harbor and Alcatraz Island.

The following day, their seven-hour flight takes them across the northern region of the United States and Lake Michigan, before landing at Toronto's Pearson International airport. They spend the next day sightseeing in Toronto, and the following morning they leave for Iceland, but in flight, Betty has one last surprise in store for the twins and changes their flight plan once again. Eleven-hours later, they cross the Atlantic Ocean and arrive in Lisbon, Portugal. Under Jacque's expert tutelage, Betty and the twins continue to spend hours at the controls of the huge Hercules cargo plane.

The days are sunny and warm, and the air smells of orange blossoms. They spend two wonderful days walking on the beach, and relaxing at their ocean front hotel, but all too soon it's time to leave paradise.

The following day, they arrive in Frankfurt, Germany, at midday and are met by their entire family, who are thrilled to see them. Everyone is excited to explore their new plane, and the twins take them on a tour, all the while bubbling over with excitement as they recount their recent adventures. Of course, they are all dying to go for a ride, so Betty suggests they fly to Prague, the capital of Czechoslovakia. It's only an hour away from Frankfurt, and they all got a chance to spend some time at the flight controls.

WHILE STUDYING AT THEIR UNIVERSITY, THE TWINS BECAME passionate glider enthusiasts, and they each owned a high-performance single seat plane, which they flew at club events throughout Europe. However, they were always a little disappointed because they could never stray too far from the airport that they departed from. When the local thermals died out, as they usually did at some point, they were forced to return to their launch site.

One sunny weekend, the twins came home to the farm to spend time with their parents. They spent the day riding their horses, and after dinner, Lotar and Chara joined them. They sat by a roaring fire on the terrace, relaxing and enjoying each other's company. Betty and Max loved hearing about their college life and, as usual, they always got around to talking about flying. The twins explained how disappointing it was to always return to the same airport that they had launched from.

Several days later, Lotar met with Betty and Max to discuss an idea that he thought might solve the twin's glider dilemma. They were only weeks away from graduating from college, and he recommended they consider buying them a new, high-performance glider as a graduation present.

Because they weren't familiar with them, he suggested they visit the local factory in Berlin to see what they were all about. When they arrived at the factory, Betty was shocked to see the futuristic looking gliders. They were made of reinforced fiberglass, had a seventy-foot wingspan, and were capable of high altitude and long-distance flights. The two pilots sit side-by-side, enveloped in a sleek plexiglass bubble that allowed for a fantastic 180-degree view.

However, its most exciting feature was its small engine, which solved the twin's problem of being tethered to the launch airport. When using the engine, they could take off without a towplane, and it had an eight-hundred-mile powered flight range. For high-altitude flying, there were two large oxygen bottles stored behind the pilot's seats. Betty was impressed by the plane, and quickly realized it was the perfect gift for the twins.

A week later, graduation day finally arrived. Long ago, Betty and Max promised the girls they would do something very special for them when they graduated, so when she told them they were treating them to a celebration dinner, they were excited, but not that surprised. She suggested they invite their boyfriends and told the twins to meet them at their company hangar at the end of the week.

Friday soon arrives, and three of their seven gigantic Hercules cargo planes are parked outside their hangar. As they wait for Lotar to ready their Gulfstream, a pickup truck arrives towing a narrow twenty-five-foot enclosed trailer with a giant red bow tied around it. It stops in front of them, and the driver walks over to the twins.

He hands each of them a key ring and surprises them. "Congratulations, ladies!"

Natalie is standing next to Max, and she throws her arms around him. "Father! Thank you."

He hugs her back. "School is hard work. Now it's time for some fun!"

Lynnetta turns to Betty. "Mother! This is incredible! Thank you!" and gives her a hug.

"Wait until you see what's inside the trailer," and Betty introduces the driver. "This is Milo."

The girls introduce themselves, then walk to the back of the trailer. Milo lifts the enclosure, and they help roll the glider out. It slides out easily, and they stare at it in astonishment. The glistening white fuselage shines in the bright sunlight. Its wings were folded back for transport, and with Milo's help, they swing them out and lock them into place. Afterword, they attach the long wing extensions, and it's fully assembled.

Milo invites them to sit in the cockpit, then shows them the biggest surprise of all. He points to a heavy chrome lever just below the instrument panel and asks Lynnetta to pull on it. When she does, the front portion of the plane's nose cone slides forward, and a hidden propeller automatically unfolds and locks into place. The twins are stunned, and he explains that the plane can take off under its own power, and best of all, it has a range of eight hundred miles when only using the engine.

As they walk around the glider, they are astonished by its high-tech features, and are dying to try it out. Natalie explains to him they are both experienced glider pilots, and he offers to take her up for a test flight. They take off and are gone for a half an hour. When they return, Lynnetta takes her turn, but it's getting late in the day, and when she returns, they put the glider back into its trailer. Milo suggests that they spend more time together later in the week, as the plane has many unique features that they need to become familiar with. They thank him, and wave goodbye as he leaves.

Betty takes them both by the arm, and they walk to the Gulfstream. "We're taking you to your favorite restaurant to celebrate your graduation."

It's an hour and a half flight, and the twins are happy to return to Paris, which they consider their second home. Their favorite restaurant overlooks the Seine River, and they have a fantastic dinner. Betty and Max have a fun time with the twins, and their dates, and they realize the girls will soon take jobs in distant cities and start their own lives. After dinner, they walk to a nearby nightclub and dance for a while before flying back that night.

A full moon is out when they arrive in Berlin, and Betty walks the girls to their cars and gives them a farewell hug. "We have one more surprise for you. Let's meet for lunch tomorrow, and Lotar will explain it to you."

They meet the following day and are doubly excited because Uncle Lotar is involved. He is well known for his adventurous spirit and outlandish ideas, and they know he has something fun planned for them. They sit down in the living room, and Lotar explains his idea. "Our heavy lift projects typically last about two weeks, and we usually fly both ways empty." The twins smile, and flash a look at each other, wondering what he's about to suggest.

"I know you love adventure, and it gave me an idea. We routinely fly near some of the world's most remote and challenging gliding sites. It would be easy to drop you off at a nearby airport for a couple of weeks and pick you up on our return flight home. You could use your plane to explore parts of the world that are completely inaccessible to most people. What do you think?"

Natalie is quick to respond. "Oh, my gosh, Uncle Lotar. That's an incredible offer!" and she looks over at her sister, who is beaming with excitement. "Of course, we'd love to!"

Betty explains their plan in more detail. "The summer is about to start, and our next cargo flight is in three weeks. We're moving heavy equipment into the mountains for a huge hydro-electric power station in Nepal, and we could drop you off in Kathmandu. From there, it's only 100 miles to the highest mountain peak in the world; Mount Everest at 29,000 feet!"

The twins are speechless, and Lotar continues. "Is three weeks enough time to get comfortable with your new plane?"

Lynnetta loves his idea. "Are you kidding? Yes, that's more than enough. Milo told us that the factory has several modification packages that are designed for extreme flying conditions. We would need those upgrades installed before we left."

A sense of adventure, and a new challenge, effects Betty like a narcotic, and she has thrived on it all her life. She explains their plan to the twins. "You can't do this alone, and your father and I want to help. Concentrate on getting the plane ready, and we will take care of the planning and logistics."

Lynnetta is relieved. "Thank you so much! It will be overwhelming just getting the plane ready."

Max continues. "Your mother and I plan to take time off, and we'll be your ground crew on your international flights. It's going to be a fun family adventure, and we're just as excited about your journey as you are."

Three weeks later, the extensive preparations by all involved are completed, and the glider has been performing extremely well. The girls fly it daily, and the factory completed the installation of the modification packages, which will allow them to fly at extreme altitudes and over long distances. They also installed an automatic locator beacon should they have to make an emergency landing in a remote area.

Betty took care of the hotel reservations, car rental, visas, and a multitude of other details, while Max chased down the weather forecasts and navigation charts of the local area. He also designed a portable eight-by-eight-foot module that will act as their command center and filled it with radio communication and weather equipment so that they can maintain contact with the girls while they are flying. The twins are excited as this will be their first flight to a famous international destination.

Soon the day of their departure arrives, and they leave Frankfurt on a 4,000-mile flight to Kathmandu, Nepal, arriving there twelve hours later. The Hercules dropped them off at the international airport and then continued on to the project work site. Max discovered a small airfield with a long grass runway outside of town, and they hired a truck to tow their plane and equipment to it.

The girls were careful and spent a few days flying the lower snow-capped mountain ranges before attempting a flight near Mount Everest. During this time, they also became experts at using their engine, especially during takeoff, and climbing to altitude. During their stay, the weather around Mount Everest was mostly clear and sunny, and their glider performed flawlessly, and beyond their wildest expectations.

Gliding fast and silently near its towering cliffs and razor-sharp ridges was a thrilling experience. When they ascended past 10,000 feet, the girls put on their oxygen masks, and caught powerful thermals that spiraled them high above the clouds and into the sun-drenched sky.

Their plane was designed for speed and the closer they flew to the mountain's rocky face, the stronger the updrafts were, and the faster they flew. Flying silently at speed, and within a hundred feet from towering vertical cliffs, was a breathtaking experience. The twins didn't attempt to fly over the summit, but they did film many of their flights.

Feeling more confident in handling their new glider, Lynnetta asked Betty to fly with her, and they spent the day high amongst the snow-covered mountains surrounding Mount Everest. She gave Betty lessons on how to handle the high-performance glider, and she was quick to catch on. Soon they were soaring silently along the craggy peaks at dizzying speeds. It was a freedom of flight that Betty had never experienced, and it thrilled her.

The following day, Natalie flew with Max, and it was an incredible experience for him as well. Two weeks later, they returned to the international airport in Kathmandu and loaded their glider into the Hercules. It had been a fabulous adventure of a lifetime for all of them.

Now seasoned pilots and explorers, the twins continued to fly to some of the most remote places on the planet. However, they had taken a year off, and graduate school would soon start. It had been an exciting time for the four of them, and Betty and Max had one last surprise planned for them. They offered to fly them to New Zealand to attend the world gliding championships.

New Zealand was world famous for its gliding conditions, as the island lies directly in the path of the Roaring Forties trade winds. The high-velocity westerly winds enable gliders to attain extremely high altitudes, and some pilots had glided distances greater than 1,300 miles.

As they had done so many times before, Betty and Max took care of the planning and logistics, and the twins set several world records for women. The evenings were an exciting time for the twins, and they socialized with famous pilots from around the world, mesmerizing them with stories of their flying adventures at some of the world's most remote destinations. Their incredible experience in New Zealand was a fantastic way to culminate their year of adventure, and it was soon time to return home.

However, the biggest surprise of their trip was yet to come. On their return flight to Germany, they stopped at nearby Melbourne, Australia. Over the years, Betty had stayed in contact with Blake Hunter, and they had a tearful reunion when they met at the airport. He introduced them to his wife, Willow, and their two handsome sons, who were about the same age as the twins. The boys eagerly showed the twins Melbourne's tourist spots, and at night they danced the evenings away at the city's hottest clubs.

Betty and Max spent several happy days with Blake and his wife, and they caught up on the many twists and turns that their lives had taken since the days following the end of the war.

CHAPTER 30
THE BEST OF TIMES

IT'S MIDSUMMER 1989. BETTY AND MAX ARE AT THEIR ESTATE overlooking the Mosel River. Even at seventy, she has a sophisticated air about her and a trim figure. Her hair is shoulder length and an elegant shade of platinum. She wears black-rimmed glasses and a black silk blouse. As for Max, he has changed little over the years except for his gray hair and glasses, which gives him a very distinguished-looking appearance. This year Betty has gone to great lengths to give Max a surprise party for his seventieth birthday. When they walk into the kitchen for breakfast, he is surprised to see that the entire house is covered with festive decorations. She hugs him. "Happy Birthday, darling!"

"What a surprise! I don't know what to say!"

"I invited Lotar and Chara to join us for dinner, and we can watch the sunset from the terrace."

At noon, there is a knock at the front door. Max goes to it and is surprised; a famous French chef, and his staff, are there to prepare an elegant dinner for them. At six o'clock, Lotar and Chara stop by and wish him happy birthday. They seat themselves at the dining room table and formally attired waiters serve them a fabulous multi-course gourmet meal.

After dinner, they retire to the terrace to watch the start of a golden summer sunset. Max lights a roaring fire in the firepit, and Betty pours everyone a brandy. He opens his presents, and afterword they sit by the fire reminiscing about their lives, and the many thrilling adventures that they all enjoyed.

Unexpectedly, music fills the house with a beautiful melody, and minutes later, a four-piece string quartet, dressed in formal attire, walks out onto the terrace, and plays for them. After a bit, the door to the great room opens, and their twin girls, husbands, and children appear and overwhelm him with love and affection. Christian and his wife, Angelina, follow them and a teary-eyed Max hugs them all. Moments later, they are followed by Adrian and Renée. He stands, happy to see their close friends, and with their arrival, the party takes on an atmosphere of excitement.

A short time later, he glances across the terrace, and walking toward him are Andy and his wife Olivia. Although much older by now, he is still handsome and distinguished looking, but walks with a cane because of his war injury. Betty and Max tearfully greet them as they hadn't seen them for over twenty years.

Following them is Shelagh, Charlie's widow, and her husband, Liam. Betty runs to her, and they hug warmly. Afterword, Betty introduces them to her twin girls.

Now that the guests have arrived, Jannik exits the kitchen, pushing a serving cart with a huge Black Forest cake covered with flickering candles. As he approaches, the group sings "Happy Birthday" in English. Max thanks everyone profusely for coming to his party, and he helps Helga serve their guests. He gives her a long hug and thanks her for being in his life.

Later in the evening, Betty walks over to the terrace railing and watches the twins and their families feeding apples to the colts, and she is overwhelmed with happiness. Sadly, early in her life, she had lost everyone in her family, and one of her lifelong dreams was to have a large family of her own; and now that dream is a reality.

As the music plays, she walks back to the crowd and stands by Max's side, listening to their friends reliving the fun times they shared in the past. By this time, the twins are dancing with their husbands, and Betty and Max join them on the dance floor. Several dances later, she pulls him to the side. "It's a beautiful evening, darling. Come and walk with me."

The sun slowly sinks into the horizon, and they walk across the green pasture, passing several mares and their colts, and finally stop at the edge of the vineyard. Betty takes his hand. "I have something to show you."

They walk out onto the massive outcropping of rock that overlooks the valley below. It's where they had their first kiss, and it was where Betty first realized Max was the one that she wanted to spend the rest of her life with. He stares in amazement at what she has created and is overwhelmed by emotion.

In front of him is a large, dark gray granite bench. Carved across the inside, and in gold lettering, is the sign of the Christian Cross, followed by an inscription in German, "*In loving memory of our parents, Wilhelm and Margarete von Hirschel*". And below that is the blue Star of David and a gold inscription in Hebrew, "*The ones we love are never gone; they live within our hearts. Your loving daughter, Elisheba Goldberg*".

To the left of the bench is a life-size granite statue of Wolfie. He is alert, and stares at something across the valley, his ears pitched forward. Max wraps his arms around her, as tears well in his eyes. "I . . . I'm speechless! It's beautiful! I still remember our first kiss here."

Betty smiles at him. "So do I." She motions toward the bench. "Come and sit with me."

Max puts his arm around her, and they gaze at the last rays of a golden sunset, and quietly enjoy the stupendous view in front of them. Betty holds his hand. "As I look back on my life, I realize that the moments when I really lived were the ones that I shared with you, the one I love," and she kisses his cheek tenderly.

EPILOGUE

IN 1990, THE BERLIN WALL CAME DOWN, AND THE SOVIETS abandoned East Germany. It had been almost forty-five years since the Allies and the Soviets divided Germany, and now the two halves were at last reunited, forming a single powerful country. For Betty, German reunification was the final step in bringing her life full circle. Along with millions of other Germans, it brought her closure, and she was finally reunited with the country, and the people, that she loved so much. Berlin was where she was born and raised, and they relocated their air cargo headquarters to Berlin's massive Tempelhof Airport.

Shortly after the war ended, Lotar found a nearly new Focke-Wulf 190, which he bought and kept in storage. In 1986, he started a total restoration, and after four years of hard work, he completed the project and flew his plane for the first time. It had been a dream of his for the last thirty-five years, and he could now relive those heady days of his youth.

Chara was the sister that Betty always wanted, and they remained life-long friends. She became an expert rider and spent a great deal of time with her stallion, Marco, although she still calls him Baby. She didn't have time to campaign him on the eventing circuit, but she rode him often on their cross-country course, and to local events. The two of them had been inseparable, and when he became older, she put him out to stud, and he spent the rest of his days running free with the other horses.

Christian, who is now known by his nickname Capi, manages Titan Heavy Lift, and he and his wife, Angelina, live in Berlin with their twin girls.

Like his father, he has a natural talent for business, and continues to expand their air cargo company by serving their client's special needs world-wide.

Betty's love affair with Arabella remained unbroken for almost thirty years. Arabella gave birth to many colts, and when she was in labor, Betty would sleep in her stall to comfort her. Arabella never tired of their trips through the forest to their alpine cabin, and she loved to graze in the deep grass at the water's edge. When she passed away, Betty buried her near the cabin, and planted an apple tree, her favorite treat, next to her grave.

Lotar and Max developed a new variety of Riesling grape that gave their brandy a unique flavor, and they became extremely successful. Along with their wine, they also sell a limited quantity of aged brandy each year.

Adrian still loves his wine business and continues to sell Dragon wine and brandy. He and Renée travel extensively to foreign countries, looking for unusual wines to offer his customers. They remain good friends with Betty and Max and ride with them whenever they can. Renée campaigned Warrior for many years, and during his incredible career, she won an Olympic Gold Medal, and countless other European Championships with him.

Dalia, Colonel Ben-Ami's wife, and Betty became close friends and she and Max spent many vacations with them in Tel-Aviv, Israel.

Over the years, Betty stayed in touch with Charlie's widow, Shelagh. After they sold Dakota Air Cargo, Shelagh returned to her home in Kildare, Ireland. Her family owns a well-known Thoroughbred stud farm, and with the help of her three brothers, she continues to operate their business with her husband Liam O'Ceallaigh.

After a year of gliding around the world, the twins returned to school, and co-authored a popular book about their yearlong gliding adventures, and dedicated it to Betty and Max.

In 1980, Lynnetta received her doctorate in aerospace engineering, and now works for the European Space Agency in Paris, France. After graduation, she married, and they had two boys.

That same year, Natalie received her doctorate in aeronautical engineering and works for a large multinational company that designs, and manufactures, military aircraft. She and her husband have a daughter and live and work in Berlin.

Betty and Gerta remained lifelong friends. Gerta, and many others in the German resistance, risked their lives to help free Germany from Nazi rule, and many of them, like her father and his friends, paid the ultimate price.

After they retired, Betty and Max remained passionate about their horses and continued to raise their beloved Hanoverians. They love to relax at their alpine cabin and enjoy the simple life and pristine surroundings of their hidden alpine valley.

Betty's favorite time of the day is at sunset, sitting in front of a blazing bonfire, talking and laughing with Max, and with the passage of time, their love continues to grow even stronger. He still plays his guitar and serenades her with her favorite songs, and afterword, they snuggle together under a warm blanket, and watch the indigo sky as it fills with glittering stars.

In her later years, Betty developed a passion for watercolor painting, and became an accomplished artist. One of her favorite places to paint is on the rocky outcropping overlooking the Mosel River. It's where she and Max first kissed, and where she can be close to their beloved Wolfie.

The End